TALES OF WISDOM

BY HOWARD SCHWARTZ

Poetry

Vessels
Gathering the Sparks
Sleepwalking Beneath the Stars

Fiction

A Blessing Over Ashes
Midrashim: Collected Jewish Parables
The Captive Soul of the Messiah: New Tales About Reb Nachman
Rooms of the Soul

Editor

Imperial Messages: One Hundred Modern Parables
Voices Within the Ark: The Modern Jewish Parables
Gates to the New City: A Treasurey of Modern Jewish Tales
Elijah's Violin & Other Jewish Fairy Tales
Miriam's Tambourine: Jewish Folktales from Around the World
Lilith's Cave: Jewish Tales of the Supernatural
The Dream Assembly: Tales of Rabbi Zalman Schachter-Shalomi
The Diamond Tree: Jewish Tales from Around the World

TALES OF WISDOM

One Hundred Modern Parables

EDITED BY HOWARD SCHWARTZ

CRESCENT BOOKS

NEW YORK • AVENEL

This 1995 edition is published by Crescent Books,
distributed by Random House Value Publishing, Inc.
40 Engelhard Avenue
Avenel, New Jersey 07001

Random House
New York • Toronto • London • Sydney • Auckland

Printed and bound in the United States of America

A CIP catalog record for this book is available from the Library of Congress.

Originally published as *Imperial Messages*

ISBN 0-517-14256-2

8 7 6 5 4 3 2 1

Acknowledgments

The editor would like to acknowledge the following persons who were kind enough to direct him to authors who were otherwise unknown to him: E. M. Beekman, Stanley Elkin, E. V. Griffith, Lyle Harris, Henry Korn, Reinhard Lettau, David Meltzer, Clarence Olson, Jerome Rothenberg, Anthony Rudolf, Robert S. Reis, Andreas Schroeder, David Shahar, Henry L. Shapiro, Theodore Solotaroff, Richard Stang, Elsie Steimnitz, Philip Stevick, Rosmarie Waldrop, and A. Leslie Wilson.

The editor and publisher would also like to acknowledge the following publishers, authors and agents for rights to reprint these parables:

"An Imperial Message" and "Before the Law" from *The Penal Colony* by Franz Kafka, translated by Willa and Edwin Muir. Translation copyright 1948 and renewed 1976 by Schocken Books, Inc. Reprinted by permission of Schocken Books, published by Pantheon Books, a division of Random House, Inc.

"The Silence of the Sirens" from *The Great Wall of China* by Franz Kafka, translated by Edwin and Willa Muir. Copyright 1946, and renewed 1974 by Schocken Books, Inc. Reprinted by permission of Schocken Books, published by Pantheon Books, a division of Random House, Inc.

"The Spider and the Fly," by Rabbi Nachman of Bratslav from *Classic Chassidic Tales,* by Meyer Levin. Reprinted by permission of the author and the author's agents, Scott Meredith Literary Agency, Inc., 580 Fifth Avenue, New York, New York, 10036.

"St. Cecilia, or the Power of Music," by Heinrich von Kleist. Translation copyright © 1975 by Henry L. Shapiro. Used by permission of Henry L. Shapiro.

"The Dream of a Ridiculous Man," by Fyodor Dostoevsky. Used by permission of the translator, David Magarshack.

"The Hermit and the Bear" from *Selected Stories* by I.L. Peretz, edited by Irving Howe and Eliezer Greenberg. Copyright © 1974 by Schocken Books Inc. Reprinted by permission of Schocken Books, published by Pantheon Books, a division of Random House, Inc.

"Everything and Nothing" and "Borges and I" from *Dreamtigers*, by Jorge Luis Borges. Copyright © 1964 by Jorge Luis Borges. Reprinted by permission of the University of Texas Press.

"The Circular Ruins," from *Labyrinths*, by Jorge Luis Borges. Copyright © 1962, 1964 by New Directions Publishing Corporation. Reprinted by permission of New Directions Publishing Corporation.

"The Sirens," "The City of Builders," and "Mr. Telleke's Conviction," by Paul van Ostaijen, from *Patriotism, Inc. and Other Tales*, by Paul van Ostaijen. Edited, translated, and annotated by E. M. Beekman. Published by the University of Massachusetts Press, Amherst, 1971. Copyright © 1971 by E. M. Beekman. Reprinted by permission of E. M. Beekman.

"My Properties" and "My King," by Henri Michaux. Translations used by permission of Basil D. Kingstone. Original language rights by permission of Editions Gallimard. Copyright © 1967 by Editions Gallimard.

"The Experimental World," "An Adventure," and "On the Scales of Osiris," from *The Marriage Feast*, by Par Lagerkvist. Copyright © 1954 by Albert Bonniers Forlag; "On the Scales of Osiris" translated by Carl Eric Lindin; "The Adventure" and "The Experimental World" translated by Alan Blair. Reprinted by permission of Farrar, Straus & Giroux and Albert Bonniers Forlag.

"Fable of the Goat" and "The Orchestra" from *Twenty-One Stories* by S.Y. Agnon, edited by Nahum N. Glatzer. Copyright © 1970 by Schocken Books, Inc. Reprinted by permission of Schocken Books, published by Pantheon Books, a division of Random House, Inc.

"The Blue Jar," from "The Young Man with the Carnation" and "The Blue Stones," from "Peter and Rosa," from *Winter's Tales*, by Isak Dinesen. Copyright © 1942 by Random House, Inc. and renewed 1970 by Johan Philip, Thomas Ingerslev c/o The Rungstedlund Foundation. Reprinted by permission of Random House, Inc. and The Bodley Head.

"The Great Mother," "The Servants," and "The Last Flower," from *The Visits of the Queen of Sheba*, by Miguel Serrano. Published by Harper & Row Publishers. Copyright © 1973 by Miguel Serrano. Reprinted by permission of Brandt & Brandt.

"The Angel and the World's Dominion," from *Tales of Angels, Spirits and Demons*. Reprinted by permission of Raphael Buber and Jerome Rothenberg.

"Jachid and Jechidah," from *Short Friday*, by Isaac Bashevis Singer. Copyright © 1961, 1962, 1963, 1964 by Isaac Bashevis Singer. Reprinted by permission of Farrar, Straus & Giroux.

"A Very Old Man With Enormous Wings," from *Leaf Storm and Other Stories*, by Gabriel Garcia Marquez. Translated from the Spanish by Gregory Rabassa. English translation copyright © 1971 by Harper & Row, Publishers. Reprinted by permission of HarperCollins Publishers.

"The Sorcerer's Son" from *The Beggar's Knife* by Rodrigo Rey Rosa. Copyright © 1985 by Rodrigo Rey Rosa and Paul Bowles. Reprinted with the permission of City Lights Books.

"The Sacrifice of the Prisoner" and "A Bloodthirsty Tiger," from *Auto-Da-Fe* by Elias Canetti. Copyright © 1964 by Elias Canetti. Reprinted by permission of Jonathan Cape Ltd.

"The Story of Lilith and Eve," by Jakov Lind. Copyright © 1975 by Jakov Lind. Reprinted by permission of the author and Harper & Row, Publishers.

"The Bride of the East," by W. S. Merwin. Reprinted by permission of W. S. Merwin and *Kayak Magazine*. Copyright © 1972 by *Kayak* Magazine.

"Sand," by W. S. Merwin, Reprinted by permission of W. S. Merwin and *Antaeus* Magazine. Copyright © 1971 by *Antaeus*. "Sand" appeared in *Antaeus* 3.

"A Fable of the Buyers," by W. S. Merwin. Reprinted by permission of W. S. Merwin and *The New Yorker* Magazine. Copyright© 1972 by The New Yorker Magazine, Inc.

"Cities and Signs," "Cities and the Dead," and "Cities and the Sky" from *Invisible Cities* by Italo Calvino, copyright © 1972 by Giulio Einaudi editore, s.p.a. English translation copyright © 1974 by Harcourt Brace Jovanovich, Inc., reprinted by permission of Harcourt Brace Jovanovich, Inc.

"The Map of Lost Objects," from *Confabulario and Other Inventions*, by Juan José Arreola. Copyright © 1964 by Juan José Arreola. Published by the University of Texas Press. Reprinted by permission of the University of Texas Press.

"Mirror and Scarf," by Edmond Jabès. Reprinted by permission of the translator, Rosmarie Waldrop.

"The Behavior of Mirrors on Easter Island," from *Cronopios and Famas*, by Julio Cortazár. Translated by Paul Blackburn. Copyright © 1969 by Random House, Inc. Reprinted by permission of Random House, Inc.

"Continuity of Parks," from *The End of the Game and Other Stories*, by Julio Cortazár. Translated by Paul Blackburn. Copyright © 1967, 1963 by Random House, Inc. Reprinted by permission of Pantheon Books, a Division of Random House, Inc.

"Shipbuilding" and "Inventions," by Christoph Meckel. Reprinted by permission of the translator, Andreas Schroeder.

"The Mapmakers of the Dead," from *Manifesto of the Dead*, by Christoph Meckel. Original text published by Verlag Eremiten-Presse of Dusseldorf. Translation published in *Dimension*. Reprinted by permission of A. Leslie Willson.

"One's Ship," from *Phantoms*, by Barton Midwood. Copyright © 1970, 1969, 1968, 1967 by Barton Midwood. Reprinted by permission of the publishers, E. P. Dutton & Co., Inc.

"Sinking Contest," by Pierre Bettencourt, from *French Writing Today*. Copyright © 1968 by Simon Watson Taylor. Reprinted by permission of Gallimand Editions and Jonathan Clowes Limited.

"The Fragrance of Shellweed," from *The Box Man*, by Kobo Abe. Translated by E. Dale Saunders. Copyright © 1974 by Alfred A. Knopf, Inc. Reprinted by permission of Alfred A. Knopf, Inc.

"The Nose," from *Tales of Good and Evil*, by Nicolai V. Gogol. Translated by David Magarshack. Copyright © 1957 by David Magarshack. Reprinted by permission of Doubleday & Company, Inc.

"Gogol's Wife," from *Gogol's Wife and Other Stories*, by Tommaso Landolfi. Copyright © 1961, 1963 by New Directions Publishing Corporation. Reprinted by permission of New Directions Publishing Corporation.

Acknowledgments ix

"Blue Notebook No. 10," "A Sonnet" and "The Connection" by Daniil Kharms, reprinted from *The Man in the Black Coat: Russian Literature of the Absurd*, translated and edited by George Gibian, Northwestern University Press, 1987. Used by permission of George Gibian.

"Dulcinea del Toboso," by Marco Denevi. Used by permission of Marco Denevi and Andreas Schroeder.

"Antimatter," from *The Childhood of an Equestrian* by Russell Edson. Copyright © 1973 by Russell Edson. Used by permission of Russell Edson.

"A Man Who Writes," from *The Very Thing That Happens* by Russell Edson. Copyright © 1964 by Russell Edson. Used by permission of Russell Edson.

"The Tower" and "The Suicide," from *The Other Side of the Mirror (El grimorio)* by Enrique Anderson Imbert. Translated by Isabel Reade. Copyright © 1966 by Southern Illinois University Press. Reprinted by permission of Southern Illinois University Press.

"Punishing the Guest," from *Obstacles*, by Reinhard Lettau. translated by Ursule Molinaro. Copyright © 1965 by Random House, Inc. Reprinted by permission of Carl Hansen Verlag.

"from *Steps*," by Jerzy N. Kosinski. Copyright © 1968 by Jerzy N. Kosinski. Reprinted by permission of Random House, Inc.

"The Imperishable Container of All Things" from *The Monday Rhetoric of the Love Club* by Marvin Cohen. Copyright © 1973 by Marvin Cohen. Reprinted by permission of New Directions Publishing Corporation.

"from *Alaap*," by Krishna Baldev Vaid. Reprinted by permission of Krishna Baldev Vaid.

"The Motorcycle Social Club," from *Dream-Work*, by Kirby Congdon. Reprinted by permission of Kirby Congdon.

"The Japanese Stonecutter," by Multatuli, from *The Oyster and the Eagle: Selected Aphorisms and Parables of Multatuli*. Edited and translated by E. M. Beekman. Published by the University of Massachusetts Press, Amherst, 1974. Translation copyright © 1975 by E. M. Beekman. Reprinted by permission of E. M. Beekman.

"Feeding the Hungry," from *Stories and Drawings*, by Roland Topor. Published by Peter Owen Ltd., London. Reprinted by permission of Peter Owen Ltd., London.

"How Wang-Fo was Saved" by Marguerite Yourcenar. From *Black Water: Anthology of Fantastic Literature*, edited by Alberto Manguel, published in the USA by Clarkson N. Potter and by Lester Orpen Dennys in Canada, 1985. Used by permission of Lucinda Vardey Agency.

"The Tree," from *The Late Man*, by Andreas Schroeder. Reprinted by permission of Andreas Schroeder.

"Women Born From Trees," from *The Testament of Cain*, by Lars Gyllensten. Reprinted by permission of Calder and Boyars, Ltd., Publishers.

"Baraka," from *The Boy Who Set the Fire*, by Mohammed Mrabet/ Paul Bowles. Reprinted by permission of Black Sparrow Press.

"I Sang in a Forest One Day," from *Tarantula*, by Bob Dylan. Copyright © 1966 by Bob Dylan. Reprinted with permission of Macmillan Publishing Co., Inc.

"The Polish Tree," by Gunter Kunert, from *Tagträume in Berlin und Andernorts*. Copyright © 1972 by Carl Hanser Verlag. Munich. Translated by Christopher Middleton, from *German Writing Today*, edited by Christopher Middleton. Copyright © 1967 by Christopher Middleton. Reprinted by permission of Carl Hanser Verlag and Penguin Books, Ltd.

"The Sheep of the Hidden Valley," by R. Yehoshua Lovaine. Copyright © 1975 by Tsvi Blanchard. Reprinted by permission of Tsvi Blanchard.

"A Myth of Asherah" and "The Book of Vessels" by Howard Schwartz. Copyright © 1991 by Howard Schwartz. Used by permission of Howard Schwartz.

"Isis" by Rachel Kubie. Copyright © 1991 by Rachel Kubie. Used by permission of Rachel Kubie.

"The Death of Rabbi Yoseph" from *The Mind of Genesis*, by David Slabotsky. Copyright © 1975 by David Slabotsky. Reprinted by permission of David Slabotsky.

"The Glass Blower," by Duane Ackerson. Reprinted by permission of Duane Ackerson.

"The Chameleon," by Milos Macourek. Translated by George Theiner, from *New Writing in Czechoslovakia*, edited by George Theiner. Copyright © 1969 by George Theiner. Reprinted by permission of Penguin Books, Ltd.

"Mr. K's Favorite Animal," from *Prosa*, Volume 5, by Bertold Brecht. Copyright © 1967 by Suhrkamp Verlag, Frankfurt am Main. All Rights Reserved. In translation, *Tales from the Calendar*, by Bertolt Brecht. Original copyright © 1949 by Gebruder Weiss Verlag, Berlin. This translation copyright © 1961 by Methuen and Co. Ltd.

"The Elephant" by Slawomir Mrozek, translated by Konrad Syrop. Copyright © 1962, 1990 by Macdonald and Co. (Publishers) Ltd. Used by permission of Grove Weidenfeld, a division of Grove Press, Inc.

"A Capsulization," from the novel *In Lieu Of* by Robert Thompson. Copyright © 1991 by Betty Thompson for the Estate of Robert Thompson. Used by permission of Betty Thompson.

"The Garden" by Paul Bowles. Copyright © 1964 by Paul Bowles. Reprinted from *Collected Stories* with the permission of Black Sparrow Press.

"*Green-sealed Messages:* 1 and 88" from *Grünverschlossene Botschaft*, by H. C. Artmann. Original rights reprinted by permission of Residenz Verlag. Number 1 translated by J. Rutherford Willems. Reprinted by permission of the translator. Number 88 translated by Derk Wynand. Reprinted by permission of the translator.

"A Considerable Purchase," from *Eine Grössere Anschaffung*, by Wolfgang Hildesheimer. Original rights copyright © 1962 by Suhrkamp Verlag, Frankfurt am Main. All Rights Reserved. Reprinted by permission of Suhrkamp Verlag. Translation used by permission of Andreas Schroeder.

"The Tramp's Sin and Charlie Chaplin," from *I Have Seen Monsters & Angels*, by Eugene Jolas. Used by permission of Maria Jolas.

"Pyramid Criticism" from "The New Egypt," copyright © 1946 by Isaac Rosenfeld, renewed © 1974 by Vasiliki Rosenfeld. From

Alpha and Omega by Isaac Rosenfeld. Used by permission of Viking Penguin, a division of Penguin Books USA Inc.

"Mummification and Space Travel," from *Limits of Space and Time*, by Britton Wilkie. Reprinted by permission of Lewis Warsh, Angel Hair Books.

"The Hot Cosmonaut," by Gust Gils. First published in *Shantih*, Vol. 2, no. 4 (Spring–Summer, 1973). Copyright © 1973 by permission of E. M. Beekman.

"Left Out" by Charles Schwartz. Copyright © 1991 by Charles Schwartz. Used by permission of Charles Schwartz.

"The Master," from *The Scale of Silence*, by Lawrence Fixel. Used by permission of Lawrence Fixel.

"The True Waiting," from *One Generation After*, by Elie Wiesel. Copyright © 1970 by Elie Wiesel. Reprinted by permission of Random House, Inc.

"Soap," by Jerome Rothenberg. Used by permission of Jerome Rothenberg.

"The Unmasking of the Apocalypse," from *The Revolution of the Pin-Ball Machines*, by Cecil Helman. Used by permission of Cecil Helman.

"Threatening Letter," by Maria Luise Kaschnitz, from *Steht Noch Dahin*. Copyright © 1970 by Insel Verlag, Frankfurt am Main. All Rights Reserved. Translation by Derk Wynand. Used by permission of the translator.

"Period," from *Selected Poems*, by Zbigniew Herbert. Translated and edited by Czeslaw Milosz and Peter Dale Scott. Copyright © 1968 by Czeslaw Milosz and Peter Dale Scott. Reprinted by permission of Penguin Books, Ltd.

"In the Land of Magic" from *Selected Writings* by Henri Michaux. Copyright © 1968 by New Directions Publishing Corporation. Reprinted by permission of New Directions Publishing Corporation.

Contents

Contents

It was now dark enough for me to see that every flower was shining with a light of its own. Indeed it was by this light that I saw them, an eternal, peculiar light, proceeding from each, and not reflected from a common source of light as in the daytime.

George MacDonald
Phantastes

Preface

The basic challenge of the parable is to write a good story in as short a space as possible. This is why, no doubt, so many of the most famous writers in this century, from Franz Kafka to Jorge Luis Borges and Isaac Bashevis Singer have at some time in their career devoted themselves to this form. These very short stories are usually scattered through their collected works, and have only rarely been gathered together (as in the case of Kafka) into a single volume. The present anthology, the first of its kind, is an attempt to bring together in one book the very best of these modern parables. Although the primary emphasis is on the writers of this century, including many contemporaries such as Jerzy Kosinski, Jakov Lind, W. S. Merwin and Italo Calvino, there is also a sampling of parables from the 19th Century, by authors such as Fyodor Dostoevsky, Nikolai Gogol, Edgar Allan Poe and George MacDonald.

The reader who comes to this collection with a preconceived notion of what a parable should be will be surprised to discover how far the modern parable has evolved from its ancient sources. But the reader who simply opens this book at random will derive the most pleasure from the wide variety of fantasies, dreams, fables and fairy-tales abounding in it. Among the seventy-three authors, representing more than twenty countries, there are, for example, five stories about angels, from the traditional fairytale of Hans Christian Anderson to the unlikely creation of Gabriel García Márquez, whose angel is a very old man with enormous wings. Then there are also four parables about trees, including one by Lars Gyllensten about women born from trees, as well as others about mirrors, ships, animals, maps, space travel, quicksand, and such legendary beings as Lilith and the Sirens.

Far from being cut and dried allegories with obvious morals, these parables more closely resemble dreams, with their strange atmosphere, unlikely settings, and unexpected twists. As in dreams, it is possible for two characters to blend into one, as happens in Jakov Lind's "The Story of Lilith and Eve," or for a man to wake one morning to find his nose has disappeared, as happens in Gogol's famous story "The Nose," or for a man to create a son out of the substance of his dreams, as does the wizard in the story "The Circular Ruins" by Jorge Luis Borges. At the same time, the authors of these stories are not simply indulging their imaginations, for the modern parable has not abandoned the aspect of the ancient parable that made it a valuable teaching story, though in most cases it has incorporated this teaching into the body of the parable rather than as an appended moral. Thus the parables of Rabbi Nachman of Bratslav, Dostoevsky, Martin Buber and Miguel Serrano, among others, make it obvious that many authors have not abandoned the moral dimension in their writings.

Finally, it is hoped that the reader will discover an affinity among the authors in this anthology that is deeper than their common interest in the modern parable. All of them are in the forefront of those who are consciously intent on preserving the elements of myth and mystery in their writings from the onslaught of realism that pervades most modern literature. For the reader for whom mythology has remained a living force this anthology should serve as a source book for further exploration of writers for whom the domain of the imagination is eminent. For a further discussion of the modern parable the reader is advised to turn to the Introduction, "Kafka and the Modern Parable."

Howard Schwartz

Kafka and the Modern Parable

Any diligent reader of modern literature will have noticed examples of short prose allegories which have appeared with increasingly frequency along with more conventional short stories in volumes published by many contemporary authors. These usually brief works have in general a strong resemblance to the parables of the ancient past, due to their use of a central or extended metaphor which has obvious allegorical implications. In particular, the parables of Franz Kafka and Jorge Luis Borges have drawn attention to this form. But, due primarily to the rigid classifications of literary genres, which for most readers limit the possibilities to the short story, the novel, lyric and epic poetry, and drama, the modern parable has so far failed to receive recognition as an independent literary form. Yet now that so many authors have successfully written in this allegorical mode, it is obvious that the parable has been resurrected as a literary genre. The purpose of this anthology is to announce this resurrection and to restore the literary dimension of this term.

In choosing the term "parable" as the most appropriate to define the works in *Imperial Messages,* I have passed over other terms which have also come to be associated with this kind of literary endeavor. Because most of these works are too short to be called short stories, the term "mini-story" has been proposed. Because of the allegorical content in most of them, the term "fable" has been brought into use. Jorge Luis Borges has suggested the term "fiction" (*ficcion*), but in the opinion of most critics he has appropriated this term for himself. The expressions "tale," "prose," and "paraprose" have also been suggested, but all of these terms have their shortcomings. Most seem descriptive rather than generic. It is the appellation "modern parable" that seems to come closest to denoting the allegorical nature and serious intent of the works written in this form.*

Perhaps the most difficult distinction to make is that between the parable and the prose poem. This latter form has also been much maligned, and is also currently experiencing a renaissance. Both parables and prose poems ordinarily make considerable use of symbolism, and hence the distinction between the two forms may in some cases be non-existent. However, as a rule it may be observed that while the prose poem makes abundant use of symbolism, as, for example, in the prose poems of Baudelaire and Rimbaud, it does not usually extend this symbolism into a single metaphor, at which point it would become allegory, which almost every modern parable makes use of such a central metaphor. Also, the narrative element in prose poetry is rarely utilized, while the modern parable, more often than not, presents a recognizable narrative. These, then, were my primary considerations in distinguishing the parable from the prose poem while selecting works for this anthology.

It is true that for many readers "parable" implies an ancient moralistic form, primarily associated with religious teachings, and in particular with the parables of Jesus. This is because the ancient parable was primarily a teaching story in which it was of central importance that the reader recognize the clear-cut moral the author intended; hence its allegorical techniques were applied to religious and moralistic ends. However, there is no requirement that limits parables to these ends, and it has been the continued use of allegorical techniques, recast in a modern mode, that has permitted the parable to evolve as have other literary forms. The modern free verse poem, for example, has little in common with the familiar metered and rhyming poem of the past. If anything has been preserved intact it is the dependence on imagery and symbolism, and in

* Due to this predominant allegorical aspect, it may appear to some readers that an even more appropriate name for the works written in this genre would simply be "modern allegories." But it is important to distinguish between the literary *device* of allegory and the literary *form* of parable.

many ways this evolution parallels that of the ancient and modern parable.

It is also possible to trace the evolution of the modern parable from a long series of spontaneous allegorical genres. Such a genealogy must go back at least to primitive mythology, and very likely even further, to dreams, the most spontaneous of all allegorical modes. Dreams have an immediacy that is fully accepted by the dreamer; there is almost no distance between the experience and the one who experiences. And myths, for those who believe in them, are inviolable. The first appearance of distance, and therefore doubt, enters with the notion of legend: that which may be true, and then again, may not. At a still further remove we evolve the folktale, the old story that is still retold, but primarily for its narrative interest rather than its likely veracity. With the folktale something of a literary consciousness enters for the first time, and this element is even more pronounced with the evolution of fairy tales, universally considered fare for children, essentially entertainment. Yet it is to be observed that all of these expressions are spontaneous. It was not until the nineteenth century that the Grimm brothers decided to write down the German folktales that had been handed down by word of mouth for centuries. Nor until that same century was it possible to identify one specific author of such stories—Hans Christian Andersen.

From this perspective the modern parable is a natural result of this evolution. Most cultures today neglect oral traditions and little spontaneous folklore seems to be produced. But the impulse which led to the cultivation and preservation of such stories has not disappeared. It has come under the domain of literary creations, expressed by authors who have transmitted into words inspirations which spring from the unconscious. It is by deriving much of its subject matter and imagery from unconscious inspiration that the modern parable has retained its spontaneous dimension. At the same time, the authors working in this genre have carried the evolution toward self-consciousness and literary refinement a step further. It is important to note that none of the authors in this anthology is anonymous—in fact, the lives, not merely the works of Dostoevsky, Poe, and Kafka, for example, are known in great detail. Likewise, all of the authors in this collection are very conscious of the style they have evolved, and though all partake of the same universal elements in drawing their inspiration, every one finds an individual means of expressing these elements. In this way individuality is not sacrificed to the underlying universality, and we are able to perceive a universal vision through the eyes of distinctly different individuals.

One critical complaint about parables and the device of allegory in general is worth considering. For many readers an allegory is a kind of symbolism where each symbol has a single point of reference. In this view the allegory is a kind of coded language that can be translated so that it has a single meaning. This is emphatically not the case with the modern parable. As with dreams, these parables must constantly be referred back to the source of their origin, the psyche. Though the external world has been greatly transformed in the past few centuries, the psyche itself changes much more slowly, and the sources and symbolism that were available to the creators of the ancient mythologies are still available to us. It is precisely this use of symbolism, so close to that found in dreams, which the authors in this anthology have made use of. And, as in dreams, there is an attempt to map out a great uncharted area, the human psyche. In that respect this book may be regarded as a kind of rough atlas, and though none of its maps (and therefore none of its cities) fully resembles any other, still all chart exactly the same City.

As to why the psyche chooses to present its symbols in the apparently obscure fashion of dreams, myths, legends, folktales, fairy tales, and literary creations, the answer is obvious: it has no other tongue with which to speak. It chooses images from the world around us and presents them in a way that refers not to the world from which they were taken, but to the psyche itself, which has incorporated them into an alphabet and made up its own language. In the ancient past the value of these messages was recognized. Dreams were widely respected as oracles, advance warnings, and statements of fact. And in our own century, once again, due in part to the advances of psychology (I am thinking especially of Carl Jung and Fritz Perls), we are again in a position to recognize in dreams an accurate barometer of our own psyches and to decipher from their imagery the symbolic intent. The poet

Charles Simic has observed that at a time when most of the outer world has been explored, it is the author who develops the tools to explore his own inner landscape who serves us best.

Thus it should not come as a surprise to the reader to learn that many of the tales in this collection had their origin in dreams. It is possible, for example, to trace the successive drafts of a number of Kafka's stories to dreams which are reported in his diaries and then transformed in the notebooks until they attain their final form. And a similar dream-like quality pervades the work of many other authors, such as George MacDonald, I. L. Peretz, Henri Michaux, S. Y. Agnon, Italo Calvino, Jerzy Kosinski and Gabriel García Márquez. Among these authors it is not uncommon for a dream to be taken as a starting point and made accessible in a literary mode. At the same time the attempt is made to remain true to the original inspiration. In addition, some of the selections included here are presented as the dreams of their protagonists, such as Dostoevsky's "The Dream of a Ridiculous Man," the first excerpt from Elias Canetti's novel *Auto-da-Fe*, entitled "The Sacrifice of the Prisoner," and the excerpt from Kobo Abé's *The Box Man*, entitled "The Fragrance of Shellweed." Jorge Luis Borges, too, has numerous instances in his stories when the dream of a character is related. The primary action in the story "The Circular Ruins" takes place entirely in the dreams of the priest of the god of fire, who sets out *to dream* himself a son and succeeds—more or less.

It should be noted that this practice of weaving a shorter work, often a parable, into a longer narrative is common, and that a number of selections in this anthology have been excerpted from such longer narratives. The most famous of these excerpts is Kafka's "Before the Law," taken from *The Trial*. Others are the parables of Dinesen, Calvino, Brecht, Artmann, Gyllensten, Rosenfeld, Kosinski, Lovaine, Vaid, Thompson, and Cohen. In most of these cases the titles were given to these selections by the editor and are used with the author's or publisher's permission.

The majority of the stories in this collection were written in this century. However, it seemed useful for many reasons to include a few examples of influential parables

written earlier. Of these, that of Rabbi Nachman of
Bratslav was written in the eighteenth century, and those
of Kleist, Dostoevsky, Gogol, Poe, MacDonald, and
Andersen all derive from the nineteenth century. Except,
perhaps, for the Andersen fairy tale, all of these parables
represent in some respect innovations in the use of allegorical narrative, and thus all set the stage for the
allegorical renaissance in this century.

Readers will also notice that certain images and symbols
often recur in these stories. It may come as a surprise, for
example, to discover that angels still provide fertile subject
matter. But after reading the parables of Andersen, Buber,
Singer, García Márquez, and Babel, it should be obvious
that the modern author is able to derive as much from the
concept of angels as did the ancients, when the belief in
their existence was taken more seriously. Working against
the conventional notion of angels, the latter three of these
stories offer a different interpretation of what it is
angels stand for at this time. The Singer story suggests
that we are all fallen angels, while the García Márquez
story may be read as a statement of the degeneration in the
belief in angels: as the belief has waned, the angel (the old
man) has become increasingly common, his wings serving
little purpose, and the doctor who examines him is astounded at the wheezing in his kidneys. Likewise, in the
Babel story the woman presses her good luck by demanding
more from the angel who is sent to her than angels can
possibly be expected to give. Other common symbols in
these stories are maps (stories by Calvino, José Arreola,
and Meckel), mirrors (Jabès, Cortazár, and Edson), ships
(Kafka, van Ostaijen, Lagerkvist, Dinesen, Meckel, and
Midwood), trees (Schroeder, Gyllensten, Kunert, and
Dylan) and animals (Peretz, Agnon, Canetti, Brecht, Macourek,
Artmann, Mrozek, and Slabotsky.) The musical metaphors in
the stories by Kleist and Agnon also lend themselves to an
interesting comparison—in more ways than one they are
Catholic and Jewish versions of the same story.

The derivation of the title of this anthology from Kafka's
parable "An Imperial Message" is not intended to imply
that Kafka was solely responsible for the evolution of
the parable from an archaic to a modern form, but rather
that it was his powerful influence which attracted other

writers and encouraged them to experiment in the form. Nor should it be assumed that the element of drawing a moral, such an essential aspect of the ancient parable, has been eliminated from the modern parable. "Parable," from the Greek *parabolē,* means literally "put next to" or "set beside," and the key literary device of both the ancient and modern parable, that of allegory, presumes a double meaning, that presented and that implied. Because aphoristic moral statements no longer sufficiently define our awareness of the world, the moral of the modern parable has been incorporated, in most cases, into the narrative itself. The difference, then, is between the explicit moral appended to the ancient parable and the implicit moral of the modern parable. Whereas with the tortise and hare we are to understand that slow determination is more effective than infrequent bursts of energy, in Poe's "The Oval Portrait" we are expected to perceive that the words on the page draw their vibrant power from a living being, whether it be the artist or his subject.

As for "An Imperial Message," it may be read as an allegory of the process any dreamer goes through in receiving messages from his unconscious mind. The king gives the message to the faithful messenger before his death, but because of the delay between the sending and the receiving, the messenger is delivering "a message from a dead man." The dead king, then, may be viewed as a symbol of the past, which preserves itself in memory and the unconscious mind, and sends messages into the future through dreams, works of art, etc. The fact that the messenger never appears with the message, although the man who dreams it to himself is certain he is on the way, signifies the fact that we can never fully comprehend the meaning of such unconscious messages, never fully receive then; i.e., we can never pin down their symbolism to a precise interpretation. It has long been understood that any true symbol can never be fully comprehended, that the circle of its meaning continues to expand. And this is equally true for a cluster of symbols around a central metaphor, as is found so often in the modern parable. Because the truths it describes are complex and not fully accessible to consciousness, the message of the modern parable never fully arrives, though the emotional response it evokes makes it clear that the message has been sent, and the longer the reader contemplates its meaning the more certain he becomes that the messenger and his message are coming closer all the time.

It is interesting to note that Kafka occasionally sought ancient sources for some of his parables. In the cases of "Paradise" and "Abraham," for example, his style is indistinguishable from that of the rabbis who invented the Midrashim which retell, with variations, basic biblical stories, filling in gaps in the narrative as a means of explaining and expanding the meaning of the original. In the parable "The Silence of the Sirens" Kafka uses this Midrashic technique to revise a basic fact about the legend of Odysseus and the Sirens—he reports that Odysseus used wax in his ears, while the original story insists he did not. And in his very short parable, "The Sirens," Kafka adds another variation to the story by attributing to the Sirens claws and sterile wombs:

> These are the seductive voices of the night; the Sirens, too, sang that way. It would be doing them an injustice to think that they wanted to seduce; they knew they had claws and sterile wombs, and they lamented this aloud. They could not help it if their laments sounded so beautiful.

Still a further variation of this legend is offered in a parable by the Belgian writer Paul van Ostaijen, writing about the same time as Kafka.* Van Ostaijen's parable, like Kafka's brief parable of the same title, is also concerned with the great suffering of the Sirens, a dimension of the legend which was not considered by previous writers who took up the subject.

In fact, one of the basic devices of the modern parable is to create this kind of Midrash, in a literary sense: to examine from a change in perspective a well-know story. The changed perspective permits the power of the old

---

* This coincidence merely confirms the impression that, as with many literary and other movements, the evolution of the modern parable had reached a point where it was ripe for experimentation. And not only the form, but even certain subjects, such as the legend of the Sirens, once again compelled attention. The recent revival of interest in the Jewish legends of Lilith and the Golem are merely additional examples of this cyclical trend.

story to be reexperienced anew, and provides a basis for reevaluating the old in light of the new. Borges, for example, in "Everything and Nothing," examines the man Shakespeare in light of his plays; Par Lagerkvist, in "The Experiment," retells the story of life inside the Garden of Eden with an unexpected twist; and Jakov Lind in his remarkable "The Story of Lilith and Eve" blends two related but divergent legends into one in a very convincing manner.

It is my hope that this anthology will serve its readers by revealing new authors and directions for them to explore, but most of all by appealing to their imagination. For it is to the power of the imagination that this collection must pay its primary tribute. Perhaps the following parable of Henri Michaux's, from the series entitled "In the Land of Magic," can express just how precarious are the spells of the imagination that the authors in this anthology are one and all attempting to invoke:

Walking on the two banks of a stream is a laborous exercise.

Rather frequently you see a man (a student in magic) going upstream that way, walking on the one bank and the other at the same time: being very preoccupied, he does not see you. For what he is performing is delicate and tolerates no inattention. He would very soon find himself back on one bank, and how disgraceful that would be!

Howard Schwartz
St. Louis

An Imperial Message
by Franz Kafka

The Emperor, so a parable runs, has sent a message to you, the humble subject, the insignificant shadow cowering in the remotest distance before the imperial sun; the Emperor from his deathbed has sent a message to you alone. He has commanded the messenger to kneel down by the bed, and has whispered the message to him; so much store did he lay on it that he ordered the messenger to whisper it back into his ear again. Then by a nod of the head he has confirmed that it is right. Yes, before the assembled spectators of his death—all the obstructing walls have been broken down, and on the spacious and loftily mounting open staircases stand in a ring the great princes of the Empire—before all these he has delivered his message. The messenger immediately sets out on his journey; a powerful, an indefatigable man; now pushing with his right arm, now with his left, he cleaves a way for himself through the throng; if he encounters resistance he points to his breast, where the symbol of the sun glitters; the way is made easier for him than it would be for any other man. But the multitudes are so vast; their numbers have no end. If he could reach the open fields how fast he would fly, and soon doubtless you would hear the welcome hammering of his fists on your door. But instead how vainly does he wear out his strength; still he is only making his way through the chambers of the innermost palace; never will he get to the end of them; and if he succeeded in that nothing would be gained; he must next fight his way down the stair; and if he succeeded in that nothing would be gained; the courts would still have to be crossed; and after the courts the second outer palace; and once more stairs and courts; and once more another palace; and so on for thousands of years; and if at last he should burst through the outermost gate—but never, never can that happen—the. imperial capital would lie before him, the center of the world, crammed to bursting with its own sediment. Nobody could fight his way through here even with a message from a dead man. But you sit at your window when evening falls and dream it to yourself.

Translated from the German
by Willa and Edwin Muir

Before the Law
by Franz Kafka

Before the Law stands a doorkeeper on guard. To this doorkeeper there comes a man from the country who begs for admittance to the Law. But the doorkeeper says that he cannot admit the man at the moment. The man, on reflection, asks if he will be allowed, then, to enter later. 'It is possible,' answers the doorkeeper, 'but not at this moment.' Since the door leading into the Law stands open as usual and the doorkeeper steps to one side, the man bends down to peer through the entrance. When the doorkeeper sees that, he laughs and says: 'If you are so strongly tempted, try to get in without my permission. But note that I am powerful. And I am only the lowest doorkeeper. From hall to hall keepers stand at every door, one more powerful than the other. Even the third of these has an aspect that even I cannot bear to look at.' These are difficulties which the man from the country has not expected to meet, the Law, he thinks, should be accessible to every man and at all times, but when he looks more closely at the doorkeeper in his furred robe, with his huge pointed nose and long, thin, Tartar beard, he decides that he had better wait until he gets permission to enter. The doorkeeper gives him a stool and lets him sit down at the side of the door. There he sits waiting for days and years. He makes many attempts to be allowed in and wearies the doorkeeper with his importunity. The doorkeeper often engages him in brief conversation, asking him about his home and about other matters, but the questions are put quite impersonally, as great men put questions, and always conclude with the statement that the man cannot be allowed to enter yet. The man, who has equipped himself with many things for his journey, parts with all he has, however valuable, in the hope of bribing the doorkeeper. The door-

keeper accepts it all, saying, however, as he takes each
gift: 'I take this only to keep you from feeling that you
have left something undone.' During all these long years
the man watches the doorkeeper almost incessantly. He
forgets about the other doorkeepers, and this one seems
to him the only barrier between himself and the Law. In
the first years he curses his evil fate aloud; later, as he
grows old, he only mutters to himself. He grows childish,
and since in his prolonged watch he has learned to know
even the fleas in the doorkeeper's fur collar, he begs the
very fleas to help him and to persuade the doorkeeper to
change his mind. Finally his eyes grow dim and he does not
know whether the world is really darkening around him
or whether his eyes are only deceiving him. But in the
darkness he can now perceive a radiance that streams im-
mortally from the door of the Law. Now his life is drawing to a close. Before he dies, all that he has experienced
during the whole time of his sojourn condenses in his mind
into one question, which he has never yet put to the doorkeeper. He beckons the doorkeeper, since he can no longer
raise his stiffening body. The doorkeeper has to bend far
down to hear him, for the difference in size between them
has increased very much to the man's disadvantage. 'What
do you want to know now?' asks the doorkeeper, 'you are
insatiable.'

'Everyone strives to attain the Law,' answers the man,
'how does it come about, then, that in all these years no
one has come seeking admittance but me?' The doorkeeper perceives that the man is at the end of his strength
and that his hearing is failing, so he bellows in his ear. 'No
one but you could gain admittance through this door,
since this door was intended only for you. I am now going
to shut it.'

Translated from the German
by Willa and Edwin Muir

The Silence of the Sirens
by *Franz Kafka*

Proof that inadequate, even childish measures, may serve to rescue one from peril.

To protect himself from the Sirens Ulysses stopped his ears with wax and had himself bound to the mast of his ship. Naturally any and every traveller before him could have done the same, except those whom the Sirens allured even from a great distance; but it was known to all the world that such things were of no help whatever. The song of the Sirens could pierce through everything, and the longing of those they seduced would have broken far stronger bonds than chains and masts. But Ulysses did not think of that, although he had probably heard of it. He trusted absolutely to his handful of wax and his fathom of chain, and in innocent elation over his little stratagem sailed out to meet the Sirens.

Now the Sirens have a still more fatal weapon than their song, namely their silence. And though admittedly such a thing has never happened, still it is conceivable that someone might possibly have escaped from their singing; but from their silence certainly never. Against the feeling of having triumphed over them by one's own strength, and the consequent exaltation that bears down everything before it, no earthly powers could have remained intact.

And when Ulysses approached them the potent songstresses actually did not sing, whether because they thought that this enemy could be vanquished only by their silence, or because the look of bliss on the face of Ulysses, who was thinking of nothing but his wax and his chains, made them forget their singing.

But Ulysses, if one may so express it, did not hear their silence; he thought they were singing and that he alone did not hear them. For a fleeting moment he saw their throats

rising and falling, their breasts lifting, their eyes filled with
tears, their lips half-parted, but believed that these were
accompaniments to the airs which died unheard around
him. Soon, however, all this faded from his sight as he fixed
his gaze on the distance, the Sirens literally vanished before his resolution, and at the very moment when they
were nearest to him he knew of them no longer.

But they—lovelier than ever—stretched their necks and
turned, let their cold hair flutter free in the wind, and
forgetting everything clung with their claws to the rocks.
They no longer had any desire to allure; all that they
wanted was to hold as long as they could the radiance that
fell from Ulysses' great eyes.

If the Sirens had possessed consciousness they would
have been annihilated at that moment. But they remained
as they had been; all that had happened was that Ulysses
had escaped them.

A codicil to the foregoing has also been handed down.
Ulysses, it is said, was so full of guile, was such a fox,
that not even the goddess of fate could pierce his armor.
Perhaps he had really noticed, although here the human
understanding is beyond its depths, that the Sirens were
silent, and opposed the afore-mentioned pretense to them
and the gods merely as a sort of shield.

Translated from the German
by Willa and Edwin Muir

4

The Spider and the Fly
by *Rabbi Nachman of Bratslav*

AND THE GREAT MOUNTAIN THAT SPOKE
IN A DREAM

Perhaps you think I will tell you everything, so that you may be able to understand my story. I will begin to tell the story.

There was a king who fought a great battle against many nations, and won the battle, and took thousands of prisoners from among all the nations. Every year, on the day of his victory, he caused a great feast to be made; and to the conqueror's festival there came princes and emperors from all the kingdoms of the world. He would have clowns at his festival, to entertain him and his guests with imitations of the different peoples of the world. The comedians would dress themselves in long cloaks, with scarves over their heads, as Arabs of the desert; and then they would appear as Turks, and as Spaniards, and they would make themselves fat as Germans, and they would make fun of whomever they pleased; and naturally they did not forget to put on long beards and to scratch themselves like Jews.

The king sat and watched the clowns, and tried to guess when they were Arabs, or Germans, or Spaniards, or Jews. Then he ordered that the Book of Nations be brought to him, and he looked in the Book of Nations to see how well the clowns had portrayed the different peoples. For the comedians, too, had looked in that book.

But while the king sat over the open volume, he noticed a spider that crept along the edge of the page; then he saw that a fly stood upon the open page. With its thin hair-like legs the spider pulled itself up the side of the book, then it reached its legs slowly over the side of the book, trying to crawl onto the page where the fly stood.

Just then a wind came and blew on the page so that it stood erect, and the spider could not reach the fly. Then the spider turned away, and for a while it crept along the table, as if it had forgotten the fly. Slowly and carefully it put out its feet, and then it stood still for a moment, as if it were waiting to hear a sound.

When the wind was gone, the page fell back to its place; then the spider turned and crept in a circle, coming nearer and nearer again to the edge of the book, until it clambered up the sides of the pages, and its little specks of eyes peered over the cliff-like top of the book onto the wide plain where the fly remained standing. And the spider lifted its claw onto the page.

Once more the wind came, and blew the page upward, and the spider fell away from the edge, and could not reach the fly. This happened several times, but at last the wind was quiet for a long while, and the spider returned to the book, and crept up the side, and placed its feet upon the open page, and drew its body up onto the page. In that instant, the wind blew hard, and turned the page over entirely upon the spider, so that he lay on his back between the pages of the book.

He tried to crawl out, but he could only crawl a little way, and he could not turn himself aright, and though he moved with all his strength he could only go a little further into the darkness that pressed upon him between the pages of the book; and there he remained, until nothing remained of him.

As for the fly, I will not tell you what he did.

But the king saw all that had happened, and he knew that what he saw was not a simple thing, but that there was a meaning intended for him in what he had seen; and it was as though he heard a message vaguely through thick walls. Then he fell into deep thought, trying to understand what had happened before his eyes; the guests at the festival saw the king was lost in thought, and did not disturb him.

For a long while the king leaned over the book, wondering, but he could not find a meaning to what he had seen; at last he became very tired, and his head leaned further over the page until it lay upon his spread arms, and he slept. Then he dreamed.

He dreamed that he sat upon his throne in his palace, and over him hung his portrait, and according to the custom in the palaces of kings, his crown hung over his portrait. He sat there, holding a precious image in his hands. Suddenly, hosts of people began to pour out of the image. He threw the thing away from him.

Then the sleeping king saw how the people that rushed out of the image turned, and climbed above him, and cut his head from his portrait. They seized his crown and hurled it into the mud. Then they ran toward him with their knives drawn, to kill him.

In that instant, a page out of the book upon which he slept stood erect and shielded him, so that the oncoming horde could do him no harm; when they had turned away, the page fell back into its place in the book.

Once more the angry people rushed to kill him, and the page stood before him and shielded him so that they had to turn back. Seven times they rushed upon him, and seven times they were prevented from harming him.

Then the king in his sleep was eager to see what was written on the leaf that had so well protected him, and what nation out of the Book of Nations might be represented there. But as he was about to look at the page, he was overcome by a terrible fear; the edges of his hair felt like ice. He began to scream.

The princes and the emperors who were his guests heard the king screaming in his sleep, and wanted to shake him that he might awake out of his frightful dream, but it was forbidden to touch the king while he slept. Then they began to shout, and to beat upon drums, and to make wild noises that might awaken the king, but he did not hear them, and only trembled, and cried out, and shouted with fear as he slept over the Book of Nations.

Then a high mountain came to him and said, "Why are you screaming so? I was asleep for many ages, and nothing could awaken me, but your screams have broken my sleep!"

"How can I keep from screaming?" cried the king. "See how all the people are assembled, how they come against me with their drawn knives! They will kill me! And I have nothing to protect me but this little sheet of paper!"

"As long as it stands before you, you have nothing to fear," said the mountain. "I too have many enemies, but that same leaf has protected me, and I am not afraid. Come, and I'll show you my enemies."

They went, and the king saw myriad upon myriad of warriors assembled at the foot of the mountain; they were shouting and dancing and loudly blowing their trumpets.

"Why do they sing so gayly, and why do they dance so triumphantly?" the king asked of the mountain.

"Each time one of them thinks of a plan by which they may come up on me, they become wild with joy, and hold a feast, and they dance and sing in triumph," said the mountain. "But the same page protects me by what is written upon it, just as you are protected."

Then the king saw that a tablet stood on the top of the mountain, but because the mountain was very high, he could not read what was written on the tablet.

Behind them, however, was another stone on which this was written: "He that has all his teeth may come up to the top of the mountain."

The king thought, "Surely there are many people who can easily go up this way." But he looked on the ground and saw that they were not pebbles, but teeth of men and beasts upon which he trod, and all over the side of the mountain there were little mounds of teeth.

For the Power of the Name had caused a grass to grow on the sides of that mountain, and this grass was such that it drew out the teeth of all those who passed over it. The enemies from below tried to ride over it on the backs of swift horses, or in wagons, thinking that thus they would not touch the grass, nevertheless their teeth fell from them, and they could go no further up against the mountain.

When the king had seen this, he returned to the place of his own dream, and saw that now his own enemies, who were the people that had rushed out of the image, took up the head of his portrait and placed it back upon the shoulders; then they took the crown out of the mud, and washed it, and hung it in its accustomed place.

And then the king woke.

At once he looked into the book, to see what was written on the page that had protected him. And he found that that page in the Book of Nations was the page of the Jews. He read carefully what was written there, and he began to understand the truth, and he said, "I will become a Jew."

But when he had become a Jew he was not yet satisfied, and cried, "The whole world must know the truth, and I will make all the peoples in the world into Jews."

But he could not think of a way by which he could show the truth to the whole world, and cause all men to become Jews, so he decided, "I will go and seek a sage who can tell me the meaning of everything in my dream, and then I shall know how to do what I want to do."

The king disguised himself as a simple traveller, and took two companions, and went out to seek a wise man.

Wherever he went he asked, "Is there anyone here who can explain a dream?" Though he travelled all over the earth, he could find no one who understood the meaning of his dream. But at last he was told of a sage who lived in a place that had no name.

When the king had been to every place that had a name, he continued to seek, and at last he reached a place where there were no hills or trees or rivers, no houses, and no beasts; and there was a man.

"What is the name of this place?" the king asked.

And the man answered him, "This place has no name." Then the king knew that he had come to the end of his journey, and that this man was the sage who could tell him the meaning of his dreams. So he told the wise man the truth about himself. "I am no simple traveller," he said, "but a king who has won many battles and conquered many nations; and now I would like to know the true meaning of my dream."

The sage answered that he could not give him the meaning of his dream, but that if the king would wait until a day that was not in a month, he might himself learn what he wanted to know. "For on that day," the wise man said, "I gather the seeds of all things and make them into a perfume. And when the perfume is spread all about you, you will have the power to see for yourself all that you desire to know."

The king said, "I will wait."

He waited. And there came a time when he no longer knew the day and the month. Then the wizard brought him a perfume, and burned the perfume until it rose all about the king. And in the cloud the king began to see.

He saw himself as he had been even before he had become himself; he saw his soul as it waited in readiness before coming down to this world, and he saw his soul being led through all the worlds above and below, while a voice cried, "If there is any one who has evil to say of this soul, let him speak!" But the soul passed through all the regions, and not one voice was raised against it. Then the king saw his soul in readiness to go down and live upon earth. But at that instant someone came hurrying, running, crying, "Hear me, God! If this soul goes down on earth, what will there remain for me to do? Why was I created!"

The king looked, to see who it was that cried out so against his soul's going to earth, and he saw that it was the Evil One himself!

And the Evil One was answered: "This soul must go down on earth. As for you, you must think of something to do." Upon this, the Evil One went away.

Then the king saw his soul being led through the high regions, from one heaven to another, until at last it stood before the Court of highest heaven, ready to take its oath to go down and live on earth. And still the Evil One had not returned. Before the soul was given oath, a messenger was sent to bring the Evil One before the Throne. The Evil One came, and brought with him a wizen old man whom he had known for a very long time. And as he came up with the bent old man, he was laughing, and chuckling, and smiling to himself, and he said, "I've thought of a way out of it all! You can let this soul go down on earth!"

Then the king saw his soul go down on earth, and he saw himself born, and he saw everything that had happened to him on earth, he saw how he had become king, and how he had gone out in battles, and slaughtered peoples, and won victories, and taken prisoners.

He saw that among the myriads of prisoners he had taken there was a beautiful maiden. The maiden possessed every loveliness that was to be found on earth, the beauty of form that was felt as sweet water under the fingers, the beauty of the eyes that was as a caress of the hands, and the beauty that is heard like the sound of bells touched by the wind. But when the king looked upon her, he saw that her beauty was not her own, but that it came forth like a perfume out of the tiny image that she wore upon herself. And it was this image that contained all forms of beauty, and because it was upon her, it seemed that all those forms of beauty were her own.

And only the very good and the very wise can go higher upon this mountain, for no more may be told.

Translated from the Yiddish, Hebrew and German sources by Meyer Levin

5

St. Cecilia, or the Power of Music

by *Heinrich von Kleist*

Around the end of the sixteenth century, when they were furiously destroying images in the Netherlands, three young brothers, students in Wittenberg, were reunited in the city of Aachen with a fourth brother who was a preacher in Antwerp. They were in town to claim a legacy from an old uncle none of them had known and, hoping their business would not take long, they stayed at an inn.

For several days the preacher told them about the very important things that had been going on in the Netherlands. Now it so happened that the nuns of the Convent of Saint Cecilia, which in those days was to be found just past the gates of the city, were about to celebrate Corpus Christi, and the four brothers, aglow with fanaticism, youth, and the example the Netherlanders had set, decided to give the city of Aachen its own taste of iconoclastic destructiveness.

The evening before the festival the preacher, who had been at the head of more than one such expedition, got together a band of young merchants' sons and students who believed in the new doctrine. They spent the night in the inn eating, drinking, and cursing the papacy and, when day broke over the towers of the city, they began their reckless proceedings by equipping themselves with all sorts of instruments of destruction. In a mood of exultation they agreed on the signal which would start them smashing the scenes from the Bible depicted on the windows, then set out for the cathedral to the ringing of its bells, confident they would find great support among the people, and determined to level it to the ground.

This is a translation of the version of this story that Kleist wrote for the *Berliner Abendblätter*. He later expanded it considerably. The longer version is better known but less incisive, and this version seemed the more appropriate for this anthology.

The Abbess, whom a friend had informed at midnight
of the danger the convent was in, tried in vain to get the
chief imperial officer of the city to send some men to protect the convent. This officer was himself an enemy of the
papacy and, covertly a believer in the new doctrine. He
turned down her request, claiming that she was imagining
things and that her convent was not in the slightest danger.

Meanwhile the time had come for the celebration to
begin, and the nuns, prayerfully and with dreadful anxiety
about what might come, made preparations for the Mass.
They were entirely without protection except for an old
beadle of seventy who stood guard with a few armed servants at the entrance of the church.

It is well known that nuns in convents, who can play all
instruments, provide their own music, and that they often
perform with a precision, understanding and sensitivity—
perhaps because of the feminine nature of this mysterious
art—not be found in orchestras whose members are men.
But now, to make things doubly disturbing, Sister Antonia,
the conductor of the orchestra, had been very ill for some
days with typhoid fever. So even without taking into account the four blasphemous brothers (who could already
be seen, enveloped in their cloaks among the pillars of the
church), the nuns were terribly worried about their performance. The Abbess had, the night before, selected a
very old Italian Mass by an unknown master which they'd
already done several times with great success, thanks to
the extraordinary piety and sincerity which had gone into
its composition. She was more determined than ever not to
be thwarted, and sent a nun to ask once more how Sister
Antonia was, only to learn that she had lost consciousness
and could not possibly conduct.

Meanwhile the situation in the cathedral had already
become most serious: over a hundred troublemakers, of
every class and age, armed with hatchets and crowbars, had
gradually gathered there; some servants standing at the
doors had been provoked in the crudest way, and extremely
shameless things had been said to individual nuns whose
pious duties had, at times, brought them into public view.
Things got so bad that the beadle went to the sacristy and
begged the Abbess on bended knee to postpone the celebration and put herself under the protection of the com-
manding officer of the city. But she was firm as a rock and

said that the festival in honor of God must take place,
reminding the beadle of his duty to defend with his life
the Mass and solemn procession that would be held in the
cathedral. And she ordered the nuns, who stood quivering
in a circle around her, to immediately begin the celebration
with an oratorio that had often been performed in the
church, although it was inferior quality.

The nuns in the organ gallery got ready to do just that—
when all of a sudden Sister Antonia appeared, looking
vigorous and healthy, though her face was a little pale, and
proposed that they proceed without delay to perform that
very old Italian work mentioned above that the Abbess
had so urgently insisted they play. When the nuns asked
in amazement how she had recovered so quickly, she replied that there was no time for idle chatter. She handed
out the copies of the score she was carrying with her and
sat down at the organ in radiant ecstasy to direct the superb music.

Then what felt like celestial peace flowed into the hearts
of the pious women; even the anxiety they had felt lent
their souls wings to fly through all the heavens of harmony.
The Mass was performed with wondrous splendor.
Throughout the expanse of the church not a single breath
was drawn during the performance. During the *Salve re-
gina* especially, and even more during the *Gloria in excelsis*, the more than three thousand people who filled the
church seemed transfixed; with the result that, in spite of
the four accursed brothers, not even the dust on the pavement was disturbed, and the convent lasted till the end
of the Thirty Years War, when, however, by a provision
of the Peace of Westphalia, it was taken away from the
Church.

But the triumph of religion was, as one could see a few
days later, much greater than even this. For the landlord
of the inn where the four brothers were staying went to
the town hall to report their strange and shocking behavior, and declared to the authorities that, to all appearances, they must have lost their wits. The young men, he
said, had come back after the end of the celebration of
Corpus Christi silent and depressed; wrapped in their dark
cloaks, they had sat round a table and asked for nothing
but bread and water; about midnight, when everything was
quiet, they had intoned the *Gloria in excelsis* with hideous,

the belief—which the Abbess for many reasons did not
dare to make public—that Saint Cecilia herself had performed this terrifying and glorious miracle. The Pope,
several years later, confirmed this view, and even at the end
of the Thirty Years' War (when the convent, as was mentioned before, was taken away from the Church), the
legend tells us that the day on which Saint Cecilia used the
mysterious power of music to rescue the convent was set
aside and honored. And during the celebration they sang,
serenely and splendidly, the *Gloria in excelsis.*

Translated from the German
by Henry L. Shapiro

gruesome voices. Then he, the landlord, had g
a light to see what was making such strange
found them sitting up at the table and still sin
the stroke of one they became quiet, lay down c
boards without saying a word, slept a few hour
up again with the sun to begin, on bread and
same dreary and dismal monastic life. Five time
lord said, he listened to them at midnight,
Gloria in excelsis with voices that rattled the
the house; no other sound ever escaped thei
Gloria was not totally devoid of musical me
way it was shrieked made it unbearable, and tl
was obliged to ask the authorities to remove fr
these men who were undoubtedly possessed by

A doctor was sent to examine the young men
them just as the landlord had described them,
attempts to discover what had struck them down
which they had entered in full possession of th
failed. Some people from town who had been s
them during the Mass were summoned to give
They testified that the brothers did indeed distur
ice at the very beginning, but that as soon as
began they became quiet and attentive, and then
the other, they sank to their knees and, like the
congregation, prayed to God.

It was right after that that Sister Antonia, tl
conductor, died of the typhoid fever which, as
before, had confined her to her bed. When tl
came, by order of the prelate of the city, to ex:
score of the work that had been performed the m
that extraordinary day, the Abbess handed it
strange and profoundly emotional state, assuring
absolutely no one knew who had really been at t
conducting the Mass. A few days earlier the cast
several other men had heard testimony which pr
the deceased had been lying in a corner of her c
convent, totally unable to move, while the music v
performed. A nun who, as her blood relation, h
chosen to be her nurse, had not budged from her
whole morning that the celebration of Corpus Ch
taken place.

Accordingly, the Archbishop of Trier, who h
told of this strange event, was the first to actually

6

The Dream of a Ridiculous Man
by Fyodor Dostoevsky

I

I am a ridiculous man. They call me a madman now. That would be a distinct rise in my social position were it not that they still regard me as being as ridiculous as ever. But that does not make me angry any more. They are all dear to me now even while they laugh at me—yes, even then they are for some reason particularly dear to me. I shouldn't have minded laughing with them—not at myself, of course, but because I love them—had I not felt so sad as I looked at them. I feel sad because they do not know the truth, whereas I know it. Oh, how hard it is to be the only man to know the truth! But they won't understand that. No, they will not understand.

And yet in the past I used to be terribly distressed at appearing to be ridiculous. No, not appearing to be, but being. I've always cut a ridiculous figure. I suppose I must have known it from the day I was born. At any rate, I've known for certain that I was ridiculous ever since I was seven years old. Afterwards I went to school, then to the university, and—well—the more I learned, the more conscious did I become of the fact that I was ridiculous. So that for me my years of hard work at the university seem in the end to have existed for the sole purpose of demonstrating and proving to me, the more deeply engrossed I became in my studies, that I was an utterly absurd person. And as during my studies, so all my life. Every year the same consciousness that I was ridiculous in every way strengthened and intensified in my mind. They always laughed at me. But not one of them knew or suspected that if there were one man on earth who knew better than anyone else that he was ridiculous, that man was I. And this—I mean, the fact that they did not know it—was the bitterest pill for me to swallow. But there I was myself at

fault. I was always so proud that I never wanted to confess
it to anyone. No, I wouldn't do that for anything in the
world. As the years passed, this pride increased in me so
that I do believe that if ever I had by chance confessed it
to any one I should have blown my brains out the same
evening. Oh, how I suffered in the days of my youth from
the thought that I might not myself resist the impulse to
confess it to my schoolfellows. But ever since I became a
man I grew for some unknown reason a little more composed in my mind, though I was more and more conscious
of that awful characteristic of mine. Yes, most decidedly
for some unknown reason, for to this day I have not been
able to find out why that was so. Perhaps it was because
I was becoming terribly disheartened owing to one circum-
stance which was beyond my power to control, namely, the
conviction which was gaining upon me that nothing in the
whole world *made any difference*. I had long felt it dawn-
ing upon me, but I was fully convinced of it only last year,
and that, too, all of a sudden, as it were. I suddenly felt
that it made *no* difference to me whether the world existed
or whether nothing existed anywhere at all. I began to be
acutely conscious that *nothing existed in my own lifetime*.
At first I couldn't help feeling that at any rate in the past
many things had existed; but later on I came to the conclusion that there had not been anything even in the past,
but that for some reason it had merely seemed to have
been. Little by little I became convinced that there would
be nothing in the future, either. It was then that I suddenly
ceased to be angry with people and almost stopped noticing them. This indeed disclosed itself in the smallest trifles.
For instance, I would knock against people while walking
in the street. And not because I was lost in thought—I had
nothing to think about—I had stopped thinking about anything at that time; it made no difference to me. Not that
I had found an answer to all the questions. Oh, I had not
settled a single question, and there were thousands of them!
But *it made no difference to me,* and all the questions disappeared.

   And, well, it was only after that that I learnt the truth. I
learnt the truth last November, on the third of November,
to be precise, and every moment since then has been im-
printed indelibly on my mind. It happened on a dismal
evening, as dismal an evening as could be imagined. I was

returning home at about eleven o'clock and I remember thinking all the time that there could not be a more dismal evening. Even the weather was foul. It had been pouring all day, and the rain too was the coldest and most dismal rain that ever was, a sort of menacing rain—I remember that—a rain with a distinct animosity towards people. But about eleven o'clock it had stopped suddenly, and a horrible dampness descended upon everything, and it became much damper and colder than when it had been raining. And a sort of steam was rising from everything, from every cobble in the street, and from every side-street if you peered closely into it from the street as far as the eye could reach. I could not help feeling that if the gaslight had been extinguished everywhere, everything would have seemed much more cheerful, and that the gaslight oppressed the heart so much just because it shed a light upon it all. I had had scarcely any dinner that day. I had been spending the whole evening with an engineer who had two more friends visiting him. I never opened my mouth, and I expect I must have got on their nerves. They were discussing some highly controversial subject, and suddenly got very excited over it. But it really did not make any difference to them. I could see that. I knew that their excitement was not genuine. So I suddenly blurted it out. "My dear fellows," I said, "you don't really care a damn about it, do you?" They were not in the least offended, but they all burst out laughing at me. That was because I had said it without meaning to rebuke them, but simply because it made no difference to me. Well, they realised that it made no difference to me, and they felt happy.

When I was thinking about the gaslight in the streets, I looked up at the sky. The sky was awfully dark, but I could clearly distinguish the torn wisps of cloud and between them fathomless dark patches. All of a sudden I became aware of a little star in one of those patches and I began looking at it intently. That was because the little star gave me an idea: I made up mind to kill myself that night. I had made up my mind to kill myself already two months before and, poor as I am, I bought myself an excellent revolver and loaded it the same day. But two months had elapsed and it was still lying in the drawer. I was so utterly indifferent to everything that I was anxious to wait for the moment when I would not be so indifferent and then kill myself. Why—I don't know. And so every night during these two months I thought of shooting myself as I was going home. I was only waiting for the right moment. And now the little star gave me an idea, and I made up my mind then and there that it should *most certainly* be that night. But why the little star gave me the idea—I don't know.

And just as I was looking at the sky, this little girl suddenly grasped me by the elbow. The street was already deserted and there was scarcely a soul to be seen. In the distance a cabman was fast asleep on his box. The girl was about eight years old. She had a kerchief on her head, and she wore only an old, shabby little dress. She was soaked to the skin, but what stuck in my memory was her little torn wet boots. I still remember them. They caught my eye especially. She suddenly began tugging at my elbow and calling me. She was not crying, but saying something in a loud, jerky sort of voice, something that did not make sense, for she was trembling all over and her teeth were chattering from cold. She seemed to be terrified of something and she was crying desperately, "Mummy! Mummy!" I turned round to look at her, but did not utter a word and went on walking. But she ran after me and kept tugging at my clothes, and there was a sound in her voice which in very frightened children signifies despair. I know that sound. Though her words sounded as if they were choking her, I realised that her mother must be dying somewhere very near, or that something similar was happening to her, and that she had run out to call someone, to find someone who would help her mother. But I did not go with her; on the contrary, something made me drive her away. At first I told her to go and find a policeman. But she suddenly clasped her hands and, whimpering and gasping for breath, kept running at my side and would not leave me. It was then that I stamped my foot and shouted at her. She just cried, "Sir! Sir! . . ." and then she left me suddenly and rushed headlong across the road: another man appeared there and she evidently rushed from me to him.

I climbed to the fifth floor. I live apart from my landlord. We all have separate rooms as in an hotel. My room is very small and poor. My window is a semicircular skylight. I have a sofa covered with American cloth, a table with books on it, two chairs and a comfortable armchair, a very old armchair indeed, but low-seated and with a high back serving as a head-rest. I sat down in the armchair, lighted the candle, and began thinking. Next door in the other room behind the partition, the usual bedlam was going on. It had been going on since the day before yesterday. A retired army captain lived there, and he had visitors —six merry gentlemen who drank vodka and played faro with an old pack of cards. Last night they had a fight and I know that two of them were for a long time pulling each other about by the hair. The landlady wanted to complain, but she is dreadfully afraid of the captain. We had only one more lodger in our rooms, a thin little lady, the wife of an army officer, on a visit to Petersburg with her three little children who had all been taken ill since their arrival at our house. She and her children were simply terrified of the captain and they lay shivering and crossing themselves all night long, and the youngest child had a sort of nervous attack from fright. This captain (I know that for a fact) sometimes stops people on Nevsky Avenue and asks them for a few coppers, telling them he is very poor. He can't get a job in the Civil Service, but the strange thing is (and that's why I am telling you this) that the captain had never once during the month he had been living with us made me feel in the least irritated. From the very first, of course, I would not have anything to do with him, and he himself was bored with me the very first time we met. But however big a noise they raised behind their partition and however many of them there were in the captain's room, it makes no difference to me. I sit up all night and, I assure you, I don't hear them at all—so completely do I forget about them. You see, I stay awake all night till daybreak, and that has been going on for a whole year now. I sit up all night in the armchair at the table—doing nothing. I read books only in the daytime. At night I sit like that without even thinking about anything in particular: some thoughts wander in and out of my mind, and I let them come and go as they please. In the night the candle burns out completely.

I sat down at the table, took the gun out of the drawer, and put it down in front of me. I remember asking myself as I put it down, "Is it to be then?" and I replied with complete certainty, "It is!" That is to say, I was going to shoot myself. I knew I should shoot myself that night for

certain. What I did not know was how much longer I
should go on sitting at the table till I shot myself. And I
should of course have shot myself, had it not been for the
little girl.

II

You see, though nothing made any difference to me, I
could feel pain, for instance, couldn't I? If anyone had
struck me, I should have felt pain. The same was true so
far as my moral perceptions were concerned. If anything
happened to arouse my pity, I should have felt pity, just
as I used to do at the time when things did make a difference to me. So I had felt pity that night: I should most
decidedly have helped a child. Why then did I not help
the little girl? Because of a thought that had occurred to
me at the time: when she was pulling at me and calling
me, a question suddenly arose in my mind and I could not
settle it. It was an idle question, but it made me angry.
What made me angry was the conclusion I drew from the
reflection that if I had really decided to do away with myself that night, everything in the world should have been
more indifferent to me than ever. Why then should I have
suddenly felt that I was not indifferent and be sorry for
the little girl? I remember that I was very sorry for her,
so much so that I felt a strange pang which was quite incomprehensible in my position. I'm afraid I am unable
better to convey that fleeting sensation of mine, but it
persisted with me at home when I was sitting at the table,
and I was very much irritated. I had not been so irritated
for a long time past. One train of thought followed another. It was clear to me that so long as I was still a human
being and not a meaningless cipher, and till I became a
cipher, I was alive, and consequently able to suffer, be
angry, and feel shame at my actions. Very well. But if, on
the other hand, I were going to kill myself in, say, two
hours, what did that little girl matter to me and what did I
care for shame or anything else in the world? I was going
to turn into a cipher, into an absolute cipher. And surely
the realisation that I should soon cease to exist *altogether*,
and hence everything would cease to exist, ought to have
had some slight effect on my feeling of pity for the little
girl or on my feeling of shame after so mean an action.

Why after all did I stamp and shout so fiercely at the little
girl? I did it because I thought that not only did I feel no
pity, but that it wouldn't matter now if I were guilty of
the most inhuman baseness, since in another two hours
everything would become extinct. Do you believe me when
I tell you that that was the only reason why I shouted like
that? I am almost convinced of it now. It seemed clear to
me that life and the world in some way or other depended
on me now. It might almost be said that the world seemed
to be created for me alone. If I were to shoot myself, the
world would cease to exist—for me at any rate. To say
nothing of the possibility that nothing would in fact exist
for anyone after me and the whole world would dissolve
as soon as my consciousness became extinct, would disappear in a twinkling like a phantom, like some integral
part of my consciousness, and vanish without leaving a
trace behind, for all this world and all these people exist
perhaps only in my consciousness.

I remember that as I sat and meditated, I began to examine all these questions which thronged in my mind one
after another from quite a different angle, and thought of
something quite new. For instance, the strange notion occurred to me that if I had lived before on the moon or on
Mars and had committed there the most shameful and dis-
honourable action that can be imagined, and had been so
disgraced and dishonoured there as can be imagined and
experienced only occasionally in a dream, a nightmare,
and if, finding myself afterwards on earth, I had retained
the memory of what I had done on the other planet, and
moreover knew that I should never in any circumstances
go back there—if that were to have happened, should I
or should I not have felt, as I looked from the earth upon
the moon, that *it made no difference* to me? Should I or
should I not have felt ashamed of that action? The questions were idle and useless, for the gun was already lying
before me and there was not a shadow of doubt in my
mind that *it* was going to take place for certain, but they
excited and maddened me. It seemed to me that I could
not die now without having settled something first. The
little girl, in fact, had saved me, for by these questions I
put off my own execution.

Meanwhile things had grown more quiet in the captain's
room: they had finished their card game and were getting

ready to turn in for the night, and now were only grumbling and swearing at each other in a halfhearted sort of way. It was at that moment that I suddenly fell asleep in my armchair at the table, a thing that had never happened to me before.

I fell asleep without being aware of it at all. Dreams, as we all know, are very curious things: certain incidents in them are presented with quite uncanny vividness, each detail executed with the finishing touch of a jeweller, while others you leap across as though entirely unaware of, for instance, space and time. Dreams seem to be induced not by reason but by desire, not by the head but by the heart, and yet what clever tricks my reason has sometimes played on me in dreams! And furthermore what incomprehensible things happen to it in a dream. My brother, for instance, died five years ago. I sometimes dream about him: he takes a keen interest in my affairs, we are both very interested, and yet I know very well all through my dream that my brother is dead and buried. How is it that I am not surprised that, though dead, he is here beside me, doing his best to help me? Why does my reason accept all this without the slightest hesitation? But enough. Let me tell you about my dream. Yes, I dreamed that dream that night. My dream of the third of November. They are making fun of me now by saying that it was only a dream. But what does it matter whether it was a dream or not, so long as that dream revealed the Truth to me? For once you have recognised the truth and seen it, you know it is the one and only truth and that there can be no other, whether you are asleep or awake. But never mind. Let it be a dream, but remember that I had intended to cut short by suicide the life that means so much to us, and that my dream—my dream—oh, it revealed to me a new, grand, regenerated, strong life!

Listen.

III

I have said that I fell asleep imperceptibly and even while I seemed to be revolving the same thoughts again in my mind. Suddenly I dreamed that I picked up the gun and, sitting in my armchair, pointed it straight at my heart—at my heart, and not at my head. For I had firmly resolved to shoot myself through the head, through the right temple, to be precise. Having aimed the gun at my breast, I paused for a second or two, and suddenly my candle, the table and the wall began moving and swaying before me. I fired quickly.

In a dream you sometimes fall from a great height, or you are being murdered or beaten, but you never feel any pain unless you really manage somehow or other to hurt yourself in bed, when you feel pain and almost always wake up from it. So it was in my dream: I did not feel any pain, but it seemed as though with my shot everything within me was shaken and everything was suddenly extinguished, and a terrible darkness descended all around me. I seemed to have become blind and dumb. I was lying on something hard, stretched out full length on my back. I saw nothing and could not make the slightest movement. All round me people were walking and shouting. The captain was yelling in his deep bass voice, the landlady was screaming and—suddenly another hiatus, and I was being carried in a closed coffin. I could feel the coffin swaying and I was thinking about it, and for the first time the idea flashed through my mind that I was dead, dead as a doornail, that I knew it, that there was not the least doubt about it, that I could neither see nor move, and yet I could feel and reason. But I was soon reconciled to that and, as usually happens in dreams, I accepted the facts without questioning them.

And now I was buried in the earth. They all went away, and I was left alone, entirely alone. I did not move. Whenever before I imagined how I should be buried in a grave, there was only one sensation I actually associated with the grave, namely, that of damp and cold. And so it was now. I felt that I was very cold, especially in the tips of my toes, but I felt nothing else.

I lay in my grave and, strange to say, I did not expect anything, accepting the idea that a dead man had nothing to expect as an incontestable fact. But it was damp. I don't know how long a time passed, whether an hour, or several days, or many days. But suddenly a drop of water, which had seeped through the lid of the coffin, fell on my closed left eye. It was followed by another drop a minute later, then after another minute by another drop, and so on. One drop every minute. All at once deep indignation

blazed up in my heart, and I suddenly felt a twinge of
physical pain in it. "That's my wound," I thought. "It's
the shot I fired. There's a bullet there. . . ." And drop
after drop still kept falling every minute on my closed
eyelid. And suddenly I called (not with my voice, for I
was motionless, but with the whole of my being) upon
Him who was responsible for all that was happening to
me:

"Whoever Thou art, and if anything more rational exists
than what is happening here, let it, I pray Thee, come to
pass here too. But if Thou art revenging Thyself for my
senseless act of self-destruction by the infamy and absurdity of life after death, then know that no torture that
may be inflicted upon me can ever equal the contempt
which I shall go on feeling in silence, though my martyrdom last for aeons upon aeons!"

I made this appeal and was silent. The dead silence
went on for almost a minute, and one more drop fell on
my closed eyelid, but I knew, I knew and believed infinitely
and unshakably that everything would without a doubt
change immediately. And then my grave was opened. I
don't know, that is, whether it was opened or dug open,
but I was seized by some dark and unknown being and
we found ourselves in space. I suddenly regained my sight.
It was a pitch-black night. Never, never had there been
such darkness! We were flying through space at a terrific
speed and we had already left the earth behind us. I did
not question the being who was carrying me. I was proud
and waited. I was telling myself that I was not afraid, and
I was filled with admiration at the thought that I was not
afraid. I cannot remember how long we were flying, nor
can I give you an idea of the time; it all happened as it
always does happen in dreams when you leap over space
and time and the laws of nature and reason, and only pause
at the points which are especially dear to your heart. All
I remember is that I suddenly beheld a little star in the
darkness.

"Is that Sirius?" I asked, feeling suddenly unable to restrain myself, for I had made up my mind not to ask any
questions.

"No," answered the being who was carrying me, "that
is the same star you saw between the clouds when you
were coming home."

I knew that its face bore some resemblance to a human face. It is a strange fact but I did not like that being, and I even felt an intense aversion for it. I had expected complete non-existence and that was why I had shot myself through the heart. And yet there I was in the hands of a being, not human of course, but which *was,* which existed. "So there is life beyond the grave!" I thought with the curious irrelevance of a dream, but at heart I remained essentially unchanged. "If I must *be* again," I thought, "and live again at someone's unalterable behest, I won't be defeated and humiliated!"

"You know I'm afraid of you and that's why you despise me," I said suddenly to my companion, unable to refrain from the humiliating remark with its implied admission, and feeling my own humiliation in my heart like the sharp prick of a needle.

He did not answer me, but I suddenly felt that I was not despised, that no one was laughing at me, that no one was even pitying me, and that our journey had a purpose, an unknown and mysterious purpose that concerned only me. Fear was steadily growing in my heart. Something was communicated to me from my silent companion—mutely but agonisingly—and it seemed to permeate my whole being. We were speeding through dark and unknown regions of space. I had long since lost sight of the constellations familiar to me. I knew that there were stars in the heavenly spaces whose light took thousands and millions of years to reach the earth. Possibly we were already flying through those spaces. I expected something in the terrible anguish that wrung my heart. And suddenly a strangely familiar and incredibly nostalgic feeling shook me to the very core: I suddenly caught sight of our sun! I knew that it could not possibly be *our* sun that gave birth to our earth, and that we were millions of miles away from our sun, but for some unknown reason I recognised with every fibre of my being that it was precisely the same sun as ours, its exact copy and twin. A sweet, nostalgic feeling filled my heart with rapture: the old familiar power of the same light which had given me life stirred an echo in my heart and revived it, and I felt the same life stirring within me for the first time since I had been in the grave.

"But if it is the sun, if it's exactly the same sun as ours," I cried, "then where is the earth?"

And my companion pointed to a little star twinkling in the darkness with an emerald light. We were making straight for it.

"But are such repetitions possible in the universe? Can that be nature's law? And if that is an earth there, is it the same earth as ours? Just the same poor, unhappy, but dear, dear earth, and beloved for ever and ever? Arousing like our earth the same poignant love for herself even in the most ungrateful of her children?" I kept crying, deeply moved by an uncontrollable, rapturous love for the dear old earth I had left behind.

The face of the poor little girl I had treated so badly flashed through my mind.

"You shall see it all," answered my companion, and a strange sadness sounded in his voice.

But we were rapidly approaching the planet. It was growing before my eyes. I could already distinguish the ocean, the outlines of Europe, and suddenly a strange feeling of some great and sacred jealousy blazed up in my heart.

"How is such a repetition possible and why? I love, I can only love the earth I've left behind, stained with my blood when, ungrateful wretch that I am, I extinguished my life by shooting myself through the heart. But never, never have I ceased to love that earth, and even on the night I parted from it I loved it perhaps more poignantly than ever. Is there suffering on this new earth? On our earth we can truly love only with suffering and through suffering! We know not how to love otherwise. We know no other love. I want suffering in order to love. I want and thirst this very minute to kiss, with tears streaming down my cheeks, the one and only earth I have left behind. I don't want, I won't accept life on any other! . . ."

But my companion had already left me. Suddenly, and without as it were being aware of it myself, I stood on this other earth in the bright light of a sunny day, fair and beautiful as paradise. I believe I was standing on one of the islands which on our earth form the Greek archipelago, or somewhere on the coast of the mainland close to this archipelago. Oh, everything was just as it is with us, except that everything seemed to be bathed in the radiance of some public festival and of some great and holy triumph attained at last. The gentle emerald sea softly lapped the shore and kissed it with manifest, visible, almost conscious love. Tall, beautiful trees stood in all the glory of their green luxuriant foliage, and their innumerable leaves (I am sure of that) welcomed me with their soft, tender rustle, and seemed to utter sweet words of love. The lush grass blazed with bright and fragrant flowers. Birds were flying in flocks through the air and, without being afraid of me, alighted on my shoulders and hands and joyfully beat against me with their sweet fluttering wings. And at last I saw and came to know the people of this blessed earth. They came to me themselves. They surrounded me. They kissed me. Children of the sun, children of their sun—oh, how beautiful they were! Never on our earth had I beheld such beauty in man. Only perhaps in our children during the very first years of their life could one have found a remote, though faint, reflection of this beauty. The eyes of these happy people shone with a bright lustre. Their faces were radiant with understanding and a serenity of mind that had reached its greatest fulfilment. Those faces were joyous; in the words and voices of these people there was a child-like gladness. Oh, at the first glance at their faces I at once understood all, all! It was an earth unstained by the Fall, inhabited by people who had not sinned and who lived in the same paradise as that in which, according to the legends of mankind, our first parents lived before they sinned, with the only difference that all the earth here was everywhere the same paradise. These people, laughing happily, thronged round me and overwhelmed me with their caresses; they took me home with them, and each of them was anxious to set my mind at peace. Oh, they asked me no questions, but seemed to know everything already (that was the impression I got), and they longed to remove every trace of suffering from my face as soon as possible.

IV

Well, you see, again let me repeat: All right, let us assume it was only a dream! But the sensation of the love of those innocent and beautiful people has remained with me for ever, and I can feel that their love is even now flowing out to me from over there. I have seen them myself. I have known them thoroughly and been convinced.

I loved them and I suffered for them afterwards. Oh, I
knew at once even all the time that there were many things
about them I should never be able to understand. To me,
a modern Russian progressive and a despicable citizen of
Petersburg, it seemed inexplicable that, knowing so much,
they knew nothing of our science, for instance. But I
soon realised that their knowledge was derived from, and
fostered by, emotions other than those to which we were
accustomed on earth, and that their aspirations, too, were
quite different. They desired nothing. They were at peace
with themselves. They did not strive to gain knowledge of
life as we strive to understand it because their lives were
full. But their knowledge was higher and deeper than the
knowledge we derive from our science; for our science
seeks to explain what life is and strives to understand it
in order to teach others how to live, while they knew how
to live without science. I understood that, but I couldn't
understand their knowledge. They pointed out their trees
to me, and I could not understand the intense love with
which they looked on them; it was as though they were
talking with beings like themselves. And, you know, I
don't think I am exaggerating in saying that they talked
with them! Yes, they had discovered their language, and
I am sure the trees understood them. They looked upon all
nature like that—the animals which lived peaceably with
them and did not attack them, but loved them, conquered
by their love for them. They pointed out the stars to me
and talked to me about them in a way that I could not
understand, but I am certain that in some curious way
they communed with the stars in the heavens, not only in
thought, but in some actual, living way. Oh, these people
were not concerned whether I understood them or not;
they loved me without it. But I too knew that they would
never be able to understand me, and for that reason I
hardly ever spoke to them about our earth. I merely kissed
the earth on which they lived in their presence, and worshipped them without any words. And they saw that and
let me worship them without being ashamed that I was
worshipping them, for they themselves loved much. They
did not suffer for me when, weeping, I sometimes kissed
their feet, for in their hearts they were joyfully aware of
the strong affection with which they would return my love.
At times I asked myself in amazement how they had man-

aged never to offend a person like me and not once arouse
in a person like me a feeling of jealousy and envy. Many
times I asked myself how I—a braggart and a liar—could
refrain from telling them all I knew of science and philosophy, of which of course they had no idea? How had it
never occurred to me to impress them with my store of
learning, or impart my learning to them out of the love I
bore them?

They were playful and high-spirited like children. They
wandered about their beautiful woods and groves, they
sang their beautiful songs, they lived on simple food—the
fruits of their trees, the honey from their woods, and the
milk of the animals that loved them. To obtain their food
and clothes, they did not work very hard or long. They
knew love and they begot children, but I never noticed
in them those outbursts of *cruel* sensuality which overtake
almost everybody on our earth, whether man or woman,
and are the only source of almost every sin of our human
race. They rejoiced in their new-born children as new
sharers in their bliss. There were no quarrels or jealousy
among them, and they did not even know what the words
meant. Their children were the children of them all, for
they were all one family. There was scarcely any illness
among them, though there was death; but their old people
died peacefully, as though falling asleep, surrounded by
the people who took leave of them, blessing them and
smiling at them, and themselves receiving with bright
smiles the farewell wishes of their friends. I never saw
grief or tears on those occasions. What I did see was love
that seemed to reach the point of rapture, but it was a
gentle, self-sufficient, and contemplative rapture. There
was reason to believe that they communicated with the departed after death, and that their earthly union was not
cut short by death. They found it almost impossible to
understand me when I questioned them about life eternal,
but apparently they were so convinced of it in their minds
that for them it was no question at all. They had no places
of worship, but they had a certain awareness of a constant,
uninterrupted, and living union with the Universe at large.
They had no specific religions, but instead they had a certain knowledge that when their earthly joy had reached
the limits imposed upon it by nature, they—both the living and the dead—would reach a state of still closer com-

munion with the Universe at large. They looked forward
to that moment with joy, but without haste and without
pining for it, as though already possessing it in the vague
stirrings of their hearts, which they communicated to each
other.

In the evening, before going to sleep, they were fond of
gathering together and singing in melodious and harmonious choirs. In their songs they expressed all the sensa-
tions the parting day had given them. They praised it and
bade it farewell. They praised nature, the earth, the sea,
and the woods. They were also fond of composing songs
about one another, and they praised each other like children. Their songs were very simple, but they sprang
straight from the heart and they touched the heart. And
not only in their songs alone, but they seemed to spend all.
their lives in perpetual praise of one another. It seemed to
be a universal and all-embracing love for each other. Some
of their songs were solemn and ecstatic, and I was scarcely
able to understand them at all. While understanding the
words, I could never entirely fathom their meaning. It
remained somehow beyond the grasp of my reason, and
yet it sank unconsciously deeper and deeper into my
heart. I often told them that I had had a presentiment of
it years ago and that all that joy and glory had been
perceived by me while I was still on our earth as a nostalgic yearning, bordering at times on unendurably poignant
sorrow; that I had had a presentiment of them all and of
their glory in the dreams of my heart and in the reveries
of my soul; that often on our earth I could not look at
the setting sun without tears. . . . That there always was
a sharp pang of anguish in my hatred of the men of our
earth; why could I not hate them without loving them too?
why could I not forgive them? And in my love for them,
too, there was a sharp pang of anguish: why could I not
love them without hating them? They listened to me, and
I could tell that they did not know what I was talking
about. But I was not sorry to have spoken to them of it,
for I knew that they appreciated how much and how
anxiously I yearned for those I had forsaken. Oh yes,
when they looked at me with their dear eyes full of love,
when I realised that in their presence my heart, too, became as innocent and truthful as theirs, I did not regret
my inability to understand them, either. The sensation of

the fullness of life left me breathless, and I worshipped them in silence.

Oh, everyone laughs in my face now and everyone assures me that I could not possibly have seen and felt anything so definite, but was merely conscious of a sensation that arose in my own feverish heart, and that I invented all those details myself when I woke up. And when I told them that they were probably right, good Lord, what mirth that admission of mine caused and how they laughed at me! Why, of course, I was overpowered by the mere sensation of that dream and it alone survived in my sorely wounded heart. But none the less the real shapes and forms of my dream, that is, those I actually saw at the very time of my dream, were filled with such harmony and were so enchanting and beautiful, and so intensely true, that on awakening I was indeed unable to clothe them in our feeble words so that they were bound as it were to become blurred in my mind; so is it any wonder that perhaps unconsciously I was myself afterwards driven to make up the details which I could not help distorting, particularly in view of my passionate desire to convey some of them at least as quickly as I could. But that does not mean that I have no right to believe that it all did happen. As a matter of fact, it was quite possibly a thousand times better, brighter, and more joyful than I describe it. What if it was only a dream? All that couldn't possibly not have been. And do you know, I think I'll tell you a secret: perhaps it was no dream at all! For what happened afterwards was so awful, so horribly true, that it couldn't possibly have been a mere coinage of my brain seen in a dream. Granted that my heart was responsible for my dream, but could my heart alone have been responsible for the awful truth of what happened to me afterwards? Surely my paltry heart and my vacillating and trivial mind could not have risen to such a revelation of truth! Oh, judge for yourselves: I have been concealing it all the time, but now I will tell you the whole truth. The fact is, I—corrupted them all!

V

Yes, yes, it ended in my corrupting them all! How it could have happened I do not know, but I remember it clearly. The dream encompassed thousands of years and left in me only a vague sensation of the whole. I only know that the cause of the Fall was I. Like a horrible trichina, like the germ of the plague infecting whole kingdoms, so did I infect with myself all that happy earth that knew no sin before me. They learnt to lie, and they grew to appreciate the beauty of a lie. Oh, perhaps, it all began *innocently*, with a jest, with a desire to show off, with amorous play, and perhaps indeed only with a germ, but this germ made its way into their hearts and they liked it. The voluptuousness was soon born, voluptuousness begot jealousy, and jealousy—cruelty. . . . Oh, I don't know, I can't remember, but soon, very soon the first blood was shed: they were shocked and horrified, and they began to separate and to shun one another. They formed alliances, but it was one against another. Recriminations began, reproaches. They came to know shame, and they made shame into a virtue. The conception of honour was born, and every alliance raised its own standard. They began torturing animals, and the animals ran away from them into the forests and became their enemies. A struggle began for separation, for isolation, for personality, for mine and thine. They began talking in different languages. They came to know sorrow, and they loved sorrow. They thirsted for suffering, and they said that Truth could only be attained through suffering. It was then that science made its appearance among them. When they became wicked, they began talking of brotherhood and humanity and understood the meaning of those ideas. When they became guilty of crimes, they invented justice, and drew up whole codes of law, and to ensure the carrying out of their laws they erected a guillotine. They only vaguely remembered what they had lost, and they would not believe that they ever were happy and innocent. They even laughed at the possibility of their former happiness and called it a dream. They could not even imagine it in any definite shape or form, but the strange and wonderful thing was that though they had lost faith in their former state of happiness and called it a fairy-tale, they longed so much to be happy and innocent once more that, like children, they succumbed to the desire of their hearts, glorified this desire, built temples, and began offering up prayers to their own idea, their own "desire," and at the same time firmly believed that it could not be realised and brought about, though they still worshipped it and adored it with tears. And yet if they could have in one way or another returned to the state of happy innocence they had lost, and if someone had shown it to them again and had asked them whether they desired to go back to it, they would certainly have refused. The answer they gave me was, "What if we are dishonest, cruel, and unjust? We *know* it and we are sorry for it, and we torment ourselves for it, and inflict pain upon ourselves, and punish ourselves more perhaps than the merciful Judge who will judge us and whose name we do not know. But we have science and with its aid we shall again discover truth, though we shall accept it only when we perceive it with our reason. Knowledge is higher than feeling, and the consciousness of life is higher than life. Science will give us wisdom. Wisdom will reveal to us the laws. And the knowledge of the laws of happiness is higher than happiness." That is what they said to me, and having uttered those words, each of them began to love himself better than anyone else, and indeed they could not do otherwise. Every one of them became so jealous of his own personality that he strove with might and main to belittle and humble it in others; and therein he saw the whole purpose of his life. Slavery made its appearance, even voluntary slavery: the weak eagerly submitted themselves to the will of the strong on condition that the strong helped them to oppress those who were weaker than themselves. Saints made their appearance, saints who came to these people with tears and told them of their pride, of their loss of proportion and harmony, of their loss of shame. They were laughed to scorn and stoned to death. Their sacred blood was spilt on the threshold of the temples. But then men arose who began to wonder how they could all be united again, so that everybody should, without ceasing to love himself best of all, not interfere with everybody else and so that all of them should live together in a society which would at least seem to be founded on mutual understanding. Whole wars were fought over this idea. All the combatants at one and the same time firmly believed that science, wisdom, and the instinct of self-preservation would in the end force mankind to unite into a harmonious and intelligent society, and therefore, to hasten matters, the "very wise" did their best to extermi-

nate as rapidly as possible the "not so wise" who did not
understand their idea, so as to prevent them from interfering with its triumph. But the instinct of self-preservation began to weaken rapidly. Proud and voluptuous men
appeared who frankly demanded all or nothing. In order
to obtain everything they did not hesitate to resort to
violence, and if it failed—to suicide. Religions were
founded to propagate the cult of non-existence and self-
destruction for the sake of the everlasting peace in noth-
ingness. At last these people grew weary of their senseless
labours and suffering appeared on their faces, and these
people proclaimed that suffering was beauty, for in suffering alone was there thought. They glorified suffering in
their songs. I walked among them, wringing my hands and
weeping over them, but I loved them perhaps more than
before when there was no sign of suffering in their faces
and when they were innocent and—oh, so beautiful! I
loved the earth they had polluted even more than when it
had been a paradise, and only because sorrow had made
its appearance on it. Alas, I always loved sorrow and
affliction, but only for myself, only for myself; for them I
wept now, for I pitied them. I stretched out my hands to
them, accusing, cursing, and despising myself. I told them
that I alone was responsible for it all—I alone; that it was
I who had brought them corruption, contamination, and
lies! I implored them to crucify me, and I taught them
how to make the cross. I could not kill myself; I had not
the courage to do it; but I longed to receive martyrdom
at their hands. I thirsted for martyrdom, I yearned for
my blood to be shed to the last drop in torment and suffering. But they only laughed at me, and in the end they began looking upon me as a madman. They justified me.
They said that they had got what they themselves wanted
and that what was now could not have been otherwise. At
last they told me that I was becoming dangerous to them
and that they would lock me up in a lunatic asylum if I
did not hold my peace. Then sorrow entered my soul with
such force that my heart was wrung and I felt as though I
were dying, and then—well, then I awoke.

It was morning, that is, the sun had not risen yet, but
it was about six o'clock. When I came to, I found myself
in the same armchair, my candle had burnt out, in the
captain's room they were asleep, and silence, so rare in

our house, reigned around. The first thing I did was to
jump up in great amazement. Nothing like this had ever
happened to me before, not even so far as the most trivial
details were concerned. Never, for instance, had I fallen
asleep like this in my armchair. Then, suddenly, as I was
standing and coming to myself, I caught sight of my gun
lying there ready and loaded. But I pushed it away from
me at once! Oh, how I longed for life, life! I lifted up my
hands and called upon eternal Truth—no, not called upon
it, but wept. Rapture, infinite and boundless rapture intoxicated me. Yes, life and—preaching! I made up my mind
to preach from that very moment and, of course, to go on
preaching all my life. I am going to preach, I want to
preach. What? Why, truth. For I have beheld truth, I have
beheld it with mine own eyes, I have beheld it in all its
glory!

And since then I have been preaching. Moreover, I
love all who laugh at me more than all the rest. Why that
is so, I don't know and I cannot explain, but let it be so.
They say that even now I often get muddled and confused
now, what will be later on? It is perfectly true. I do get
muddled and confused and it is quite possible that I shall
be getting worse later. And, of course, I shall get muddled several times before I find out how to preach, that is,
what words to use and what deeds to perform, for that is
all very difficult! All this is even now as clear to me as
daylight, but, pray, tell me who does not get muddled and
confused? And yet all follow the same path, at least all
strive to achieve the same thing, from the philosopher to
the lowest criminal, only by different roads. It is an old
truth, but this is what is new: I cannot even get very much
muddled and confused. For I have beheld the Truth. I
have beheld it and I know that people can be happy and
beautiful without losing their ability to live on earth. I will
not and I cannot believe that evil is the normal condition
among men. And yet they all laugh at this faith of mine.
But how can I help believing it I have beheld it—the
Truth—it is not as though I had invented it with my mind:
I have beheld it, I have beheld it, and the *living image* of
it has filled my soul for ever. I have beheld it in all its
glory and I cannot believe that it cannot exist among men.
So how can I grow muddled and confused? I shall of course
lose my way and I'm afraid that now and again I may

speak with words that are not my own, but not for long:
the living image of what I beheld will always be with me
and it will always correct me and lead me back on to the
right path. Oh, I'm in fine fettle, and I am of good cheer.
I will go on and on for a thousand years, if need be. Do
you know, at first I did not mean to tell you that I corrupted them, but that was a mistake—there you have my
first mistake! But Truth whispered to me that I was *lying,*
and so preserved me and set me on the right path. But I'm
afraid I do not know how to establish a heaven on earth,
for I do not know how to put it into words. After my
dream I lost the knack of putting things into words. At
least, onto the most necessary and most important words.
But never mind, I shall go on and I shall keep on talking,
for I have indeed beheld it with my own eyes, though I
cannot describe what I saw. It is this the scoffers do not
understand. "He had a dream," they say, "a vision, a hallucination!" Oh dear, is this all they have to say? Do they
really think that is very clever? And how proud they are!
A dream! What is a dream? And what about our life? Is
that not a dream too? I will say more: even—yes, even if
this never comes to pass, even if there never is a heaven
on earth (that, at any rate, I can see very well!), even
then I shall go on preaching. And really how simple it all
is: in one day, *in one hour,* everything could be arranged.
at once! The main thing is to love your neighbour as yourself—that is the main thing, and that is everything, for
nothing else matters. Once you do that, you will discover
at once how everything can be arranged. And yet it is an
old truth, a truth that has been told over and over again,
but in spite of that it finds no place among men! "The
consciousness of life is higher than life, the knowledge of
happiness is higher than happiness"—that is what we have
to fight against! And I shall, I shall fight against it! If
only we all wanted it, everything could be arranged
immediately.

And—I did find that little girl. . . . And I shall go on!
I shall go on!

Translated from the Russian
by David Magarshack

7

The Oval Portrait
by Edgar Allan Poe

The chateau into which my valet had ventured to make forcible entrance, rather than permit me, in my desperately wounded condition, to pass a night in the open air, was one of those piles of commingled gloom and grandeur which have so long frowned among the Appenines, not less in fact than in the fancy of Mrs. Radcliffe. To all appearance it had been temporarily and very lately abandoned. We established ourselves in one of the smallest and least sumptuously furnished apartments. It lay in a remote turret of the building. Its decorations were rich, yet tattered and antique. Its walls were hung with tapestry and bedecked with manifold and multiform armorial trophies, together with an unusually great number of very spirited modern paintings in frames of rich golden arabesque. In these paintings, which depended from the walls not only in their main surfaces, but in very many nooks which the bizarre architecture of the chateau rendered necessary—in these paintings my incipient delirium, perhaps, had caused me to take deep interest; so that I bade Pedro to close the heavy shutters of the room—since it was already night—to light the tongues of a tall candelabrum which stood by the head of my bed—and to throw open far and wide the fringed curtains of black velvet which enveloped the bed itself. I wished all this done that I might resign myself, if not to sleep, at least alternately to the contemplation of these pictures, and the perusal of a small volume which had been found upon the pillow, and which purported to criticise and describe them.

Long—long I read—and devoutly, devotedly I gazed. Rapidly and gloriously the hours flew by, and the deep midnight came. The position of the candelabrum displeased me, and outreaching my hand with difficulty, rather than disturb my slumbering valet, I placed it so as to throw its rays more fully upon the book.

But the action produced an effect altogether unanticipated. The rays of the numerous candles (for there were many) now fell within a niche of the room which had hitherto been thrown into deep shade by one of the bedposts. I thus saw in vivid light a picture all unnoticed before. It was the portrait of a young girl just ripening into womanhood. I glanced at the painting hurriedly, and then closed my eyes. Why I did this was not at first apparent even to my own perception. But while my lids remained thus shut, I ran over in mind my reason for so shutting them. It was an impulsive movement to gain time for thought—to make sure that my vision had not deceived me—to calm and subdue my fancy for a more sober and more certain gaze. In a very few moments I again looked fixedly at the painting.

That I now saw aright I could not and would not doubt; for the first flashing of the candles upon that canvas had seemed to dissipate the dreamy stupor which was stealing over my senses, and startle me at once into waking life.

The portrait, I have already said, was that of a young girl. It was a mere head and shoulders, done in what is technically termed a *vignette* manner; much in the style of the favorite heads of Sully. The arms, the bosom and even the ends of the radiant hair, melted imperceptibly into the vague yet deep shadow which formed the background of the whole. The frame was oval, richly gilded and filagreed in *Moresque*. As a thing of art nothing could be more admirable than the painting itself. But it could have been neither the execution of the work, nor the immortal beauty of the countenance, which had so suddenly and so vehemently moved me. Least of all, could it have been that my fancy, shaken from its half slumber, had mistaken the head for that of a living person. I saw at once that the peculiarities of the design, of the *vignetting,* and of the frame, must have instantly dispelled such idea—must have prevented even its momentary entertainment. Thinking earnestly upon these points, I remained, for an hour perhaps, half sitting, half reclining, with my vision riveted upon the portrait. At length, satisfied with the true secret of its effect, I fell back within the bed. I had found the spell of the picture in an absolute *life-likeliness* of expression, which at first startling, finally confounded, subdued and appalled me. With deep and reverent awe I replaced the candelabrum in its former position. The cause of my deep agitation being thus shut from view, I sought eagerly the volume which discussed the paintings and their histories. Turning to the number which designated the oval portrait, I there read the vague and quaint words which follow:

"She was a maiden of rarest beauty, and not more lovely than full of glee. And evil was the hour when she saw, and loved, and wedded the painter. He, passionate, studious, austere, and having already a bride in his Art: she a maiden of rarest beauty, and not more lovely than full of glee: all light and smiles, and frolicksome as the young fawn: loving and cherishing all things: hating only the Art which was her rival: dreading only the pallet and brushes and other untoward instruments which deprived her of the countenance of her lover. It was thus a terrible thing for this lady to hear the painter speak of his desire to portray even his young bride. But she was humble and obedient, and sat meekly for many weeks in the dark high turret-chamber where the light dripped upon the pale canvas only from overhead. But he, the painter, took glory in his work, which went on from hour to hour and from day to day. And he was a passionate, and wild and moody man, who became lost in reveries; so that he *would* not see that the light which fell so ghastlily in that lone turret withered the health and the spirits of his bride, who pined visibly to all but him. Yet she smiled on and still on, uncomplainingly, because she saw that the painter, (who had high renown,) took a fervid and burning pleasure in his task, and wrought day and night to depict her who so loved him, yet who grew daily more dispirited and weak. And in sooth some who beheld the portrait spoke of its resemblance in low words, as of a mighty marvel, and a proof not less of the power of the painter than of his deep love for her whom he depicted so surpassingly well. But at length, as the labor drew nearer to its conclusion, there were admitted none into the turret; for the painter had grown wild with the ardor of his work, and turned his eyes from the canvas rarely, even to regard the countenance of his wife. And he *would* not see that the tints which he spread upon the canvas were drawn from the cheeks of her who sat beside him. And when many weeks had passed, and but little remained to do, save one brush upon the mouth and one tint upon the eye, the spirit of the lady again flickered up as the flame within the socket of the lamp. And then the brush was given, and then the tint was placed; and, for one moment, the painter stood entranced before the work which he had wrought; but in the next, while he yet gazed, he grew tremulous and very pallid, and aghast, and crying with a loud voice, "This is indeed *Life* itself!" turned suddenly to regard his beloved: —*She was dead.*"

8

The Castle

A Parable by George MacDonald

On the top of a high cliff, forming part of the base of a great mountain, stood a lofty castle. When or how it was built, no man knew; nor could any one pretend to understand its architecture. Every one who looked upon it felt that it was lordly and noble; and where one part seemed not to agree with another, the wise and modest dared not to call them incongruous, but presumed that the whole might be constructed on some higher principle of architecture than they yet understood. What helped them to this conclusion was that no one had ever seen the whole of the edifice; that even of the portion best known, some part or other was always wrapt in thick folds of mist from the mountain; and that, when the sun shone upon this mist, the parts of the building that appeared through the vaporous veil, were strangely glorified in their indistinctness, so that they seemed to belong to some aerial abode in the land of the sunset; and the beholders could hardly tell whether they had ever seen them before, or whether they were now for the first time partially revealed.

Nor, although it was inhabited, could certain information be procured as to its internal construction. Those who dwelt in it often discovered rooms they had never entered before; yea, once or twice, whole suites of apartments, of which only dim legends had been handed down from former times. Some of them expected to find one day secret places, filled with treasures of wondrous jewels, amongst which they hoped to light upon Solomon's ring, which had for ages disappeared from the earth, but which had controlled the spirits, and the possession of which made a man simply what a man should be, the king of the world. Now and then, a narrow, winding stair, hitherto untrodden, would bring them forth on a new turret, whence new pros-

pects of the circumjacent country were spread out before
them. How many more of these there might be, or how
much loftier, no one could tell. Nor could the foundations
of the castle in the rock on which it was built be determined with the smallest approach to precision. Those of
the family who had given themselves to exploring in that
direction, found such a labyrinth of vaults and passages,
and endless successions of down-going stairs, out of one
underground space into a yet lower, that they came to the
conclusion that at least the whole mountain was perforated
and honeycombed in this fashion. They had a dim consciousness, too, of the presence, in those awful regions,
of beings whom they could not comprehend. Once, they
came upon the brink of a great black gulf, in which the
eye could see nothing but darkness: they recoiled in horror; for the conviction flashed upon them that that gulf
went down into the very central spaces of the earth, of
which they had hitherto been wandering only in the upper
crust; nay, that the seething blackness before them had
relations mysterious, and beyond human comprehension,
with the far-off voids of space, into which the stars dare
not enter.

At the foot of the cliff whereon the castle stood, lay a
deep lake, inaccessible save by a few avenues, being surrounded on all sides with precipices, which made the water
look very black, although it was as pure as the night-sky.
From a door in the castle, which was not to be otherwise
entered, a broad flight of steps, cut in the rock, went down
to the lake, and disappeared below its surface. Some
thought the steps went to the very bottom of the water.

Now in this castle there dwelt a large family of brothers
and sisters. They had never seen their father or mother.
The younger had been educated by the elder, and these by
an unseen care and ministration, about the sources of which
they had, somehow or other, troubled themselves very
little, for what people are accustomed to, they regard as
coming from nobody; as if help and progress and joy and
love were the natural crops of Chaos or old Night. But
Tradition said that one day—it was utterly uncertain *when*
—their father would come, and leave them no more; for
he was still alive, though where he lived nobody knew. In
the meantime all the rest had to obey their eldest brother,
and listen to his counsels.

But almost all the family was very fond of liberty, as
they called it; and liked to run up and down, hither and
thither, roving about, with neither law nor order, just
as they pleased. So they could not endure their brother's
tyranny, as they called it. At one time they said that he
was only one of themselves, and therefore they would
not obey him; at another, that he was not like them, and
could not understand them, and *therefore* they would not
obey him. Yet, sometimes, when he came and looked
them full in the face, they were terrified, and dared not
disobey, for he was stately, and stern and strong. Not one
of them loved him heartily, except the eldest sister, who
was very beautiful and silent, and whose eyes shone as if
light lay somewhere deep behind them. Even she, although
she loved him, thought him very hard sometimes; for when
he had once said a thing plainly, he could not be persuaded
to think it over again. So even she forgot him sometimes,
and went her own ways, and enjoyed herself without him.
Most of them regarded him as a sort of watchman, whose
business it was to keep them in order; and so they were
indignant and disliked him. Yet they all had a secret feeling that they ought to be subject to him; and after any
particular act of disregard, none of them could think, with
any peace, of the old story about the return of their father
to his house. But indeed they never thought much about it,
or about their father at all; for how could those who cared
so little for their brother, whom they saw every day, care
for their father whom they had never seen?—One chief
cause of complaint against him was that he interfered with
their favourite studies and pursuits; whereas he only sought
to make them give up trifling with earnest things, and seek
for truth, and not for amusement, from the many wonders
around them. He did not want them to turn to other studies, or to eschew pleasures; but, in those studies, to seek
the highest things most, and other things in proportion to
their true worth and nobleness. This could not fail to be
distasteful to those who did not care for what was higher
than they. And so matters went on for a time. They
thought they could do better without their brother; and
their brother knew they could not do at all without him,
and tried to fulfill the charge committed into his hands.

At length, one day, for the thought seemed to strike
them simultaneously, they conferred together about giving

a great entertainment in their grandest rooms to any of
their neighbours who chose to come, or indeed to any inhabitants of the earth or air who would visit them. They
were too proud to reflect that some company might defile
even the dwellers in what was undoubtedly the finest palace
on the face of the earth. But what made the thing worse,
was, that the old tradition said that these rooms were to be
kept entirely for the use of the owner of the castle. And,
indeed, whenever they entered them, such was the effect
of their loftiness and grandeur upon their minds, that they
always thought of the old story, and could not help believing it. Nor would the brother permit them to forget it
now; but, appearing suddenly amongst them, when they
had no expectation of being interrupted by him, he re-
buked them, both for the indiscriminate nature of their
invitation, and for the intention of introducing any one,
not to speak of some who would doubtless make their appearance on the evening in question, into the rooms kept
sacred for the use of the unknown father. But by this time
their talk with each other had so excited their expectations
of enjoyment, which had previously been strong enough,
that anger sprung up within them at the thought of being
deprived of their hopes, and they looked each other in the
eyes; and the look said: "We are many, and he is one—let
us get rid of him, for he is always finding fault, and
thwarting us in the most innocent pleasures;—as if we
would wish to do anything wrong!" So without a word
spoken, they rushed upon him; and although he was
stronger than any of them, and struggled hard at first, yet
they overcame him at last. Indeed some of them thought
he yielded to their violence long before they had the mastery
of him; and this very submission terrified the more tender-
hearted among them. However, they bound him; carried
him down many stairs, and, having remembered an iron
staple in the wall of a certain vault, with a thick rusty
chain attached to it, they bore him thither, and made the
chain fast around him. There they left him, shutting the
great gnarring brazen door of the vault, as they departed
for the upper regions of the castle.

Now all was in a tumult of preparation. Every one was
talking of the coming festivity; but no one spoke of the
deed they had done. A sudden paleness overspread the
face, now of one, and now of another; but it passed

away, and no one took any notice of it; they only plied
the task of the moment the more energetically. Messengers
were sent far and near, not to individuals or families, but
publishing in all places of concourse a general invitation
to any who chose to come on a certain day, and partake
for certain succeeding days, of the hospitality of the dwellers in the castle. Many were the preparations immediately
begun for complying with the invitation. But the noblest
of their neighbours refused to appear; not from pride, but
because of the unsuitableness and carelessness of such a
mode. With some of them it was an old condition in the
tenure of their estates, that they should go to no one's
dwelling except visited in person, and expressly solicited.
Others, knowing what sorts of persons would be there, and
that, from a certain physical antipathy, they could scarcely
breathe in their company, made up their minds at once not
to go. Yet multitudes, many of them beautiful and innocent as well as gay, resolved to appear.

Meanwhile the great rooms of the castle were got in
readiness—that is, they proceeded to deface them with
decorations; for there was a solemnity and stateliness
about them in their ordinary condition, which was at once
felt to be unsuitable for the light-hearted company so soon
to move about in them with the self-same carelessness with
which men walk abroad within the great heavens and hills
and clouds. One day, while the workmen were busy, the
eldest sister, of whom I have already spoken, happened
to enter, she knew not why. Suddenly the great idea of the
mighty halls dawned upon her, and filled her soul. The
so-called decorations vanished from her view, and she
felt as if she stood in her father's presence. She was at
once elevated and humbled. As suddenly the idea faded and
fled, and she beheld but the gaudy festoons and draperies
and paintings which disfigured the grandeur. She wept and
sped away. Now it was too late to interfere, and things
must take their course. She would have been but a Cas-
sandra-prophetess to those who saw but the pleasure before them. She had not been present when her brother was
imprisoned; and indeed for some days had been so wrapt
in her own business, that she had taken but little heed of
anything that was going on. But they all expected her to
show herself when the company was gathered; and they

had applied to her for advice at various times during their
operations.

At length the expected hour arrived, and the company
began to assemble. It was a warm summer evening. The
dark lake reflected the rose-coloured clouds in the west,
and through the flush rowed many gaily-painted boats,
with various coloured flags, towards the massy rock on
which the castle stood. The trees and flowers seemed already asleep, and breathing forth their sweet dream-breath.
Laughter and low voices rose from the breast of the lake
to the ears of the youths and maidens looking forth ex-
pectant from the lofty windows. They went down to the
broad platform at the top of the stairs in front of the door
to receive their visitors. By degrees the festivities of the
evening commenced. The same smiles flew forth both at
eyes and lips, darting like beams through the gathering
crowd. Music, from unseen sources, now rolled in billows,
now crept in ripples through the sea of air that filled the
lofty rooms. And in the dancing halls, when hand took
hand, and form and motion were moulded and swayed by
the indwelling music, it governed not these alone, but, as
the ruling spirit of the place, every new burst of music
for a new dance swept before it a new and accordant
odour, and dyed the flames that glowed in the lofty lamps
with a new and accordant stain. The floors bent beneath
the feet of the time-keeping dancers. But twice in the evening some of the inmates started, and the pallor occasionally
common to the household overspread their faces, for they
felt underneath them a counter-motion to the dance, as if
the floor rose slightly to answer their feet. And all the
time their brother lay below in the dungeon, like John the
Baptist in the castle of Herod, when the lords and captains sat around, and the daughter of Herodias danced
before them. Outside, all around the castle, brooded the
dark night unheeded; for the clouds had come up from all
sides, and were crowding together overhead. In the unfre-
quent pauses of the music, they might have heard, now and
then, the gusty rush of a lonely wind, coming and going
no one could know whence or whither, born and dying unexpected and unregarded.

But when the festivities were at their height, when the
external and passing confidence which is produced between
superficial natures by a common pleasure, was at the full,

a sudden crash of thunder quelled the music, as the thunder quells the noise of the uplifted sea. The windows were driven in, and torrents of rain, carried in the folds of a rushing wind, poured into the halls. The lights were swept away; and the great rooms, now dark within, were darkened yet more by the dazzling shoots of flame from the vault of blackness overhead. Those that ventured to look out of the windows saw, in the blue brilliancy of the quick-following jets of lightning, the lake at the foot of the rock, ordinarily so still and so dark, lighted up, not on the surface only, but down to half its depth; so that, as it tossed in the wind, like a tortured sea of writhing flames, or incandescent half-molten serpents of brass, they could not tell whether a strong phosphorescence did not issue from the transparent body of the waters, as if earth and sky lightened together, one consenting source of flaming utterance.

Sad was the condition of the late plastic mass of living form that had flowed into shape at the will and law of the music. Broken into individuals, the common transfusing spirit withdrawn, they stood drenched, cold, and benumbed, with clinging garments; light, order, harmony, purpose departed, and chaos restored; the issuings of life turned back on their sources, chilly and dead. And in every heart reigned that falsest of despairing convictions, that this was the only reality, and that was but a dream. The eldest sister stood with clasped hands and down-bent head shivering and speechless, as if waiting for something to follow. Nor did she wait long. A terrible flash and thunder-peal made the castle rock; and in the pausing silence that followed, her quick sense heard the rattling of a chain far off, deep down; and soon the sound of heavy footsteps, accompanied with the clanking of iron, reached her ear. She felt that her brother was at hand. Even in the darkness, and amidst the bellowing of another deep-bosomed cloud-monster, she knew that he had entered the room. A moment after, a continuous pulsation of angry blue light began, which, lasting for some moments, revealed him standing amidst them, gaunt, haggard, and motionless; his hair and beard untrimmed, his face ghastly, his eyes large and hollow. The light seemed to gather around him as a centre. Indeed some believed that it throbbed and radiated from his person, and not from the stormy heavens above them. The lightning had rent the wall of his prison, and released the iron staple of his chain which he had wound about him like a girdle. In his hand he carried an iron fetter-bar, which he had found on the floor of the vault. More terrified at his aspect than at all the violence of the storm, the visitors, with many a shriek and cry, rushed out into the tempestuous night. By degrees, the storm died away. Its last flash revealed the forms of the brothers and sisters lying prostrate, with their faces on the floor, and that fearful shape standing motionless amidst them still.

Morning dawned, and there they lay, and there he stood. But at a word from him, they arose and went about their various duties, though listlessly enough. The eldest sister was the last to rise; and when she did, it was only by a terrible effort that she was able to reach her room, where she fell again on the floor. There she remained lying for days. The brother caused the doors of the great suite of rooms to be closed, leaving them just as they were, with all the childish adornment scattered about, and the rain still falling in through the shattered windows. "Thus let them lie," said he, "till the rain and frost have cleansed them of paint and drapery: no storm can hurt the pillars and arches of these halls."

The hours of this day went heavily. The storm was gone, but the rain was left; the passion had departed, but the tears remained behind. Dull and dark the low misty clouds brooded over the castle and the lake, and shut out all the neighbourhood. Even if they had climbed to the loftiest known turret, they would have found it swathed in a garment of clinging vapour, affording no refreshment to the eye, and no hope to the heart. There was one lofty tower that rose sheer a hundred feet above the rest, and from which the fog could have been seen lying in a grey, mass beneath; but that tower they had not yet discovered, nor another close beside it, the top of which was never seen, nor could be, for the highest clouds of heaven clustered continually around it. The rain fell continuously, though not heavily, without; and within, too, there were clouds from which dropped the tears which are the rain of the spirit. All the good of life seemed for the time departed, and their souls lived but as leafless trees that had forgotten the joy of the summer, and whom no wind prophetic of spring had yet visited. They moved about mechanically, and had not strength enough left to wish to die.

The next day the clouds were higher, and a little wind blew through such loopholes in the turrets as the false improvements of the inmates had not yet filled with glass, shutting out, as the storm, so the serene visitings of the heavens. Throughout the day, the brother took various opportunities of addressing a gentle command, now to one and now to another of his family. It was obeyed in silence. The wind blew fresher through the loopholes and the shattered windows of the great rooms and found its way, by unknown passages, to faces and eyes hot with weeping. It cooled and blessed them.—When the sun arose the next day, it was in a clear sky.

By degrees, everything fell into the regularity of subordination. With the subordination came increase of freedom. The steps of the more youthful of the family were heard on the stairs and in the corridors more light and quick than ever before. Their brother had lost the terrors of aspect produced by his confinement, and his commands were issued more gently, and oftener with a smile, than in all their previous history. By degrees his presence was universally felt through the house. It was no surprise to any one at his studies, to see him by his side when he lifted up his eyes, though he had not before known that he was in the room. And although some dread still remained, it was rapidly vanishing before the advances of a firm friendship. Without immediately ordering their labours, he always influenced them, and often altered their direction and objects. The change soon evident in the household was remarkable. A simple, nobler expression was visible on all the countenances. The voices of the men were deeper, and yet seemed by their very depth more feminine than before; while the voices of the women were softer and sweeter, and at the same time more full and decided. Now the eyes had often an expression as if their sight was absorbed in the gaze of the inward eyes; and when the eyes of two met, there passed between those eyes the utterance of a conviction that both meant the same thing. But the change was, of course to be seen more clearly, though not more evidently, in individuals.

One of the brothers, for instance, was very fond of astronomy. He had his observatory on a lofty tower, which stood pretty clear of the others, towards the north and east. But hitherto, his astronomy, as he had called it, had been more of the character of astrology. Often, too, he might have been seen directing a heaven-searching telescope to catch the rapid transit of a fiery shooting-star, belonging altogether to the earthly atmosphere, and not to the serene heavens. He had to learn that the signs of the air are not the signs of the skies. Nay, once, his brother surprised him in the act of examining through his longest tube a patch of burning heath upon a distant hill. But now he was diligent from morning till night in the study of the laws of the'truth that has to do with stars; and when the curtain of the sunlight was about to rise from before the heavenly worlds which it had hidden all day long, he might be seen preparing his instruments with that solemn countenance with which it becometh one to look into the mysterious harmonies of Nature. Now he learned what law and order and truth are, what consent and harmony mean; how the individual may find his own end in a higher end, where law and freedom mean the same thing, and the purest certainty exists without the slightest constraint. Thus he stood on the earth, and looked to the heavens.

Another, who had been much given to searching out the hollow places and recesses in the foundations of the castle, and who was often to be found with compass and ruler working away at a chart of the same which he had been in process of constructing, now came to the conclusion, that only by ascending the upper regions of his abode, could he become capable of understanding what lay beneath; and that, in all probability, one clear prospect, from the top of the highest attainable turret, over the castle as it lay below, would reveal more of the idea of its internal construction, than a year spent in wandering through its subterranean vaults. But the fact was, the desire to ascend wakening within him had made him forget what was beneath; and having laid aside his chart for a time at least, he was now to be met in every quarter of the upper parts, searching and striving upward, now in one direction, now in another; and seeking, as he went, the best outlooks into the clear air of outer realities.

And they began to discover that they were all meditating different aspects of the same thing; and they brought together their various discoveries, and recognized the likeness between them; and the one thing often explained the other, and combining with it helped to a third. They grew in consequence more and more friendly and loving; so that every now and then, one turned to another and said, as in surprise, "Why, you are my brother!"—"Why, you are my sisfer!" And yet they had always known it.

The change reached to all. One, who lived on the air of sweet sounds, and who was almost always to be found seated by her harp or some other instrument, had, till the late storm, been generally merry and playful, though sometimes sad. But for a long time after that, she was often found weeping, and playing little simple airs which she had heard in childhood—backward longings, followed by fresh tears. Before long, however, a new element manifested itself in her music. It became yet more wild, and sometimes retained all its sadness, but it was mingled with anticipation and hope. The past and the future merged in one; and while memory yet brought the rain-cloud, expectation threw the rainbow across its bosom—and all was uttered in her music, which rose and swelled, now to defiance, now to victory; then died in a torrent of weeping.

As to the eldest sister, it was many days before she recovered from the shock. At length, one day, her brother came to her, took her by the hand led her to an open window, and told her to seat herself by it, and look out. She did so; but at first saw nothing more than an unsympathizing blaze of sunlight. But as she looked, the horizon widened out, and the dome of the sky ascended, till the grandeur seized upon her soul, and she fell on her knees and wept. Now the heavens seemed to bend lovingly over her, and to stretch out wide cloud-arms to embrace her; the earth lay like the bosom of an infinite love beneath her, and the wind kissed her cheek with an odour of roses. She sprang to her feet, and turned, in an agony of hope, expecting to behold the face of the father, but there stood only her brother, looking calmly though lovingly on her emotion. She turned again to the window. On the hilltops rested the sky: Heaven and Earth were one; and the prophecy awoke in her soul, that from betwixt them would the steps of the father approach.

Hitherto she had seen but Beauty; now she beheld truth. Often had she looked on such clouds as these, and loved the strange ethereal curves into which the winds moulded them; and had smiled as her little pet sister told her what curious animals she saw in them, and tried to point them out to her. Now they were as troops of angels, jubilant over her new birth, for they sang, in her soul, of beauty, and truth, and love. She looked down, and her little sister knelt beside her.

She was a curious child, with black glittering eyes, and dark hair; at the mercy of every wandering wind; a frolicsome, daring girl, who laughed more than she smiled. She was generally in attendance on her sister, and was always finding and bringing her strange things. She never pulled a primrose, but she knew the haunts of all the orchis tribe, and brought from them bees and butterflies innumerable, as offerings to her sister. Curious moths and glow-worms were her greatest delight; and she loved the stars, because they were like the glow-worms. But the change had affected her too; for her sister saw that her eyes had lost their glittering look, and had become more liquid and transparent. And from that time she often observed that her gaiety was more gentle, her smile more frequent, her laugh less bell-like; and although she was a wild as ever, there was more elegance in her motions, and more music in her voice. And she clung to her sister with far greater fondness than before.

The land reposed in the embrace of the warm summer days. The clouds of heaven nestled around the towers of the castle; and the hearts of its inmates became conscious of a warm atmosphere—of a presence of love. They began to feel like the children of a household, when the mother is at home. Their faces and forms grew daily more and more beautiful, till they wondered as they gazed on each other. As they walked in the gardens of the castle, or in the country around, they were often visited, especially the eldest sister, by sounds that no one heard but themselves, issuing from woods and waters; and by forms of love that lightened out of flowers, and grass, and great rocks. Now and then the young children would come in with a slow, stately step, and, with great eyes that looked as if they would devour all the creation, say that they had met the father amongst the trees, and that he had kissed them; "And," added one of them once, "I grew so big!" But when others went out to look, they could see no one. And some said it must have been the brother, who grew more and more beautiful, and loving, and reverend, and who had lost all traces of hardness, so that they wondered they could ever have thought him stern and harsh. But the eldest sister held her peace, and looked up, and her eyes filled with tears. "Who can tell," thought she, "but the little children know more about it than we?"

Often, at sunrise, might be heard their hymn of praise to their unseen father, whom they felt to be near, though they saw him not. Some words thereof once reached my ear through the folds of the music in which they floated, as in an upward snow-storm of sweet sounds. And these are some of the words I heard—but there was much I seemed to hear, which I could not understand, and some things which I understood but cannot utter again.

"We thank thee that we have a father, and not a maker; that thou hast begotten us, and not moulded us as images of clay; that we have come forth of thy heart, and have not been fashioned by thy hands. It *must* be so. Only the heart of a father is able to create. We rejoice in it, and bless thee that we know it. We thank thee for thyself. Be what thou art—our root and life, our beginning and end, our all in all. Come home to us. Thou livest; therefore we live. In thy light we see. Thou art—that is all our song."

Thus they worship, and love, and wait, Their hope and expectation grow ever stronger and brighter, that one day, ere long, the Father will show himself amongst them, and thenceforth dwell in his own house for evermore. What was once but an old legend has become the one desire of their hearts.

And the loftiest hope is the surest of being fulfilled.

9

The Hermit and the Bear

by I. L. Peretz

Once there was a man who could not abide evil. So he turned the little shop he kept over to his wife, shut himself up in a room in his house, and immersed himself in Torah and prayer—studying the revealed scripture and the Kabbalah as well.

But even at home, in his very own household, he saw evil. Finally thinking the matter over, he decided to become a hermit, left his home, and went to study in a corner of the synagogue.

He sits in the synagogue, but the world's evil follows him there. Sometimes a night watchman comes in to warm himself at the stove, or a wanderer comes in to sleep, or a sleepless man blunders into the synagogue—and they sit around the stove talking—but whatever they talk about, the end is always evil upon evil.

Again, the hermit ponders the matter and leaves town to go out into the world to look for a city without evil. And he doesn't find one. It's the same world wherever he goes.

So he gives up on civilization and travels from forest to forest, over hills and valleys until, far from all human habitation, he comes to a stream. What the river is called he does not know, but on its bank there stand the ruins of an ancient palace.

Well, he settles there and busies himself with the Kabbalah. But there's no way to escape from evil. The river sometimes runs wild, overturning boats, tearing up hunks of meadow and even newly sown fields. As for what goes on among the fish—a constant warfare.

So hermit has no peace and cannot sleep. As for running away—there's no place left to run.

He lies there and thinks and thinks, trying to fathom

where the source of so much evil might be; and so comes
to the conclusion that evil happens because the soul of the
world is asleep.

That's not such a wild thought as it seems. For instance, consider the small world of man. So long as a man's
soul is awake, he does what is fitting, according to plan
and according to reason. All his limbs obey his soul. But
when a man is asleep, then the soul—the master of the
body—dozes off; and the body starts thrashing about, without order, without purpose. Every limb goes off on its own:
one hand here, the other there; the head for itself, the
body for itself—all without reason.

One can get badly hurt that way!

And evil is reasonless. The world thrashes, convulsed
without order; and the soul of the world is asleep. Every
separate bit of the world looks out for itself, not for the
welfare of all.

Do you understand? Right or wrong, this is what the
hermit thought.

So he concludes that there is only thing to do: to wake
the soul of the world. Once it is awake, then order will
reign. The conflicts, the convulsions, the thrashing about
of the world's limbs will stop.

But how does one wake the soul of the world? For *that*
there are ideas in the holy books. There are certain things
to say and to do. It takes some fervent meditation. One
has to dedicate oneself to the task wholeheartedly and with
devotion. If not, the words fly off into thin air—into
nothing.

Clearly, something must be created that has wings and a
soul; something that knows where to fly and what to ask
for when it gets there. Of course, during the day, it's
not possible to create it. No sooner do you get deeply involved in thought, than a crow caws, a bird sings, or one
hears a distant peasant cursing the hard soil for dulling his
plow.

The right time is at night, especially at midnight.

So that's what the hermit does—night after night until
he senses that he's getting somewhere.

But the angry river-spirit becomes aware of what he's
doing and says: "No peace for him!" No sooner is the
hermit engrossed in his meditation, than the river-spirit
flings himself about, making the river seethe and roar and

heave its waves against the banks until the hermit's deep
thoughts are as topsy-turvy as the boatman overturned
down river in the commotion.

The hermit, then, who is not eager to go looking for
another ruin beside some other river (Who knows how
long that would take or whether he'd find what he's looking for?); the hermit, then, sees that he must move the
river, river-spirit and all, because, after all, evil is still
multiplying and destroying the world.

Well—moving the river is a small mattter for the hermit.
He has a holy spell for that. All it takes is some additional
fasting, some deep meditation, and the river moves.

Which puts the river-spirit into a fiery rage; but too bad
for him. The holy spell has been spoken. And yet, the
spirit wants revenge; so he agitates the river even more
and makes the waves grow huge. Then, snatching a swollen wave, he flings it toward the bank, toward the ruins.

And the wave turns into a bear. A hairy black bear with
bloodshot eyes that runs around the ruins, roaring and
snarling, interfering with the hermit's meditations once
again.

What's to be done? He's not going to kill the bear. That
would be evil. Because, in truth, how is the bear guilty of
anything? It lives; let it live!

Well, it occurs to the hermit to quiet the bear. To make
something decent of him, so that, bear though he is, he
will understand what it's all about.

The hermit decides to elevate the bear. He will change
him and enlighten his soul.

So, one morning early, the hermit climbs to the top of
his ruin and stands there looking down at the bear. No
sooner does the bear see him than he falls into a dreadful
rage. Digging the ground with his forepaws, he roars and
growls and leaps about, his mouth foaming, glaring with
bloodshot eyes at the hermit; and the hermit, his eyes filled
with loving kindness, looks down at the bear. And there's
a war between the two sets of eyes—the hermit's brim-
ming with love and pity, the bear's filled with hatred and
rage. But the hermit's eyes are the stronger. Slowly, slowly,
they begin to conquer those of the bear.

The conflict between the two pairs of eyes, between the
two hearts and the two souls, lasts a long time until, when
the sun is in the east, the struggle is over; and when it is

high in the heavens, the bear lies humbly before the ruin like a submissive dog; and when the sun sets, the bear rises quietly and sends the hermit a tenderly pleading look and approaches the gate of the ruins where it knocks quietly, whining like a dog to be let in.

The hermit has won. The hairy beast has given up, and his whining means to say: "Let me come to you. Let me serve you like a dog. I'll lie at your feet; I'll lick your hands, and look faithfully into your eyes, and anticipate your every desire; and when you are deep in meditation, I'll be nice and quiet beside you—I won't even catch flies."

The hermit opens the gate. The bear approaches him and lies down quietly at his feet. And his eyes say: "You are my God, My hopes are in you. I believe in you. Your thoughts are holy. With your meditations you will rebuild the world." And the hermit lovingly caresses the bear, the bear he has himself created, the bear that believes in him.

And he begins to muse, desiring to be immersed in his thoughts once more, to meditate on what is needful to wake the soul of the world.

But there is nothing left for him to think. He himself no longer possesses his former soul, because in the same measure that the bear has ascended to him, he has descended to the bear.

He senses a weariness in all his limbs; his eyelids grow heavy. Falteringly, he goes to his bed, and the bear follows him and lies down beside him.

There is no end to evil. The bear has become partly human, and the human, partly a bear. And a saint who lies down with a bear cannot wake the soul of the world.

Translated from the Yiddish by Leonard Wolf

10

Everything and Nothing

by Jorge Luis Borges

There was no one in him; behind his face (which even in poor paintings of the period is unlike any other) and his words, which were copious, imaginative, and emotional, there was nothing but a little chill, a dream not dreamed by anyone. At first he thought everyone was like him, but the puzzled look on a friend's face when he remarked on that emptiness told him he was mistaken and convinced him forever that an individual must not differ from his species. Occasionally he thought he would find in books the cure for his ill, and so he learned the small Latin and less Greek of which a contemporary was to speak. Later he thought that in the exercise of an elemental human rite he might well find what he sought, and he let himself be initiated by Anne Hathaway one long June afternoon. At twenty-odd he went to London. Instinctively, he had already trained himself in the habit of pretending that he was someone, so it would not be discovered that he was no one. In London he hit upon the profession to which he was predestined, that of the actor, who plays on stage at being someone else. His playacting taught him a singular happiness, perhaps the first he had known; but when the last line was applauded and the last corpse removed from the stage, the hated sense of unreality came over him again. He ceased to be Ferrex or Tamburlaine and again became a nobody. Trapped, he fell to imagining other heroes and other tragic tales. Thus, while in London's bawdyhouses and taverns his body fulfilled its destiny as body, the soul that dwelled in it was Caesar, failing to heed the augurer's admonition, and Juliet, detesting the lark, and Macbeth, conversing on the heath with the witches, who are also the fates. Nobody was ever as many men as that man, who like the Egyptian Proteus managed to exhaust all the possible shapes of being. At times he slipped into some corner of his work a confession, certain that it would not be deciphered; Richard affirms that in his single person he plays many parts, and Iago says with strange words. "I am not what I am." His passages on the fundamental identity of existing, dreaming, and acting are famous.

Twenty years he persisted in that controlled hallucination, but one morning he was overcome by the surfeit and the horror of being so many kings who die by the sword and so many unhappy lovers who converge, diverge, and melodiously agonize. That same day he disposed of his theater. Before a week was out he had returned to the village of his birth where he recovered the trees and the river of his childhood and he did not bind them to those others his muse had celebrated, those made illustrious by mythological allusions and Latin phrases. He had to be someone; he became a retired impresario who has made his fortune and who interests himself in loans, lawsuits, and petty usury. In this character he dictated the arid final will and testament that we know, deliberately excluding from it every trace of emotion and of literature. Friends from London used to visit his retreat, and for them he would take on again the role of poet.

The story goes that, before or after he died, he found himself before God and he said: "I, who have been so many men in vain, want to be one man: myself." The voice of God replied from a whirlwind: "Neither am I one self; I dreamed the world as you dreamed your work, my Shakespeare, and among the shapes of my dream are you, who, like me, are many persons—and none."

Translated from the Spanish by Mildred Boyer

11

The Circular Ruins

by Jorge Luis Borges

And if he left off dreaming about you . . .
Through the Looking Glass, VI

N o one saw him disembark in the unanimous night, no one
saw the bamboo canoe sinking into the sacred mud, but
within a few days no one was unaware that the silent man
came from the South and that his home was one of the infinite villages upstream, on the violent mountainside, where
leprosy is infrequent. The truth is that the obscure man
kissed the mud, came up the bank without pushing aside
(probably without feeling) the brambles which dilacerated
his flesh, and dragged himself, nauseous and bloodstained,
to the circular enclosure crowned by a stone tiger or horse,
which once was the color of fire and now was that of ashes.
This circle was a temple, long ago devoured by fire, which
the malarial jungle had profaned and whose god no longer
received the homage of men. The stranger stretched out
beneath the pedestal. He was awakened by the sun high
above. He evidenced without astonishment that his wounds
had closed; he shut his pale eyes and slept, not out of bodily
weakness but out of determination of will. He knew that
this temple was the place required by his invincible purpose; he knew that, downstream, the incessant trees had
not managed to choke the ruins of another propitious
temple, whose gods were also burned and dead; he knew
that his immediate obligation was to sleep. Towards midnight he was awakened by the disconsolate cry of a bird.
Prints of bare feet, some figs and a jug told him that men
of the region had respectfully spied upon his sleep and were
solicitous of his favor or feared his magic. He felt the chill
of fear and sought out a burial niche in the dilapidated
wall and covered himself with some unknown leaves.

The purpose which guided him was not impossible, though it was supernatural. He wanted to dream a man: he wanted to dream him with minute integrity and insert him into reality. This magical project had exhausted the entire content of his soul; if someone had asked him his own name or any trait of his previous life, he would not have been able to answer. The uninhabited and broken temple suited him, for it was a minimum of visible world; the nearness of the peasants also suited him, for they would see that his frugal necessities were supplied. The rice and fruit of their tribute were sufficient sustenance for his body, consecrated to the sole task of sleeping and dreaming.

At first, his dreams were chaotic; somewhat later, they were of a dialectical nature. The stranger dreamt that he was in the center of a circular amphitheater which in some way was the burned temple: clouds of silent students filled the gardens; the faces of the last ones hung many centuries away and at a cosmic height, but were entirely clear and precise. The man was lecturing to them on anatomy, cosmography, magic; the countenances listened with eagerness and strove to respond with understanding, as if they divined the importance of the examination which would redeem one of them from his state of vain appearance and interpolate him into the world of reality. The man, both in dreams and awake, considered his phantoms' replies, was not deceived by impostors, divined a growing intelligence in certain perplexities. He sought a soul which would merit participation in the universe.

After nine or ten nights, he comprehended with some bitterness that he could expect nothing of those students who passively accepted his doctrines, but that he could of those who, at times, would venture a reasonable contradiction. The former, though worthy of love and affection, could not rise to the state of individuals; the latter preexisted somewhat more. One afternoon (now his afternoons too were tributaries of sleep, now he remained awake only for a couple of hours at dawn) he dismissed the vast illusory college forever and kept one single student. He was a silent boy, sallow, sometimes obstinate, with sharp features which reproduced those of the dreamer. He was not long disconcerted by his companions' sudden elimination; his progress, after a few special lessons, astounded his teacher. Nevertheless, ca-

tastrophe ensued. The man emerged from sleep one day
as if from a viscous desert, looked at the vain light of
afternoon, which at first he confused with that of dawn,
and understood that he had not really dreamt. All that
night and all day, the intolerable lucidity of insomnia
weighed upon him. He tried to explore the jungle, to exhaust himself; amidst the hemlocks, he was scarcely able
to manage a few snatches of feeble sleep, fleetingly mottled
with some rudimentary visions which were useless. He tried
to convoke the college and had scarcely uttered a few
brief words of exhortation, when it became deformed and
was extinguished. In his almost perpetual sleeplessness, his
old eyes burned with tears of anger.

He comprehended that the effort to mold the incoherent
and vertiginous matter dreams are made of was the most
arduous task a man could undertake, though he might
penetrate all the enigmas of the upper and lower orders:
much more arduous than weaving a rope of sand or coin-
ing the faceless wind. He comprehended that an initial
failure was inevitable. He swore he would forget the
enormous hallucination which had misled him at first, and
he sought another method. Before putting it into effect, he
dedicated a month to replenishing the powers his delirium
had wasted. He abandoned any premeditation of dreaming
and, almost at once, was able to sleep for a considerable
part of the day. The few times he dreamt during this
period, he did not take notice of the dreams. To take up
his task again, he waited until the moon's disk was perfect.
Then, in the afternoon, he purified himself in the waters
of the river, worshiped the planetary gods, uttered the law-
ful syllables of a powerful name and slept. Almost immediately, he dreamt of a beating heart.

He dreamt it as active, warm, secret, the size of a closed
fist, of garnet color in the penumbra of a human body as
yet without face or sex; with minute love he dreamt it, for
fourteen lucid nights. Each night he perceived it with
greater clarity. He did not touch it, but limited himself to
witnessing it, observing it, perhaps correcting it with his
eyes. He perceived it, lived it, from many distances and
many angles. On the fourteenth night he touched the pul-
monary artery with his finger, and then the whole heart,
inside and out. The examination satisfied him. Deliberately,
he did not dream for a night; then he took the heart again,

invoked the name of a planet and set about to envision another of the principal organs. Within a year he reached the skeleton, the eyelids. The innumerable hair was perhaps the most difficult task. He dreamt a complete man, a youth, but this youth could not rise nor did he speak nor could he open his eyes. Night after night, the man dreamt him as asleep.

In the Gnostic cosmogonies, the demiurge knead and mold a red Adam who cannot stand alone; as unskillful and crude and elementary as this Adam of dust was the Adam of dreams fabricated by the magician's nights of effort. One afternoon the man almost destroyed his work, but then repented. (It would have been better for him had he destroyed it.) Once he had completed his supplications to the numina of the earth and the river, he threw himself down at the feet of the effigy which was perhaps a tiger and perhaps a horse, and implored its unknown succor. That twilight, he dreamt of the statue. He dreamt of it as a living, tremulous thing: it was not an atrocious mongrel of tiger and horse, but both these vehement creatures at once and also a bull, a rose, tempest. This multiple god revealed to him that its earthy name was Fire, that in the circular temple (and in other of its kind people had rendered it sacrifices and cult and that it would magically give life to the sleeping phantom, in such a way that all creatures except Fire itself and the dreamer would believe him to be a man of flesh and blood. The man was ordered by the divinity to instruct his creature in its rites, and send him to the other broken temple whose pyramids survived downstream, so that in this deserted edifice a voice might give glory to the god. In the dreamer's dream, the dreamed one awoke.

The magician carried out these orders. He devoted a period of time (which finally comprised two years) to revealing the arcana of the universe and of the fire cult to his dream child. Inwardly, it pained him to be separated from the boy. Under the pretext of pedagogical necessity, each day he prolonged the hours he dedicated to his dreams. He also redid the right shoulder, which was perhaps deficient. At times, he was troubled by the impression that all this had happened before . . . In general, his days were happy; when he closed his eyes, he would think: *Now I shall be with my son.* Or, less often: *The child I have engendered awaits me and will not exist if I do not go to him.*

Gradually, he accustomed the boy to reality. Once he ordered him to place a banner on a distant peak. The following day, the banner flickered from the mountain top. He tried other analogous experiments, each more daring than the last. He understood with certain bitterness that his son was ready—and perhaps impatient—to be born. That night he kissed him for the first time and sent him to the other temple whose debris showed white downstream, through many leagues of inextricable jungle and swamp. But first (so that he would never know he was a phantom, so that he would be thought a man like others) he instilled into him a complete oblivion of his years of apprenticeship.

The man's victory and peace were dimmed by weariness. At dawn and at twilight, he would prostrate himself before the stone figure, imagining perhaps that his unreal child was practicing the same rites, in other circular ruins, downstream; at night, he would not dream, or would dream only as all men do. He perceived the sounds and forms of the universe with a certain colorlessness: his absent son was being nurtured with these diminutions of his soul. His life's purpose was complete; the man persisted in a kind of ecstasy. After a time, which some narrators of his story prefer to compute in years and others in lustra, he was awakened one midnight by two boatmen; he could not see their faces, but they told him of a magic man in a temple of the North who could walk upon fire and not be burned. The magician suddenly remembered the words of the god. He recalled that, of all the creatures of the world, fire was the only one that knew his son was a phantom. This recollection, at first soothing, finally tormented him. He feared his son might meditate on his abnormal privilege and discover in some way that his condition was that of a mere image. Not to be a man, to be the projection of another man's dream, what a feeling of humiliation, of vertigo! All fathers are interested in the children they have procreated (they have permitted to exist) in mere confusion or pleasure; it was natural that the magician should fear for the future of that son, created in thought, limb by limb and feature by feature, in a thousand and one secret nights.

The end of his meditations was sudden, though it was foretold in certain signs. First (after a long drought) a faraway cloud on a hill, light and rapid as a bird; then, toward the south, the sky which had the rose color of the leopard's mouth; then the smoke which corroded the metallic nights; finally, the panicky flight of the animals. For what was happening had happened many centuries ago. The ruins of the fire god's sanctuary were destroyed by fire. In a birdless dawn the magician saw the concentric blaze close round the wall. For a moment, he thought of taking refuge in the river, but then he knew that death was coming to crown his old age and absolve him of his labors. He walked into the shreds of flame. But they did not bite into his flesh, they caressed him and engulfed him without heat or combustion. With relief, with humiliation, with terror, he understood that he too was a mere appearance, dreamt by another.

Translated from the Spanish
by James E. Irby

12

Borges and I

by Jorge Luis Borges

It's the other one, it's Borges, that things happen to. I stroll about Buenos Aires and stop, perhaps mechanically now, to look at the arch of an entrance or an iron gate. News of Borges reaches me through the mail and I see his name on an academic ballot or in a biographical dictionary. I like hourglasses, maps, eighteenth-century typography, the taste of coffee, and Stevenson's prose. The other one shares these preferences with me, but in a vain way that converts them into the attributes of an actor. It would be too much to say that our relations are hostile; I live, I allow myself to live, so that Borges may contrive his literature and that literature justifies my existence. I do not mind confessing that he has managed to write some worthwhile pages, but those pages cannot save me, perhaps because the good part no longer belongs to anyone, not even to the other one, but rather to the Spanish language or to tradition. Otherwise, I am destined to be lost, definitively, and only a few instants of me will be able to survive in the other one. Little by little I am yielding him everything, although I am well aware of his perverse habit of falsifying and exaggerating. Spinoza held that all things long to preserve their own nature: the rock wants to be rock forever and the tiger, a tiger. But I must live on in Borges, not in myself—if indeed I am anyone—though I recognize myself less in his books than in many others, or than in the laborious strumming of a guitar. Years ago I tried to free myself from him and I passed from lower-middle-class myths to playing games with time and infinity, but those games are Borges' now, and I will have to conceive something else. Thus my life is running away, and I lose everything and everything belongs to oblivion, or to the other one.

I do not know which of us two is writing this page.

*Translated from the Spanish
by Mildred Boyer*

13

The Sirens

by Paul van Ostaijen

Not so long ago sailors succeeded in catching the sirens, a few miles south of the Azores. The sirens whistled heart-rendingly, but the sailors, being literally deaf, remained unaffected. They wanted to purge the seas of these dangerous creatures and locked the sirens in a dark closed-off corner of the hold. In the harbors where their ship moored, after they had told of their catch, they were treated by seamen with jubilation and hurrahs. And since sailors believe that a captured siren is a talisman, they had no problem selling the sirens in Lisbon, Liverpool, and Rotterdam. But only deaf sailors could lodge the sirens in the darkest corner of the ship's hold, the others knowing themselves unequal to the task.

Everyone knows that sea captains are people who want to exploit everything to their own advantage. So it was to be with the captured sirens. A round opening was made in the wall of the sirens' brig, and from this opening a pipe carried the sirens' whistling far above the deck, above the sea, above the stream and the city. To make the sirens whistle when it was useful or pleasing to them, the seamen made a thin lance ending in three sharp needles. These needles were dipped in poppy juice and were thrust into the body of the captured sirens through a small opening in the brig. Poppy juice, when absorbed, produces an indescribable longing for space and an unlimited sadness. In sirens it awakens their memory of distant seas, their former power over men, and an ultimate sadness in which, as in another dimension, lie all of space and all delusions of power. Then the sirens scream very loudly. The endless vibrations of the whistling shot sharply across the ship into space, suspended above the stream and the city. Seamen and people on shore say in the middle of their revels, it's twelve, the sirens whistled, the new year begins.

Yet, despite their captivity, the sirens have not relinquished their power. True, they are no longer able to entice blue jackets to the depths of the deep sea, where their song is an untimely death amidst the wonder of anemones and seaweeds, shells and coral. But those who have once heard the whistling of the sirens high over the city, cannot for the rest of their lives suppress their longing for this lament. They have, like the mouse to the cat, fallen prey to the harbor, where they know the ships and the sirens.

Translated from the Dutch
by E. M. Beekman

14

The City of Builders

by *Paul van Ostaijen*

"Well, tearing down is really quite easy."
(*A commonplace in committees, etc.*)

—Isn't it true, to tear down is easy? Anybody can tear down without the least bit of know-how. You get to work with a pick and shovel and the demolition is finished in no time at all. Not only are you through with the demolition, but you can also say, the job is done. Such a profession is, as everyone will admit, quite easy. But not to tear anything down and build, to keep always building, with a vengeance, that is something entirely different, you gentlemen wreckers. Naturally, you are so hardened in wickedness that you can't even understand the joy which lies locked in constant, ever constant building.

The gentlemen senators who held the fate of the free seaport of Creixcroll in their hands were, from that point of view, fanatics about building and—it seemed to them a necessary corollary—enemies of any tearing down. Hence they decided to apply to the city of Creixcroll their philosophy of life, the antithetical conception in regard to building and tearing down. They didn't doubt at all that the city would thereby reach a period of great glory not known for centuries. The mayor of Creixcroll issued a police ordinance, which forbade all Creixcrollers to tear down anything—be it merely one stone of a chicken coop. Heavy penalties would hit those who dared tamper with the regulation. The senate, on the other hand, designed an enormous premium system to support all those who by building would contribute to leading the city of Creixcroll toward her period of glory. In order to scare everyone away from the disastrous vandalism of tearing down, the medieval punishment of pillory was reinstituted in Creixcroll's judicial system. He who dared to tear anything down was pilloried. This wise measure was taken in order to impress on the growing generation from childhood on the positive value of building, next to a contempt for the base and easy wrecker's work.

Basically, Creixcroll's citizens saw much truth in this. For that matter, if anyone spoke to them about the glory of their city, he always found them to be an obedient audience and perhaps useful material. That was also the case in this instance. The Creixcrollers rushed to work, i.e., to building. To be sure, soon there existed in the city a terrible shortage of architects, masons, carpenters, and all the other skilled men from branches connected with the building industry. After a short time things had already gone so far in Creixcroll that the literal professions were, so to speak, simply abolished. The young gentlemen from the better classes and from the middle class became architects, engineers, or building contractors, while all the working men switched to the building industry. No luxury trade seemed to be a match for the building industry, and no one could therefore guarantee its workers a decent income. Luxury items were no longer desired. If a Creixcroller had money to spare, he would invest it in a building. Gold and jewelry, a cozy house, and a linen closet filled to the topmost shelf—which used to be the ideal of all female Creixcrollers—were relinquished as being useless. Building had become the "measure of all things." The wealth of a person was measured according to the number of buildings he was constructing or, in the worst case, had constructed for him. Since the old harbor Creixcroll was financially a well-established city, her inhabitants had large reserves at their disposal. And all these reserves, up to that time primarily invested in bonds from solid overseas states, were used to finance this splendid, "uplifting" period of history. Everybody invested whatever he owned in liquid assets in buildings. As a matter of course Creixcroll's senate had to come up with something to provide the city with the necessary number of bakers and butchers. Galley slaves were called upon for this purpose.

If in the beginning usefulness, i.e., the necessity for and the need for buildings, still played the decisive role, this pragmatic consideration soon disappeared and the Creixcrollers built only pour *l'amour de l'art,* the glory of their

city, the way it had been represented to them by the
philosophers of the building theory. The Creixcrollers built
therefore simply for the joy of building. They built so
much that, after a short period of exertion of this indus-
trious people, there were dozens of all possible kinds of
buildings to spare, houses, palaces, concert halls, and
churches. After three years of this sustained effort the
city of Creixcroll had, among others, five court houses,
eight city halls, ten slaughterhouses, as many asylums for
stray dogs, and seventy churches, of which forty-five could
not be used at present, and furthermore an enormous number of empty houses. The building of privies along public
roads also got its turn now and then, in such a way that, in
this respect also, the city of Creixcroll was well supplied
in an exemplary fashion. Creixcroll's senate supported all
these efforts as much as possible. It also had countless buildings erected at its own expense, including these privies.
What was supposed to happen to all these building reserves would become clear in the future.

Against the objection of "uselessness" an architect had
already found a technically brilliant answer, namely the
building of an "abstract building," as he called it. The
owner could, according to circumstances, convert this
abstract building into a department store, a concert hall
or a cafeteria.

As far as the wreckers were concerned, they were forced
to notice, to their dismay, that the magistrates did not
allow anyone to mock their ordinances. A pigeon fancier
who had given up his hobby, thereby following for that
matter the inclination of all Creixcrollers, and who now
thought that he could tear down his dovecot, saw the
offence punished with an entire day in the pillory. The
following incident, however, gave cause for a lengthy legal
explanation. An owner had a sock-worn house in the old
center of the city. Like all Creixcrollers he liked the glory
óf his city and thought to contribute to its glory by answering the building order in kind. Since open land within
Creixcroll's city limits had become scarce and, on top of
that, because of the heavy demand was very highly priced,
this owner decided to tear down his wretch of a house in
order to erect a new one on the same spot. Sure. As soon
as the workmen had made so much as a gesture indicating
they might want to start the demolition, a police squad

stood ready. They brought the whole bunch, owner, architect, and workmen, to the police station. From this action stemmed—for the Creixcroll of that time—a very famous trial. The owner deluded himself in thinking he had a strong position. He thought that the tearing down of a house was surely legal, when in place of this old house a new one would be erected. How can you possibly build a skyscraper on top of a medieval corbiestep. Even more so when the corbiestep, even without this experiment, would collapse under the weight of years. The owner argued that, in his judgment, he had done the city a service, for in the street where his house stood it was really not safe for either passers-by or occupants.

"This proposition is absolutely wrong," remarked the President of the Building Tribunal—an organism dealing exclusively with the execution of ordinances concerning building and wrecking. "For we should never forget that the Creixcrollers who have steered our city onto a new course started with the idea that tearing down is easy, hence unworthy of a people such as ours, and that building, always building, is the one and only ideal which a superb city such as Creixcroll can aim for. No matter what reasons one could provide to motivate tearing things down, they are a priori invalid. Tearing down is, categorically, a reprehensible deed." And so the owner was sentenced, after the tribunal had accepted the mitigating circumstances presented by the defense, to twenty years' imprisonment. It is only natural that he, too, like all wreckers, was chained to the pillory immediately after the sentence had been pronounced. His guard, however, his head full of plans for the "abstract building" which he would build very soon, forgot the fellow in the pillory. The unfortunate owner, after fourteen days of the most painful hardships, perished there.

Want rapidly increased in the city of Creixcroll—we mean a want of land to build on. It became urgent to do something about it. The magistrates decided that now the builders of Creixcroll simply had to attack the public squares—the health of the Creixcrollers wouldn't go all that easily to the dogs. However great the emergency might become, the citizens only needed to get it firmly in their head that now, just as before, tearing down would be severely punished. If you could not find any land anymore, you simply had to prop up the old building which you owned in such a manner that it could support the weight of a larger number of stories. If the house would give way despite being propped up, you simply had to accept this natural phenomenon. The rubble could not be cleared away, however, no matter what. The ruins too had to prove the activities of Creixcroll.

A further cause of this intense building activity was that each Creixcroller began to feel himself an expert on construction. And so it happened that in the statistical returns of the city of Creixcroll the cause, "accidents," soon took first place. For that matter, the word "accident" had lost its original meaning. In Creixcroll one understood "accident" only to mean the fact of perishing in the collapse of a building.

In the end it became a bit much for some Creixcrollers. Especially after the builders were busily building the public squares chock-full, a movement was formed which, hesitantly at first, was called the Anti-Building Movement. The propagandists of this movement tried to demonstrate that it really was no fun to live in a city which was being re-created into a forest of houses—an unhealthy forest—and that it was necessary as soon as possible to put a stop to this building activity, which they called a mania.

As soon as the Building Tribunal had been informed of this rebellious talk they arrested the leader of the Anti-Building Movement. The Supreme Court, which had the jurisdiction in cases of treason, was assigned to the case. Since, according to the jury and judges, treason was proven as clearly as water from a well, it was quite unnecessary to make an elaborate trial out of his case. The sentence was the death penalty. The Court decided to administer it later by means of the rack. A didactic feast would be made from this putting on the rack, to teach all minds with rebellious tendencies a good lesson once and for all. A prophet is not without honor, save in his own country, thought the Anti-Building man.

Then the unexpected happened.

—Your honor, said the executioner, where can I set up the rack?

—In Central Square, answered the judge.

—Central Square! Central Square! You know, I'm sure, that Central Square exists only in name now.

—Put the rack where you want it, Hapmans.

—Sure, easier said than done, your honor, sir. There is no square larger than an apron in the city.

—What?

—I am saying that we cannot put this traitor, this rotten slob, on the rack, because we cannot set up the rack anywhere.

Indeed. The didactic feast had to be postponed. The zealots of the Anti-Building Movement used this occasion to incite the Creixcrollers:

—We don't speak for our cause. But think about it for a moment—the authorities arrange a beautiful feast. For the first time in ages you will be able to enjoy the rack as a public recreation. And what happens? The feast is off because we don't have a square. If you had followed his advice, you would have had a square at this moment, and you would have been able to put him very neatly to the rack.

A gang of Creixcrollers, with the executioner Hapmans among them, marched at night on the prison, rightfully angered by the idiotic organization of the present regime, and liberated the agitator. The next day he was placed at the head of the Senate of the city of Creixcroll.

—What do the people want? he asked from the balcony of the city hall.

—Squares! it rolled like a plainsong against him.

—You won't escape us for a second time, said a voice behind him. It was Hapmans. He stuck, defined in that sense by his job, strictly to the letter of the law.

Translated from the Dutch
by E. M. Beekman

Mr. Telleke's Conviction

by *Paul van Ostaijen*

It needed many convincing proofs from his acquaintances before Mr. Telleke decided to make a trip in an express train. Yet despite these proofs he still stuck to his opinion. That thing moves too fast. That has to result in accidents. If you put your feet quickly one in front of the other you're sure to fall. Exactly the same thing would happen to an express train.

But Telleke had allowed himself to be convinced. It's not that those accidents rarely happen, but it does mean that he too could have a go at it.

Telleke was now in the express train. He jumped, walked to the window and yelled: the train's going too fast. There's definitely going to be an accident.

Telleke wanted to prevent accidents. He also yelled: my fellow passengers, watch out, there's definitely going to be an accident.—After that and in order to escape that miserable fate he threw himself out of the window of the express train.

Before entering the realm of eternity he thought: that's really what I always had in mind. Even my direst attempt to avoid the accident did not make any difference.

Translated from the Dutch
by E. M. Beekman

My Properties
by *Henri Michaux*

In my properties it's all flat, nothing moves; and if there is a shape here or there, then where does the light come from? No shadow.

Sometimes when I have time, I observe, holding my breath; lying in wait; and if I see something emerge, I take off like a bullet and leap onto the spot; but the head, for it's most often a head, ducks back into the swamp; quickly I take aim, it's mud, perfectly ordinary mud or sand, sand . . .

It doesn't open onto a beautiful sky either. Although there is nothing overhead, it seems, you have to walk bent over as if in a low tunnel.

These properties are my only properties and I have lived in them since my childhood and I can say that very few people possess poorer ones.

Often I wanted to lay out fine avenues in them, I would make a great park . . .

Not that I like parks, but—still.

At other times (it's an obsession of mine, unwearying, which grows again after every failure), I see in outside life or in a picture book an animal I like, a tufted heron for example, and I tell myself: now that would look nice on my properties and besides it might multiply, and I take a sheaf of notes and learn about all that makes up the life of the animal. My documentation becomes vaster and vaster. But when I try to transport it onto my properties, it is always lacking some essential organs. I struggle. I I already feel that this won't succeed either; and as for multiplying, on my properties, things don't multiply, I know that only too well. I concern myself with the new arrival's food, its air, I plant trees for it, I sow grass, but such are my detestable properties that if I turn away, or somebody calls me outside a moment, when I come back there's nothing left, or only a layer of ashes which just might reveal one last speck of scorched moss—just might.

But sometimes it comes alive, life stirs. It's visible, it's certain. I had always had a feeling there was something in it, I feel full of high spirits. But here comes a woman from outside; and riddling me with pleasures without number but so close together it lasts only a moment, and carrying me away at the same time for a trip many, many times around the world . . . (Whereas I didn't dare ask her to tour my properties, in the state of poverty and almost non-existence they are in). Well! on the other hand, promptly harassed by so many travels on which I don't understand anything and which were only a perfume, I get away from her, cursing women yet again, and completely lost on the planet, I weep for my properties which are nothing, but which still represent familiar ground, and don't give me that impression of *absurdity* I find everywhere.

Translated from the French
by Basil D. Kingstone

17

My King

by Henri Michaux

In my night I besiege my King. I get up bit by bit and I wring his neck.

He regains strength. I attack him again and wring his neck once more.

I shake him and shake him like an old plum tree, and his crown trembles on his head.

And yet he is my King, I know it and he knows it, and I am most certainly in his service.

But in the night, the passion of my hands strangles him unceasingly. No cowardice, though, I come with bare hands and I squeeze his kingly neck.

And he's my King, whom I have been strangling in vain for so long in the secrecy of my little room; his face turns blue at first but in no time becomes natural again, and his head is raised again, every night, every night.

In the secrecy of my little room, I fart in my King's face. Then I burst out laughing. He tries to keep a calm expression, washed clean of all insult. But I fart without stopping in his face, except to turn around and look at him, and burst out laughing in his noble face, which tries to keep its majesty.

That's how I behave towards him; endless beginning of my obscure life.

And now I throw him to the ground, and sit on his face —his dignified face disappears—my rough pants with the oil spots, and my butt—to call it by its right name—sit unembarrassed on that face made to rule.

And I don't hesitate, oh no, to turn left and right, any time I like and even more, without bothering about his eyes or his nose getting in the way. I only go away once I'm tired of sitting.

And if I turn around, his imperturable face rules still.

I slap him, I slap him, then I wipe his nose like a child's, in derision.

And yet it's quite obvious that he is the King, and I am his subject, his only subject.

I kick his ass out of my room. I cover him with kitchen refuse and garbage. I break dishes under his feet. I stuff his ears with vulgar and well-chosen insults, to really hit him deeply and shamefully, especially filthy and detailed Neapolitan slanders, the mere statement of which is a stain one cannot get rid of, a foul coat made to measure: the real liquid manure of existence.

Well, I have to begin all over again the next day.

He's come back; he's there. He's always there. He cannot get out and stay out. He absolutely has to impose his damned royal presence on me in my room, which is small enough already . . .

Translated from the French
by Basil D. Kingstone

18

The Experimental World
by *Par Lagerkvist*

Once upon a time there was a world which was not intended to be a real, proper world but which was only meant to experiment with this and that, where one could see by trial and error how everything turned out, what could be made of it. It was to be like a laboratory, a research station where various suggestions and ideas could be tried out to see what they were worth. If anything chanced to give a satisfactory result, proved to be perfect, then it was to be used elsewhere.

A start was made with a little of everything. Plants and trees were set out and tended, fertilized with sun. They grew a bit, then they died out and mouldered away, others had to be started. Many animals were tried, they did fairly well, they developed; but then all at once they stopped where they were or crept back almost to where they had begun; everything came to a standstill. But it didn't matter very much; failures were only to be expected. Some things were not so bad for all that, and much was learned.

Then it was seen what could be done with human beings. It didn't go at all well. They grew a bit, but then they slipped back again. They could be got so that they seemed almost perfect, whole nations, great and noble, but all at once they slipped back, proved to be nothing but animals. But it didn't matter very much; failures were only to be expected. The earth was full of bones from all kinds of human beings who had turned out badly, from nations that had been a failure. But quite a lot was learned about how it should not be.

Then came the idea to try just one or two; it was no use with such a lot of people. A boy- and a girl-child were chosen who were to grow up in the most beautiful parts of the earth. They were allowed to run about in the woods

and romp, play under the trees and take delight in everything. They were allowed to become a young man and
woman who loved one another, their happiness was complete, their eyes met as openly as if their love had been
but a clear summer's day. Even all the human failures
around them saw that there was an unaccountable splendour about them which made them different from everything else in the world. And they rejoiced at it; they could
do that at least. Love drew the two lovers together. It
could not remain merely as a beautiful earthly day; it rose
up into a light where the young people felt dizzy, where
they had to shut their eyes or be blinded; their hearts
thumped, their lips quivered. They lay under the rose trees
in the most beautiful part of the earth, in a wonderful
night which had been provided for them. And they fell
asleep in bliss, in the ecstasy and perfect beauty of love,
locked in each other's arms. They awakened no more;
they were dead. They were to be used elsewhere.

Translated from the Swedish
by Alan Blair

19

The Adventure

by Pär Lagerkvist

A ship with black sails came to take me away. And I went on board willingly enough. I might just as well take a little trip; I was young and carefree and had a longing for the sea. We put out from the coast, which soon disappeared behind us, and the ship was borne steadily along by a fresh wind. Those of the crew with whom I came in contact were stern and grave; we had little to say to each other on board. We sailed and sailed day and night for a long time and on the same course. We did not come across any land. We sailed on year after year; the sea was black, the wind good. There was no sign of land. At last I thought this was strange and asked one of the crew what was the reason. He answered that there was no world any longer. It was annihilated, had sunk down into the depths. There was only ourselves.

I thought that was exciting. We kept on sailing for a long time. The sea lay void. The wind filled the black sails. Everything was empty; there were only the depths below us. Then a frightful storm burst. The sea roared and heaved all around us. We fought in the darkness. The storm did not cease, nor the darkness. Year after year it continued. The clouds trailed across the black sails; everything was black and empty and desolate. We fought in the night, in anguish and need, wrought-up, lacerated, without daring to hope any more.

Then at last we heard the deafening roar of breakers. We were cast by a mighty wave against a rocky island which rose out of the sea. The ship was broken to pieces; we clung to the rock. The wreckage and shreds of sail floated about; we clung fast to the ground. At long last it grew light and we could see. The little island on which we had been saved was rugged and dark. There was only a single storm-blown tree, no flowers or verdure. We clung fast. We were happy. We laid our cheeks to the ground and wept for joy. It was the world beginning to rise up out of the depths again.

Translated from the Swedish
by Alan Blair

20

On the Scales of Osiris

by Par Lagerkvist

And the Great King over two kingdoms awakened as
from a deep sleep in his grave chamber, which was filled
with all the things of the earth, in order to step before
the throne of Osiris. Around him there were gathered all
the riches of life, all that which is given to the chosen,
wagons of cedar inlaid with gold and ivory, war chariots
of copper ornamented with reliefs of victory, couches for
resting borne by gilded cows with the sun disk between
their horns, precious gems in bowls of onyx and jade,
shimmering sealed alabaster jars with oils and ointments.
Slaves of both sexes carved in wood and small as dolls performed their duties, served marvellous courses, raised the
walls of his palace, carried home his quarry and his fal-
cons after the hunt, hoisted his sails on the sacred river.
He looked about and did not understand.

At his feet knelt his body servant with his hands pressed
against his breast, ready to hear his commands. Ethiopian
slaves butchered a sheep and prepared it at the hearth, har-
vested the fields and drove the oxen at the water wheel.
Dancing girls in transparent garments danced for him with
their arms lifted above their heads to the music of flutes
and harps.

What was this? He could not remember. In a common
bowl of clay, unlike anything else there, lay some blackened
grains of corn. Servants were occupied in baking bread,
wool carding, spinning and weaving. On a basin of gold
lay pearls and sparkling precious stones. He understood
nothing, did not recognize anything. In the centre his own
statue was throned. He did not know who it was. On the
pale chalkstone walls of the grave chamber his whole life
was pictured, all his power and glory, his victories over
his enemies, his armies and chiefs, and he himself trium-

phant on his chariot riding over the trampled corpses of
his foes while the falcon of Horus lifted the looped cross,
the sacred mark of life, before his eyes.

What did this mean? He could not explain. The life of
the earth lived in all its splendour around him, all that
which he had wanted to carry along, all that which he had
thought important to have here. All was as he had decided. But he did not now know what the meaning of it
was. He stood there and looked about as in an unknown
world. His glance was as if touched by a hand which had
taken away the interpretation of the pictures; his soul was
as a subterranean well without surface.

Then his lifeless glance happened to fall on a small gilded
image of a woman who radiated light before him through
the dimness. She did not awaken any memories in him,
not even one. She was as unknown to him as anything
there. But within him something moved when he looked
at her, as if something were still alive. He went nearer and
gazed at the image. She sat with her hands resting on her
small knees and her large earthy eyes met his questioning
glance. No, he did not know her. But there rose within
him something like a mighty wave which filled his breast.
He did not know what it was, but it was something great
and strange; it gripped him with a secret power. It was
something wonderful and incomprehensible, something
which lived.

The gold flakes came off when he touched her. Filled his
hands with sparkling dust.

Long he stood there in the twilight by her image. Then
he lifted his empty eyes and, with his hand on his breast,
he entered before the throne of Osiris.

Translated from the Swedish
by Carl Eric Lindin

21

Fable of the Goat

by S. Y. Agnon

The tale is told of an old man who groaned from his heart. The doctors were sent for, and they advised him to drink goat's milk. He went out and bought a she-goat and brought her into his home. Not many days passed before the goat disappeared. They went out to search for her but did not find her. She was not in the yard and not in the garden, not on the roof of the House of Study and not by the spring, not in the hills and not in the fields. She tarried several days and then returned by herself; and when she returned, her udder was full of a great deal of milk, the taste of which was as the taste of Eden. Not just once, but many times she disappeared from the house. They would go out in search for her and would not find her until she returned by herself with her udder full of milk that was sweeter than honey and whose taste was the taste of Eden.

One time the old man said to his son, "My son, I desire to know where she goes and whence she brings this milk which is sweet to my palate and a balm to all my bones."

His son said to him, "Father, I have a plan."

He said to him, "What is it?"

The son got up and brought a length of cord. He tied it to the goat's tail.

His father said to him, "What are you doing, my son?"

He said to him, "I am tying a cord to the goat's tail, so that when I feel a pull on it I will know that she has decided to leave, and I can catch the end of the cord and follow her on her way."

The old man nodded his head and said to him, "My son, if your heart is wise, my heart too will rejoice."

The youth tied the cord to the goat's tail and minded it carefully. When the goat set off, he held the cord in his

hand and did not let it slacken until the goat was well on
her way and he was following her. He was dragged along
behind her until he came to a cave. The goat went into
the cave, and the youth followed her, holding the cord.
They walked thus for an hour or two, or maybe even a
day or two. The goat wagged her tail and bleated, and the
cave came to an end.

When they emerged from the cave, the youth saw lofty
mountains, and hills full of the choicest fruit, and a fountain of living waters that flowed down from the mountains; and the wind wafted all manner of perfumes. The
goat climbed up a tree by clutching at the ribbed leaves.
Carob fruits full of honey dropped from the tree, and she
ate of the carobs and drank of the garden's fountain.

The youth stood and called to the wayfarers: "I adjure
you, good people, tell me where I am, and what is the
name of this place?"

They answered him, "You are in the Land of Israel,
and you are close by Safed."

The youth lifted up his eyes to the heavens and said,
"Blessed be the Omnipresent, blessed be He who has
brought me to the Land of Israel." He kissed the soil and
sat down under the tree.

He said, "Until the day breathe and the shadows flee
away, I shall sit on the hill under this tree. Then I shall go
home and bring my father and mother to the Land of
Israel." As he was sitting thus and feasting his eyes on the
holiness of the Land of Israel, he heard a voice proclaim-
ing:

"Come, let us go out to greet the Sabbath Queen."

And he saw men like angels, wrapped in white shawls,
with boughs of myrtle in their hands, and all the houses
were lit with a great many candles. He perceived that the
eve of Sabbath would arrive with the darkening, and that
he would not be able to return. He uprooted a reed and
dipped it in gallnuts, from which the ink for the writing of
Torah scrolls is made. He took a piece of paper and wrote
a letter to his father:

"From the ends of the earth I lift up my voice in song
to tell you that I have come in peace to the Land of Israel.
Here I sit, close by Safed, the holy city, and I imbibe its
sanctity. Do not inquire how I arrived here but hold onto
this cord which is tied to the goat's tail and follow the

footsteps of the goat; then your journey will be secure, and you will enter the Land of Israel."

The youth rolled up the note and placed it in the goat's ear. He said to himself: When she arrives at Father's house, Father will pat her on the head, and she will flick her ears. The note will fall out, Father will pick it up and read what is written on it. Then he will take up the cord and follow the goat to the Land of Israel.

The goat returned to the old man, but she did not flick her ears, and the note did not fall. When the old man saw that the goat had returned without his son, he clapped his hands to his head and began to cry and weep and wail, "My son, my son, where are you? My son, would that I might die in your stead, my son, my son!"

So he went, weeping and mourning over his son, for he said, "An evil beast has devoured him, my son is assuredly rent in pieces!"

And he refused to be comforted, saying, "I will go down to my grave in mourning for my son."

And whenever he saw the goat, he would say, "Woe to the father who banished his son, and woe to her who drove him from the world!"

The old man's mind would not be at peace until he sent for the butcher to slaughter the goat. The butcher came and slaughtered the goat. As they were skinning her, the note fell out of her ear. The old man picked up the note and said, "My son's handwriting!"

When he had read all that his son had written, he clapped his hands to his head and cried, "*Vay! Vay!* Woe to the man who robs himself of his own good fortune, and woe to the man who requites good with evil!"

He mourned over the goat many days and refused to be comforted, saying, "Woe to me, for I could have gone up to the Land of Israel in one bound, and now I must suffer out my days in this exile!"

Since that time the mouth of the cave has been hidden from the eye, and there is no longer a short way. And that youth, if he has not died, shall bear fruit in his old age, full of sap and richness, calm and peaceful in the Land of the Living.

Translated from the Hebrew
by Barney Rubin

22

The Orchestra
by S. Y. Agnon

1

I had been busy that entire year. Every day, from morning until midnight, I would sit at my table and write—at
times out of habit, and at times stimulated by the pen. We
sometimes dare to call this divine inspiration. I therefore
became oblivious to all other affairs; and I would recall
them only to postpone them. But on the eve of Rosh ha-
Shanah I said to myself: A new year is approaching, and
I have left many letters unattended. Let me sit down and
reply to them, and enter the new year without obligations.

I proceeded on that day as on every other, save that I
am regularly accustomed to arise at dawn, and that day I
arose three hours earlier. For this is a night when one
arises especially early for penitential prayers on the theme
of "Remember the Covenant."

Before I sat down to take care of the letters, I reflected:
A new year is approaching, and one ought to enter it
clean, but if time does not permit me to go and bathe in
the river, because of these letters, I will take a hot bath.

At that moment Charni happened to be visiting us. The
same old Charni who usually boasts to me that she served
in my grandfather's house long before I was born. Charni
said: "Your wife is busy with holiday preparations, and
you are placing extra burdens upon her. Come to our
house and I will prepare you a hot bath." I liked her suggestion; after all, I needed a haircut in honor of the
Rosh ha-Shanah festival, and on the way to the barber I
would stop off and bathe.

I examined the letters and weighed which of them ought
to be answered first. Since they were many and the time
was short, it was impossible to answer in one day all that

many men had written to me in the course of an entire
year, and I decided to pick out the most important ones,
then to deal with those of middling importance, and afterwards with the least important. While I stood deliberating,
it occurred to me that I should get rid of the trivial letters
first, in order to be free for the more important ones.

Trivia tend to be frustrating. Because a matter is trivial
and has no substance, it is difficult to handle. If there is a
trace of substance, it lies in what the author of the letter
had in mind and what answer he expected. As much as I
knew that I had nothing to say in reply, my desire to
answer increased, for if I left them unattended, they would
trouble me. Their very existence is a burden, for I remember them and come to trivial thoughts.

I picked up a pen to write, but my mind was blank.
How strange! The entire year I write effortlessly, and now
that I have to write two or three inconsequential lines, my
pen refuses to cooperate. I put that letter down and
picked up another.

This letter was no letter, but a ticket to an concert con-
ducted by the king of musicians. I have heard that the
minds of those who hear him are transformed. There
actually was a man who used to go to all the concerts but
got nothing out of them; he used to think that he did not
appreciate music until he chanced upon a concert of
this conductor. He said afterward: "Now I know that I
do understand music, but that all musicians whom I have
heard until now do not know what music is." I took the
concert ticket and put it in my pocket.

2

The days before a holiday are brief—some of them because sundown is early and others because holiday preparations are heavy. All the more so the day before Rosh
ha-Shanah, which is short in itself and is sped by preparations for the Day of Judgment. By noon I hadn't managed to answer so much as a single letter. I put the letters
aside and said to myself that what I had not managed to
do before Rosh ha-Shanah I would do in the days between
Rosh ha-Shanah and the Day of Atonement. It would have
been good to enter a new year free of obligations, but what

was I to do when trivial letters did not instruct me how
they were to be answered.

I got up and went to my grandfather's house to bathe
before the holiday, for Charni had prepared me there a
hot bath. But when I got to the house, I found the door
locked. I walked around and around the house, and each
time I reached the door, I stopped and knocked. A neighbor peeked out from behind her curtains and said: "Are
you looking for Charni? Charni went to the market to
buy fruit for the holiday benediction." I continued walking around the house until Charni arrived.

By rights the old lady should have apologized for making me wait and robbing me of my time. But not only
didn't she excuse herself, she stood and chattered. If I
remember correctly, she told about finding a pomegranate
which was partly squashed, yet its seeds had not separated.

Suddenly three sounds were heard from the tower of
the Council house. I looked at my watch and saw that it
was already three o'clock. My watch is always in dispute
with the tower of the Council house, and today it made
peace with it. And it seemed that the Heavens were agree-
ing with them. Had I tarried so long on the way, and been
detained walking around the house? In any case, three
hours had passed and scarcely two and a half remained
before the New Year's festival began. And this old woman
was standing and chattering about a pomegranate that was
squashed and about its seeds that had not separated.

I interrupted her and asked: "Have you prepared the
bath for me, and is the water heated?" Charni set down
her basket and exclaimed: "God in Heaven, I had intended to prepare a bath for you!" I said: "And you
haven't done it?" She replied: "Not yet, but I will do
it right away." I urged: "Hurry, Charni, hurry. The day
doesn't stand still." She picked between her teeth with
her finger and said: "You don't have to rush me. I know
that time doesn't stand still, and neither will I. Look, I
am already on my way in to make the fire and warm up
some water. You practically have your hot bath." I took
a walk in front of the house while waiting for the water
to heat.

The old judge passed by me. I remembered a question
that I had meant to ask him, but I was afraid to get involved with him and so not manage to cleanse myself for

the holiday; for this judge, once you turn to him, will not
let you go. I postponed my question for another time, and
did not turn to him. In order to occupy myself, I took out
the ticket and noticed that the concert was for the eve of
Rosh ha-Shanah. Isn't it strange that I, who am not a
concert-goer, should be invited to a concert on the eve of
Rosh ha-Shanah!

I put the ticket back in my pocket, and resumed pacing
in front of the house.

Ora, my little relative, came by, whose voice was as
sweet as the sound of the violin, and who looked like a
violin which the musician had leaned against an unstable
wall, and the wall collapsed upon it. I looked closely at her
and saw that she was depressed. I asked her: "What have
you been doing, Ora? You look like a little fawn that went
to the fountain and found no water." Ora said: "I'm leaving here." I asked: "Why are you leaving? What's your
reason? You have always wanted to see this magnificent
conductor, and now that he has come to conduct our
orchestra, you are leaving." Ora burst into tears and said:
"Uncle, I don't have a ticket." I laughed good-heartedly
and said to her: "Let me wipe away your tears." I looked
at her affectionately, and thought how lucky I was to be
able to gratify this dear child, who found music more
delightful than all the delights in the world, and was most
enthralled with the famous conductor who was this evening
conducting the great chorus. I put my hand in my pocket
to take out the ticket and give it to Ora. And again I
smiled good-heartedly, like one who has the power to do
good. But Ora, who did not know my generous intentions,
threw herself about my neck and kissed me goodbye. I
became distracted, forgot what I was about, and didn't
give Ora the ticket. And while I was standing there, be-
wildered, Charni came and called me.

The oven was flaming, the bath clean and clear, and the
bath water leaped and rose to meet me. But I hadn't the
strength to bathe. Even my time was not with me. I said
to my brother: You bathe, for I am a weak person, and if
I bathe in hot water, I have to rest afterwards, and there
isn't enough time. I left the bath and went home. In order
to be more comfortable, I removed my hat from my head
and carried it in my hand. A passing wind mussed my
hair. Where were my brains? For in the hour that I stood

and waited for the bath, I could have gone to the barber's. I lifted my eyes and looked up at the sky. The sun was already about to set. I went home with a heavy heart. My daughter came out to meet me, dressed in her holiday best. She pointed her finger into space and said: "Light." I thought to myself: What is she saying? The sun has already set, and hasn't left a trace of light behind. Or perhaps she meant the candle that was kindled in honor of the festival. I looked at the candles and realized that the festival had already begun, and I had better run to the House of Prayer. My daughter stared at my old clothes and put her little hands on her new dress to cover it, so as not to shame her father in his old garments. And her eyes were on the verge of tears, both for herself who wore a new dress when her father was dressed in old clothes, and for her father who wore old clothes at a time when the New Year had arrived.

3

After dinner I went outside. The heavens were black, but many stars glittered in them and lit up their darkness. Not a man was outdoors, and all the houses were sunk in sleep. And I too started to doze off. But this sleep was not really sleep, for I could feel that my feet were walking. And I kept walking and walking like this until I arrived at a certain place and heard the sound of music, and I knew I had reached the concert hall. I took out my ticket and entered.

The hall was full. Men and women violinists, men and women drummers, trumpeters, and players of a variety of instruments all stood, dressed in black, and played incessantly. The great conductor was not to be seen in the hall, but the musicians played as if someone were standing over them and waving his baton. And all the men and women musicians were my friends and acquaintances, whom I knew from all the places I had ever lived. How did it happen that all my acquaintances came together in one place and in one chorus?

I came upon a place, sat down, and concentrated. Each man and woman was playing for himself. However, all the melodies joined to form a single song. And every man and woman was bound to his instrument, and the instruments were fastened to the floor, and each one thought that he alone was bound, and was ashamed to ask his neighbor to release him. Or perhaps the players knew that they were fastened to their instruments, and their instruments fastened to the floor, but thought that it was by their free choice that they and their instruments were so bound, and it was by their free choice that they played. One thing was clear, that though their eyes were on their instruments, their eyes did not see what their hands were doing, for all alike were blind. And I fear that perhaps even their ears did not hear what they were playing, and that from much playing they had grown deaf.

I slid out of my seat and crept toward the door. The door was open, and a man whom I had not noticed upon entering was standing at the entrance. He was like all other door-keepers; but there was about him something like the air of that same old judge, who, once you have turned to him, does not let you go.

I said to him: "I would like to leave." He plucked the word out of my mouth and replied in my voice: "To leave? What for?" I said to him: "I have prepared myself a bath, and am in a hurry lest it grow cold." He replied in a voice that would have terrified even a man stronger than I, and said to me: "It's flaming. It's flaming. Your brother has already been scalded by it." I replied, apologetically: "I was occupied with correspondence, and didn't have time to take my bath." He asked: "With what letters were you occupied?" I took out a letter and showed him. He bent over me and said: "But I wrote that letter." I replied: "I intended to answer you." He looked at me and asked: "What did you intend to answer?" My words hid because of his voice, and my eyes closed, and I began to grope with my hands. Suddenly I found myself standing before my house.

My daughter came out and said: "Let me bring you a candle." I answered her: "Do you really think the candle will light my darkness?" By the time she had gone to bring it, the fire escaped from the furnace and blazed around about. And some woman stood before the furnace heaping wood on the fire. Because of the fire and the smoke, I could not look on. And I didn't see if it was old Charni who stood before the furnace, or if it was my young relative Ora who heaped up the fire.

A terror descended upon me, and I stood as if fixed to
the earth. My spirit grew despondent within me that, at
the time when all who sleep were sleeping, I should be so
awake. In truth, not I alone was awake, but also the stars
in heaven were awake with me. And by the light of the
stars of heaven I saw what I saw. And because my spirit
was lowly, my words hid in my mouth.

Translated from the Hebrew
by Judah Stampfer

23

The Blue Jar

by Isak Dinesen

There was once an immensely rich old Englishman who had been a courtier and a councillor to the Queen and who now, in his old age, cared for nothing but collecting ancient blue china. To that end he travelled to Persia, Japan and China, and he was everywhere accompanied by his daughter, the Lady Helena. It happened, as they sailed in the Chinese Sea, that the ship caught fire on a still night, and everybody went into the lifeboats and left her. In the dark and the confusion the old peer was separated from his daughter. Lady Helena got up on deck late, and found the ship quite deserted. In the last moment a young English sailor carried her down into a lifeboat that had been forgotten. To the two fugitives it seemed as if fire was following them from all sides, for the phosphorescence played in the dark sea, and, as they looked up, a falling star ran across the sky, as if it was going to drop into the boat. They sailed for nine days, till they were picked up by a Dutch merchantman, and came home to England.

The old lord had believed his daughter to be dead. He now wept with joy, and at once took her off to a fashionable watering-place so that she might recover from the hardships she had gone through. And as he thought it must be unpleasant to her that a young sailor, who made his bread in the merchant service, should tell the world that he had sailed for nine days alone with a peer's daughter, he paid the boy a fine sum, and made him promise to go shipping in the other hemisphere and never come back. 'For what,' said the old nobleman, 'would be the good of that?'

When Lady Helena recovered, and they gave her the news of the Court and of her family, and in the end also

told her how the young sailor had been sent away never
to come back, they found that her mind had suffered
from her trials, and that she cared for nothing in all the
world. She would not go back to her father's castle in its
park, nor go to Court, nor travel to any gay town of the
continent. The only thing which she now wanted to do
was to go, like her father before her, to collect rare blue
china. So she began to sail, from one country to the other,
and her father went with her.

In her search she told the people with whom she
dealt that she was looking for a particular blue colour,
and would pay any price for it. But although she bought
many hundred blue jars and bowls, she would always
after a time put them aside and say: 'Alas, alas, it is not
the right blue.' Her father, when they had sailed for many
years, suggested to her that perhaps the colour which she
sought did not exist. 'O God, Papa,' said she, 'how can
you speak so wickedly? Surely there must be some of it
left from the time when all the world was blue.'

Her two old aunts in England implored her to come
back, still to make a great match. But she answered them:
'Nay, I have got to sail. For you must know, dear aunts,
that it is all nonsense when learned people tell you that
the seas have got a bottom to them. On the contrary, the
water, which is the noblest of the elements, does, of
course, go all through the earth, so that our planet really
floats in the ether, like a soapbubble. And there, on the
other hemisphere, a ship sails, with which I have got to
keep pace. We two are like the reflection of one another,
in the deep sea, and the ship of which I speak is always
exactly beneath my own ship, upon the opposite side of
the globe. You have never seen a big fish swimming underneath a boat, following it like a dark-blue shade in the
water. But in that way this ship goes, like the shadow
of my ship, and I draw it to and fro wherever I go, as the
moon draws the tides, all through the bulk of the earth. If
I stopped sailing, what would those poor sailors who make
their bread in the merchant service do? But I shall tell you
a secret,' she said. 'In the end my ship will go down, to
the centre of the globe, and at the very same hour the
other ship will sink as well—for people call it sinking,
although I can assure you that there is no up and down

in the sea—and there, in the midst of the world, we two shall meet.'

Many years passed, the old lord died and Lady Helena became old and deaf, but she still sailed. Then it happened, after the plunder of the summer palace of the Emperor of China, that a merchant brought her a very old blue jar. The moment she set eyes on it she gave a terrible shriek. 'There it is!' she cried. 'I have found it at last. This is the true blue. Oh, how light it makes one. Oh, it is as fresh as a breeze, as deep as a deep secret, as full as I say not what.' With trembling hands she held the jar to her bosom, and sat for six hours sunk in contemplation of it. Then she said to her doctor and her lady-companion: 'Now I can die. And when I am dead you will cut out my heart and lay it in the blue jar. For then everything will be as it was then. All shall be blue round me, and in the midst of the blue world my heart will be innocent and free, and will beat gently, like a wake that sings, like the drops that fall from an oar blade.' A little later she asked them: 'Is it not a sweet thing to think that, if only you have patience, all that has ever been, will come back to you?' Shortly afterwards the old lady died.

24

The Blue Stones

by Isak Dinesen

There was once a skipper who named his ship after his wife. He had the figure-head of it beautifully carved, just like her, and the hair of it gilt. But his wife was jealous of the ship. 'You think more of the figure-head than of me,' she said to him. 'No,' he answered, 'I think so highly of her because she is like you, yes, because she is you yourself. Is she not gallant, full-bosomed; does she not dance in the waves, like you at our wedding? In a way she is really even kinder to me than you are. She gallops along where I tell her to go, and she lets her long hair hang down freely, while you put up yours under a cap. But she turns her back to me, so that when I want a kiss I come home to Elsinore.' Now once, when this skipper was trading at Trankebar, he chanced to help an old native King to flee traitors in his own country. As they parted the King gave him two big blue, precious stones, and these he had set into the face of his figure-head, like a pair of eyes to it. When he came home he told his wife of his adventure, and said: 'Now she has your blue eyes too.' 'You had better give me the stones for a pair of earrings,' said she. 'No,' he said again, 'I cannot do that, and you would not ask me to if you understood.' Still the wife could not stop fretting about the blue stones, and one day, when her husband was with the skippers' corporation, she had a glazier of the town take them out, and put two bits of blue glass into the figure-head instead, and the skipper did not find out, but sailed off to Portugal. But after some time the skipper's wife found that her eyesight was growing bad, and that she could not see to thread a needle. She went to a wise woman, who gave her ointments and waters, but they did not help her and in the end the old woman shook her head, and told her that this was a rare and incurable disease, and that she was going blind. 'Oh, God,' the wife then cried, 'that the ship was back in the harbour of Elsinore. Then I should have the glass taken out, and the jewels put back. For did he not say that they were my eyes?' But the ship did not come back. Instead the skipper's wife had a letter from the Consul of Portugal, who informed her that she had been wrecked, and gone to the bottom with all hands. And it was a very strange thing, the Consul wrote, that in broad daylight she had run straight into a tall rock, rising out of the sea.

The Great Mother
by *Miguel Serrano*

In the beginning, the Great Mother looked at herself in a mirror. Then she looked at a second mirror and at a third. In this way all mothers came into being. The Great Mother had eyes like the depths of an abyss, but those of the other mothers were as blue as the sky.

In the ancient city of Amber, next to the Temple of Kali, a priest wearing a red tunic and with feet covered with the blood of sacrifices, explained these things to me. And so I came to know that I had not one mother but many.

Since my life seems to have been so much like an abyss and to be more and more like one, I am trying to look within myself to discover the coffin of the original Great Mother. I will open it and inside I will probably find that she has taken the form of somebody else. Perhaps she will be the Queen of Sheba; possibly even Jesus Christ. Whatever form she takes will be the form of my soul.

Of course when one opens a coffin, one destroys it. Nevertheless a delicate odour of cedarwood will come forth.

Translated from the Spanish
by Frank MacShane

The Servants
by Miguel Serrano

One day while at a party conversing about all these things, I noticed that somebody had left a cigarette case behind. I picked it up and saw that it had many compartments, one of which was for cigarette holders. It looked quite old and was almost falling apart. One of the holders in the case was for smoking opium and was decorated with an almost illegible inscription. For a long while I wondered whether or not I should use it; I hesitated because it seemed to me that cigarette holders are too private and personal to be used by other people.

I walked up and down thinking about the matter and after a while a friend came up to me. Without my having to explain anything, he said to me: 'As usual, you are trying to profit from somebody else's work. You are really very stupid.'

Immediately I understood what he meant, and so I answered: 'I see that you are Melchizdek. You're right: I am stupid. On the other hand, you are not. For myself, I have never known how to do the intermediate steps, and I'm even ignorant of what is essential. There's no use in my studying because I never remember anything. Therefore I must turn to you because you know. Thanks to your wisdom the Queen of Sheba came back. But when you die I'm going to have you thrown into your pot of chemicals. I am quite willing to admit that I'm afraid the Queen of Sheba may discover how much you know and how little I know.'

While I was speaking, the orchestra began to play some old music, and so when I was finished I asked my friend not to go away but to sit with me and listen to it. I told him there was a secret rhythm that lay behind the notes we heard, and I explained that it was the rhythm of drums played by negroes. I told him that if he stayed with me, we would create something remarkable between us. He of course was an alchemist, but I felt within me all that was necessary for the creation of our artificial being. In addition, I could sense the presence of all the 'works and days of hands'. At one end were the red hands, next came the yellow and the white, and over all were the black hands for they were the ones that played the drums.

A dead woman then came up to us and began to prophesy and warn us, but when we looked at her hands we saw they were lined. Then we knew she was an impostor, for death removes the lines from all hands.

The truth is that I came to understand a good deal at this party. I knew who the servants were, and knew that as we use them so they use us and indeed alter us, as do the black children along the beaches of Madras. I realized that one cannot be everything at once. One is either a scientist or a man who understands the essence. One is either Melchizedek or Solomon.

As I left I thanked all the servants, nodding my head to all of them, men and women, children and animals, to all who since my childhood have been modelling and sustaining me with their multicoloured hands, preparing me for matrimony and death.

Translated from the Spanish
by Frank MacShane

The Last Flower
by Miguel Serrano

Even though you are *married*, you will have to die one day. Everybody has to die. The difference for the person who is *married* is this: that a youth will come carrying a flower which he will touch to your lips and to your forehead. Possibly the flower will come alone. If it does, then you will leap directly into that flower and remain there. It seems a difficult feat, but it is the result of hard work and of the waiting you have endured during your life, especially the waiting for your wedding. But it really makes no difference whether the youth comes; because the flower you enter is the final fruit of your soul and your ultimate creation.

Translated from the Spanish
by Frank MacShane

The Angel
by *Hans Christian Andersen*

"Whenever a good child dies, an angel of God comes down from heaven, takes the dead child in his arms, spreads out his great white wings, and flies with him over all the places which the child has loved during his life. Then he gathers a large handful of flowers which he carries up to the Almighty, that they may bloom more brightly in heaven than they do on earth. And the Almighty presses the flowers to His heart, but He kisses the flower that pleases Him best, and it receives a voice and is able to join the song of the chorus of bliss."

These words were spoken by an angel of God as he carried a dead child up to heaven, and the child listened as if in a dream. Then they passed over well-known spots where the little one had often played, and through beautiful gardens full of lovely flowers.

"Which of these shall we take with us to heaven to be transplanted there?" asked the angel.

Close by grew a slender, beautiful rosebush, but some wicked hand had broken the stem, and the half-opened rosebuds hung all faded and withered on the trailing branches.

"Poor rosebush!" said the child. "Let us take it with us to heaven, that it may bloom above in God's garden."

The angel took up the rosebush. Then he kissed the child and the little one half-opened his eyes. The angel gathered also some beautiful flowers, as well as a few humble buttercups and heartsease.

"Now we have flowers enough," said the child, but the angel only nodded. He did not fly upward to heaven.

It was night and quite still in the great town. Here they remained, and the angel hovered over a small narrow street in which lay a large heap of straw, ashes, and sweepings

from houses of people who had moved away. There lay
fragments of plates, pieces of plaster, rags, old hats, and
other rubbish. Amidst all of this confusion, the angel pointed to the pieces of a broken flowerpot, and to a lump of
earth which had fallen out of it. The earth had been kept
from falling to pieces by the roots of a withered field
flower which had been thrown amongst the rubbish.

"We will take this with us," said the angel. "I will tell
you why as we fly along."

And as they flew the angel related the history.

"Down in that narrow lane, in a low cellar, lived a poor
sick boy. He had been afflicted from his childhood, and
even in his best days he could just manage to walk up
and down the room on crutches once or twice, but no
more. During some days in summer the sunbeams would
lie on the floor of the cellar for about half an hour. In
this spot the poor sick boy would sit warming himself in
the sunshine and watching the red blood through his
delicate fingers as he held them before his face. Then he
would say he had been out, though he knew nothing of
the green forest in its spring verdure till a neighbor's son
brought him a green bough from a beech tree. This he
would place over his head, and fancy that he was in the
beechwood while the sun shone and the birds caroled
gaily. One spring day the neighbor's boy brought him some
field flowers, and among them was one to which the roots
still adhered. This he carefully planted in a flowerpot, and
placed in a window seat near his bed. And the flower
had been planted by a fortunate hand, for it grew, put
forth fresh shoots, and blossomed every year. It became
a splendid flower garden to the sick boy, and his little
treasure upon earth. He watered it and cherished it, and
took care it should have the benefit of every sunbeam that
found its way into the cellar, from the earliest morning
ray to the evening sunset. The flower entwined itself even
in his dreams. For him it bloomed; for him it spread its
perfume. And it gladdened his eyes, and to the flower he
turned, even in death, when the Lord called him. He has
been one year with God. During that time the flower has
stood in the window, withered and forgotten, till cast out
among the sweepings into the street, on the day the lodgers
moved. And this poor flower, withered and faded as it is,
we have added to our nosegay, because it gave more real

joy than the most beautiful flower in the garden of a queen."

"But how do you know all this?" asked the child whom the angel was carrying to heaven.

"I know it," said the angel, "because I myself was the poor sick boy who walked upon crutches, and I know my own flower well."

Then the child opened his eyes and looked into the glorious happy face of the angel, and at the same moment they found themselves in that heavenly home where all is happiness and joy. And God pressed the dead child to His heart, and wings were given him so that he could fly with the angel, hand in hand. Then the Almighty pressed all the flowers to His heart. But He kissed the withered field flower and it received a voice. Then it joined in the song of the angels, who surrounded the throne, some near, and others in a distant circle, but all equally happy. They all joined in the chorus of praise, both great and small—the good, happy child and the poor field flower, that once lay withered and cast away on a heap of rubbish in a narrow dark street.

Translated from the Danish
by E. V. Lucas and H. B. Paull

29

The Angel and the World's Dominion
by Martin Buber

There was a time when the Will of the Lord, Whose hand
has the power to create and destroy all things, unleashed
an endless torrent of pain and sickness over the Earth.
The air grew heavy with the moisture of tears, and a dim
exhalation of sighs clouded it over. Even the legions that
surround His throne were not immune to the hovering
sadness. One angel, in fact, was so deeply moved by the
sufferings he saw below, that his soul grew quite restless.
When he lifted his voice in song with the others, a note of
perplexity sounded among the strains of pure faith; his
thoughts rebelled and contended with the Lord. He could
no longer understand why death and deprivation need serve
as connecting links in the great Chain of Events. Then
one day, he felt to his horror that the eye of All-Being
was piercing his own eye and uncovering the confusion in
his heart. Pulling himself together, he came before the
Lord, but when he tried to talk, his throat dried up. Nevertheless, the Lord called him by name and gently touched
his lips. Then the angel began to speak. He begged God to
place the administration of the Earth in his hands for a
year's time, that he might lead it to an era of well-being.
The angelic bands trembled at this audacity. But at that
same moment, Heaven grew radiant with the brightness of
God's smile. He looked at the suppliant with great love,
as He announced His agreement. When the angel stood
up again, he too was shining.

And so a year of joy and sweetness visited the Earth.
The shining angel poured the great profusion of his merciful heart over the most anguished of her children, on those
who were benumbed and terrified by want. The groans of
the sick and dying no longer disturbed the world's deep,
surging harmony. The angel's companion in the steely
armor, who only a short time before had been rushing and

roaring through the air, stepped aside now, waiting pee-
vishly with lowered sword, relieved of his official duties.
The Earth floated through a fecund sky that left her with
the burden of new vegetation. When summer was at its
height, people moved singing through the full, yellow
fields; never had such abundance existed in the memory
of living man. At harvest time, it seemed likely that the
walls would burst or the roofs fly off, if they were going
to find room to store their crops.

Proud and contented, the shining angel basked in his
own glory. For by the time the first snow of winter covered
the valleys, and dominion over the Earth reverted into
God's hands, he had parcelled out such an enormous
bounty, that the sons of the Earth would surely be enjoying his gifts for many years to come.

But one cold day, late in the year, a multitude of voices
rose heavenwards in a great cry of anguish. Frightened
by the sound, the angel journied down to the Earth and,
dressed as a pilgrim, entered the first house along the way.
The people there, having threshed the grain and ground it
into flour, had then started baking bread—but, alas, when
they took the bread out of the oven, it fell to pieces, and
the pieces were unpalatable; they filled the mouth with a
disgusting taste, like clay. And this was precisely what the
angel found in the second house and in the third and
everywhere that he set foot. People were lying on the
floor, tearing their hair and cursing the King of the World,
who had deceived their miserable hearts with His false
blessing.

The angel flew away and collapsed at his Master's feet.
Lord, he cried, help me to understand where my power
and judgment were lacking.

Then God raised his voice and spoke: Behold a truth
which is know to me, and only to me from the beginning
of time, a truth too deep and dreadful for your delicate,
generous hands, my sweet apprentice—it is this, that the
Earth must be nourished with putrefaction and covered
with shadows that its seeds may bring forth—and it is
this, that souls must be made fertile with flood and sorrow, that through them the Great Work may be born.

Translated from the German
by Jerome Rothenberg

30

Jachid and Jechidah

by Isaac Bashevis Singer

In a prison where souls bound for Sheol—Earth they call it there—await destruction, there hovered the female soul Jechidah. Souls forget their origin. Purah, the Angel of Forgetfulness, he who dissipates God's light and conceals His face, holds dominion everywhere beyond the Godhead. Jechidah, unmindful of her descent from the Throne of Glory, had sinned. Her jealousy had caused much trouble in the world where she dwelled. She had suspected all female angels of having affairs with her lover Jachid, had not only blasphemed God but even denied him. Souls, she said, were not created but had evolved out of nothing: they had neither mission nor purpose. Although the authorities were extremely patient and forgiving, Jechidah was finally sentenced to death. The judge fixed the moment of her descent to that cemetery called Earth.

The attorney for Jechidah appealed to the Superior Court of Heaven, even presented a petition to Metatron, the Lord of the Face. But Jechidah was so filled with sin and so impenitent that no power could save her. The attendants seized her, tore her from Jachid, clipped her wings, cut her hair, and clothed her in a long white shroud. She was no longer allowed to hear the music of the spheres, to smell the perfumes of Paradise and to meditate on the secrets of the Torah, which sustain the soul. She could no longer bathe in the wells of balsam oil. In the prison cell, the darkness of the nether world already surrounded her. But her greatest torment was her longing for Jachid. She could no longer reach him telepathically. Nor could she send a message to him, all of her servants having been taken away. Only the fear of death was left to Jechidah.

Death was no rare occurrence where Jechidah lived but it befell only vulgar, exhausted spirits. Exactly what happened to the dead, Jechidah did not know. She was convinced that when a soul descended to Earth it was to extinction, even though the pious maintained that a spark of life remained. A dead soul immediately began to rot and was soon covered with a slimy stuff called semen. Then a grave digger put it into a womb where it turned into some sort of fungus and was henceforth known as a child. Later on, began the tortures of Gehenna: birth, growth, toil. For according to the morality books, death was not the final stage. Purified, the soul returned to its source. But what evidence was there for such beliefs? So far as Jechidah knew, no one had ever returned from Earth. The enlightened Jechidah believed that the soul rots for a short time and then disintegrates into a darkness of no return.

Now the moment had come when Jechidah must die, must sink to Earth. Soon, the Angel of Death would appear with his fiery sword and thousand eyes.

At first Jechidah had wept incessantly but then her tears had ceased. Awake or asleep she never stopped thinking of Jachid. Where was he? What was he doing? Whom was he with? Jechidah was well aware he would not mourn for her for ever. He was surrounded by beautiful females, sacred beasts, angels, seraphim, cherubs, ayralim, each one with powers of seduction. How long could someone like Jachid curb his desires? He, like she, was an unbeliever. It was he who had taught her that spirits were not created, but were products of evolution. Jachid did not acknowledge free will, nor believe in ultimate good and evil. What would restrain him? Most certainly he already lay in the lap of some other divinity, telling those stories about himself he had already told Jechidah.

But what could she do? In this dungeon all contact with the mansions ceased. All doors were closed: neither mercy, nor beauty entered her. The one way from his prison led down to Earth, and to the horrors called flesh, blood marrow, nerves, and breath. The God-fearing angels promised resurrection. They preached that the soul did not linger forever on Earth, but that after it had endured its punishment, it returned to the Higher Sphere. But Jechidah, being a modernist, regarded all of this as superstition. How would a soul free itself from the corruption of the body? It was scientifically impossible. Resurrection was a dream, a silly comfort of primitive and frightened souls.

2

One night as Jechidah lay in a corner brooding about Jachid and the pleasures she had received from him, his kisses, his caresses, the secrets whispered in her ear, the many positions and games into which she had been initiated, Dumah, the thousand-eyed Angel of Death, looking just as the Sacred Books described him, entered bearing a fiery sword.

"Your time has come, little sister," he said.

"No further appeal is possible?"

"Those who are in this wing always go to Earth."

Jachidah shuddered. "Well, I am ready."

"Jechidah, repentance helps even now. Recite your confession."

"How can it help? My only regret is that I did not transgress more," said Jechidah rebelliously.

Both were silent. Finally Dumah said, "Jechidah, I know you are angry with me. But is it my fault, sister? Did I want to be the Angel of Death? I too am a sinner, exiled from a higher realm, my punishment to be the executioner of souls. Jechidah, I have not willed your death, but be comforted. Death is not as dreadful as you imagine. True, the first moments are not easy. But once you have been planted in the womb, the nine months that follow are not painful. You will forget all that you have learned here. Coming out of the womb will be a shock; but childhood is often pleasant. You will begin to study the lore of death, clothed in a fresh, pliant body, and soon will dread the end of your exile."

Jechidah interrupted him. "Kill me if you must, Dumah, but spare me your lies."

"I am telling you the truth, Jechidah. You will be absent no more than a hundred years, for even the wickedest do not suffer longer than that. Death is only the preparation for a new existence."

"Dumah, please. I don't want to listen."

"But it is important for you to know that good and evil exist there too and that the will remains free."

"What will? Why do you talk such nonsense?"

"Jechidah, listen carefully. Even among the dead there are laws and regulations. The way you act in death will

determine what happens to you next. Death is a laboratory
for the rehabilitation of souls."

"Make an end of me, I beseech you."

"Be patient, you still have a few more minutes to live
and must receive your instructions. Know, then, that one
may act well or evilly on Earth and that the most perni-
cious sin of all is to return a soul to life."

This idea was so ridiculous that Jechidah laughed despite her anguish.

"How can one corpse give life to another?"

"It's not as difficult as you think. The body is composed
of such weak material that a mere blow can make it dis-
integrate. Death is no stronger than a cobweb; a breeze
blows and it disappears. But it is a great offense to destroy
either another's death or one's own. Not only that, but
you must not act or speak or even think in such a way as
to threaten death. Here one's object is to preserve life, but
there it is death that is succoured."

"Nursery tales. The fantasies of an executioner."

"It is the truth, Jechidah. The Torah that applies to
Earth is based on a single principle: Another man's death
must be as dear to one as one's own. Remember my words.
When you descend to Sheol, they will be of value to you."

"No, no, I won't listen to any more lies." And Jechidah
covered her ears.

3

Years passed. Everyone in the higher realm had forgotten Jechidah except her mother who still continued to
light memorial candles for her daughter. On Earth Jechidah had a new mother as well as a father, several brothers
and sisters, all dead. After attending a high school, she
had begun to take courses at the university. She lived in a
large necropolis where corpses are prepared for all kinds
of mortuary functions.

It was spring, and Earth's corruption grew leprous with
blossoms. From the graves with their memorial trees and
cleansing waters arose a dreadful stench. Millions of creatures, forced to descend into the domains of death, were
becoming flies, butterflies, worms, toads, frogs. They buzzed, croaked, screeched, rattled, already involved in the
death struggle. But since Jechidah was totally inured to

the habits of Earth, all this seemed to her part of life. She sat on a park bench staring up at the moon, which from the darkness of the nether world is sometimes recognized as a memorial candle set in a skull. Like all female corpses, Jechidah yearned to perpetuate death, to have her womb become a grave for the newly dead. But she couldn't do that without the help of a male with whom she would have to copulate in the hatred which corpses call love.

As Jechidah sat staring into the sockets of the skull above her, a white-shrouded corpse came and sat beside her. For a while the two corpses gazed at each other, thinking they could see, although all corpses are actually blind. Finally the male corpse spoke:

"Pardon, Miss, could you tell me what time it is?"

Since deep within themselves all corpses long for the termination of their punishment, they are perpetually concerned with time.

"The time?" Jechidah answered. "Just a second." Strapped to her wrist was an instrument to measure time but the divisions were so minute and the symbols so tiny that she could not easily read the dial. The male corpse moved nearer to her.

"May I take a look? I have good eyes."

"If you wish."

Corpses never act straightforwardly but are always sly and devious. The male corpse took Jechidah's hand and bent his head toward the instrument. This was not the first time a male corpse had touched Jechidah but contact with this one made her limbs tremble. He stared intently but could not decide immediately. Then he said: "I think it's ten minutes after ten."

"Is it really so late?"

"Permit me to introduce myself. My name is Jachid."

"Jachid? Mine is Jechidah."

"What an odd coincidence."

Both hearing death race in their blood were silent for a long while. Then Jachid said: "How beautiful the night is!"

"Yes, beautiful!"

"There's something about spring that cannot be expressed in words."

"Words can express nothing," answered Jechidah.

As she made this remark, both knew they were destined to lie together and to prepare a grave for a new corpse.

The fact is, no matter how dead the dead are there remains some life in them, a trace of contact with that knowledge which fills the universe. Death only masks the truth. The sages speak of it as a soap bubble that bursts at the touch of a straw. The dead, ashamed of death, try to conceal their condition through cunning. The more moribund a corpse the more voluble it is.

"May I ask where you live?" asked Jachid.

Where have I see him before? How is it his voice sounds so familiar to me? Jechidah wondered. *And how does it happen that he's called Jachid? Such a rare name.*

"Not far from here." she answered.

"Would you object to my walking you home?"

"Thank you. You don't have to. But if you want . . . It is still too early to go to bed."

When Jachid rose, Jechidah did, too. Is this the one I have been searching for? Jechidah asked herself, the one destined for me? But what do I mean by destiny? According to my professor, only atoms and motion exist. A carriage approached them and Jechidah heard Jachid say:

"Would you like to take a ride?"

"Where to?"

"Oh, just around the park."

Instead of reproving him as she intended to, Jechidah said: "It would be nice. But I don't think you should spend the money."

"What's money? You only live once."

The carriage stopped and they both got in. Jechidah knew that no self-respecting girl would go riding with a strange young man. What did Jachid think of her? Did he believe she would go riding with anyone who asked her? She wanted to explain that she was shy by nature, but she knew she could not wipe out the impression she had already made. She sat in silence, astonished at her behavior. She felt nearer to the stranger than she ever had to anyone. She could almost read his mind. She wished the night would continue for ever. Was this love? Could one really fall in love so quickly? And am I happy? she asked herself. But no answer came from within her. For the dead are always melancholy, even in the midst of gaiety. After a while Jechidah said: "I have a strange feeling I have experienced all this before."

"*Déjà vu*—that's what psychology calls it."

"But maybe there's some truth to it . . ."

"What do you mean?"

"Maybe we've known each other in some other world."
Jachid burst out laughing. "In what world? There is
only one, ours, the earth."

"But maybe souls do exist."

"Impossible. What you call the soul is nothing but vibrations of matter, the product of the nervous system. I should
know, I'm a medical student." Suddenly he put his arm
around her waist. And although Jechidah had never permitted any male to take such liberties before, she did not
reprove him. She sat there perplexed by her acquiescence,
fearful of the regrets that would be hers tomorrow. I'm
completely without character, she chided herself. But he is
right about one thing. If there is no soul and life is nothing but a short episode in an eternity of death, then why
shouldn't one enjoy oneself without restraint? If there is
no soul, there is no God, free will is meaningless. Morality,
as my professor says, is nothing but a part of the ideologi-
cal superstructure.

Jechidah closed her eyes and leaned back against the
upholstery. The horse trotted slowly. In the dark all the
corpses, men and beasts, lamented their death—howling,
laughing, buzzing, chirping, sighing. Some of the corpses
staggered, having drunk to forget for a while the tortures
of hell. Jechidah had retreated into herself. She dozed off,
then awoke again with a start. When the dead sleep they
once more connect themselves with the source of life. The
illusion of time and space, cause and effect, number and
relation ceases. In her dream Jechidah had ascended again
into the world of her origin. There she saw her real mother,
her friends, her teachers. Jachid was there, too. The two
greeted each other, embraced, laughed and wept with joy.
At that moment, they both recognized the truth, that death
on Earth is temporary and illusory, a trial and a means of
purification. They traveled together past heavenly mansions, gardens, oases for convalescent souls, forests for
divine beasts, islands for heavenly birds. No, our meeting
was not an accident, Jechidah murmured to herself. There
is a God. There is a purpose in creation. Copulation, free
will, fate—all are part of His plan. Jachid and Jechidah
passed by a prison and gazed into its window. They saw a
soul condemned to sink down to Earth. Jechidah knew that

this soul would become her daughter. Just before she woke up, Jechidah heard a voice:

"The grave and the grave digger have met. The burial will take place tonight."

Translated from the Yiddish
by the Author and Elizabeth Pollet

A Very Old Man With Enormous Wings

by Gabriel García Márquez

A TALE FOR CHILDREN

On the third day of rain they had killed so many crabs inside the house that Pelayo had to cross his drenched courtyard and throw them into the sea, because the newborn child had a temperature all night and they thought it was due to the stench. The world had been sad since Tuesday. Sea and sky were a single ash-gray thing and the sands of the beach, which on March nights glimmered like powered light, had become a stew of mud and rotten shellfish. The light was so weak at noon that when Pelayo was coming back to the house after throwing away the crabs, it was hard for him to see what it was that was moving and groaning in the rear of the courtyard. He had to go very close to see that it was an old man, a very old man, lying face down in the mud, who, in spite of his tremendous efforts, couldn't get up, impeded by his enormous wings.

Frightened by that nightmare, Pelayo ran to get Elisenda, his wife, who was putting compresses on the sick child, and he took her to the rear of the courtyard. They both looked at the fallen body with mute stupor. He was dressed like a ragpicker. There were only a few faded hairs left on his bald skull and very few teeth in his mouth, and his pitiful condition of a drenched great-grandfather had taken away any sense of grandeur he might have had. His huge buzzard wings, dirty and half-plucked, were forever entangled in the mud. They looked at him so long and so closely that Pelayo and Elisenda very soon overcame their

surprise and in the end found him familiar. Then they
dared speak to him, and he answered in an incomprehensible dialect with a strong sailor's voice. That was how they
skipped over the inconvenience of the wings and quite in-
telligently concluded that he was a lonely castaway from
some foreign ship wrecked by the storm. And yet, they
called in a neighbor woman who knew everything about
life and death to see him, and all she needed was one look
to show them their mistake.

"He's an angel," she told them. "He must have been
coming for the child, but the poor fellow is so old that the
rain knocked him down."

On the following day everyone knew that a flesh-and-
blood angel was held captive in Pelayo's house. Against
the judgment of the wise neighbor woman, for whom angels in those times were the fugitive survivors of a celestial
conspiracy, they did not have the heart to club him to
death. Pelayo watched over him all afternoon from the
kitchen, armed with his bailiff's club, and before going to
bed he dragged him out of the mud and locked him up with
the hens in the wire chicken coop. In the middle of the
night, when the rain stopped, Pelayo and Elisenda were
still killing crabs. A short time afterward the child woke
up without a fever and with a desire to eat. Then they
felt magnanimous and decided to put the angel on a raft
with fresh water and provisions for three days and leave
him to his fate on the high seas. But when they went out
into the courtyard with the first light of dawn, they found
the whole neighborhood in front of the chicken coop having fun with the angel, without the slightest reverence,
tossing him things to eat through the openings in the wire
as if he weren't a supernatural creature but a circus
animal.

Father Gonzaga arrived before seven o'clock, alarmed
at the strange news. By that time onlookers less frivolous
than those at dawn had already arrived and they were
making all kinds of conjectures concerning the captive's
future. The simplest among them thought that he should
be named mayor of the world. Others of sterner mind felt
that he should be promoted to the rank of five-star general
in order to win all wars. Some visionaries hoped that he
could be put to stud in order to implant on earth a race
of winged wise men who could take charge of the universe.

But Father Gonzaga, before becoming a priest, had been a robust woodcutter. Standing by the wire, he reviewed his catechism in an instant and asked them to open the door so that he could take a close look at that pitiful man who looked more like a huge decrepit hen among the fascinated chickens. He was lying in a corner drying his open wings in the sunlight among the fruit peels and breakfast leftovers that the early risers had thrown him. Alien to the impertinences of the world, he only lifted his antiquarian eyes and murmured something in his dialect when Father Gonzaga went into the chicken coop and said good morning to him in Latin. The parish priest had his first suspicion of an imposter when he saw that he did not understand the language of God or know how to greet His ministers. Then he noticed that seen close up he was much too human: he had an unbearable smell of the outdoors, the back side of his wings was strewn with parasites and his main feathers had been mistreated by terrestrial winds, and nothing about him measured up to the proud dignity of angels. Then he came out of the chicken coop and in a brief sermon warned the curious against the risks of being ingenuous. He reminded them that the devil had the bad habit of making use of carnival tricks in order to confuse the unwary. He argued that if wings were not the essential element in determining the difference between a hawk and an airplane, they were even less so in the recognition of angels. Nevertheless, he promised to write a letter to his bishop so that the latter would write to his primate so that the latter would write to the Supreme Pontiff in order to get the final verdict from the highest courts.

His prudence fell on sterile hearts. The news of the captive angel spread with such rapidity that after a few hours the courtyard had the bustle of a marketplace and they had to call in troops with fixed bayonets to disperse the mob that was about to knock the house down. Elisenda, her spine all twisted from sweeping up so much marketplace trash, then got the idea of fencing in the yard and charging five cents admission to see the angel.

The curious came from far away. A traveling carnival arrived with a flying acrobat who buzzed over the crowd several times, but no one paid any attention to him because his wings were not those of an angel but, rather, those of a sidereal bat. The most unfortunate invalids on earth came in search of health: a poor woman who since childhood had been counting her heartbeats and had run out of numbers; a Portuguese man who couldn't sleep because the noise of the stars disturbed him; a sleepwalker who got up at night to undo the things he had done while awake; and many others with less serious ailments. In the midst of that shipwreck disorder that made the earth tremble, Pelayo and Elisenda were happy with fatigue, for in less than a week they had crammed their rooms with money and the line of pilgrims waiting their turn to enter still reached beyond the horizon.

The angel was the only one who took no part in his own act. He spent his time trying to get comfortable in his borrowed nest, befuddled by the hellish heat of the oil lamps and sacramental candles that had been placed along the wire. At first they tried to make him eat some mothballs, which, according to the wisdom of the wise neighbor woman, were the food prescribed for angels. But he turned them down, just as he turned down the papal lunches that the penitents brought him, and they never found out whether it was because he was an angel or because he was an old man that in the end he ate nothing but eggplant mush. His only supernatural virtue seemed to be patience. Especially during the first days, when the hens pecked at him, searching for the stellar parasites that proliferated in his wings, and the cripples pulled out feathers to touch their defective parts with, and even the most merciful threw stones at him, trying to get him to rise so they could see him standing. The only time they succeeded in arousing him was when they burned his side with an iron for branding steers, for he had been motionless for so many hours that they thought he was dead. He awoke with a start, ranting in his hermetic language and with tears in his eyes, and he flapped his wings a couple of times, which brought on a whirlwind of chicken dung and lunar dust and a gale of panic that did not seem to be of this world. Although many thought that his reaction had been one not of rage but of pain, from then on they were careful not to annoy him, because the majority understood that his passivity was not that of a hero taking his ease but that of a cataclysm in repose.

Father Gonzaga held back the crowd's frivolity with

formulas of maidservant inspiration while awaiting the arrival of a final judgment on the nature of the captive. But the mail from Rome showed no sense of urgency. They spent their time finding out if the prisoner had a navel, if his dialect had any connection with Aramaic, how many times he could fit on the head of a pin, or whether he wasn't just a Norwegian with wings. Those meager letters might have come and gone until the end of time if a providential event had not put an end to the priest's tribulations.

It so happened that during those days, among so many other carnival attractions, there arrived in town the traveling show of the woman who had been changed into a spider for having disobeyed her parents. The admission to see her was not only less than the admission to see the angel, but people were permitted to ask her all manner of questions about her absurd state and to examine her up and down so that no one would ever doubt the truth of her horror. She was a frightful tarantula the size of a ram and with the head of a sad maiden. What was most heartrending, however, was not her outlandish shape but the sincere affliction with which she recounted the details of her misfortune. While still practically a child she had sneaked out of her parents' house to go to a dance, and while she was coming back through the woods after having danced all night without permission, a fearful thunderclap rent the sky in two and through the crack came the lightning bolt of brimstone that changed her into a spider. Her only nourishment came from the meatballs that charitable souls chose to toss into her mouth. A spectacle like that, full of so much human truth and with such a fearful lesson, was bound to defeat without even trying that of a haughty angel who scarcely deigned to look at mortals. Besides, the few miracles attributed to the angel showed a certain mental disorder, like the blind man who didn't recover his sight but grew three new teeth, or the paralytic who didn't get to walk but almost won the lottery, and the leper whose sores sprouted sunflowers. Those consolation miracles, which were more like mocking fun, had already ruined the angel's reputation when the woman who had been changed into a spider finally crushed him completely. That was how Father Gonzaga was cured forever of his insomnia and Pelayo's courtyard went back to being as empty as dur-

ing the time it had rained for three days and crabs walked
through the bedrooms.

The owners of the house had no reason to lament. With
the money they saved they built a two-story mansion with
balconies and gardens and high netting so that crabs
wouldn't get in during the winter, and with iron bars on
the windows so that angels wouldn't get in. Pelayo also set
up a rabbit warren close to town and gave up his job as
bailiff for good, and Elisenda bought some satin pumps
with high heels and many dresses of iridescent silk, the
kind worn on Sunday by the most desirable women in
those times. The chicken coop was the only thing that
didn't receive any attention. If they washed it down with
creolin and burned tears of myrrh inside it every so often,
it was not in homage to the angel but to drive away the
dungheap stench that still hung everywhere like a ghost
and turning the new house into an old one. At first,
when the child learned to walk, they were careful that he
not get too close to the chicken coop. But then they began
to lose their fears and got used to the smell, and before the
child got his second teeth he'd gone inside the chicken coop
to play, where the wires were falling apart. The angel was
no less standoffish with him than with other mortals, but
he tolerated the most ingenious infamies with the patience
of a dog who had no illusions. They both came down
with chicken pox at the same time. The doctor who took
care of the child couldn't resist the temptation to listen to
the angel's heart, and he found so much whistling in the
heart and so many sounds in his kidneys that it seemed
impossible for him to be alive. What surprised him most,
however, was the logic of his wings. They seemed so natural on that completely human organism that he couldn't
understand why other men didn't have them too.

When the child began school it had been some time
since the sun and rain had caused the collapse of the
chicken coop. The angel went dragging himself about
here and there like a stray dying man. They would drive
him out of the bedroom with a broom and a moment later
find him in the kitchen. He seemed to be in so many
places at the same time that they grew to think that he'd
been duplicated, that he was reproducing himself all
through the house, and the exasperated and unhinged
Elisenda shouted that it was awful living in that hell full

of angels. He could scarcely eat and his antiquarian eyes had also become so foggy that he went about bumping into posts. All he had left were the bare cannulae of his last feathers. Pelayo threw a blanket over him and extended him the charity of letting him sleep in the shed, and only then did they notice that he had a temperature at night, and was delirious with the tongue twisters of an old Norwegian. That was one of the few times they became alarmed, for they thought he was going to die and not even the wise neighbor woman had been able to tell them what to do with dead angels.

And yet he not only survived his worst winter, but seemed improved with the first sunny days. He remained motionless for several days in the farthest corner of the courtyard, where no one would see him, and at the beginning of December some large, stiff feathers began to grow on his wings, the feathers of a scarecrow, which looked more like another misfortune of decrepitude. But he must have known the reason for those changes, for he was quite careful that no one should notice them, that no one should hear the sea chanteys that he sometimes sang under the stars. One morning Elisenda was cutting some bunches of onions for lunch when a wind that seemed to come from the high seas blew into the kitchen. Then she went to the window and caught the angel in his first attempts at flight. They were so clumsy that his fingernails opened a furrow in the vegetable patch and he was on the point of knocking the shed down with the ungainly flapping that slipped on the light and couldn't get a grip on the air. But he did manage to gain altitude. Elisenda let out a sigh of relief, for herself and for him, when she saw him pass over the last houses, holding himself up in some way with the risky flapping of a senile vulture. She kept watching him even when she was through cutting the onions and she kept on watching until it was no longer possible for her to see him, because then he was no longer an annoyance in her life but an imaginary dot on the horizon of the sea.

Translated from the Spanish
by Gregory Rabassa

The Sorcerer's Son
by Rodrigo Rey Rosa

In the shade of a tree near the center of the square a group of people had gathered. One man with a pale, greenish complexion seemed to be describing an involved fight. It was almost impossible to understand his words. His gestures were wide and violent; he touched his face, indicating his eyelids, bared his breast and a long scar that traversed his belly.

Later that night they explained that he was a sorcerer, and that what he had been relating that afternoon was the story of the birth of his son. He had told them that one morning when he stooped over to drink in the river, he had seen his face in the water. It was transformed: his eyes had been gouged out, and his lips were mixed up with his nose. He shook his head, and managed to see himself again as he really was. An aching had started up inside him. Walking with difficulty, at times even having to crawl, he moved upward along the path and came to a cave. He went in and sat down, breathless. On his abdomen he saw, or thought he saw, a fire burning. The flame leaned eastward, although there was no wind. He remained there in the dark for seven days, without eating, drinking or moving. One morning before dawn two tiny women the size of a head visited him. They danced, or struggled desperately, on top of his abdomen. At the end, one of them lay dead, near his groin. The other slashed open his belly with a stone blade and hid inside the wound, carrying the body of the other with her. When the sorcerer thought he was already dead, a bird like a ray of light flew out of his belly. It described a white circle and then a red one, above his body, and disappeared into the distant sky.

Translated from the Spanish
by Paul Bowles

The Sacrifice of the Prisoner
by *Elias Canetti*

That night he saw a man standing, fast bound, on the terrace of a temple, defending himself with wooden clubs from the savage attacks of two upright jaguars on his left and right. Both animals were decked with strange streamers in all colours. They gnashed their teeth, roared and rolled their eyes so wildly that it made the blood run cold. The sky was black and narrow, and had hidden his stars in his pocket. Tears of glass trickled out of the eyes of the prisoner and splintered into a thousand pieces as they reached the pavement. But as nothing further happened, the savage combat grew boring and made the spectator yawn. Then by chance his eye fell on the feet of the jaguars. They had human feet. Aha, thought the spectator —lanky, learned man—these are sacrificial priests of ancient Mexico. They are performing a sacred comedy. The victim knows well that he must die in the end. The priests are disguised as jaguars but I see through them at once.

The jaguar on the right seized a heavy stone wedge and drove it into the victim's heart. One edge of it clove sharp through the breast bone. Kien closed his eyes, dazzled. He thought, the blood must spirt up to the very sky; he sternly disapproved of this medieval barbarism. He waited until he thought the blood must have ceased to flow, then opened his eyes. Oh horrible: from the cleft victim's wounded breast a book appeared, another, a third, many. There was no end to it, they fell to the ground, they were clutched at by viscous flames. The blood had set fire to the wood, the books were burning. 'Shut your breast!' shouted Kien to the prisoner, 'Shut your breast!' He gesticulated with his hands; 'you must do it like this, quickly, quickly!' The prisoner understood; with a terrific jerk he freed himself of his bonds and clutched both his hands over his heart; Kien breathed again.

Then suddenly the victim tore his bosom wide open. Books poured forth in torrents. Scores, hundreds, they were beyond counting; the flames licked up towards the paper; each one wailed for help; a fearful shrieking rose on all sides. Kien stretched out his arms to the books, now blazing to heaven. The altar was much further off than he had thought. He took a couple of strides and was no nearer. He must run if he was to save them alive. He ran and fell; this cursed shortness of breath; it came of neglecting his physical health; he could tear himself into pieces with rage. A useless creature, when there was need of him he was no use. Those miserable wretches! Human sacrifices he had heard of—but books, books! Now at last he was at the altar. The fire singed his hair and eyebrows. The wood pyre was enormous; from the distance he had thought it quite small. They must be in the very centre of the fire. Into it then, you coward, you swaggerer, you miserable sinner!

But why blame himself? He was in the middle of it. *Where are you? Where are you?* The flames dazzled him. And what the devil was this, wherever he reached out, he could get hold of nothing but shrieking human beings. They clutched hold of him with all their strength. He hurled them from him, they came back to him. They crept to him from below and entwined his knees; from above his head burning torches rained down on him. He was not looking up yet he saw them clearly. They seized on his ears, his hair, his shoulders. They enchained him with their bodies. Bedlam broke lose. 'Let me go,' he shouted, 'I don't know you. What do you want with me! How can I rescue the books!'

But one of them had thrown himself against his mouth, and clung fast to his tightly closed lips. He wanted to speak again, but he could not open his mouth. He implored them in his mind: *I can't save them! I can't save them!* He wanted to cry, but where were his tears? His eyes too were fast closed; human beings were pressing against them too. He tried to step free of them, he lifted his right leg high in the air; in vain, it was dragged back again, dragged down by a burden of burning human kind, dragged down by a leaden weight. He abhorred them, these greedy creatures; could they not be satisfied with the life they had had? He loathed them. He would have liked to hurt them, torment them, reproach them; he could do nothing, nothing! Not for one moment did he forget why he was there. They might hold his eyes forcibly shut, but in his spirit he could see mightily. He saw a book growing in every direction at once until it filled the sky and the earth and the whole of space to the very horizon. At its edges a reddish glow, slowly, quickly, devoured it. Proud, silent, uncomplaining, it endured a martyr's death. Men screamed and shrieked, the book burnt without a word. Martyrs do not cry out, saints do not cry out.

Then a voice spoke; in it was all knowledge, for it was the voice of God: 'There are no books here. All is vanity.' And at once Kien knew that the voice spoke truth. Lightly, he threw off the burning mob and jumped out of the fire. He was saved. Did it hurt them? Terribly, he answered himself, but not so much as people usually think. He was extraordinarily happy about the voice. He could see himself, dancing from the altar. At a little distance, he turned round. He was tempted to laugh at the empty fire.

Then he stood still, lost in contemplation of Rome. He saw the mass of struggling limbs; the air was thick with the smell of burning flesh. How stupid men are! He forgot his anger. A single step, and they could save themselves.

Suddenly, he did not know how it could have happened, the men were changed into books. He gave a great cry and rushed, beside himself, in the direction of the fire. He ran, panted, scolded himself, leaped into the flames and was again surrounded by those imploring human bodies. Again the terror seized him, again God's voice set him free, again he escaped and watched again from the same place the same scene. Four times he let himself be fooled. The speed with which events succeeded each other increased each time. He knew that he was bathed in sweat. Secretly he began to long for the breathing space allowed him between one excitement and the next. In the fourth pause, he was overtaken by the Last Judgment. Gigantic wagons, high as houses, as mountains, high as the heavens, closed in from two, ten, twenty, from all sides upon the devouring altar. The voice, harsh and destructive, mocked him: 'Now come the books! Kien cried out and woke.

Translated from the German
by C. V. Wedgwood

A Bloodthirsty Tiger
by Elias Canetti

A bloodthirsty tiger lusting for men once disguised itself in the skin and dress of a young maiden. Weeping, it stood at a street corner and was so beautiful that a learned man came along. She lied to him cunningly, and out of pity he took her to his house, as one of his many wives. He was a very brave man and loved to sleep with her. One night she threw off her maiden's skin and tore open his breast. She ate his heart and vanished through the window. She left her shining white skin on the floor behind her. Both were found by one of the other wives who screamed her throat sore asking for an elixir of life. She went down to the most powerful man of the country, a madman who lived in the filth of the market-place, and for long hours rolled about at his feet. He spat into her hand for all the world to see, and she had to drink it. She wept and sorrowed day after day, for she loved the dead man though he had no heart. From the shame she had drunk for him, there grew a new heart out of the warm soil of her bosom. She gave it to the man and he came back to her.

Translated from the German
by C. V. Wedgwood

The Story of Lilith and Eve

by Jakov Lind

Before God created Eve, the legend tells us, he created Lilith, but Lilith left Adam, as she could never agree with him, in smaller and larger matters, while Eve became Adam's true wife, that is, a woman who is always in agreement with her man. Lilith left, but not for good. The legend tells us she returns to haunt Adam as lust.

Once upon a time there was a man who was haunted by Lilith. The demon had disguised herself in the clothes of an ordinary, simple, agreeable Woman and came to visit Adam when he was alone.

Why are you on your own? Lilith asked. Where is your woman, the one who came to replace me?

She is out in the country, she went to visit relatives, and she will return soon. She will not be pleased to find you here, for she fears you.

Why should my sister be afraid of me? asked Lilith. I am as simple in my heart as she is. I am as good and kind as she is. I love my parents and I love my children, the same as she. But I don't think as she does, our difference is hidden in the mind, not in our bodies.

I believe you, said Adam, and I love you, but I need a peaceful life.

Have it your way, said Lilith, have your peaceful life. I am just your other woman, and I will not leave you, but will love you as I always did.

Adam looked into her eyes and said no more. Her eyes were like doors wide open into a world he had almost forgotten, and he stepped inside.

They were in each other's arms and mouth when Eve returned. Lilith and Adam are united, she thought. Stay with me sister. I will bring food to your bed. She brought

food and drink to the bed for them and retired to a far
corner of the house, where she crouched at the stove to
keep herself warm, and went into a trance. She left her
own body and entered the body of her sister Lilith and
thus she embraced and kissed Adam and felt his love for
her as she had never known it before.

But I am your Eve, said Lilith. Why do you love me
so passionately? You never loved me with such passion
before.

Adam laughed and said: You will leave with dawn and
I will not see you for a long time. If I am passionate it's
because our happiness is but short.

How can you say that? said Lilith. I will be here tomorrow and the day after and so for the rest of your life. Why
do you love me so passionately? Do you think I am the one
I look? I am Eve speaking through my sister's mouth.

You are joking, laughed Adam, I know you will leave
at the dawn and will not be back for quite some time.

Lilith, who was Eve now, kissed him and said: I wish
this were so, but alas I cannot leave you. I will stay with
you, because you are full of fire for this other woman
whose body I have now taken over. Look at me carefully
and tell me whether you don't see that I am your wife
Eve?

Eve sits in the far corner of the house, said Adam. But
when he looked he could not see her there. What he saw
were the flames from the stove.

36

The Bride of the East
by W. S. *Merwin*

A girl fell in love with the East and said she would marry no other. When her father heard of this he went to talk with her. He described to her all the kingdoms of the earth. He told her of the pleasures of the South, he was eloquent in praise of the glories of the North, he lifted a corner of the horizon to let her catch a single glimpse of the West. But she would not look and would not listen.

"Why the East?" her father said.

"Everything comes from him," she answered.

"But the East cannot marry you," her father said, as gently as he could. She sat still, at the window.

"The East cannot even come to you," her father went on.

"He can," she said.

"You would not be here," her father said. "You would be far away, to the west of here."

"He would see me," she answered.

"Even if you were still visible you would be too far to recognize. a very small black figure sitting in a frame full of darkness, travelling backwards into a mountain."

"I will not have gone," she said. "I will have waited."

"You can't wait," he answered.

"Why not?"

"Even now you're going."

"It's not true."

"Each time you sleep you wake up farther away."

"Farther from where?"

"From here."

"I don't care."

"Farther from the East."

"I've stopped sleeping." And it was true. Ever since

she had fallen in love she had sat awake all night, every
night, looking out of the east window.

"Each time you blink your eyes, when you open them
you are farther."

"Only from here," she said.

"From the East," he insisted.

"No," she said. "He can go faster."

"Nothing is faster than you when you close your eyes."

"He'd be there."

"He wouldn't stay."

"And I've stopped closing them." It was true. As she
sat looking out of the window, her eyes never blinked,
day or night.

"I want you to go to sleep now, and tomorrow we can
talk about other things," her father said.

"I don't want to sleep," she said. "You just don't want
me to marry the East. Why don't you want me to marry
the East?"

"I want you to marry someone from here."

"I don't want anybody from here."

"You will."

"I can't even see them. I look at their faces and all I
see is holes."

"That's because your head is full of the East. But it
will be different in the morning, you'll see."

"Besides, I've stopped looking at them." It was true.
All she looked at now was the sky beyond the frame of
the window facing east, which was then growing dark.

"I suppose that when you look at my face you see nothing but a hole too," he said. It was a trick to make her
turn and look at him, but she was used to his tricks, and
never took her eyes from the window. "But we're all becoming that way. You too," he said. "We're fading away
so that we can't be seen at all. We're beginning to look
just like air, so that even if he could come here he wouldn't
be able to find you."

It was another trick to make her look, but she knew it.

"He's already found me," she said. At this her father
was startled, for a moment. Then he grew angry, which
is not always an aid to illumination.

"I don't believe you," he said, harshly because it was
not wholly true.

"And you will never marry him," he added, with deliberate cruelty.

"I'm already his bride," she said.

This made her father still more angry.

"It's impossible," he insisted. But nothing would change her thoughts nor turn her gaze from the window.

"Very well," her father said. "Wait for him." And he sent for men to brick up the east window. But she was still there the next morning. And the next evening, and the following morning. She was still there when the bells rang for Sunday, and she was still there when they rang for Easter. She was still there when they rang for her brother's wedding and when they tolled for her mother's passing, and when they rang for her father's burial, and for her brother's death, and others' deaths, and fires in the city, and storms in summer, and sieges and victories and griefs, and when the walls fell behind her because the place had stood uninhabited and untended for so long, the roof letting in until the beams rotted and then moss rooted along them and led the way down and the light followed and she was still there sitting by the bricked-up east window from which not a single brick had fallen, because scar tissue holds longer than the original. But she noticed nothing until they took down the east wall too, finally, because it was unsafe, and because they wanted the stones from the window-frame, and the space, in which to put something else, and then of course the bricks fell at her feet and she stood up and held out her hands toward the east, and feeling nothing there, took a step forward.

It is one of her withered hands that you feel occasionally on your arm, a second at a time, in an episode that must surely last for more than one life. Often it is dark when her finger touches you, and so you may not at first notice that she is blind, and is groping with both hands, in one direction. She is looking for the brick wall beyond which is the East, whose image is still in her breast, but the bricks have gone, and while they were there she had lost her ability to see anything except the darkness of the east, which looks like other darkness. But once she touches you she seems at once to know where she is going, and she leads you through the dark tree-lined square to an unlit doorway. It appears to you that there is a scorpion on one side of the doorway and a worm on the other side. They are bowing to each other, but straighten as you approach, and are heard saying to each other, as you pass through,

"My old friend." (This is the scorpion.)

"My very old friend." (This is the worm, answering.)

"I never wanted bones."

"Neither did I." (The worm again.)

"I'm better off without them."

"That's what I say to myself. If I say anthing."

"You should consider having eyes, though."

"What would I want with eyes?"

"You'd see."

"Who needs to see?"

"The bride of the East."

"What for? Only the East can pass through this door and live."

But you are not the East. You are subject to every wind that blows. And as you turn to tell her, she is not there.

37

Sand

by W. S. Merwin

An ant was born in an hourglass. Before it hatched out there was nothing to notice—and who would have looked, who would have suspected that one instant in each measure of time was an egg? And after the ant had emerged, it was too late to ask whether the birth was a mistake, or any of its circumstances. Anyway, there was no one to ask, except those nameless hosts, his brothers, at once much older and much younger than he was, who nudged and ground past him, rustling toward the neck of the glass, and fell, and lay blind, deaf, and dreamless in the mountain made of each other, and would never hatch, though the mountain itself turned over again and again and sent them smoking down from its tip like souls into time. Besides, it never occurred to him that there was a question to ask. He did not know that things ever had been or ever could be any different, and whatever capacity for speech he may have been born with slept on inside him like a grain of sand.

There was nothing to eat. But he had never been told about hunger, and ants, particularly those of his species, can subsist for long periods, sometimes for generations, without consuming other life of any kind. The same was true of thirst, dry though that place surely was, made of nothing but those rocks his family. Whatever discomfort he may have become aware of, arising either from hunger or thirst, seemed to him to be like something that we would no doubt call a memory, returning inexplicably to trouble him in a new life, and certain to fade. It stirred in him like some ghost from his days as a grain of sand, but he could not remember what use it had been to him then. And he would hold it to him and save it for a while, as though there were a danger of losing it. He would hold it, trying to understand it, not knowing that

it was pain. Something of the kind was true also of
breathing. No doubt he thought he was breathing. But
then he knew nothing of breath. What, after all, reached
him through the glass? The light. The darkness. Sounds.
Gravity. The desire to climb. What reached the grains of
sand? Light. Darkness. Vibrations. Gravity. No one knows
what else.

His brothers tried to crush him. He tried to count them.
He could see that they were not infinite. But he could
never start at the beginning. He would count them as they
edged past him faster and faster. He had no names for
numbers, but he tried to count the brothers even so as he
was borne along with them, as he climbed on their
shoulders, as he swam on their heads, falling with them.
He tried to count them as they fell on him and rolled after
him to the foot of the next mountain, to the glass. He
would start to the top again at once, trying to count them
as they slipped under his feet. He would climb, counting,
till the mountain turned over, and then he would begin
again. Each time the mountain flowed out from under him
he delayed the falling for an instant, and a measure of
time paused while he clung to the neck of the glass, climbing on sand. Then everything went on just the same.

No one hand told him about time. He did not know why
he was trying to count. He did not know what a number,
a final sum, would tell him, what use it would be to him,
what he would call it, where he would put it. He did not
know that they were not his real brothers. He thought he
was a grain of sand.

He did not know that he was alone.

38

A Fable of the Buyers

by W. S. *Merwin*

A man walked down the street with three dreams for sale. Of course he would not tell anyone what they were. He even said that he couldn't, because the dreams wouldn't be the same for them. He couldn't tell them anything about the dreams at all. They were there like straws to be drawn. Everyone hopes for better dreams than his own, and people bought them. The dreams were to be opened in private, the buyers were told. They were printed on exactly the same paper, which was made to dissolve as it was read, or to dissolve anyway if someone tried to keep it without reading it, like a talisman, so that it might produce its dream that way, as everything can do if the right spirit approaches it. A little later they would return to sight in the man's hand.

People who bought the dreams sometimes met each other later and tired to compare which dreams they had bought. Very suspiciously, at first. Very cautiously, with hints back and forth. Everyone found out after a while that the other person seemed to have bought a different dream. But then it turned out finally that there were too many of them in the same room for them all to have had different dreams, and they started arguing with each other. For they had all seen that there were only three dreams in the man's hand.

But with each person each dream clearly had been different. And still the buyers wanted to know which of the three dreams they had had. They tried everything. They classified by means of every triad they could think of. They divided each other into three factions, which never seemed accurate enough. They kept changing sides, and never forgiving each other. Eventually, in order to check, two of them tried to read the same dream at the same time, and it disappeared at once, entirely, and never reappeared in the man's hand. That happened again and the man was left with only one.

"Now won't the others come back at all?" he was asked.

"No," he said. "But it doesn't matter. They were all copies of the same dream."

"Will you sell us that one?" they asked.

"No," he said. "I'm going to give it back."

"Which one it it?" they asked, almost in unison.

For none of them had learned anything at all. What can you learn from a bought dream?

39

The Mountain of Signs

by Antonin Artaud

The land of the Tarahumara is full of signs, shapes, and natural effigies which do not seem to be mere products of accident, as if the gods, whose presence here is everywhere felt, had wished to signify their powers through these strange signatures in which the human form is hunted down from every side.

Indeed, there is no lack of places on earth where Nature, impelled by a kind of intelligent caprice, has carved human shapes. But here it is a different matter: for here it is on the entire *geographic area of a race* that Nature *has intentionally spoken.*

And the strange fact is that those who pass this way, as if stricken with an unconscious paralysis, seal their senses so as to know nothing of this. That Nature, by a strange caprice, should quite suddenly reveal a man's body being tortured on a rockface, one might at first suppose to be a mere caprice, a caprice signifying nothing. But when, day in and day out on horseback, this intelligent spell is cast repeatedly, and *Nature stubbornly manifests the same idea;* when the same pathetic shapes recur; when the heads of well-known gods appear on the rockfaces and a theme of death emerges of which man bears the burden—and in response to the drawn and quartered form of the human, there are, *becoming less obscure* and more freed from a petrifying substance, those forms of the gods who have forever tormented him,—when a whole country develops on stone a philosophy parallel to that of men; when one realizes that the original men used a sign language and that one rediscovers this language enormously magnified on the rocks, then indeed, one can no longer suppose this to be a caprice, a mere caprice signifying nothing.

If the major part of the Tarahumara race is indigenous,

and if, as they claim, they fell out of the sky in the Sierra, one could say that they fell into a Nature already prepared. And this Nature wanted to think as man thinks. And as she *evolved* from men, likewise she also *evolved* from rocks.

I saw this naked man they were torturing, nailed to a rock, with certain forms at work over him even as the sun was evaporating them; but I don't know by what miracle of optics the man beneath them remained complete, though exposed to the same light.

Whether it was the mountain or myself which was haunted, I cannot say, but I saw similar optical miracles during this periplus across the mountain, and they confronted me at least once every day.

Maybe I was born with a body as tortured and counterfeited as that of the immense mountain; but it was a body whose obsessions might be useful: and it occurred to me in the mountain that it might be just useful to have an *obsession for counting.* There wasn't a shadow but I had it counted, when I sensed it turning, hovering around something or other; and it frequently happened that in adding up these shadows I made my way back to some strange hearths.

I saw in the mountain a naked man leaning out of a huge window. His head was nothing but an enormous hole, a sort of circular cavity, where successively and according to the hour, the sun or moon appeared. He had his right arm outstretched like a bar, and the left was also like a bar but drowned in shadows and folded inward.

His ribs could be counted, there were seven on either side. In place of his navel, there gleamed a brilliant triangle, made of what? I could not really tell. It was as if Nature had chosen this mountainside to lay bare her imprisoned flints.

Now, though his head was empty, the indentations of the rock on every side imposed on him a definite expression, the nuances of which changed with the changes of hour and light.

This forward stretching right arm, edged with a ray of light, did not indeed point in any commonplace direction . . . And I questioned what it portended!

It was not quite noon when I encountered this vision; I was on horseback and rapidly advancing. However, I was instantly aware that I was not dealing with graven images, but with a predetermined play of light which had *superimposed itself* upon the stone relief.

This likeness was known to the Indians; to me, it appeared by its composition, its structure, to be governed by the same principle by which this fragmented mountain was governed. In the line that arm made, I saw a rock-girt village.

And I saw that the stones all had the shape of a woman's bosom with two breasts perfectly delineated.

Eight times I saw the repetition of a single rock, which cast two shadows on the ground; I twice saw the same animal head holding its own likeness in its jaws and devouring it; I saw, dominating the village, a sort of huge phallic tooth with three stones at its summit and four holes on its outer face; and I saw, according to their principle, all these forms pass little by little into reality.

I seemed to read everywhere a tale of childbirth amid war, a tale of genesis and chaos, with all these bodies of gods which were carved like men, and these truncated human statues. Not one shape that was intact, not one body that did not appear as if it came out of a recent massacre, not one group where I could avoid reading the struggle that divided it.

I found drowned men, half-nibbled away by the stones, and on the rocks higher up, other men engaged in driving them off. Elsewhere, a statue of Death loomed huge, holding in its hand a little child.

There is in the Kabbala a music of Numbers, and this music which reduces material chaos to its prime elements explains by a kind of grandiose mathematics how Nature orders and directs the birth of forms she brings forth out of chaos. And all I beheld seemed to be governed by a Number. The statues, the shapes, the shadows all yielded a number,—such as 3, 4, 7, or 8,—which kept recurring. The truncated female torsos were 8 in number; the phallic tooth had, as I have said, three stones and four holes; the evaporated forms were 12 in number, et cetera. I repeat, these forms may be assumed natural, granted, but their repetition is far from natural. And what is even less natural is that these forms of their land are repeated by the Tarahumara in their rituals and dance. And these dances result from no mere accident, but they are governed by the same

secret mathematics, the same concern for a subtle play of
Numbers which governs the entire Sierra.

Now this inhabited Sierra, which breathes a metaphysical
system into its rocks, has been strewn by the Tarahumara
with signs, signs which are perfectly conscious, intelligent,
and concerted.

At every crossroads one sees trees *deliberately* burnt
into the shape of crosses, or of beings, and often these
beings are doubles, and confront each other, as if to express the essential *duality* of things; and I saw this duality
reduced to its prime elements in a sign . . . enclosed in a
ring, which struck me as having been branded on a tall
pine tree with a red-hot iron; other trees bore spears, trefoils, acanthus leaves surrounded with crosses; here and
there, in sunken places, corridors choked with rocks, rows
of Egyption ankhs deployed in files; and the doors of
Tarahumara houses displayed the Maya world-symbol: two
facing triangles whose points are joined by a bar; and this
bar is the Tree of Life passing through the center of
Reality.

Thus, as I was making my way across the mountain,
these spears, these crosses, these trefoils, these leafy hearts,
these composite crosses, these triangles, these beings which
confront and oppose each other to signify their eternal
war, their division, their duality, awakened in me strange
memories. I recall suddenly that there were in History
certain Sects which had incrusted the rockfaces with
identical signs, and the members of these Sects wore these
signs carved in jade, hammered in iron, or chased. And it
occurs to me that this symbolism hides a Science. And it
seems strange to me that the primitive Tarahumara people,
whose rituals and thought are older than the Flood, could
have already possessed this Science long before the first
Legend of the Grail appeared, long before the Rose-
crucian Sect was founded.

Translated from the French
by David Rattray

40

Cities and Signs
by Italo Calvino

You walk for days among trees and among stones. Rarely does the eye light on a thing, and then only when it has recognized that thing as the sign of another thing: a print in the sand indicates the tiger's passage; a marsh announces a vein of water; the hibiscus flower, the end of winter. All the rest is silent and interchangeable; trees and stones are only what they are.

Finally the journey leads to the city of Tamara. You penetrate it along streets thick with signboards jutting from the walls. The eye does not see things but images of things that mean other things: pincers point out the tooth-drawer's house; a tankard, the tavern; halberds, the barracks; scales, the grocer's. Statues and shields depict lions, dolphins, towers, stars: a sign that something—who knows what?—has as its sign a lion or a dolphin or a tower or a star. Other signals warn of what is forbidden in a given place (to enter the alley with wagons, to urinate behind the kiosk, to fish with your pole from the bridge) and what is allowed (watering zebras, playing bowls, burning relatives' corpses). From the doors of the temples the gods' statutes are seen, each portrayed with his attributes— the cornucopia, the hourglass, the medusa—so that the worshiper can recognize them and address his prayers correctly. If a building has no signboard or figure, its very form and the position it occupies in the city's order suffice to indicate its function: the palace, the prison, the mint, the Pythagorean school, the brothel. The wares, too, which the vendors display on their stalls are valuable not in themselves but as signs of other things: the embroidered headband stands for elegance; the gilded planquin, power; the volumes of Averroes, learning; the ankle bracelet, voluptuousness. Your gaze scans the streets as if they were

written pages: the city says everything you must think,
makes you repeat her discourse, and while you believe
you are visiting Tamara you are only recording the names
with which she defines herself and all her parts.

However the city may really be, beneath this thick
coating of signs, whatever it may contain or conceal, you
leave Tamara without having discovered it. Outside, the
land stretches, empty, to the horizon; the sky opens, with
speeding clouds. In the shape that chance and wind give
the clouds, you are already intent on recognizing figures:
a sailing ship, a hand, an elephant. . . .

Translated from the Italian
by William Weaver

41

Cities and the Dead
by Italo Calvino

Never in all my travels had I ventured as far as Adelma. It was dusk when I landed there. On the dock the sailor who caught the rope and tied it to the bollard resembled a man who had soldiered with me and was dead. It was the hour of the wholesale fish market. An old man was loading a basket of sea urchins on a cart; I thought I recognized him; when I turned, he had disappeared down an alley, but I realized that he looked like a fisherman who, already old when I was a child, could no longer be among the living. I was upset by the sight of a fever victim huddled on the ground, a blanket over his head: my father a few days before his death had yellow eyes and a growth of beard like this man. I turned my gaze aside; I no longer dared look anyone in the face.

I thought: "If Adelma is a city I am seeing in a dream, where you encounter only the dead, the dream frightens me. If Adelma is a real city, inhabited by living people, I need only continue looking at them and the resemblances will dissolve, alien faces will appear, bearing anguish. In either case it is best for me not to insist on staring at them."

A vegetable vendor was weighing a cabbage on a scales and put it in a basket dangling on a string a girl lowered from a balcony. The girl was identical with one in my village who had gone mad for love and killed herself. The vegetable vendor raised her face: she was my grandmother.

I thought: "You reach a moment in life when, among the people you have known, the dead outnumber the living. And the mind refuses to accept more faces, more expressions: on every new face you encounter, it prints the old forms, for each one it finds the most suitable mask."

The stevedores climbed the steps in a line, bent beneath demijohns and barrels; their faces were hidden by sackcloth hoods; "Now they will straighten up and I will recognize them," I thought, with impatience and fear. But I could not take my eyes off them; if I turned my gaze just a little toward the crowd that crammed those narrow streets, I was assailed by unexpected faces, reappearing from far away, staring at me as if demanding recognition, as if to recognize me, as if they had already recognized me. Perhaps, for each of them, I also resembled someone who was dead. I had barely arrived at Adelma and I was already one of them, I had gone over to their side, absorbed in that kaleidscope of eyes, wrinkles, grimaces.

I thought: "Perhaps Adelma is the city where you arrive dying and where each finds again the people he has known. This means I, too, am dead." And I also thought: "This means the beyond is not happy."

Translated from the Italian
by William Weaver

42

Cities and the Sky
by *Italo Calvino*

In Eudoxia, which spreads both upward and down, with winding alleys, steps, dead ends, hovels, a carpet is preserved in which you can observe the city's true form. At first sight nothing seems to resemble Eudoxia less than the design of that carpet, laid out in symmetrical motives whose patterns are repeated along straight and circular lines, interwoven with brilliantly colored spires, in a repetition that can be followed throughout the whole woof. But if you pause and examine it carefully, you become convinced that each place in the carpet corresponds to a place in the city and all the things contained in the city are included in the design, arranged according to their true relationship, which escapes your eye distracted by the bustle, the throngs, the shoving. All of Eudoxia's confusion, the mules' braying, the lampblack stains, the fish smell is what is evident in the incomplete perspective you grasp; but the carpet proves that there is a point from which the city shows its true proportions, the geometrical scheme implicit in its every, tiniest detail.

It is easy to get lost in Eudoxia: but when you concentrate and stare at the carpet, you recognize the street you were seeking in a crimson or indigo or magenta thread which, in a wide loop, brings you to the purple enclosure that is your real destination. Every inhabitant of Eudoxia compares the carpet's immobile order with his own image of the city, and anguish of his own, and each can find, concealed among the arabesques, an answer, the story of his life, the twists of fate.

An oracle was questioned about the mysterious bond between two objects so dissimilar as the carpet and the city. One of the two objects—the oracle replied—has the form the gods gave the starry sky and the orbits in which the worlds revolve; the other is an approximate reflection, like every human creation.

For some time the augurs had been sure that the carpet's harmonious pattern was of divine origin. The oracle was interpreted in this sense, arousing no controversy. But you could, similarly, come to the opposite conclusion: that the true map of the universe is the city of Eudoxia, just as it is, a stain that spreads out shapelessly, with crooked streets, houses that crumble one upon the other amid clouds of dust, fires, screams in the darkness.

Translated from the Italian
by William Weaver

The Map of Lost Objects
by Juan José Arreola

The man who sold me the map was not the least bit odd. Just an ordinary-type fellow, perhaps a little sick. He simply accosted me like those vendors you meet on the street. He asked very little money for his map; he wanted to get rid of it at any cost. When he offered to give me a demonstration I accepted out of curiosity, because it was Sunday and I didn't have anything else to do. We went to a nearby spot to look for the sad object that perhaps he himself had thrown there, sure that nobody would pick it up: a rose-colored, celluloid comb, studded with lots of little stones. I still keep it among a dozen such trinkets, and I am especially fond of it because it was the first link in the chain. I regret that I have not kept along with it the other things I sold and the coins I spent. Since that time I have been living off of whatever I find through the map. Quite a wretched life, true, but it has freed me forever from all worry. Fortunately, now and then a lost woman, who mysteriously adjusts herself to my modest means, appears on the map.

Translated from the Spanish
by George D. Schall

Mirror and Scarf

by Edmond Jabès

*"We will gather images and images of
images until the last—which is blank.
This one we will agree on."*
Reb Carasso.

Mardohai Simhon claimed the silk scarf he wore around
his neck was a mirror.

"Look," he said, "my head is separated from my body
by a scarf. Who dares give me the lie if I say I walk with
a knotted mirror under my chin?

"The scarf reflects a face, and you think it is made of
flesh.

"Night is the mirror. Day the scarf. Moon and sun reflected features. But my true face, brothers, where was it
lost?"

At his death, a large scar was discovered on his neck.

The meaning of this anecdote was discussed by the
rabbis.

Reb Alphandery, in his authority as dean, spoke first.

"A double mirror," he said, "separates us from the Lord,
so that God sees Himself when trying to see us, and we,
when trying to see Him, see only our own face."

"Is appearance no more than the reflections thrown
back and forth by a set of mirrors?" asked Reb Ephraim.
"You are no doubt alluding to the soul, Reb Alphandery,
in which we see ourselves mirrored. But the body is the
place of the soul, just as the mountain is the bed of the
brook. The body has broken the mirror."

"The brook," continued Reb Alphandery, "sleeps on the
summit. The brook's dream is of water, as is the brook. It
flows for us. Our dreams extend us.

"Do you not remember this phrase of Reb Alsem's:

'We live out the dream of creation, which is God's dream. Evenings, our own dreams snuggle down into it like sparrows in their nests?' "

"And did not Reb Hames write: 'Birds of night, my dreams explore the immense dream of the sleeping universe?' "

"Are dreams the limpid discourse between the facets of a crystal block?" continued Reb Ephraim. "The world is of glass. You know it by its brilliance, night or day."

"The earth turns in a mirror. The earth turns in a scarf," replied Reb Alphandery.

"The scarf of a dandy with a nasty scar," said Reb Ephraim.

> (*"Words are inside breath, as the earth is inside time."*
> Reb Mares.)

And Yukel said:

"The bundle of the Wandering Jew contains the earth and more than one star."

"Whatever contains is itself contained," said Reb Mawas.
The story I told you, as well as the commentaries it inspired, will be recorded in the book of the eye. The ladder urges us beyond ourselves. Hence its importance. But in a void, where do we place it?

> (*God is sculpted.*"
> Reb Moyal.)

Translated from the French
by Rosmarie Waldrop

The Behavior of Mirrors on Easter Island

by Julio Cortazár

When you set up a mirror on the western side of Easter Island, it runs backwards. When you set one up on the eastern side of the island, it runs forward. Delicate surveys may discover the point at which that mirror will run on time, but finding the point at which that mirror works correctly is no guarantee that that point will serve for any other, since mirrors are subject to the defects of the individual substances of which they are made and react the way they really and truly want to. So that Solomon Lemos, an anthropologist on fellowship from the Guggenheim Foundation, looking into the mirror to shave, saw himself dead of typhus—this was on the eastern side of the island. And at the same time a tiny mirror which he'd forgotten on the western side of Easter Island (it'd been dropped between some stones) reflected for no one Solomon Lemos in short pants on his way to school, then Solomon Lemos naked in a bathtub being enthusiastically soaped by his mummy and daddy, then Solomon Lemos goin da-da-da, to the thrilled delight of his Aunt Remeditos on a cattle ranch in Trenque Lanquen county.

Translated from the Spanish
by Paul Blackburn

Continuity of Parks

by *Julio Cortazár*

He had begun to read the novel a few days before. He
had put it down because of some urgent business con-
ferences, opened it again on his way back to the estate by
train; he permitted himself a slowly growing interest in the
plot, in the characterizations. That afternoon, after writing
a letter giving his power of attorney and discussing a matter of joint ownership with the manager of his estate, he
returned to the book in the tranquillity of his study which
looked out upon the park with its oaks. Sprawled in his
favorite armchair, its back toward the door—even the
possibility of an intrusion would have irritated him, had he
thought of it—he let his left hand caress repeatedly the
green velvet upholstery and set to reading the final chap-
ters. He remembered effortlessly the names and his mental
image of the characters; the novel spread its glamour over
him almost at once. He tasted the almost perverse pleasure
of disengaging himself line by line from the things around
him, and at the same time feeling his head rest comfortably
on the green velvet of the chair with its high back, sensing
that the cigarettes rested within reach of his hand, that
beyond the great windows the air of afternoon danced
under the oak trees in the park. Word by word, licked up
by the sordid dilemma of the hero and heroine, letting himself be absorbed to the point where the images settled
down and took on color and movement, he was witness to
the final encounter in the mountain cabin. The woman arrived first, apprehensive; now the lover came in, his face
cut by the backlash of a branch. Admirably, she stanched
the blood with her kisses, but he rebuffed her caresses, he
had not come to perform again the ceremonies of a secret
passion, protected by a world of dry leaves and furtive
paths through the forest. The dagger warmed itself against

his chest, and underneath liberty pounded, hidden close. A lustful, panting dialogue raced down the pages like a rivulet of snakes, and one felt it had all been decided from eternity. Even to those caresses which writhed about the lover's body, as though wishing to keep him there, to dissuade him from it; they sketched abominably the frame of that other body it was necessary to destroy. Nothing had been forgotten: alibis, unforeseen hazards, possible mistakes. From this hour on, each instant had its use minutely assigned. The cold-blooded, twice-gone-over re-examination of the details was barely broken off so that a hand could caress a cheek. It was beginning to get dark.

Not looking at one another now, rigidly fixed upon the task which awaited them, they separated at the cabin door. She was to follow the trail that led north. On the path leading in the opposite direction, he turned for a moment to watch her running, her hair loosened and flying. He ran in turn, crouching among the trees and hedges until, in the yellowish fog of dusk, he could distinguish the avenue of trees which led up to the house. The dogs were not supposed to bark, they did not bark. The estate manager would not be there at this hour, and he was not there. He went up the three porch steps and entered. The woman's words reached him over the thudding of blood in his ears: first a blue chamber, then a hall, then a carpeted stairway. At the top, two doors. No one in the first room, no one in the second. The door of the salon, and then, the knife in hand, the light from the great windows, the high back of an armchair covered in green velvet, the head of the man in the chair reading a novel.

Translated from the Spanish
by Paul Blackburn

47

Inventions
by Christoph Meckel

Now I don't want you to believe that the act of inventing, as I pursue it, is any old arbitrary science. It isn't anymore than whaling or farming is. My inventions aren't based on any of the customary gimmicks and make no use of the credulity or lack of imagination of the people. Nor are they often linked with any specific purpose such as to insult or to disarm. I don't approach anyone with my inventions, I therefore don't disarm them. Whoever is envious of me will most probably be insulted, but to this I hasten to add: the ability to invent is not an enviable one.

If I believed that it would be a good thing to let an orchestra pass through a resort at this particular time and under these particular circumstances—what could stop me from making it happen? Of course I would need incontestable reasons; say the death of an alderman or the drowning of a strange lady who smelled of money or much property—that would be enough to induce me. Immediately the first drummers appear.

Of course there are people who can invent and conjure up quite thoughtlessly. Those are virtuosos; people who can depend on a large repertoire of ideas. They are usually amazingly productive, they stack mountains upon mountains to an altitude four times their original height, change coal freighters into submarines, and, in time of danger, submarines into coal freighters. For the entertainment of their guests they can drag islands up out of bays, lakes and ponds, and they manage it all perfectly cheerfully as a joke, or even out of boredom.

As for me, I never do anything out of boredom. If I were bored I could search for a companion as long as I liked; he would not appear. Not even his card.

There is the thing about rabbits. I could bring out a rab-

bit, a respectable, almost exemplary rabbit for which I
know all the specifications. But what do I care about
rabbits. I, for one, would rather create elephants.

I could also manage a donkey, but where would I put
him? He'd be condemned to a life of uselessness, would
degenerate to leading a dissolute life, probably starve or
die of a thrashing, and I would have to travel to the South
to account for him—for that reason alone I'd rather suppress him.

Translated from the German
by Andreas Schroeder

48

Shipbuilding
by Christoph Meckel

I have my own original and infallible method for inventing ships: I have my ship appear from a little spring as a small bark canoe. Then, depending on the size and current of the various creeks, I carefully let it grow, very slowly, so that nothing unforeseen will happen and force me to back-track.

Once in the creeks I allow it to float along at a leisurely pace, enjoying its adventures with the trout and the bow-nets. I must consider the fact that my ship will pass through duck ponds and village streams where the women wash their clothes; therefore I keep its scale small. I let it float along without funnel or masts, without sail or wheel, concealing the fact that these things will soon belong to it, since it could conceivably become a little impatient. At this point, however, it is already as large as a rowboat.

When it has reached those rivers which influence the provincial geography in some decisive way, I allow the first funnels and antenna-like masts to appear. But I must keep within certain limits, not overlooking the fact that viaducts and suspension bridges are considerable hindrances. By this time my ship has grown to the size of a barge.

In the large rivers which indicate their importance by rapids and frequent ice-floes, I am no longer niggardly over its dimensions and fit it out with sail and funnels; I permit a larger number of cabins, expand the holds and increase the number of ship's officers.

By the time it reaches those deltas and estuaries which begin to prefigure the ocean's endlessness, my ship is complete from figurehead to flagmast, and as the ocean receives it, it lacks only a name.

At this point I leave my ship. While the figurehead murmurs my name so as not to forget, the crew hardly remembers me. And suddenly I am seized by a furious anguish and rather than to see my ship fade into the distance I travel back to the mountains, plug the spring (if it hasn't already dried up) and take up position in front of another, lying in wait day and night for the next small canoe to come floating up.

But as for my finest ships, I've never allowed them to enter reality. They rest inside the mountains and dream of light, of the blustering charm of rivers and seas, of huge mast ornaments and white sail dresses, Not until some earthquake splits the mountains and a volcano makes the effort to burst the rock will anyone discover my secret compartment: countless tiny ships surrounded by pompous shadow-plated rock, waiting in the darkness to attain visibility.

Translated from the German
by Andreas Schroeder

The Mapmakers of the Dead
by *Christoph Meckel*

The mapmakers of the realm of the dead—they want finally to be certain of something—differ surprisingly in their opinions. There are some who make out that the frontier is a mountain range, others that it an ocean, and others who think that the realm is round. They simply cannot agree. So they disperse, rush away in swarms, scatter far and wide into the desert, and go off in search. They make swimming motions, in order to ascertain, perhaps, that there is water, perhaps in order to be raised up and carried along by a wave; they frantically hope that they will stumble and fall, for this would mean that stones were there, which might indicate the existence of a mountain. But eventually they move forward in their usual way, completely content in their conviction that the frontiers must be sought farther off.

Those who believe that the realm is round stay behind in an enviable state of inertia. Sometimes a group of mountain-seekers will cross their horizon; their hurry tells that they still have not found the hoped-for frontiers. Or the ocean-seekers appear, quivering with zeal, traversing the void in an insistent hurry. A thousand questions. The immense inquisitiveness of the inert. And, disavowing any weakness, busily waving, the others reply: We have found traces, indications, hints! Just a little more patience!

*Translated from the German
by Christopher Middleton*

One's Ship
by Barton Midwood

I am up to my calves in the sea, the very beginnings of the sea which stretches before me out to the edge of the sky. My ship, my tiny ship moored in the shallows, rocks back and forth anxiously, like a schoolboy. The waves lap at its side, the cool waters, Ah, let us go, let us set forth, my ship!

But I am detained. All the women have gathered on the beachhead. We must deal with them, my ship and I. All want to make passage with us. They are shrieking, moaning, imploring. Each woman presents a plaintive convincing case. Each, it is clear from their arguments, deserves beyond the shadow of a doubt to accompany me. They love me, they cry. Of course! I am irresistible. My rudder is golden, my sails ample, I have shapely legs. On the beach, with the wind blowing in my thin hair, I make an appealing picture. I am the captain of a noble craft, of everything in fact in sight. I am the only man for miles around. I am needed, that's clear. But how should I take them all, these lovely creatures? There is room for but one companion and frankly I am loath to take anyone beside myself. I am selfish, utterly. The wind blows in my hair. I turn to them and raise my arms for silence. I shall speak. A hush falls. All eyes grow round and soft and fix me tenderly. The tears flow. It is touching. The back of my shirt bellies like a sail.

"Ladies," I say, "I should like to speak to you individually. Form a line!"

They fight for first place. They pull one another's hair. They make an undignified spectacle. At last, however, they are in single file, a long line that runs back from the shore, across the beach, out to the road, and . . . to the ends of the earth for all I know. Nevertheless, I shall give them audience, each one. I must be fair!

I bid the first come forward.

"Yvonne!" I cry. "Come here, my dear. I love you passionately. Let me touch you."

I caress her thighs, she throws her arms around my neck, and we kiss so unconscionably long and hard that we fall to the ground and roll in the sand. We have no regard. One forgets oneself. There is nothing to be done.

"Have no fear," I whisper as we stand up and brush the sand from our mouths. "You are the one. I shall take you with me."

She kisses me lightly on the forehead, holding my face in her hands and standing just on her toes. Then she retires to a shady spot beneath a palm and waits, contentedly. From her purse she takes an orange and sucks it. She stares at me over it from under lowered loving brows.

"Next!"

Elsa steps forward. She runs at me, leaps into the air, locking her legs around my waist, wraps her arms around my neck, those slender tan arms with the light down, and kisses me precisely on the lips.

"You are the one," I whisper. "Have no fear."

She too retires to a palm and sucks an orange. They have all brought oranges. It must be the season.

Shy and blushing comes Natalie. She looks at the ground. She falls in a faint at my feet. I lift her in my arms and lave her forehead with handfuls of the sea. She comes to.

"Be happy," she says in a swoon. "I am so embarrassed. All these people . . . oh, oh, forgive us. I love you so. You are not in debt to me. I shall always love you. You must take who you please."

And then she falls to crying, her lips wet with her tears on my neck.

"Natalie," I say, "you are not like the others. I shall take you with me. Have no fear."

Ecstatically she too retires to a palm. She eats an apple however. She is different.

So it goes. Three, four, five days pass in this way— talking, embracing, promising, eating apples and oranges. I have spoken to one and a half billion women—yes! I have counted assiduously. I have promised each one that I shall take her with me. It is difficult to say no. How does one say no when one is intoxicated with saying yes? Saying

yes is my whiskey. It burns so pleasantly. And after the
first few, the rest go down so easily! Yes, yes, yes! It is
only no that tastes bitter in my mouth. And what do I
care for bitterness? What do I care for . . .

I know. You will say, "He is a fool. He does not know
how to handle his affairs. He does not appreciate fully the
efficacy of saying no. He is a sensualist and cares for
nothing but the moment. He has not a practical vision. He
will cause nothing but anguish in this world with his infer-
nal yes."

And so be it! Say it! I know all that! And I care not!

They sit there now, my pretty little one and a half
billion; I face them with my hands on my hips. What now?
I could make a dash for the ship but they would be on me,
crawling over the deck, before I could hoist the mainsail.
They would destroy the ship in a moment. I know something about crowds.

I turn my back to them. Bobbing up and down in the
sea are the lovely mermaids with the long flowing hair—
light green hair, with streaks of blonde that shimmer in
the sun. Breasts high and firm, bellies silky, these creatures
are not half fish as the mythologies say. Under the surface
of the waters, from the waist down, they are womanly,
with sleek strong legs. The poets have cunningly perpe-
trated that half fish business on the public in order to discourage exploitation.

"Ladies," I announce, suddenly, whirling around. "I
must test the ship. I must take a brief spin about the
harbor. I shall return shortly. And then the chosen one
will join me . . ."

This pronouncement seems to disconcert them. There is
a sullen suspicious murmur of disapproval. I walk very
cautiously to the ship. I make no sudden movement that
might alarm them. I walk slowly, slowly, cautiously, as a
man who walks past a mad dog. I attempt to make myself
invisible. I hold my breath.

The mainsail is up. I push off, I glide . . . glide upon
the waters. I am safe, free! I glide, glide! I laugh! I wave
my handkerchief in farewell! I am safe! Out of touch! The
mermaids beckon me with their arms, their heads tilted
slightly upward. They burst into a chorus of song—an
ethereal song, fathomless and sea-struck. I cannot whistle
that tune, but I hear it in my dreams—every note I know.

I have heard it, every note, before. Why then can I not whistle it? I am not a bad whistler. In fact, I am rather musical. I know, like the palm of my hand, the music at the bottom of things.

There is a rustling sound below—footsteps coming up the ladder from the hold. A woman climbs on deck. She has a child cradled in her arms and a fierce expression in her eyes. Of course. One hopes beyond hope. There is no escape. One knew it all along. The mermaids make piteous lament! Their song is swallowed in the roar of the sea. There is a storm coming out of the west. There is always a storm coming out of the west; one accepts that. One never examines one's ship carefully enough. One escapes the beach, one escapes half the world, but never looks thoroughly enough into the nooks and crannies of one's own ship. One is a shithead. One hates oneself. One is not one. One is multitudinous.

"Well!" says one. "What the hell are you doing here on one's ship? And who's the brat? Never mind! Take the raft! Paddle yourselves back to shore! One is displeased! Do you hear? Displeased!"

Without a word she loosens the chains from the raft and kicks it into the sea.

"The raft!" I cry. "What have you done?"

She says nothing. Her eyes accuse me. One is made to feel guilty by those eyes. And then the brat sets to howling. A vicious discourteous little monster. And then the storm is coming out of the west . . . one has set off; one is on one's voyage.

I sit on the deck, hang my hands limply over the edge . . . the mermaids kiss my fingertips. I go on but I know not where I go. A return to the beach is out of the question. I entertain thoughts of pushing the stowaways overboard, but they are tenacious. And then, perhaps, yes, perhaps I need them for ballast. I comfort myself with these thoughts. I contrive reasons for needing them. That is how one's mind works. One has them, one cannot rid oneself easily of them—at least not without committing a heinous crime—so one contrives reasons for needing them. One always needs what one has. If ever one allows oneself to think one does not need what one has, then one is . . .

Sinking Contest
by *Pierre Bettencourt*

In La Mancha province, I possess seven and a half acres of quicksands on which I organize sinking contests. The prizes in the lottery, totalling about a million, are not to be sniffled at. From the first issue of tickets, competitors rushed to take part.

'The rules are very simple,' I tell them, 'the last to disappear wins.'

They stepped forward and were each in turn sucked up by the sands. Those who struggled sank more quickly than the others. Most of them, suddenly scared out of their wits and bitterly regretting their rash involvement in this venture, yelled for me to come and extricate them. One by one, their heads disappeared. A few arms still stuck out from the surface. Then nothing. Only a big, strapping fellow from Roussillon, just across the border, was more or less holding his own at shoulder level, a broad smile on his face: 'I think I've won,' he called out to me rather breathlessly.

From the cement strip on which I was standing I had only to throw him the rope. But I calculated rapidly that my million would come in very useful in subsidizing the invention of fresh enterprises, and that after all I was the only witness of the victory of this lad who had already sunk so deep that he could no longer turn his head to verify the fact that the surface around him was empty. From where I was standing I made violent signals to him as if to explain there was still another competitor left, right behind him.

I shall never forget the look of hatred he shot at me before disappearing.

Translated from the French
by Simon Watson Taylor

The Fragrance of Shellweed
by Kobo Abé

I wonder if you've heard about shellweed. It may be this grass with thorny leaves like twists of firecrackers that covers the whole rocky slope where I am now sitting.

When you smell the fragrance of shellweed they say you dream of being a fish.

The story should be taken with a grain of salt, I feel, but it's not implausible. As shellweed prefers swampy land containing considerable salt, naturally it grows readily at the seashore, and it is not particularly surprising that there should be a tradition of its odor producing dreams of fish. Furthermore, according to one explanation, the alkaloids in its pollen bring about a floating sensation that resembles dizziness; and since at the same time it irritates the respiratory membranes, it is also possible, apparently, to have the hallucination of drowning in water.

But if that were all, it would not be particularly surprising. What's worrisome about a shellweed dream is not so much the dream itself as the problem of awakening from it. With a real fish there's no way of knowing, but they say that the passage of time that the dream fish experiences is quite different from when it is awake. The speed is remarkably slower, and one has the feeling that a few terrestrial seconds are drawn out to several days or several weeks.

Nevertheless, thanks to the strangeness of the dream scenery, one at first takes the utmost delight in the lightness of one's body, subtracted as if from gravity, sporting among the undulating seaweed in the shadows of rocks, passing through strips of light limned by the lens of the waves, chasing after schools of trusting fish. As one is light oneself, one feels as if the world itself has become buoyant. One is completely liberated from bodily afflictions

171

caused by gravity—drooping belly, stiffness of shoulders and neck, pain in the knee joints, falling arches—and one frolics around as if one were at least ten years younger. The lightness intoxicates the dream fish like alcohol.

But unless the fish is real, every case of intoxication sobers up and ultimately palls. In the sluggish flow of time, boredom soon becomes unbearable. It should not be too hard to imagine the feeling of irritation the completely bored dream fish experiences, the lack of resistance as if its five senses were numbed. Soon the free lightness of substance gradually begins to pall. One's whole body is wrapped round and round, as if forced into a restrictive garment in the shape of a fish. The soles of the feet send out feelers, seeking the sense of resistance they are used to when walking on land. The joints begin to recall fondly the heaviness of the various tissues and musculature that govern them. There is an unreasonable desire to walk. And suddenly one is amazed to realize that one lacks the legs necessary to do so.

But legs aren't the only thing lacking. No ears, no neck, no shoulders, and more than anything else, no arms. An inexpressible sense of deficiency. Quite definitely because the arms have been torn off. No curiosity can ultimately be satisfied unless one can check by touching with one's hands. If one wants really to know another person, if one does not know him with one's fingers, push him, punch him, bend him, tear at him, one can scarcely claim to know him completely. One wants to touch, to pass one's hands all over him. The bag of scales is insufferable for the fish. It strains to tear it off, but all it can do is to open its gills wide, raise its dorsal fin rigid, and trail a cord several inches long of pepper-colored excrement.

Writhing in a pain that floods to the very tips of its toes, the sham fish suddenly arrives at the fatal suspicion that he is perhaps fake. The instant doubt begins, everythings becomes very strange. When one has the body of a fish, without any vocal cords to begin with, to say nothing of hands or feet, one is plagued in one's use of such words. Double perception is as irritating as an itch.

Perhaps all such happenings are dream sequences.

Nevertheless, the dream is too long. It has been going on for so long that one can no longer remember when it started. However protracted, one will supposedly awaken from it sometime.

To ascertain that one is dreaming, the first thing—and it's reliable, for I have tried it several times myself—is to give the back of the hand a good pinch. But unfortunately a fish doesn't have nails to pinch with, nor a hand to pinch the back of. If that doesn't work, you can jump heroically from a steep cliff. That too I remember having succeeded at any number of times. Certainly if a fish is capable of that, there's no particular inconvenience in not having arms or legs. But what kind of a fall would a sea fish have?

I have never, of course, heard of a fish falling. Even a dead fish floats to the surface. It's much more complicated than a balloon falling in air. As far as the descent is concerned, it's a reverse fall. A reverse fall . . .

Indeed, does such a way of waking from a dream exist? I suppose a fish may well drown in air by falling in reverse, upward, toward the sky. The danger of death is the same. It's the same as a fall on land, and one of necessity awakens from the dream.

Yet once having pushed his thinking this far, the fake fish, with a timidity unexpected in a cold-blooded animal, still hesitates. They say that when one is able to realize that one is dreaming one is already near the end of the dream. The fish has done all he can do to wake up, and although it is waiting a while longer to see just what will happen, it will not influence the outcome.

The fake fish decided to wait. His very determination touched with the pallidness of the sea seemed to have paled.

Days, weeks passed, and the time had come for the fake fish to reach his decision. A storm had broken. A great tropical storm bore down, causing the bottom of the sea to tremble. Great waves rose, making the timid and indecisive fake fish demonstrate what little courage he had. But he was in no hurry to die. He simply gave himself over to the movement of the waves.

Suddenly a wave crest like the blades of fifty electric saws marshaled horizontally bore down on him. Sweeping the fake fish before it, it broke momentously against the cliffs and tossed the fish high into the air. And the fake fish drowned in the atmosphere.

Now I wonder if he awoke from his dream. No, one

does not have a shellweed dream so casually. It is altogether different from an ordinary one. As the fake fish
died before awakening, he could not expect to awaken
from his dream again. He still had to go on dreaming until
after he died. Ultimately the dead fake fish apparently
would exist forever as a fake fish, as if it had received
the latest freezing treatment. They say that among those
fish tossed up onto the seashore after the storm there were
not a few unlucky ones who had fallen asleep suffocated
by the flowers of the shellweed.

Translated from the Japanese
by E. Dale Saunders

53

The Nose

by Nicolai V. Gogol

I

A most extraordinary thing happened in Petersburg on the twenty-fifth of March. The barber, Ivan Yakovlevich, who lives on the Voznessensky Avenue (his surname is lost, and even on his signboard, depicting a gentlemen with a lathered face and bearing the inscription: "Also lets blood," no surname appears)—the barber Ivan Yakovlevich woke up rather early and inhaled the smell of hot bread. Raising himself a little in bed, he saw that his wife, a highly respectable lady who was very fond of a cup of coffee, was taking out of the oven some freshly baked bread.

"I won't have coffee today, my dear," said Ivan Yakovlevich. "Instead I'd like some hot bread with onions."

(That is to say, Ivan Yakovlevich would have liked both, but he knew that it was absolutely impossible to ask for two things at once; for his wife disliked such absurd whims.)

"Let the fool eat bread," his wife thought to herself. "All the better for me: there'll be an extra cup of coffee left." And she flung a loaf on the table.

After putting on, for propriety's sake, his frock coat over his shirt, Ivan Yakovlevich sat down at the table, sprinkled some salt, peeled two onions, picked up a knife, and, assuming a solemn expression, began cutting the bread. Having cut it in two, he had a look into the middle of one of the halves and, to his astonishment, noticed some white object there. Ivan Yakovlevich prodded it carefully with the knife and felt it with a finger. "It's solid," he said to himself. "What on earth can it be?"

He dug his fingers into the bread and pulled out—a
nose! Ivan Yakovlevich's heart sank: he rubbed his eyes
and felt it again: a nose! There could be no doubt about
it: it was a nose! And a familiar nose, too, apparently.
Ivan Yakovlevich looked horrified. But his horror was
nothing compared to the indignation with which his wife
was overcome.

"Where have you cut off that nose, you monster?" she
screamed angrily. "Blackguard! Drunkard! I shall inform
the police against you myself. What a cutthroat! Three
gentlemen have told me already that when you are shaving them you pull so violently at their noses that it is a
wonder they still remain on their faces!"

But Ivan Yakovlevich was more dead than alive. He
recognised the nose as belonging to no other person than
the Collegiate Assessor Kovalyov, whom he shaved every
Wednesday and every Sunday.

"Wait, my dear, I'll wrap it in a rag and put it in a
corner: let it stay there for a bit and then I'll take it
out."

"I won't hear of it! What do you take me for? Keep a
cutoff nose in my room? You heartless villain, you! All
you know is to strop your razor. Soon you won't be fit
to carry out your duties at all, you whoremonger, you
scoundrel, you! You don't expect me to answer to the police for you, do you? Oh, you filthy wretch, you block-
head, you! Out with it! Out! Take it where you like, only
don't let me see it here again!"

Ivan Yakovlevich stood there looking utterly crushed.
He thought and thought and did not know what to think.

"Damned if I know how it happened," he said at last,
scratching behind his ear. "Did I come home drunk last
night? I'm sure I don't know. And yet the whole thing is
quite impossible—it can't be true however you look at it:
for bread is something you bake, and a nose is something
quite different. Can't make head or tail of it!"

Ivan Yakovlevich fell silent. The thought that the police
might find the nose at his place and charge him with having cut it off made him feel utterly dejected. He could already see the scarlet collar, beautifully embroidered with
silver, the sabre—and he trembled all over. At last he got
his trousers and boots, pulled on these sorry objects, and,

accompanied by his wife's execrations, wrapped the nose in a rag and went out into the street.

He wanted to shove it under something, either under the seat by the gates or drop it, as it were, by accident and then turn off into a side street. But as ill luck would have it, he kept coming across people he knew, who at once addressed him with the question: "Where are you off to?" or "Who are you going to shave so early in the morning?"—so that he could not find a right moment for getting rid of it. On one occasion he did succeed in dropping it, but a policeman shouted to him from the distance, pointing to it with his halberd: "Hey, you, pick it up! You've dropped something!" And Ivan Yakovlevich had to pick up the nose and put it in his pocket. He was overcome by despair, particularly as the number of people in the streets was continually increasing with the opening of the stores and the small shops.

He decided to go to the Issakiyevsky Bridge, for it occurred to him that he might be able to throw it into the Neva. But I'm afraid I am perhaps a little to blame for not having so far said something more about Ivan Yakovlevich, an estimable man in many respects.

Ivan Yakovlevich, like every other Russian working man, was a terrible drunkard. And though every day he shaved other people's chins, he never bothered to shave his own. Ivan Yakovlevich's frock coat (he never wore an ordinary coat) was piebald; that is to say, it was black, but covered all over with large brown, yellow, and grey spots; his collar was shiny; and instead of three buttons only bits of thread dangled from his coat. Ivan Yakovlevich was a great cynic, and every time the Collegiate Assessor Kovalyov said to him: "Your hands always stink, Ivan Yakovlevich," he would reply with the question: "Why should they stink, sir?" "I don't know why, my dear fellow," the Collegiate Assessor would say, "only they do stink." And after taking a pinch of snuff, Ivan Yakovlevich would lather him for that all over his cheeks, under the nose, behind his ears, and under his beard, in short, wherever he fancied.

This worthy citizen had in the meantime reached Issakiyevsky Bridge. First of all he looked round cautiously, then he leaned over the parapet, as though anxious to see whether there were a great many fishes swimming by, and

as he did so he stealthily threw the rag with the nose into
the river. He felt as though a heavy weight had been lifted
from his shoulders: Ivan Yakovlevich even grinned. Instead
of going to shave the chins of civil servants, he set off
towards an establishment which bore the inscription: "Tea
and Victuals," intending to ask for a glass of punch,
when he suddenly noticed at the end of the bridge a
police inspector of noble exterior, with large whiskers, with
a three-cornered hat, and with a sabre. He stood rooted
to the spot; meanwhile the police officer beckoned to him
and said: "Come here, my man!"

Knowing the rules, Ivan Yakovlevich took off his cap
some way off and, coming up promptly, said: "I hope
your honour is well."

"No, no, my good man, not 'your honour.' Tell me,
what were you doing there on the bridge?"

"Why, sir, I was going to shave one of my customers
and I just stopped to have a look how fast the current was
running."

"You're lying, sir, you're lying! You won't get off with
that. Answer my question, please!"

"I'm ready to shave you two or even three times a
week, sir, with no conditions attached," replied Ivan
Yakovlevich.

"No, my dear sir, that's nothing! I have three barbers
who shave me and they consider it a great honour, too.
You'd better tell me what you were doing there!"

Ivan Yakovlevich turned pale. . . . But here the incident is completely shrouded in a fog and absolutely nothing
is known of what happened next.

II

Collegiate Assessor Kovalyov woke up fairly early and
muttered, "Brrr . . ." with his lips, which he always did
when he woke up, though he could not say himself why
he did so. Kovalyov stretched and asked for the little looking glass standing on the table. He wanted to look at the
pimple which had appeared on his nose the previous evening, but to his great astonishment, instead of his nose, he
saw a completely empty, flat place! Frightened, Kovalyov
asked for some water and rubbed his eyes with a towel:
there was no nose! He began feeling with his hand and

pinched himself to see whether he was still asleep: no, he
did not appear to be asleep. The Collegiate Assessor
Kovalyov jumped out of bed and shook himself: he had
no nose! He immediately told his servant to help him dress
and rushed off straight to the Commissioner of Police.

Meanwhile we had better say something about Kovalyov
so that the reader may see what sort of a person this Collegiate Assessor was. Collegiate Assessors who receive that
title in consequence of their learned diplomas cannot be
compared with those Collegiate Assessors who obtain this
rank in the Caucasus. They are two quite different species.
Learned Collegiate Assessors . . . But Russia is such a
wonderful country that if you say something about one
Collegiate Assessor, all the Collegiate Assessors, from Riga
to Kamchatka, will most certainly think that you are refer-
ring to them. The same, of course, applies to all other
callings and ranks. Kovalyov was a Caucasian Collegiate
Assessor. He had obtained that rank only two years earlier
and that was why he could not forget it for a moment;
and to add to his own importance and dignity, he never
described himself as a Collegiate Assessor, that is to say,
a civil servant of the eighth rank, but always as a major,
that is to say, by the corresponding rank in the army.
"Look here, my good woman," he used to say when he
met a peasant woman selling shirt fronts in the street, "you
go to my house—I live on Sadovaya Street—and just ask:
Does Major Kovalyov live here? Anyone will show you."
But if he met some pretty little minx, he'd give her besides
a secret instruction, adding: "You just ask for Major
Kovalyov's apartment, darling." And that is why we, too,
will in future refer to this Collegiate Assessor as Major
Kovalyov.

Major Kovalyov was in the habit of taking a stroll on
Nevsky Avenue every day. The collar of his shirt front
was always extremely clean and well starched. His whiskers were such as one can still see nowadays on provincial
district surveyors, architects, and army doctors, as well as
on police officers performing various duties and, in general, on all gallant gentlemen who have full, ruddy cheeks
and are very good at a game of boston: these whiskers go
right across the middle of the cheek and straight up to
the nose. Major Kovalyov wore a great number of cor-
nelian seals, some with crests and others which had en-

graved on them: Wednesday, Thursday, Monday, and so
on. Major Kovalyov came to Petersburg on business, to
wit, to look for a post befitting his rank: if he were lucky,
the post of a vice-governor, if not, one of an administrative clerk in some important department. Major Kovalyov
was not averse to matrimony, either, but only if he could
find a girl with a fortune of two hundred thousand. The
reader can, therefore, judge for himself the state in which
the major was when he saw, instead of a fairly handsome
nose of moderate size, a most idiotic, flat, smooth place.

As misfortune would have it, there was not a single cab
to be seen in the street and he had to walk, wrapping himself in his cloak and covering his face with a handkerchief,
as though his nose were bleeding. "But perhaps I imagined
it all," he thought. "It's impossible that I could have lost
my nose without noticing it!" He went into a pastry cook's
for the sole purpose of having a look at himself in a mirror.
Fortunately, there was no one in the shop: the boys were
sweeping the rooms and arranging the chairs; some of
them, sleepy-eyed, were bringing in hot cream puffs on
trays; yesterday's papers, stained with coffee, were lying
about on tables and chairs. "Well, thank God, there's nobody here," he said. "Now I can have a look." He went
timidly up to the mirror and looked. "Damn it," he said,
disgusted, "the whole thing is too ridiculous for words! If
only there'd be something instead of a nose, but there's
just nothing!"

Biting his lips with vexation, Kovalyov went out of
the pastry cook's and made up his mind, contrary to his
usual practice, not to look or smile at anyone. Suddenly he
stopped dead in his tracks at the front doors of a house; a
most inexplicable thing happened before his very eyes: a
carriage drew up before the entrance, the carriage door
opened, and a gentleman in uniform jumped out and,
stooping, rushed up the steps. Imagine the horror and, at
the same time, amazement of Kovalyov when he recognised that this was his own nose! At this extraordinary sight
everything went swimming before his eyes. He felt that he
could hardly stand on his feet; but he made up his mind
that, come what may, he would wait for the gentleman's
return to the carriage. He was trembling all over as though
in a fever. Two minutes later the nose really did come out.
He wore a gold-embroidered uniform with a large stand-up

collar, chamois-leather breeches, and a sword at his side. From his plumed hat it could be inferred that he was a State Councillor, a civil servant of the fifth rank. Every-thing showed that he was going somewhere to pay a visit. He looked round to the right and to the left, shouted to his driver, who had driven off a short distance, to come back, got into the carriage, and drove off.

Poor Kovalyov nearly went out of his mind. He did not know what to think of such a strange occurrence. And, in-deed, how was it possible for a nose which had only the day before been on his face and which could neither walk nor drive—to be in a uniform! He ran after the carriage which, luckily, did not go far, stopping before the Kazan Cathedral.

He hastened into the cathedral, pushing his way through the crowd of beggarwomen with bandaged faces and only two slits for the eyes, at whom he used to laugh so much before, and went into the church. There were only a few worshippers inside the church; they were all standing near the entrance. Kovalyov felt so distraught that he was un-able to pray and he kept searching with his eyes for the gentleman in the State Councillor's uniform. At last he saw him standing apart from the other worshippers. The nose was hiding his face completely in his large stand-up collar and was saying his prayers with the expression of the ut-most piety.

"How am I to approach him?" thought Kovalyov. "It is clear from everything, from his uniform, from his hat, that he is a State Councillor. I'm damned if I know how to do it!"

He went up to him and began clearing his throat; but the nose did not change his devout attitude for a moment and carried on with his genuflections.

"Sir," said Kovalyov, inwardly forcing himself to take courage, "Sir——"

"What do you want?" answered the nose, turning round.

"I find it strange, sir, I—I believe you ought to know your proper place. And all of a sudden I find you in church of all places! You—you must admit that——"

"I'm sorry but I can't understand what you are talking about. . . . Explain yourself."

"How can I explain it to him?" thought Kovalyov and, plucking up courage, began: "Of course—er—you see—I

—I am a major and—and you must admit that it isn't
right for—er—a man of my rank to walk about without a
nose. I mean—er—a tradeswoman selling peeled oranges
on Voskressensky Bridge can sit there without a nose; but
for a man like me who expects to obtain the post of a
governor, which without a doubt he will obtain and—er—
besides, being received in many houses by ladies of good
position, such as Mrs. Chekhtaryov, the widow of a State
Councillor, sir, and many others—er——Judge for yourself, sir, I mean, I—I don't know"—Major Kovalyov
shrugged his shoulders—" I am sorry but if one were to
look upon it according to the rules of honour and duty—
er—you can understand yourself, sir——"

"I don't understand anything, sir," replied the nose.
"Please explain yourself more clearly."

"Sir," said Kovalyov with a consciousness of his own
dignity, "I don't know how to understand your words. It
seems to me the whole thing is perfectly obvious. Or do
you wish—I mean, you are my own nose, sir!"

The nose looked at the major and frowned slightly.

"You are mistaken, sir. I am *myself*. Besides, there can
be no question of any intimate relationship between us. I
see, sir, from the buttons of your uniform that you are
serving in a different department."

Having said this, the nose turned away and went on
praying.

Kovalyov was utterly confounded, not knowing what to
do or even what to think. At that moment he heard the
agreeable rustle of a lady's dress; an elderly lady, her dress
richly trimmed with lace, walked up to them, accompanied
by a slim girl in a white dress, which looked very charming
on her slender figure, and in a straw-coloured hat, as light
as a pastry puff. Behind them, opening a snuffbox, stood
a tall flunkey with enormous whiskers and quite a dozen
collars on his Cossack coat.

Kovalyov came nearer, pulled out the cambric collar of
his shirt front, straightened the seals hanging on his gold
watch chain and, turning his head this way and that and
smiling, turned his attention to the ethereal young lady
who, like a spring flower, bent forward a little, as she
prayed, and put her little white hand with its semi-trans-
parent fingers to her forehead to cross herself. The smile
on Kovalyov's face distended a little more when he caught

sight under her pretty hat of a chin of dazzling whiteness and part of her cheek, suffused with the colour of the first spring rose. But suddenly he sprang back as though he had burnt himself. He recollected that, instead of a nose, he had absolutely nothing on his face, and tears started to his eyes. He turned round, intending to tell the gentleman in uniform plainly that he was merely pretending to be a State Councillor, that he was a rogue and an imposter and nothing else than his own nose. . . . But the nose was no longer there: he had managed to gallop off, no doubt to pay another visit. . . .

That plunged Kovalyov into despair. He left the church and stopped for a moment under the colonnade, carefully looking in all directions to see whether he could catch sight of the nose anywhere. He remembered very well that he wore a hat with a plume and a gold-embroidered uniform; but he had not noticed his cloak, nor the colour of his carriage, nor his horses, nor even whether he had a footman behind him and, if so, in what livery. Besides, there were so many carriages careering backwards and forwards that it was difficult to distinguish one from another. But even if he had been able to distinguish any of them, there was no way of stopping it. It was a lovely, sunny day. There were hundreds of people on Nevsky Avenue. A whole flowery cascade of ladies was pouring all over the pavement from the Police Bridge to the Anichkin Bridge. There he saw coming a good acquaintance of his, a civil servant of the seventh rank, whom he always addressed as lieutenant colonel, especially in the presence of strangers. And there was Yaryzhkin, the head clerk in the Senate, a great friend of his, who always lost points when he went eight at boston. And here was another major, who had received the eighth rank of Collegiate Assessor in the Caucasus, waving to him to come up. . . .

"Oh, hell!" said Kovalyov. "Hey, cabby, take me straight to the Commissioner of Police!"

Kovalyov got into the cab and kept shouting to the driver: "Faster! Faster!"

"Is the Police Commissioner at home?" he asked, entering the hall.

"No, sir," replied the janitor. "He's just gone out."

"Well of all thing!"

"Yes sir," the janitor added, "he's not been gone so

long, but he's gone all right. If you'd come a minute
earlier, you'd probably have found him at home."

Without taking his handkerchief off his face, Kovalyov
got into the cab and shouted in an anguished voice:

"Drive on!"

"Where to, sir?" asked the cabman.

"Straight ahead!"

"Straight ahead, sir? But there's a turning here; to right
or to left?"

This question stumped Kovalyov and made him think
again. A man in his position ought first of all apply to the
City Police Headquarters, not because they dealt with matters of this kind there, but because instructions coming
from there might be complied with much more quickly than
those coming from any other place; to seek satisfaction
from the authorities of the department in which the nose
claimed to be serving would have been unreasonable, for
from the nose's replies he perceived that nothing was
sacred to that individual and that he was quite capable of
telling a lie just as he had lied in denying that he had ever
seen him. Kovalyov was, therefore, about to tell the cabman to drive him to Police Headquarters, when it again
occurred to him that this rogue and impostor, who had
treated him in such a contumelious way, might take advantage of the first favourable opportunity and slip out of
town, and then all his searches would be in vain or, which
God forbid, might go on for a whole month. At last it
seemed that Heaven itself had suggested a plan of action
to him. He decided to go straight to a newspaper office
and, while there was still time, put in an advertisement
with a circumstantial description of the nose so that anyone meeting it might bring it to him at once or, at any
rate, let him know where it was. And so, having made up
his mind, he told the cabman to drive him to the nearest
newspaper office and all the way there he kept hitting the
cabman on the back with his fist, repeating, "Faster, you
rogue! Faster, you scoundrel!" "Good Lord, sir, what are
you hitting me for?" said the cabman, shaking his head
and flicking with the rein at the horse, whose coat was as
long as a lap dog's. At last the cab came to a stop and
Kovalyov ran panting into a small reception room where
a grey-haired clerk, in an old frock coat and wearing spec-

tacles, sat at a table, with a pen between his teeth, counting some coppers.

"Who receives advertisements here?" cried Kovalyov. "Oh, good morning!"

"How do you do?" said the clerk, raising his eyes for a moment and dropping them again on the carefully laid out heaps of coppers before him.

"I should like to insert——"

"One moment, sir, I must ask you to wait a little," said the clerk, writing down a figure on a piece of paper with one hand and moving two beads on his abacus with the other.

A footman with galloons on his livery and a personal appearance which showed that he came from an aristocratic house, was standing beside the clerk with a note in his hand. He thought it an opportune moment for displaying his knowledge of the world.

"Would you believe it, sir," he said, "the little bitch isn't worth eighty copecks, and indeed I shouldn't give even eight copecks for her, but the countess dotes on her, sir, she simply dotes on her, and that's why she's offering a hundred roubles to anyone who finds her! Now, to put it politely, sir, just as you and me are speaking now, you can never tell what people's tastes may be. What I mean is that if you are a sportsman, then keep a pointer or a poodle, don't mind spending five hundred or even a thousand roubles, so long as your dog is a good one."

The worthy clerk listened to this with a grave air and at the same time kept counting the number of letters in the advertisement the footman had brought. The room was full of old women, shop assistants, and house porters—all with bits of paper in their hands. In one a coachman of sober habits was advertised as being let out on hire; in another an almost new, secondhand carriage, brought from Paris in 1814, was offered for sale; in still others were offered for sale: a serf girl of nineteen, experienced in laundry work and suitable for other work, a well-built open carriage with only one spring broken, a young, dappled-grey, mettlesome horse of seventeen years of age, a new consignment of turnip and radish seed from London, a summer residence with all the conveniences, including two boxes for horses and a piece of land on which an excellent birchwood or pinewood could be planted; there was

also an advertisement containing a challenge to those who
wished to purchase old boot soles with an invitation to
come to the auction rooms every day from eight o'clock
in the morning to three o'clock in the afternoon. The
room, in which all these people were crowded, was very
small and the air extremely thick; but the Collegiate Assessor Kovalyov did not notice the bad smell because he
kept the handkerchief over his face and also because his
nose was at the time goodness knows where.

"Excuse me, sir," he said at last with impatience, "it's
very urgent. . . ."

"Presently, presently," said the grey-haired gentleman,
flinging their notes back to the old women and the house
porters. "Two roubles forty copecks! One moment, sir!
One rouble sixty-four copecks! What can I do for you?"
he said at last, turning to Kovalyov.

"Thank you, sir," said Kovalyov. "You see, I've been
robbed or swindled, I can't so far say which, but I should
like you to put in an advertisement that anyone who brings
the scoundrel to me will receive a handsome reward."

"What is your name, sir?"

"What do you want my name for? I'm sorry I can't give
it to you. I have a large circle of friends: Mrs. Chekh-
taryov, the widow of a State Councillor, Pelageya Grigor-
yevna Podtochin, the widow of a first lieutenant. . . . God
forbid that they should suddenly find out! You can simply
say: a Collegiate Assessor or, better still, a gentleman of
the rank of major."

"And is the runaway your house serf?"

"My house serf? Good Lord, no! That wouldn't have
been so bad! You see, it's my—er—nose that has run
away from me. . . ."

"Dear me, what a strange name! And has this Mr.
Nosov robbed you of a large sum of money?"

"I said nose, sir, nose! You're thinking of something
else! It is my nose, my own nose that has disappeared I
don't know where. The devil himself must have played a
joke on me!"

"But how did it disappear? I'm afraid I don't quite
understand it."

"I can't tell you how it happened. The worst of it is
that now it is driving about all over the town under the
guise of a State Councillor. That's why I should like you

to insert an advertisement that anyone who catches him
should bring him at once to me. You can see for yourself, sir that I cannot possibly carry on without such a
conspicuous part of myself. It's not like some little toe
which no one can see whether it is missing or not once
I'm wearing my boots. I call on Thursdays on Mrs.
Chekhtaryov, the widow of a State Councillor. Mrs. Podtochin, the widow of a first lieutenant, and her pretty
daughter are also good friends of mine, and you can
judge for yourself the position I am in now. I can't go
and see them now, can I?"

The clerk pursed his lips tightly which meant that he
was thinking hard.

"I'm sorry, sir," he said at last, after a long pause, "but
I can't possibly insert such an advertisement in the papers."

"What? Why not?"

"Well, you see, sir, the paper might lose its reputation.
If everyone were to write that his nose had run away,
why—— As it is, people are already saying that we are
publishing a lot of absurd stories and false rumours."

"But why it is so absurd? I don't see anything absurd
in it."

"It only seems so to you. Last week, for instance, a
similar thing happened. A civil servant came to see me
just as you have now. He brought an advertisement, it
came to two roubles and seventy-three copecks, but all it
was about was that a poodle with a black coat had run
away. You wouldn't think there was anything in that,
would you? And yet it turned out to be a libellous statement. You see, the poodle was the treasurer of some insti-
tution or other. I don't remember which."

"But I am not asking you to publish an advertisement
about a poodle, but about my own nose, which is the
same as about myself."

"No, sir, I cannot possibly insert such an advertisement."

"Not even if my own nose really has disappeared?"

"If it's lost, then it's a matter for a doctor. I'm told there
are people who can fit you with a nose of any shape you
like. But I can't help observing, sir, that you are a gentleman of a merry disposition and are fond of pulling a
person's leg."

"I swear to you by all that is holy! Why, if it has come
to that, I don't mind showing you."

"Don't bother, sir," said the clerk, taking a pinch of snuff. "Still," he added, unable to suppress his curiosity, "if it's no bother, I'd like to have a look."

The Collegiate Assessor removed the handkerchief from his face.

"It is very strange, indeed!" said the clerk. "The place is perfectly flat, just like a pancake from a frying pan. Yes, quite incredibly flat."

"Well, you won't dispute it now, will you? You can see for yourself that you simply must insert it. I shall be infinitely grateful to you and very glad this incident has given me the pleasure of making your acquaintance. . . ."

It may be seen from that that the major decided to lay it on a bit thick this time.

"Well, of course, it's easy enough to insert an advertisement," said the clerk, "but I don't see that it will do you any good. If you really want to publish a thing like that, you'd better put it in the hands of someone skilful with his pen and let him describe it as a rare natural phenomenon and publish it in *The Northern Bee*"—here he took another pinch of snuff—"for the benefit of youth"—here he wiped his nose—"or just as a matter of general interest."

The Collegiate Assessor was utterly discouraged. He dropped his eyes and glanced at the bottom of the newspaper where the theatrical announcements were published; his face was ready to break into a smile as he read the name of a very pretty actress, and his hand went automatically to his pocket to feel whether he had a five-rouble note there, for, in Kovalyov's opinion, officers of the higher ranks ought to have a seat in the stalls—but the thought of his nose spoilt it all!

The clerk himself appeared to be touched by Kovalyov's embarrassing position. Wishing to relieve his distress a little, he thought it proper to express his sympathy in a few words.

"I'm very sorry indeed, sir," he said, "that such a thing should have happened to you. Would you like a pinch of snuff? It relieves headaches, dispels melancholy moods, and it is even a good remedy against haemorrhoids."

Saying this, the clerk offered his snuffbox to Kovalyov, very deftly opening the lid with the portrait of a lady in a hat on it.

This unintentional action made Kovalyov lose his patience.

"I can't understand, sir," he said angrily, "how you can joke in a matter like this! Don't you see I haven't got the thing with which to take a pinch of snuff? To hell with your snuff! I can't bear the sight of it now, and not only your rotten beresina brand, but even if you were to offer me rappee itself!"

Having said this, he walked out of the newspaper office, greatly vexed, and went to see the police inspector of his district, a man who had a great liking for sugar. At his home, the entire hall, which was also the dining room, was stacked with sugar loaves with which local tradesmen had presented him out of friendship. When Kovalyov arrived, the police inspector's cook was helping him off with his regulation top boots; his sabre and the rest of his martial armour were already hung peaceably in the corners of the room, and his three-year-old son was playing with his awe-inspiring three-cornered hat. He himself was getting ready to partake of pleasures of peace after his gallant, warlike exploits.

Kovalyov walked in at the time when he stretched, cleared his throat, and said: "Oh, for a couple of hours of sleep!" It could, therefore, be foreseen that the Collegiate Assessor could have hardly chosen a worse time to arrive; indeed, I am not sure whether he would have got a more cordial reception even if he had brought the police inspector several pounds of sugar or a piece of cloth. The inspector was a great patron of the arts and manufactures, but he preferred a bank note to everything else. "This is something," he used to say. "There is nothing better than that: it doesn't ask for food, it doesn't take up a lot of space, there's always room for it in the pocket, and when you drop it, it doesn't break."

The inspector received Kovalyov rather coldly and said that after dinner was not the time to carry out investigations and that nature herself had fixed it so that after a good meal a man had to take a nap (from which the Collegiate Assessor could deduce that the inspector was not unfamiliar with the sayings of the ancient sages), and that a respectable man would not have his nose pulled off.

A bull's eye! . . . It must be observed that Kovalyov was extremely quick to take offence. He could forgive any-

thing people said about himself, but he could never forgive
an insult to his rank or his calling. He was even of the
opinion that any reference in plays to army officers or civil
servants of low rank was admissible, but that the censor-
ship ought not to pass any attack on persons of higher
rank. The reception given him by the police inspector disconcerted him so much that he tossed his head and said
with an air of dignity, with his hands slightly parted in a
gesture of surprise: "I must say that after such offensive
remarks, I have nothing more to say. . . ." and went out.

He arrived home hardly able to stand on his feet. By
now it was dusk. After all these unsuccessful quests his
rooms looked melancholy or rather extremely disgusting to
him. On entering the hall, he saw his valet Ivan lying on
his back on the dirty leather sofa and spitting on the ceiling and rather successfully aiming at the same spot. Such
an indifference on the part of his servant maddened him;
he hit him on the forehead with his hat, saying: "You pig,
you're always doing something stupid!"

Ivan jumped up and rushed to help him off with his
cloak.

On entering his room, the major, tired and dejected,
threw himself into an armchair and, at last, after several
sighs, said:

"Lord, oh Lord, why should I have such bad luck? If
I had lost an arm or a leg, it would not be so bad; if I had
lost my ears, it would be bad enough, but still bearable;
but without a nose a man is goodness knows what, neither
fish, nor flesh, nor good red herring—he isn't a respectable
citizen at all! He is simply something to take and chuck
out of the window! If I had had it cut off in battle or in
a duel or had been the cause of its loss myself, but to lose
it without any reason whatever, for nothing, for absolutely
nothing! . . . But not," he added after a brief reflection,
"it can't be. It's inconceivable that a nose should be lost,
absolutely inconceivable. I must be simply dreaming or
just imagining it all. Perhaps by some mistake I drank,
instead of water, the spirits which I rub on my face after
shaving. Ivan, the blithering fool, did not take it away and
I must have swallowed it by mistake."

To convince himself that he was not drunk, the major
pinched himself so painfully that he cried out. The pain
completely convinced him that he was fully awake and

that everything had actually happened to him. He went
up slowly to the looking glass and at first screwed up his
eyes with the idea that perhaps he would see his nose in
its proper place; but almost at the same moment he
jumped back, saying: "What a horrible sight!"

And, indeed, the whole thing was quite inexplicable. If
he had lost a button, a silver spoon, his watch, or something
of the kind, but to lose—and in his own apartment, too!
Taking all the circumstances into consideration, Major
Kovalyov decided that he would not be far wrong in assuming that the whole thing was the fault of no other person than Mrs. Podtochin, who wanted him to marry her
daughter. He was not himself averse to flirting with her,
but he avoided a final decision. But when Mrs. Podtochin
told him plainly that she would like her daughter to marry
him, he quietly hung back with his compliments, declaring
that he was still too young, that he had to serve another
five years, as he had decided not to marry till he was exactly forty-two. That was why Mr. Podtochin, out of revenge no doubt, had made up her mind to disfigure him
and engaged some old witch to do the foul deed, for he
simply refused to believe that his nose had been cut off:
no one had entered his room, and his barber, Ivan Yakovlevich, had shaved him on Wednesday, and during the
whole of that day and even on Thursday his nose was intact—he remembered that, he knew that for certain; besides, he would have felt pain and the wound could not
possibly have healed so quickly and become as smooth as
a pancake. He made all sorts of plans in his head: to issue
a court summons against her or to go to see her and confront her with the undeniable proof of her crime. His
thoughts were interrupted by a gleam of light through all
the cracks of the door, which let him know that Ivan had
lighted a candle in the hall. Soon Ivan himself appeared,
carrying the candle in front of him and lighting the whole
room brightly. Kovalyov instinctively seized his handkerchief and covered the place where his nose had been only
the day before so that the stupid fellow should not stand
there gaping, seeing his master so strangely transformed.

Ivan had scarcely had time to go back to his cubby-
hole when an unfamiliar voice was heard in the hall,
saying:

"Does the Collegiate Assessor Kovalyov live here?"

"Come in," said Kovalyov, jumping up quickly and opening the door. "Major Kovalyov is here."

A police officer of a handsome appearance, with whiskers that were neither too dark nor too light and with fairly full cheeks, came in. It was, in fact, the same police officer who, at the beginning of this story, had been standing at the end of Issakiyevsky Bridge.

"Did you lose your nose, sir?"

"That's right."

"It's been found now."

"What are you saying?" cried Major Kovalyov.

He was bereft of speech with joy. He stared fixedly at the police officer who was standing before him and whose full lips and cheeks reflected the flickering light of the candle.

"How was it found?"

"By a most extraordinary piece of luck, sir. It was intercepted just before he was leaving town. It was about to get into the stagecoach and leave for Riga. He even had a passport made out in the name of a certain civil servant. And the funny thing is that at first I was myself inclined to take him for a gentleman. But luckily I was wearing my glasses at the time and I saw at once that it was a nose. You see, sir, I am shortsighted, and if you were to stand in front of me I would just see that you have a face, but would not be able to make out either your nose or your beard or anything else for that matter. My mother-in-law, that is to say, my wife's mother, can't see anything, either."

Kovalyov was beside himself with excitement.

"Where is it? Where? I'll go at once!"

"Don't trouble, sir. Realising how much you must want it, I brought it with me. And the funny part about it is that the chief accomplice in this affair is the scoundrel of a barber on Voznessensky Avenue, who is now locked up in a cell at the police station. I've suspected him for a long time of theft and drunkenness and, as a matter of fact, he stole a dozen buttons from a shop only the other day. Your nose, sir, is just as it was."

At these words, the police officer put his hand in his pocket and pulled out the nose wrapped in a piece of paper.

"Yes, yes, it's my nose!" cried Kovalyov. "It's my nose all right! Won't you have a cup of tea with me, sir?"

"I'd be very glad to, sir, but I'm afraid I'm rather in a hurry. I have to go to the House of Correction from here. Food prices have risen a great deal, sir. . . . I have my mother-in-law, that is to say, my wife's mother, living with me and, of course, there are the children. My eldest, in particular, is a very promising lad, sir. A very clever boy he is, sir, but I haven't the means to provide a good education for him—none at all. . . ."

Kovalyov took the hint and, snatching up a ten-rouble note from the table, thrust it into the hand of the police officer, who bowed and left the room, and almost at the same moment Kovalyov heard his voice raised in the street, where he was boxing the ears of a foolish peasant who had happened to drive with his cart on to the boulevard.

After the departure of the police officer, the Collegiate Assessor remained for a time in a sort of daze, and it was only after several minutes that he was able to recover his senses, so overwhelmed was he by his joy at the unexpected recovery of his nose. He took the newly found nose very carefully in both his cupped hands and examined it attentively once more.

"Yes, it's my nose all right!" said Major Kovalyov. "There's the pimple on the left side which I only got the other day."

The major almost laughed with joy. But nothing lasts very long in the world, and that is why even joy is not so poignant after the first moment. A moment later it grows weaker still and at last it merges imperceptibly into one's ordinary mood, just as a circle made in the water by a pebble at last merges into its smooth surface. Kovalyov began to ponder and he realised that the matter was not at an end: the nose had been found, but it had still to be affixed, to be put back in its place.

"And what it if doesn't stick?"

At this question that he had put to himself the major turned pale.

With a feeling of indescribable panic he rushed up to the table and drew the looking glass closer to make sure that he did not stick his nose on crookedly. His hands trembled. Carefully and with the utmost circumspection he

put it back on its former place. Oh horror! The nose did
not stick! . . . He put it to his mouth, breathed on it to
warm it a little, and once more put it back on the smooth
place between his two cheeks; but, try as he might, the
nose refused to stick.

"Come on, come on! Stick, you idiot!" he kept saying
to it.

But the nose, as though made of wood, kept falling
down on the table with so strange a sound that it might
have been cork. The major's face contorted spasmodically.
"Won't it adhere?" he asked himself in a panic. But though
he kept putting it back on its own place a great many
times, his efforts were as unavailing as ever.

He called Ivan and sent him for the doctor, who occupied the best flat on the ground floor of the same house.
The doctor was a fine figure of a man; he had wonderful
pitch-black whiskers, a fresh, healthy wife, he ate fresh
apples in the morning and kept his mouth quite extraordinarily clean, rinsing it every morning for nearly three
quarters of an hour and brushing his teeth with five different kinds of toothbrushes. The doctor came at once.
After asking how long it was since the accident, he lifted
up Major Kovalyov's face by the chin and gave a fillip with
his thumb, on the spot where the nose had been, with such
force that the major threw back his head so violently that
he hit the wall. The doctor said that it was nothing and,
after advising him to move away from the wall a little,
told him to bend his head to the right. After feeling the
place where the nose had been, he said: "H'm!" Then he
told him to bend his head to the left, and again said:
"H'm!" In conclusion he gave him another fillip with the
thumb so that the major tossed his head like a horse whose
teeth are being examined. Having carried out this experiment, the doctor shook his head and said:

"No, I'm afraid it can't be done! You'd better remain
like this, for it might be much worse. It is, of course, quite
possible to affix your nose. In fact, I could do it right now.
But I assure you that it might be the worse for you."

"How do you like that! How am I to remain without a
nose?" said Kovalyov. "It can't possibly be worse than
now. It's—it's goodness only knows what! How can I show
myself with such a horrible face? I know lots of people of
good social position. Why, today I have been invited to

two parties. I have a large circle of friends: Mrs. Chekh-taryov, the widow of a State Councillor, Mrs. Podtochin, the widow of an army officer—though after what she did to me now I shall have no further dealings with her except through the police. Do me a favour, Doctor," said Kovalyov in an imploring voice. "Is there no way at all? Stick it on somehow. It may not be quite satisfactory, but so long as it sticks I don't mind. I could even support it with a hand in an emergency. Besides, I don't dance, so that I could hardly do any harm to it by some inadvertent movement. As for my gratitude for your visits, you may be sure that I will recompense you as much as I can. . . ."

"Believe me, sir," said the doctor neither in too loud nor in too soft a voice, but in a very persuasive and magnetic one, "I never allow any selfish motives to interfere with the treatment of my patients. This is against my principles and my art. It is true I charge for my visits, but that is only because I hate to offend by my refusal. Of course, I could put your nose back, but I assure you on my honour, if you won't belive my words, that it will be much worse. You'd better leave it to nature. Wash it often with cold water, and I assure you that without a nose you will be as healthy as with one. As for your nose, I'd advise you to put it in a bottle of spirits or, better still, pour two spoon-fuls of aqua fortis and warmed-up vinegar into the bottle, and you'd be able to get a lot of money for it. I might take it myself even, if you won't ask too much for it."

"No, no," cried the desperate Major Kovalyov, "I'd rather it rotted away!"

"I'm sorry," said the doctor, taking his leave, "I wish I could be of some help to you, but there's nothing I can do! At least you saw how anxious I was to help you."

Having said this, the doctor left the room with a dignified air. Kovalyov did not even notice his face, and in his profound impassivity only caught sight of the cuffs of his spotlessly clean white shirt peeping out of his black frock coat.

On the following day he decided, before lodging his complaint, to write to Mrs. Podtochin a letter with a request to return to him without a fight what she had taken away from him. The letter was as follows:

Dear Mrs. Podtochin,

I cannot understand your strange treatment of me. I assure you that, by acting like this, you will gain nothing and will certainly not force me to marry your daughter. Believe me, I know perfectly well what happened to my nose and that you, and no one else, are chief instigator of this affair. Its sudden detachment from its place, its flight, and its disguise, first in the shape of a civil servant and then in its own shape, is nothing more than the result of witchcraft employed by you or by those who engage in the same honourable occupations as yourself. For my part, I deem it my duty to warn you that if the aforementioned nose is not back in its usual place today, I shall be forced to have recourse to the protection and the safeguard of the law.

However, I have the honour of remaining, madam, with the utmost respect

Your obedient servant,

Platon Kovalyov

Dear Platon Kuzmich,

Your letter has greatly surprised me. To be quite frank, I never expected it, particularly as regards your unjust reproaches. I wish to inform you that I have never received the civil servant you mention, neither in disguise nor in his own shape. It is true, Filipp Ivanovich Potachkin used to come to see me. And though he did ask me for my daughter's hand and is a man of good and sober habits and of great learning, I have never held out any hopes to him. You also mention your nose. If you mean by that that I wished to put your nose out of joint, that is, to give you a formal refusal, I am surprised that you should speak of such a thing when, as you know perfectly well, I was quite of the contrary opinion and if you should now make a formal proposal to my daughter, I should be ready to satisfy you immediately for that has always been my dearest wish, in the hope of which

I remain always at your service,

Pelageya Podtochin

"No," said Kovalyov, after he had read the letter, "she had certainly nothing to do with it. It's impossible! The letter is not written as a guilty person would have written it." The Collegiate Assessor was an expert on such things, for, while serving in the Caucasus, he had several times been under judicial examination. "How then, in what way, did it happen? The devil alone can sort it out!" he said at last, utterly discouraged.

Meanwhile the rumours about this extraordinary affair spread all over the town and, as usually happens, not without all sorts of embellishments. At that time people's minds were particularly susceptible to anything of an extraordinary nature: only a short time before everybody had shown a great interest in the experiments of magnetism. Besides, the story of the dancing chairs in Konyushennaya Street was still fresh in people's minds, and it is therefore not surprising that people soon began talking about the Collegiate Assessor Kovalyov's nose which, it was alleged, was taking a walk on Nevsky Avenue at precisely three o'clock in the afternoon. Thousands of curious people thronged Nevsky Avenue every day. Someone said that the nose was in Junker's Stores, and such a crowd of people collected at the stores that the police had to be called to restore order. One enterprising, bewhiskered businessman of respectable appearance, who was selling all sorts of dry pasties at the entrance to the theatre, had purposely made beautiful wooden benches on which it was perfectly safe to stand and invited people to use them for eighty copecks each. One highly estimable colonel, who had left his home earlier than usual so that he could see the nose, pushed his way through the crowd with great difficulty but, to his great indignation, he saw in the window of the stores, instead of the nose, an ordinary woollen sweater and a lithograph of a girl pulling up her stocking and a dandy, with a small beard and an open waistcoat, peeping at her from behind a tree—a picture that had hung in the same place for over ten year. On stepping back from the window, he said with vexation: "One should not be allowed to create a disturbance among the common people by such stupid and improbable stories."

Then the rumour spread that Major Kovalyov's nose was not taking a walk on Nevsky Avenue but in Tavrichesky Gardens and that he had been there for a long time;

in fact, that when the Persian Prince Khozrev Mirza had lived there he had greatly marvelled at that curious freak of nature. A few students of the Surgical Academy set off there. One highly aristocratic lady wrote a letter to the head keeper of the gardens specially to ask him to show that rare phenomenon to her children and, if possible, with instructive and edifying explanations for young boys.

All men about town, without whom no important social gathering is complete, who liked to amuse the ladies and whose stock of amusing stories had been entirely used up at the time, were extremely glad of all this affair. A small section of respectable and well-meaning people were highly dissatisfied. One gentleman declared indignantly that he failed to understand how in our enlightened age such absurd stories could be spread abroad and that he was surprised the government paid no attention to it. This gentleman evidently was one of those gentlemen who would like to involve the government in everything, even in his daily tiffs with his wife. After that—but here again a thick fog descends on the whole incident, and what happened afterwards is completely unknown.

III

The world is full of all sorts of absurdities. Sometimes there is not even a semblance of truth: suddenly the very same nose, which had been driving about disguised as a State Councillor and had created such an uproar in town, found itself, as if nothing had happened, on its accustomed place again, namely, between the two cheeks of Major Kovalyov. This happened on the seventh of April. Waking up and looking quite accidentally into the mirror, he saw —his nose! He grabbed it with his hand—it was his nose all right! . . . "Aha!" said Kovalyov, and nearly went leaping barefoot all over the room in a roisterous dance in his joy. But Ivan, who entered just then, prevented him. He told Ivan to bring in some water for washing at once and, while washing, glanced once again into the mirror: he had a nose! While wiping himself with a towel, he again glanced into the mirror: he had a nose!

"Have a look, Ivan, there seems to be a pimple on my nose," he said, thinking to himself: "Won't it be awful if

Ivan were to say, No, sir, there's no pimple and no nose,
either!"

But Ivan said: "There's nothing, sir. I can't see no pimple. Nothing at all on your nose, sir."

"That's good, damn it!" said the major to himself, snapping his fingers.

At that moment the barber Ivan Yakovlevich poked his
head through the door, but as timidly as a cat which had
just been thrashed for the theft of suet.

"Tell me first of all—are your hands clean?" Kovalyov
shouted to him from the other end of the room.

"They are clean, sir."

"You're lying!"

"I swear they are clean, sir!"

"Very well, they'd better be!"

Kovalyov sat down. Ivan Yakovlevich put a napkin
round him and in a twinkling, with the aid of his brush
alone, transformed his whole beard and part of his cheek
into the sort of cream that is served in a merchant's home
at a name-day party.

"Well, I never!" said Ivan Yakovlevich to himself as he
glanced at the nose. Then he bent his head to the other
side and looked at the nose sideways. "Well. I'm damned,"
he went on, looking at the nose for some considerable
time. "Dear, oh dear, just think of it!" At last, gently and
as cautiously as can only be imagined, he raised two
fingers to grasp it by its end. Such was Ivan Yakovlevich's
system.

"Mind, mind what you're doing!" cried Kovalyov.

Ivan Yakovlevich was utterly discouraged, perplexed,
and confused as he had never been confused before. At last
he began carefully titillating him with the razor under the
beard, and though he found it difficult and not at all convenient to shave without holding on to the olfactory organ,
he did at last overcome all the obstacles by pressing his
rough thumb against the cheek and the lower jaw and
finished shaving him.

When everything was ready, Kovalyov hastened to dress
at once, took a cab, and drove straight to the nearest
pastry cook's. On entering, he at once shouted to the boy
at the other end of the shop: "Boy, a cup of chocolate!"
and immediately went up to the looking glass: he had a
nose all right! He turned round gaily and glanced ironi-

cally, screwing up one eye a little, at two military gentlemen, one of whom had a nose no bigger than a waistcoat
button. After that he set off for the office of the department where he was trying to obtain the post of vice-
governor or, if unsuccessful, of an administrative clerk. On
passing through the reception room, he glanced into the
looking glass: he had a nose all right! Then he went to
see another Collegiate Assessor, a man who was very
fond of sneering at people, to whom he often used to say
in reply to his biting remarks: "Oh, away with you! I
know you, Mr. Pinprick!" On the way he thought: "If the
major does not split his sides with laughter when he sees
me, it's a sure sign that everything is in its proper place."
But the Collegiate Assessor showed no signs of merriment.
"It's perfect, perfect, damn it!" thought Kovalyov to himself. On the way back he met Mrs. Podtochin and her
daughter, greeted them, and was met with joyful exclama-
tions, which again proved to him that there was nothing
wrong with him. He talked a long time with them and,
taking out his snuffbox deliberately, kept stuffing his nose
with snuff at both entrances for a great while, saying to
himself: "There, I'm putting on this show specially for
you, stupid females! And I won't marry your daughter
all the same. Flirt with her—by all means, but nothing
more!" And Major Kovalyov took his walks after that as
if nothing had happened. He was to be seen on Nevsky
Avenue, in the theatres—everywhere. And his nose, too,
just as if nothing had happened, remained on his face,
without as much as a hint that he had been playing truant.
And after that Major Kovalyov was always seen in the
best of humour, smiling, running after all the pretty ladies,
and once even stopping before a little shop in the Arcade
and buying himself a ribbon of some order for some mysterious reason, for he had never been a member of any
order.

So that is the sort of thing that happened in the northern
capital of our far-flung Empire. Only now, on thinking it
all over, we can see that there is a great deal that is improbable in it. Quite apart from the really strange fact of
the supernatural displacement of the nose and its appearance in various parts of the town in the guise of a State
Councillor, how did Kovalyov fail to realise that he could
not advertise about his nose in a newspaper? I am not say-

ing that because I think that advertisement rates are too high—that's nonsense, and I am not at all a mercenary person. But it's improper, awkward, not nice! And again—how did the nose come to be in a loaf of bread and what about Ivan Yakovlevich? No, that I cannot understand, I simply cannot understand it! But what is even stranger and more incomprehensible than anything is that authors should choose such subjects. I confess that is entirely beyond my comprehension. It's like—no, I simply don't understand it. In the first place it's of no benefit whatever to our country, and in the second place—but even in the second place there's no benefit whatever. I simply don't know what to make of it. . . .

And yet, in spite of it all, though, of course, we may take for granted this and that and the other—may even—But then where do you not find all sorts of absurdities? All the same, on second thoughts, there really is something in it. Say what you like, but such things do happen—not often, but they do happen.

1835–36

Translated from the Russian
by David Magarshack

54

Gogol's Wife
by Tommaso Landolfi

At this point, confronted with the whole complicated affair of Nikolai Vassilevitch's wife, I am overcome by hesitation. Have I any right to disclose something which is unknown to the whole world, which my unforgettable friend himself kept hidden from the world (and he had his reasons), and which I am sure will give rise to all sorts of malicious and stupid misunderstandings? Something, moreover, which will very probably offend the sensibilities of all sorts of base, hypocritical people, and possibly of some honest people too, if there are any left? And finally, have I any right to disclose something before which my own spirit recoils, and even tends toward a more or less open disapproval?

But the fact remainse that, as a biographer, I have certain firm obligations. Believing as I do that every bit of information about so lofty a genius will turn out to be of value to us and to future generations, I cannot conceal something which in any case has no hope of being judged fairly and wisely until the end of time. Moreover, what right have we to condemn? Is it given to us to know, not only what intimate needs, but even what higher and wider ends may have been served by those very deeds of a lofty genius which perchance may appear to us vile? No indeed, for we understand so little of these privileged natures. "It is true," a great man once said, "that I also have to pee, but for quite different reasons."

But without more ado I will come to what I know beyond doubt, and can prove beyond question, about this controversial matter, which will now—I dare to hope—no longer be so. I will not trouble to recapitulate what is already known of it, since I do not think this should be necessary at the present stage of development of Gogol studies.

Let me say it at once: Nikolai Vassilevitch's wife was
not a woman. Nor was she any sort of human being, nor
any sort of living creature at all, whether animal or vegetable (although something of the sort has sometimes been
hinted). She was quite simply a balloon. Yes, a balloon;
and this will explain the perplexity, or even indignation, of
certain biographers who were also the personal friends of
the Master, and who complained that, although they often
went to his house, they never saw her and "never even
heard her voice." From this they deduced all sorts of dark
and disgraceful complications—yes, and criminal ones too.
No, gentlemen, everything is always simpler than it appears. You did not hear her voice simply because she
could not speak, or to be more exact, she could only speak
in certain conditions, as we shall see. And it was always,
except once, in tête-à-tête with Nikolai Vassilevitch. So let
us not waste time with any cheap or empty refutations but
come at once to as exact and complete a description as
possible of the being or object in question.

Gogol's so-called wife was an ordinary dummy made of
thick rubber, naked at all seasons, buff in tint, or as is
more commonly said, flesh-colored. But since women's
skins are not all of the same color, I should specify that
hers was a light-colored, polished skin, like that of certain
brunettes. It, or she, was, it is hardly necessary to add, of
feminine sex. Perhaps I should say at once that she was
capable of very wide alterations of her attributes without,
of course, being able to alter her sex itself. She could
sometimes appear to be thin, with hardly any breasts and
with narrow hips more like a young lad than a woman, and
at other times to be excessively well-endowed or—let us
not mince matters—fat. And she often changed the color
of her hair, both on her head and elsewhere on her body,
though not necessarily at the same time. She could also
seem to change in all sorts of other tiny particulars, such
as the position of moles, the vitality of the mucous membranes and so forth. She could even to a certain extent
change the very color of her skin. One is faced with the
necessity of asking oneself who she really was, or whether
it would be proper to speak of a single "person"—and in
fact we shall see that it would be imprudent to press this
point.

The cause of these changes, as my readers will already

have understood, was nothing else but the will of Nikolai Vassilevitch himself. He would inflate her to a greater or lesser degree, would change her wig and her other tufts of hair, would grease her with ointments and touch her up in various ways so as to obtain more or less the type of woman which suited him at that moment. Following the natural inclinations of his fancy, he even amused himself sometimes by producing grotesque or monstrous forms; as will be readily understood, she became deformed when inflated beyond a certain point or if she remained below a certain pressure.

But Gogol soon tired of these experiments, which he held to be "after all, not very respectful" to his wife, whom he loved in his own way—however inscrutable it may remain to us. He loved her, but which of these incarnations, we may ask ourselves, did he love? Alas, I have already indicated that the end of the present account will furnish some sort of an answer. And how can I have stated above that it was Nikolai Vassilevitch's will which ruled that woman? In a certain sense, yes, it is true; but it is equally certain that she soon became no longer his slave but his tyrant. And here yawns the abyss, or if you prefer it, the Jaws of Tartarus. But let us not anticipate.

I have said that Gogol obtained with his manipulations *more or less the* type of woman which he needed from time to time. I should add that when, in rare cases, the form he obtained perfectly incarnated his desire. Nikolai Vassilevitch fell in love with it "exclusively," as he said in his own words, and that this was enough to render "her" stable for a certain time—until he fell out of love with "her." I counted no more than three or four of these violent passions—or, as I suppose they would be called today, infatuations—in the life (dare I say in the conjugal life?) of the great writer. It will be convenient to add here that a few years after what one may call his marriage, Gogol had even given a name to his wife. It was Caracas, which is, unless I am mistaken, the capital of Venezuela. I have never been able to discover the reason for this choice: great minds are so capricious!

Speaking only of her normal appearance, Caracas was what is called a fine woman—well built and proportioned in every part. She had every smallest attribute of her sex properly disposed in the proper location. Particularly worthy of attention were her genital organs (if the adjective is permissible in such a context). They were formed by means of ingenious folds in the rubber. Nothing was forgotten, and their operation was rendered easy by various devices, as well as by the internal pressure of the air.

Caracas also had a skeleton, even though a rudimentary one. Perhaps it was made of whalebone. Special care had been devoted to the construction of the thoracic cage, of the pelvic basin and of the cranium. The first two systems were more or less visible in accordance with the thickness of the fatty layer, if I may so describe it, which covered them. It is a great pity that Gogol never let me know the name of the creator of such a fine piece of work. There was an obstinacy in his refusal which was never quite clear to me.

Nikolai Vassilevitch blew his wife up through the anal sphincter with a pump of his own invention, rather like those which you hold down with your two feet and which are used today in all sorts of mechanical workshops. Situated in the anus was a little one-way valve, or whatever the correct technical description would be, like the mitral valve of the heart, which, once the body was inflated, allowed more air to come in but none to go out. To deflate, one unscrewed a stopper in the mouth, at the back of the throat.

And that, I think, exhausts the description of the most noteworthy peculiarities of this being. Unless perhaps I should mention the splendid rows of white teeth which adorned her mouth and the dark eyes which, in spite of their immobility, perfectly simulated life. Did I say simulate? Good heavens, simulate is not the word! Nothing seems to be the word, when one is speaking of Caracas! Even these eyes could undergo a change of color, by means of a special process to which, since it was long and tiresome, Gogol seldom had recourse. Finally, I should speak of her voice, which it was only once given to me to hear. But I cannot do that without going more fully into the relationship between husband and wife, and in this I shall no longer be able to answer to the truth of everything with absolute certitude. On my conscience I could not—so confused, both in itself and in my memory, is that which I now have to tell.

Here, then, as they occur to me, are some of my memories.

The first and, as I said, the last time I ever heard Caracas speak to Nikolai Vassilevitch was one evening when we were absolutely alone. We were in the room where the woman, if I may be allowed the expression, lived. Entrance to this room was strictly forbidden to everybody. It was furnished more or less in the Oriental manner, had no windows and was situated in the most inaccessible part of the house. I did know that she could talk, but Gogol had never explained to me the circumstances under which this happened. There were only the two of us, or three, in there. Nikolai Vassilevitch and I were drinking vodka and discussing Butkov's novel. I remember that we left this topic, and he was maintaining the necessity for radical reforms in the laws of inheritance. We had almost forgotten her. It was then that, with a husky and submissive voice, like Venus on the nuptial couch, she said point-blank: "I want to go poo poo."

I jumped, thinking I had misheard, and looked across at her. She was sitting on a pile of cushions against the wall; that evening she was a soft, blonde beauty, rather well-covered. Her expression seemed commingled of shrewdness and slyness, childishness and irresponsibility. As for Gogol, he blushed violently and, leaping on her, stuck two fingers down her throat. She immediately began to shrink and to turn pale; she took on once again that lost and astonished air which was especially hers, and was in the end reduced to no more than a flabby skin on a perfunctory bony armature. Since, for practical reasons which will readily be divined, she had an extraordinarily flexible backbone, she folded up almost in two, and for the rest of the evening she looked up at us from where she had slithered to the floor, in utter abjection.

All Gogol said was: "She only does it for a joke, or to annoy me, because as a matter of fact she does not have such needs." In the presence of other people, that is to say of me, he generally made a point of treating her with a certain disdain.

We went on drinking and talking, but Nikolai Vassilevitch seemed very much disturbed and absent in spirit. Once he suddenly interrupted what he was saying, seized my hand in his and burst into tears. "What can I do now?"

he exclaimed. You understand, Foma Paskalovitch, that I loved her?"

It is necessary to point out that it was impossible, except by a miracle, ever to repeat any of Caracas' forms. She was a fresh creation every time, and it would have been wasted effort to seek to find again the exact proportions, the exact pressure, and so forth, of a former Caracas. Therefore the plumpish blonde of that evening was lost to Gogol from that time forth forever; this was in fact the tragic end of one of those few loves of Nikolai Vassilevitch, which I described above. He gave me no explanation; he sadly rejected my proffered comfort, and that evening we parted early. But his heart had been laid bare to me in that outburst. He was no longer so reticent with me, and soon had hardly any secrets left. And this, I may say in parenthesis, caused me very great pride.

It seems that things had· gone well for the "couple" at the beginning of their life together. Nikolai Vassilevitch had been content with Caracas and slept regularly with her in the same bed. He continued to observe this custom till the end, saying with a timid smile that no companion could be quieter or less importunate than she. But I soon began to doubt this, especially judging by the state he was sometimes in when he woke up. Then, after several years, their relationship began strangely to deteriorate.

All this, let it be said once and for all, is no more than a schematic attempt at an explanation. About that time the woman actually began to show signs of independence or, as one might say, of autonomy. Nikolai Vassilevitch had the extraordinary impression that she was acquiring a personality of her own, indecipherable perhaps, but still distinct from his, and one which slipped through his fingers. It is certain that some sort of continuity was established between each of her appearances—between all those brunettes, those blondes, those redheads and auburn-headed girls, between those plump, those slim, those dusky or snowy or golden beauties, there was a certain something in common. At the beginning of this chapter I cast some doubt on the propriety of considering Caracas as a unitary personality; nevertheless I myself could not quite, whenever I saw her, free myself of the impression that, however unheard of it may seem, this was fundamentally the

same woman. And it may be that this was why Gogol felt
he had to give her a name.

An attempt to establish in what precisely subsisted the
common attributes of the different forms would be quite
another thing. Perhaps it was no more and no less than
the creative afflatus of Nikolai Vassilevitch himself. But
no, it would have been too singular and strange if he had
been so much divided off from himself, so much averse to
himself. Because whoever she was, Caracas was a disturbing presence and even—it is better to be quite clear—
a hostile one. Yet neither Gogol nor I ever succeeded in
formulating a remotely tenable hypothesis as to her true
nature; when I say formulate, I mean in terms which
would be at once rational and accessible to all. But I
cannot pass over an extraordinary event which took place
at this time.

Caracas fell ill of a shameful disease—or rather Gogol
did—though he was not then having, nor had he ever
had, any contact with other women. I will not even try to
describe how this happened, or where the filthy complaint
came from; all I know is that it happened. And that my
great, unhappy friend would say to me: "So, Foma
Paskalovitch, you see what lay at the heart of Caracas; it
was the spirit of syphilis."

Sometimes he would even blame himself in a quite
absurd manner; he was always prone to self-accusation.
This incident was a real catastrophe as far as the already
obscure relationship between husband and wife, and the
hostile feelings of Nikolai Vassilevitch himself, were concerned. He was compelled to undergo long-drawn-out and
painful treatment—the treatment of those days—and the
situation was aggravated by the fact that the disease in
the woman did not seem to be easily curable. Gogol deluded himself for some time that, by blowing his wife up
and down and furnishing her with the most widely divergent aspects, he could obtain a woman immune from the
contagion, but he was forced to desist when no results
were forthcoming.

I shall be brief, seeking not to tire my readers, and also
because what I remember seems to become more and more
confused. I shall therefore hasten to the tragic conclusion.
As to this last, however, let there be no mistake. I must

once again make it clear that I am very sure of my ground.
I was an eyewitness. Would that I had not been!

The years went by. Nikolai Vassilevitch's disease for his
wife became stronger, though his love for her did not
show any signs of diminishing. Toward the end, aversion
and attachment struggled so fiercely with each other in
his heart that he became quite stricken, almost broken
up. His restless eyes, which habitually assumed so many
different expressions and sometimes spoke so sweetly to
the heart of his interlocutor, now almost always shone
with a fevered light, as if he were under the effect of a
drug. The strangest impulses arose in him, accompanied
by the most senseless fears. He spoke to me of Caracas
more and more often, accusing her of unthinkable and
amazing things. In these regions I could not follow him,
since I had but a sketchy acquaintance with his wife,
and hardly any intimacy—and above all since my sensi-
bility was so limited compared with his. I shall accordingly
restrict myself to reporting some of his accusations, without reference to my personal impressions.

"Believe it or not, Foma Paskalovitch," he would, for
example, often say to me: "Believe it or not, *she's aging!*"
Then, unspeakably moved, he would, as was his way,
take my hands in his. He also accused Caracas of giving
herself up to solitary pleasures, which he had expressly
forbidden. He even went so far as to charge her with
betraying him, but the things he said became so extremely
obscure that I must excuse myself from any further account of them.

One thing that appears certain is that toward the end
Caracas, whether aged or not, had turned into a bitter
creature, querulous, hypocritical and subject to religious
excess. I do not exclude the possibility that she may have
had an influence on Gogol's moral position during the last
period of his life, a position which is sufficiently well
known. The tragic climax came one night quite unexpectedly when Nikolai Vassilevitch and I were celebrating
his silver wedding one of the last evenings we were to spend
together, I neither can or should attempt to set down what
it was that led to his decision, at a time when to all appearances he was resigned to tolerating his consort. I
know not what new events had taken place that day. I

shall confine my self to the facts; my readers must make
what they can of them.

That evening Nikolai Vassilevitch was unusually agitated.
His distaste for Caracas seemed to have reached an un-
precedented intensity. The famous "pyre of vanities"—
the burning of his manuscripts—had already taken place;
I should not like to say whether or not at the instigation
of his wife. His state of mind had been further inflamed
by other causes. As to this physical condition, this was
ever more pitiful, and strengthened my impression that
he took drugs. All the same, he began to talk in a more
or less normal way about Belinsky, who was giving him
some trouble with his attacks on the *Selected Correspondence*. Then suddenly, tears rising to his eyes, he interrupted himself and cried out: "No. No. It's too much. I
can't go on any longer," as well as other obscure and dis-
connected phrases which he would not clarify. He seemed
to be talking to himself. He wrung his hands, shook his
head, got up and sat down again after having taken four
or five anxious steps round the room. When Caracas appeared, or rather when we went in to her later in the
evening in her Oriental chamber, he controlled himself no
longer and begain to behave like an old man, if I may so
express myself, in his second childhood, quite giving way
to his absurd impulses. For instance, he kept nudging me
and winking and senselessly repeating: "There she is,
Foma Paskalovitch; there she is!" Meanwhile she seemed
to look up at us with a disdainful attention. But behind
these "mannerisms" one could feel in him a real repugnance, a repugnance which had, I suppose, now reached
the limits of the endurable. Indeed . . .

After a certain time Nikolai Vassilevitch seemed to
pluck up courage. He burst into tears, but somehow they
were more manly tears. He wrung his hands again, seized
mine in his, and walked up and down, muttering: "That's
enough! We can't have any more of this. This is an unheard of thing. How can such a thing be happening to
me? How can a man be expected to put up with *this?*"

He then leapt furiously upon the pump, the existence of
which he seemed just to have remembered, and, with it in
his hand, dashed like a whirlwind to Caracas. He inserted
the tube in her anus and began to inflate her. . . . Weeping
the while, he shouted like one possessed: "Oh, how I love

her, how I love her, my poor, poor darling! . . . But she's
going to burst! Unhappy Caracas, most pitiable of God's
creatures! But die she must!"

Caracas was swelling up. Nikolai Vassilevitch sweated,
wept and pumped. I wished to stop him but, I know not
why, I had not the courage. She began to become deformed and shortly assumed the most monstrous aspect;
and yet she had not given any signs of alarm—she was
used to these jokes. But when she began to feel unbearably
full, or perhaps when Nikolai Vassilevitch's intentions
became plain to her, she took on an expression of bestial
amazement, even a little beseeching, but still without
losing that disdainful look. She was afraid, she was even
committing herself to his mercy, but still she could not
believe in the immediate approach of her fate; she could
not believe in the frightful audacity of her husband. He
could not see her face because he was behind her. But I
looked at her with fascination, and did not move a finger.

At last the internal pressure came through the fragile
bones at the base of her skull, and printed on her face an
indescribable rictus. Her belly, her thighs, her lips, her
breasts and what I could see of her buttocks had swollen to
incredible proportions. All of a sudden she belched, and
gave a long hissing groan; both these phenomena one could
explain by the increase in pressure, which had suddenly
forced a way out through the valve in her throat. Then
her eyes bulged frantically, threatening to jump out of
their sockets. Her ribs flared wide apart and were no
longer attached to the sternum, and she resembled a
python digesting a donkey. A donkey, did I say? An ox!
An elephant! At this point I believed her already dead,
but Nikolai Vassilevitch, sweating, weeping and repeating:
"My dearest! My beloved! My best!" continued to pump.

She went off unexpectedly and, as it were, all of a piece.
It was not one part of her skin which gave way and the
rest which followed, but her whole surface at the same
instant. She scattered in the air. The pieces fell more or
less slowly, according to their size, which was in no case
above a very restricted one. I distinctly remember a piece
of her cheek, with some lip attached, hanging on the corner of the mantelpiece. Nikolai Vassilevitch stared at me
like a madman. Then he pulled himself together and, once
more with furious determination, he began carefully to

collect those poor rags which once had been the shining
skin of Caracas, and all of her.

"Good-by, Caracas," I thought I heard him murmur,
'Good-by! You were too pitiable!" And then suddenly and
quite audibly: "The fire! The fire! She too must end up in
the fire." He crossed himself—with his left hand, of course.
Then, when he had picked up all those shriveled rags,
even climbing on the furniture so as not to miss any, he
threw them straight on the fire in the hearth, where they
began to burn slowly and with an excessively unpleasant
smell. Nikolai Vassilevitch, like all Russians, had a passion for throwing important things in the fire.

Red in the face, with an inexpressible look of despair,
and yet of sinister triumph too, he gazed on the pyre of
those miserable remains. He had seized my arm and was
squeezing it convulsively But those traces of what had once
been a being were hardly well alight when he seemed yet
again to pull himself together, as if he were suddenly
remembering something or taking a painful decision. In
one bound he was out of the room.

A few seconds later I heard him speaking to me through
the door in a broken, plaintive voice: "Foma Paskalovitch,
I want you to promise not to look. *Golubchik*, promise
not to look at me when I come in."

I don't know what I answered, or whether I tried to
reassure him in any way. But he insisted, and I had to
promise him, as if he were a child, to hide my face
against the wall and only turn round when he said I might.
The door then opened violently and Nikolai Vassilevitch
burst into the room and ran to the fireplace.

And here I must confess my weakness, though I consider it justified by the extraordinary circumstances. I
looked round before Nikolai Vassilevitch told me I could;
it was stronger than me. I was just in time to see him
carrying something in his arms, something which he
threw on the fire with all the rest, so that it suddenly flared
up. At that, since the desire to *see* had entirely mastered
every other thought in me, I dashed to the fireplace. But
Nikolai Vassilevitch placed himself between me and it
and pushed me back with a strength of which I had not
believed him capable. Meanwhile the object was burning
and giving off clouds of smoke. And before he showed

any sign of calming down there was nothing left but a heap of silent ashes.

The true reason why I wished to see was because I had already glimpsed. But it was only a glimpse, and perhaps I should not allow myself to introduce even the slightest element of uncertainty into this true story. And yet, an eyewitness account is not complete without a mention of that which the witness knows with less than complete certainty. To cut a long story short, that something was a baby. Not a flesh and blood baby, of course, but more something in the line of a rubber doll or a model. Something, which, to judge by its appearance, could have been called *Caracas' son.*

Was I mad too? That I do not know, but I do know that this was what I saw, not clearly, but with my own eyes. And I wonder why it was that when I was writing this just now I didn't mention that when Nikolai Vassilevitch came back into the room he was muttering between his clenched teeth: "Him too! Him too!"

And that is the sum of my knowledge of Nikolai Vassilevitch's wife. In the next chapter I shall tell what happened to him afterwards, and that will be the last chapter of his life. But to give an interpretation of his feelings for his wife, or indeed for any thing, is quite another and more difficult matter, though I have attempted it elsewhere in this volume, and refer the reader to that modest effort. I hope I have thrown sufficient light on a most controversial question and that I have unveiled the mystery, if not of Gogol, then at least of his wife. In the course of this I have implicitly given the lie to the insensate accusation that he ill-treated or even beat his wife, as well as other like absurdities. And what else can be the goal of a humble biographer such as the present writer but to serve the memory of that lofty genius who is the object of his study?

Translated from the Italian
by Wayland Young

Blue Notebook No. 10

by Daniil Kharms

There was once a red-haired man who had no eyes and no ears. He also had no hair, so he was called red-haired only in a manner of speaking.

He wasn't able to talk, because he didn't have a mouth. He had no nose, either.

He didn't even have any arms or legs. He also didn't have a stomach, and he didn't have a back, and he didn't have a spine, and he also didn't have any other insides. He didn't have anything. So it's hard to understand whom we're talking about.

So we'd better not talk about him any more.

Translated from the Russian
by George Gibian

A Sonnet

by *Daniil Kharms*

An amazing thing happened to me: I suddenly forgot which came first, 7 or 8.

I went to my neighbors and asked them what they thought about that.

I was really amazed when they told me that they too couldn't remember the counting sequence. They remembered 1, 2, 3, 4, 5, and 6, but they forgot what came after that.

We all went into the grocery store at the corner of Znamensky and Basseynaya streets and asked the cashier. The cashier smiled sadly, took a tiny little hammer out of her mouth, and slightly twitching her nose, said, "I think 7 comes after 8 in those cases when 8 comes after 7."

We thanked the cashier and ran joyfully out of the store. But then, thinking over the cashier's words, we again fell silent, because her words turned out to make no sense.

What were we to do? We went into the summer park and counted trees. But after we reached 6, we stopped and argued. Some thought 7 came next, and others that 8 came next.

We argued for a long time, but fortunately a little boy fell off a park bench and broke both jaws. This distracted us from our argument.

Then we all went home.

Translated from the Russian
by George Gibian

The Connection
by Daniil Kharms

Philosopher!

1. I am writing to you in answer to your letter which you are about to write to me in answer to my letter which I wrote to you.

2. A violinist bought a magnet and was carrying it home. Along the way, hoods jumped him and knocked his cap off his head. The wind picked up the cap and carried it down the street.

3. The violinist put the magnet down and ran after the cap. The cap fell into a puddle of nitric acid and dissolved.

4. In the meantime, the hoods picked up the magnet and hid.

5. The violinist returned home without a coat and without a cap, because the cap had dissolved in the nitric acid, and the violinist, upset by losing his cap, had left his coat in the streetcar.

6. The conductor of the streetcar took the coat to a secondhand shop and exchanged it there for sour cream, groats, and tomatoes.

7. The conductor's father-in-law ate too many tomatoes, became sick, and died. The corpse of the conductor's father-in-law was put in the morgue, but it got mixed up, and in place of the conductor's father-in-law, they buried some old woman.

8. On the grave of the old woman, they put a white post with the inscription "Anton Sergeevich Kondratev."

9. Eleven years later, the worms had eaten through the post, and it fell down. The cemetery watchman sawed the post into four pieces and burned it in his stove. The wife of the cemetery watchman cooked cauliflower soup over that fire.

10. But when the soup was ready, a fly fell from the wall, directly into the pot with this soup. They gave the soup to the beggar Timofey.

11. The beggar Timofey ate the soup and told the beggar Nikolay that the cemetery watchman was a good-natured man.

12. The next day the beggar Nikolay went to the cemetery watchman and asked for money. But the cemetery watchman gave nothing to the beggar Nikolay and chased him away.

13. The beggar Nikolay became very angry and set fire to the cemetery watchman's house.

14. The fire spread from the house to the church, and the church burned down.

15. A long investigation was carried on but did not succeed in determining the cause of the fire.

16. In the place where the church had stood a club was built, and on the day the club opened a concert was organized, at which the violinist who fourteen years earlier had lost his coat performed.

17. In the audience sat the son of one of those hoods who fourteen years before had knocked the cap off that violinist.

18. After the concert was over, they rode home in the same streetcar. In the streetcar behind theirs the driver was the same conductor who once upon a time had sold the violinist's coat in a secondhand shop.

Translated from the Russian
by George Gibian

Dulcinea del Toboso

by *Marco Denevi*

She read so many novels that she ended up losing her mind. She had people call her Dulcinea del Toboso (her name was really Aldonza Lorenza), she thought she was a princess (she was a peasant's daughter), she imagined herself as young and beautiful (she was forty years old and her face was scarred by smallpox). Finally, she invented a lover for herself to whom she gave the name don Quixote de la Mancha. She said that don Quixote had departed for far away kingdoms in search of adventures and danger, both to perform worthy deeds and to be able, on his return, to marry a damsel of her noble character. She spent all her time peering out the window waiting for the return of the nonexistent knight. Alonso Quijano, a poor devil who loved her, struck on the idea of passing himself off as don Quixote. He put on an old suit of armor, mounted his nag, and set forth to repeat the deeds which Dulcinea attributed to her lover. When sure of the success of his strategy, he returned to Toboso; Dulcinea had died.

Translated from the Spanish
by Susan Herman Price

Antimatter
by *Russell Edson*

On the other side of a mirror there's an inverse world, where the insane go sane; where bones climb out of the earth and recede to the first slime of love.

And in the evening the sun is just rising.

Lovers cry because they are a day younger, and soon childhood robs them of their pleasure.

In such a world there is much sadness which, of course, is joy . . .

A Man Who Writes
by *Russell Edson*

A man had written *head* on his forehead, and *hand* on each hand, and *foot* on each foot.

His father said, stop stop stop, because the redundancy is like having two sons, which is two sons too many, as in the first instance which is one son too many.

The man said, may I write *father* on father?

Yes, said father, because one father is tired of bearing it all alone.

Mother said, I'm leaving if all these people come to dinner.

But the man wrote *dinner* all over the dinner.

When dinner was over father said to his son, will you write *belch* on my belch?

The man said, I will write *God bless everyone* on God.

The Tower
by *Enrique Anderson Imbert*

Solness proposed this time to build the highest tower in the world, at whose mast would wave the green flag of our planet in its rotations before the box seats of the galaxy.

It was necessary to dig an abyss and fix into the spongy insides of the earth a foundation that would support the weight.

With workmen and cranes he burrowed down like a mole; and his ambition kept pushing him toward the antipodes. At each new depth he would imagine that the lookout of the skyscraper would rise nearer to the stars; and the stars he could now see from below at all hours, jumping with agile feet over the opening.

And in that gloomy niche and with the smell of firedamp they all died, at the top of an upside-down tower, lustrous as seeds.

Translated from the Spanish
by Isabel Reade

The Suicide

by *Enrique Anderson Imbert*

At the foot of the open Bible—where was marked in red the verse that would explain everything—he aligned the letters: to his wife, to the judge, to his friends. Then he drank the poison and went to bed.

Nothing. In an hour he got up and looked at the bottle. Yes, it was the poison. He was so sure! He increased the dosage and drank another glass. He went back to bed. Another hour. He was not dying. Then he shot his revolver against his temple. What joke was this? Someone— but who, when?—someone had exchanged his poison for water, his bullets for blank cartridges. He shot the four other bullets against his temple. Useless. He closed the Bible, gathered up the letters and went out of the room just as the owner of the hotel, servants and curious people were running up, alarmed at the noise of the five shots.

Arriving at his house he found his wife poisoned and his five children on the floor, each with a bullet wound in the temple.

He took the kitchen knife, bared his stomach and began slashing at himself. The blade would sink into the soft flesh and then come out clean as water, and the flesh would regain its smoothness like water after a fish is caught.

He poured naphtha over his clothes and the matches would go out hissing.

He ran to the balcony, and before jumping he could see a crowd of men and women lying in the street, bleeding from their knifed stomachs, amid the flames of the burning city.

Translated from the Spanish
by Isabel Reade

Punishing the Guest
by Reinhard Lettau

For several weeks the guest had kept them waiting in vain for his arrival. The spacious house was ready to receive him, the bed in the sumptuous guest suite had been made up with the finest linen, flowers had been put in vases, the kitchen was filled with an aroma of salads mixed by expert hands, but the guest wasn't arriving. The first hours of unfulfilled expectation were the most painful—at what point could they be sure that the guest was no longer arriving? He was coming from afar and had announced his arrival for an indefinite hour that afternoon.

Since then, well-composed cables had postponed his arrival from day to day. His explanations grew more substantial, the words were more and more carefully chosen, and when a superbly phrased excuse arrived on the morning of the third day, they had to admit secretly that these cables made the guest's delays almost fascinating. Each time a new arrival drew near, they surprised themselves thinking that a new wire would be preferable to the mere arrival of the guest himself, because the reasons for his delays were so varied and unexpected that all soon began to say that the guest's actual arrival would have come as an anticlimax.

Obviously the daily recurrence of fruitless waiting, that would drop to zero only to rise again telegraphically, disturbed the order of the household. It was especially painful when a new cable delayed the arrival for a couple of hours or half a day, and all preparations had to be halted, or at least interrupted. The hosts had to resort to hasty interim arrangements and often a new wire resetting the guest's announced arrival would throw them into utmost excitement. At that point, the salads, that the previous cable had threatened with wilting, had been devoured, the

silver trays had been stacked away, the house wasn't ready
any more. It's not surprising that, after a week, the possibility of the guest's failing to arrive was included in the
preparations for his arrival. The periodical preparation for
the guest's possible non-arrival required a different set-up.
Much had to be taken into consideration and planned for,
but there was one other alternative: to keep the house in
a state of permanent readiness. But in order to achieve
this, the hosts would have had to leave their house, keep-
ing it untouched by the changing course of events, and
watch the guest's actual arrival, perhaps from a neighboring house—their ready house in constant view.

The hosts' mood turned sour when they realized that
the guest had kept them waiting for two weeks. At first,
the constant announcements of his arrival for the next
day or the next hour might have given an impression of
optimism; but by now there was little doubt that the clas-
sical period of his cable-literature was apparently over.
On the seventeenth day, toward noon, they received a
cable: "Arriving immediately," and spontaneously invited
by telephone all the friends and neighbors who had been
supposed to be present at the reception of the guest from
the start. Together with the neighbors and friends a tele-
graph boy arrived at the house, delivering a threadbare
epic by the once-again-not-arriving visitor.

The friends entered the house, chatting loudly in expectation of the guest. This splendid summer day was certainly deserving of praise, they remarked, and walked
straight through the house into the garden. Here they
stood together on tender strips of lawn, lauding their host's
horticultural talents. Nothing, they cried, could spoil their
mood, nor did they manifest any disappointment when
their host proceeded to read them the just-received cable
—on the contrary: they immediately wanted all the pre-
ceding messages read to them as well. This was done, and
great hilarity broke out when they discovered that the
twelfth telegram from the vainly awaited guest had been
sent from a town nearby, that the guest must therefore
have passed through the area, whereas his most recent
messages had come from Hammerfest.

The idea to play at arrival-of-the-guest came from Mrs.
Saatmantel, a voluminous widow. It was applauded by all
and Theodore, the oldest son of the house, jumped from

a kitchen window, tiptoed around the driver's box and mounted a rented vehicle that transported him in no time in front of the parental house. A servant opened the carriage door for him; waving a weary left hand toward the house, he handed the servant an impressive tip. On the terrace he was embraced and introduced all around. He gave lengthy accounts of the unpleasantness of his delays, drank a number of highballs, and in the general gaiety no one paid particular attention to the fact that the real guest, a Mr. Flugbeil, had actually arrived in the meantime and was standing among the servants. When Flugbeil had reached the house shortly after Theodore, well-informed friends had dragged him into the cellar and clad him in butler's livery. To this day he is serving with zeal, although he's been known to turn pale occasionally when there is talk of a guest arriving.

Translated from the German
by Ursule Molinaro

from *Steps*
by *Jerzy Kosinski*

There were several of us, all archeological assistants, working on one of the islands with a professor who for years had been excavating remnants of an ancient civilization that had flourished fifteen centuries before our era.

It was an advanced civilization, the professor claimed, but at some point a massive catastrophe had wiped it out. He had challenged the prevailing theory that a disastrous earthquake, followed by a tidal wave, had struck the island. We were collecting fragments of pottery, sifting through ashes for the remains of artifacts, and unearthing building materials, all of which the professor catalogued as evidence to support his as yet unpublished work.

After a month I decided to leave the excavations and visit a neighboring island. In my haste to catch the ferry I left without my paycheck, but I obtained the promise that it would be forwarded on the next mail skiff. I could live for one day on the money I had with me.

After arriving I spent the entire day sightseeing. The island was dominated by a dormant volcano, its broad slopes covered with porous lava rock, weathered to form a poor but arable soil.

I walked down to the harbor; an hour before sunset, when the air was cooling, the fishing boats put out for the night. I watched them slide over the calm, almost waveless water until their long, low forms vanished from sight. The islands suddenly lost the light reflected from their rocky spines and grew stark and black. And then, as though drawn silently beneath the surface, they disappeared one by one.

On the morning of the second day I went down to the quay to meet the mail skiff. To my consternation my paycheck had not arrived. I stood on the dock, wondering

how I was going to live and whether I would even be able
to leave the island. A few fishermen sat by their nets,
watching me; they sensed that something was wrong.
Three of them approached and spoke to me. Not understanding, I replied in the two languages I knew: their
faces became sullen and hostile, and they abruptly turned
away. That evening I took my sleeping bag down to the
beach and slept on the sand.

In the morning I spent the last of my money on a cup
of coffee. After strolling up the winding streets behind the
port, I walked through the scrubby fields to the nearest
village. The villagers sat in the shade, covertly watching
me. Hungry and thirsty, I returned to the beach again,
walking beneath a blazing sun. I had nothing to barter for
food or money: no watch, no fountain pen, no cuff links,
no camera, no wallet. At noon, when the sun stood high
and the villagers sheltered in their cottges, I went to the
police station. I found the island's solitary policeman doz-
ing by the telephone. I woke him, but he seemed reluctant
to understand even my simplest gesture. I pointed to his
phone, pulling out my empty pockets; I made signs and
drew pictures, even miming thirst and hunger. All this
had no effect: the policeman showed neither interest nor
understanding, and the phone remained locked. It was
the only one on the island; the guidebook I had read had
even bothered to note the fact.

In the afternoon I strolled around the village, smiling
at the inhabitants, hoping to be offered a drink or to be
invited to a meal. No one returned my greeting; the villagers turned away and the storekeepers simply ignored
me. The church was on the largest island of the group
and I had no means of getting there to ask for food and
shelter. I returned to the beach as if expecting help to
rise up from the sea. I was famished and exhausted. The
sun had brought on a pounding headache, I felt waves of
vertigo. Unexpectedly I caught the sound of people talking
in an alien language. Turning, I saw two women sitting
close to the water. Folds of gray, heavily veined fat hung
from their thighs and upper arms; their full, pendulous
breasts were squashed in outsize brassieres.

They sunbathed sprawling on their beach towels surrounded by picnic equipment: food baskets, thermos flasks,
parasols, and nets full of fruit. A pile of books, heaped up

alongside, conspicuously displayed library numbers. They were evidently tourists staying with a local family. I approached them slowly but directly, anxious not to alarm them. They stopped talking, and I greeted them smilingly, using my languages in turn. They replied in another one. We had no common language, but I was very conscious of the proximity of food. I sat down beside them as though I had understood I had been invited. When they began to eat I eyed the food; they either did not notice this or ignored my intense stare. After a few minutes the woman I judged to be the older offered me an apple. I ate it slowly, trying to conceal my hunger and hoping for something more solid. They watched me intently.

It was hot on the beach and I dozed off. But I woke when the two women pulled themselves to their feet, their shoulders and back red from the sun. Rivulets of perspiration streaked the sand that clung to their flabby thighs, the fat slid over their hips as they braced themselves to stoop and collect their belongings. I helped them. With flirtatious nods they set off along the inner rim of the beach; I followed.

We reached the house they occupied. On entering I was hit by another wave of vertigo; I stumbled on a step and collapsed. Laughing and chattering, the women undressed me and maneuvered me onto a large, low bed. Still dazed, I pointed to my stomach. There was no delay: they rushed to bring me meat, fruit, and milk. Before I could finish the meal, they had drawn the curtains and torn off their bathing suits. Naked, they fell upon me. I was buried beneath their heavy bellies and broad backs; my arms were pinioned; my body was manipulated, squeezed, pressed, and thumped.

I was at the dock at dawn. The mail skiff came in, but there was neither a check nor a letter for me. I stood there watching the boat recede into the hot sun that dissolved the morning mist, revealing one by one the distant islands.

65

The Imperishable Container
of All Current Pasts

by Marvin Cohen

I discover, in my girl, layers and layers of mineral deposits, archaeological strata from her encounters with previous men. These physically encumber my right of entry, and I ask her why she collects such outworn trophies. She sighs, and says, "I venerate the past. It has such masculine endurance."

"All fine and well," I agree, "but it impedes me. See, I'm left in the cold. How can I force my way in?" "Push harder," she suggests. But ah, so many things in the way! They thwart my active principle, and I say, "I'll remain outside, where the space is cleared of insurmountable obstacles." "Very well," she agrees, and extracts from her shrine a sample of the accumulated debris, which she examines with both hands. "That was Harry," she says, sighing with fond remembrance. How loyal she is to the ghastly vigor of traditional emblems kept forever in her museum of private erotica! Yet, at all hours, she's open to the public. The crowd is uncontrollable, and traffic regulations must be put into effect. Coming and going pedestrians stumble upon the remnants of their timeless ancestors, in her legend of impure, but popular, precedence.

The clutter doesn't discourage visitors. They leave their calling cards, and are filed in that amazing perservative. She's a conservatory, where the past bulges with immense lingerings. Additions are daily recorded, to stagger an impotent future. The world overfills itself, and teems with fertile overgrowth. She's due for an internal cleansing, to sweep clear the dated and admit the endless present. Let her restore her storage to the flow of successive newness. Then movement is possible, and a vital avenue of penetration.

"Try again," she implores. I strain, and then plunge into the dizzy totality of historical disorder; it's like building a housing project on a monumental cemetery whose inhabitants, according to the latest fossil explorations, belong bonily to each epoch of retreating phases ranging to the evolutionary source itself, when living forms, squirming out of mud, oozed at the sight of my girl and first settled into her ample beginnings, which were to accommodate, in her mania for collecting, all subsequent species.

I'm the latest, but by no means the last. She ages only into an enlarged youth: the capacious wholeness of her widening warehouse is that interior female to unlimited containment. Nothing, once in, goes out whole again; and what remains is for the ages.

from *Alaap*

by *Krishna Baldev Vaid*

One night I saw a warm naked corpse lying next to me. I was pleased. It was a fresh and beautiful corpse. I wasn't afraid of it. Every night I sleep alone. My luck has taken a turn tonight.

The moon peeping through the window was my friend.

I hugged my corpse hard. I kissed her eyes, her lips, her nipples. Again and again. I caressed her hair, massaged her thighs, kneaded every inch of her body. Again and again. I did all that a healthy man can do with a dead body. Again and again.

Next morning when I woke up there was no naked corpse next to me. Instead there was a stale woman fully clothed. What possessed you last night, she asked.

I was so surprised and enraged that my teeth disappeared.

I closed my eyes and turned away from her. For a long time I lay there dead. When I got up my mirror was there taunting me.

If I had teeth I might have laughed.

Translated from the Hindi
by the author

The Motorcycle Social Club
by *Kirby Congdon*

After a run, we all meet at the Club—those of us who haven't broken down, dropped their bikes, or gotten hurt, injured or killed. We play pool and drink, and move in even strides about the room, showing off the thick backs of our curving thighs, gleaming where the black leather stretches tight. We spend the evening sending messages— flowers, emergency telegrams and time-bombs—with our eyes. When we pair off, we are casual and conceal the excitement we feel at our public but silent commitment to destruction. The veteran members disappear one by one to recover in hometowns, or to wait in hospitals or graves. But the membership grows, though the initiations become more stringent. The local people laugh nervously at our public image, or they ask, Where will it all end? But the game, underneath, is serious and there is no end. In the land of plenty, death grows, fertilized and lush. And we get drunk on the habit-forming perfumes of its secret and majestic, its black and addictive blooms, and each flower broken off sheds a glittering shower of hard new seeds. There's the fascination. To join the Club is difficult; to be a member is final and permanent. Meanwhile, as we wait for our own last night, we drink and play pool.

The Japanese Stonecutter
by *Multatuli*

There was once a man who hewed stones from the rock. His labor was very hard, and he labored much, but his wages were slight and he was not content.

He sighed because his labor was hard, and he cried: Oh, I wish I were rich so I could rest on a couch with a cover of silk.

And an angel came from heaven, saying: You are what you have said.

And he was rich. And he did rest on a couch and the cover was of silk.

And the king of the land went by, with horsemen in front of his carriage. And behind the carriage there were also horsemen and a golden parasol was held over the head of the king.

And when the rich man saw this he was vexed that no golden parasol was held over his own head. And he was not content.

He sighed and cried: I wish to be king.

And an angel came from heaven, saying: You are what you have said.

And he was king. And many horsemen rode in front of his carriage, and there were also horsemen behind his carriage, and a golden parasol was held over his head.

And the sun shone hot rays and scorched the earth so that the grass shoots withered.

And the king complained that the sun burnt his face and that it excelled him in power. And he was not content.

He sighed and cried: I wish to be the sun.

And an angel came from heaven, saying: You are what you have said.

And he was the sun. And he directed his rays upward and down, to the right and to the left, everywhere. And he scorched the grass shoots on earth and the countenances of kings who were on earth.

And a cloud placed itself between him and the earth, and the rays of the sun bounced back from it.

And he grew wroth that his power was resisted and he complained that the cloud excelled him in power. And he was not content.

He wished to be the cloud which was so powerful.

And an angel came from heaven, saying: You are what you have said.

And he became a cloud and placed himself between the sun and the earth, and caught the rays so that the grass grew green.

And the cloud rained large drops on the earth, causing the rivers to swell and floods to carry the herds away.

And he destroyed the fields with much water.

And he fell upon a rock which did not yield. And he splashed in great streams, but the rock did not yield.

And he grew wroth because the rock would not yield and the power of his streams was in vain. And he was not content.

He cried: That rock has been given power which excels mine. I wish to be that rock.

And an angel came from heaven, saying: You are what you have said.

And he did become rock and did not move when the sun shone nor when it rained.

And then there came a man with a pick and with a chisel and with a heavy hammer and he hewed stones out of the rock.

And the rock said: How can it be that this man has power that excels mine and hews stones out of my lap? And he was not content.

He cried: I am weaker than he. . . . I wish to be that man.

And an angel came from heaven, saying: You are what you have said.

And he was a stone cutter. And he hewed stones from the rock, with hard labor, and he labored very hard for small wages, and he was content.

Translated from the Dutch
by E. M. Beekman

69

Feeding the Hungry
by Roland Topor

You're bound to think I'm a liar: but I've never felt hungry. I don't know what hunger means. As far back as I can remember I've never known what it was like. I eat, of course, but without appetite. I feel absolutely nothing, not even distaste. I just eat.

People often ask me, 'How do you manage to eat, then?' I have to admit that I don't know. What happens usually is that I'm sitting at a table and there's a plateful of food in front of me. Since I'm rather absent-minded I very soon forget about it. When I think about it again, the plate is empty. That's what happens.

Does this mean that I eat under hypnosis, in some kind of dissociated state? Certainly not. I said that this is what usually happens. But not always. Sometimes I remember the plate of food in front of me. But that doesn't stop me from emptying it all the same.

Naturally, I've tried fasting. But that didn't work. I got thinner and thinner. I gave up just in time. A little longer and I would have died of hunger without knowing it. This experience frightened me so much that I now eat all the time. That way I don't worry. I'm tall and strong, and I have to keep the machine going. For other people, hunger provides a warning; since I am deprived of it I have to be doubly careful. As I said earlier, I'm absent-minded. To forget would be fatal. I prefer to eat all the time: it's safer. I realize too that when I don't eat I become nervous and irritable, and don't know what to do about it. Instead, I smoke too much and drink too much, which is bad.

In the street I am frequently accosted by gaunt men dressed in rags. They gaze at me with fever-bright eyes and stammer out, 'We're hungry!' I look at them with hatred. They eat only a crust of dry bread once a month, if that, but they enjoy it. 'Hungry, are you?' I say to them nastily. 'You're lucky.'

Sobs rattle in their throats. Shudders wrack them. Eventually they move off with slow, hesitant steps. As for me, I go into the first restaurant I see. Will the miracle occur? My heart beats fast as I swallow the first mouthful. A terrible despair overwhelms me. Nothing. Nothing at all. No appetite. I take my revenge by eating furiously, like someone drowning their sorrow in drink.

I leave the restaurant weighed down with food and hatred. For I'm becoming bitter. I'm beginning to detest other people, people who are hungry. I hate them. So they're hungry, are they? I hope they die of hunger! I shan't be sorry for them! After all, thinking about people who are hungry while I'm eating is the only pleasure left to me.

Translated from the French
by Margaret Crosland and David LeVay

70

How Wang-Fo Was Saved

by *Marguerite Yourcenar*

The old painter Wang-Fo and his disciple Ling were wandering along the roads of the Kingdom of Han.

They made slow progress because Wang-Fo would stop at night to watch the stars and during the day to observe the dragonflies. They carried hardly any luggage, because Wang-Fo loved the image of things and not the things themselves, and no object in the world seemed to him worth buying, except brushes, pots of lacquer and China ink, and rolls of silk and rice paper. They were poor, because Wang-Fo would exchange his paintings for a ration of boiled millet, and paid no attention to pieces of silver. Ling, his disciple, bent beneath the weight of a sack full of sketches, bowed his back with respect as if he were carrying the heavens' vault, because for Ling the sack was full of snow-covered mountains, torrents in spring, and the face of the summer moon.

Ling had not been born to trot down the roads, following an old man who seized the dawn and captured the dusk. His father had been a banker who dealt in gold, his mother the only child of a jade merchant who had left her all his worldly possessions, cursing her for not being a son. Ling had grown up in a house where wealth made him shy: he was afraid of insects, of thunder and the face of the dead. When Ling was fifteen, his father chose a bride for him, a very beautiful one because the thought of the happiness he was giving his son consoled him for having reached the age in which the night is meant for sleep. Ling's wife was as frail as a reed, childish as milk, sweet as saliva, salty as tears. After the wedding, Ling's parents became discreet to the point of dying, and their son was left alone in a house painted vermilion, in the company of his young wife who never stopped smiling and a plum tree that blossomed every spring with pale-pink flowers. Ling loved this woman of a crystal-clear heart as one loves a mirror that will never tarnish, or a talisman that will protect one forever. He visited the teahouses to follow the dictates of fashion, and only moderately favored acrobats and dancers.

One night, in the tavern, Wang-Fo shared Ling's table. The old man had been drinking in order to better paint a drunkard, and he cocked his head to one side as if trying to measure the distance between his hand and his bowl. The rice wine undid the tongue of the taciturn craftsman, and that night Wang spoke as if silence were a wall and words the colors with which to cover it. Thanks to him, Ling got to know the beauty of the drunkards' faces blurred by the vapors of hot drink, the brown splendor of the roasts unevenly brushed by tongues of fire, and the exquisite blush of wine stains strewn on the tablecloths like withered petals. A gust of wind broke the window: the downpour entered the room. Wang-Fo leaned out to make Ling admire the livid zebra stripes of lightning, and Ling, spellbound, stopped being afraid of storms.

Ling paid the old painter's bill, and as Wang-Fo was both without money and without lodging, he humbly offered him a resting place. They walked away together; Ling held a lamp whose light projected unexpected fires in the puddles. That evening, Ling discovered with surprise that the walls of his house were not red, as he had always thought, but the color of an almost rotten orange. In the courtyard, Wang-Fo noticed the delicate shape of a bush to which no one had paid any attention until then, and compared it to a young woman letting down her hair to dry. In the passageway, he followed with delight the hesitant trail of an ant along the cracks in the wall, and Ling's horror of these creatures vanished into thin air. Realizing that Wang-Fo had just presented him with the gift of a new soul and a new vision of the world, Ling respectfully offered the old man the room in which his father and mother had died.

For many years now, Wang-Fo had dreamed of painting the portrait of a princess of olden days playing the lute under a willow. No woman was sufficiently unreal to be his model, but Ling would do because he was not a woman. Then Wang-Fo spoke of painting a young prince shooting an arrow at the foot of a large cedar tree. No young man of the present was sufficiently unreal to serve as his model, but Ling got his own wife to pose under the plum tree in the garden. Later on, Wang-Fo painted her in a fairy costume against the clouds of twilight, and the young woman wept because it was an omen of death. As Ling came to prefer the portraits painted by Wang-Fo to the young woman herself, her face began to fade, like a flower exposed to warm winds and summer rains. One morning, they found her hanging from the branches of the pink plum tree: the ends of the scarf that was strangling her floated in the wind, entangled with her hair. She looked even more delicate than usual, and as pure as the beauties celebrated by the poets of days gone by. Wang-Fo painted her one last time, because he loved the green hue that suffuses the face of the dead. His disciple Ling mixed the colors and the task needed such concentration that he forgot to shed tears.

One after the other, Ling sold his slaves, his jades, and the fish in his pond to buy his master pots of purple ink that came from the West. When the house was emptied, they left it, and Ling closed the door of his past behind him. Wang-Fo felt weary of a city where the faces could no longer teach him secrets of ugliness or beauty, and the master and his disciple walked away together down the roads of the Kingdom of Han.

Their reputation preceded them into the villages, to the gateway of fortresses, and into the atrium of temples where restless pilgrims halt at dusk. It was murmured that Wang-Fo had the power to bring his paintings to life by adding a last touch of color to their eyes. Farmers would come and beg him to paint a watchdog, and the lords would ask him for portraits of their best warriors. The priests honored Wang-Fo as a sage; the people feared him as a sorcerer. Wang enjoyed these differences of opinion which gave him the chance to study expressions of gratitude, fear, and veneration.

Ling begged for food, watched over his master's rest, and took advantage of the old man's raptures to massage his feet. With the first rays of the sun, when the old man was still asleep, Ling went in pursuit of timid landscapes hidden behind bunches of reeds. In the evening, when the master, disheartened, threw down his brushes, he would carefully pick them up. When Wang became sad and spoke of his old age, Ling would smile and show him the solid trunk of an old oak; when Wang felt happy and made jokes, Ling would humbly pretend to listen.

One day, at sunset, they reached the outskirts of the Imperial City and Ling sought out and found an inn in which Wang-Fo could spend the night. The old man wrapped himself up in rags, and Ling lay down next to him to keep him warm because spring had only just begun and the floor of beaten earth was still frozen. At dawn, heavy steps echoed in the corridors of the inn; they heard the frightened whispers of the innkeeper and orders

shouted in a foreign, barbaric tongue. Ling trembled, remembering
that the night before, he had stolen a rice cake for his master's
supper. Certain that they would come to take him to prison, he
asked himself who would help Wang-Fo ford the next river on
the following day.

The soldiers entered carrying lanterns. The flames gleaming
through the motley paper cast red and blue lights on their leather
helmets. The string of a bow quivered over their shoulders, and
the fiercest among them suddenly let out a roar for no reason at
all. A heavy hand fell on Wang-Fo's neck, and the painter could
not help noticing that the soldiers' sleeves did not match the
color of their coats.

Helped by his disciple, Wang-Fo followed the soldiers, stum-
bling along uneven roads. The passing crowds made fun of these
two criminals who were certainly going to be beheaded. The
soldiers answered Wang's questions with savage scowls. His
bound hands hurt him, and Ling in despair looked smiling at his
master, which for him was a gentler way of crying.

They reached the threshold of the Imperial Palace, whose
purple walls rose in broad daylight like a sweep of sunset. The
soldiers led Wang-Fo through countless square and circular
rooms whose shapes symbolized the seasons, the cardinal points,
the male and the female, longevity, and the prerogatives of
power. The doors swung on their hinges with a musical note,
and were placed in such a manner that one followed the entire
scale when crossing the palace from east to west. Everything
combined to give an impression of superhuman power and
subtlety, and one could feel that here the simplest orders were as
final and as terrible as the wisdom of the ancients. At last, the
air became thin and the silence so deep that not even a man
under torture would have dared to scream. A eunuch lifted a
tapestry; the soldiers began to tremble like women, and the
small troop entered the chamber in which the Son of Heaven sat
on a high throne.

It was a room without walls, held up by thick columns of blue
stone. A garden spread out on the far side of the marble shafts,
and each and every flower blooming in the greenery belonged to
a rare species brought here from across the oceans. But none of
them had any perfume, so that the Celestial Dragon's meditations would not be troubled by fine smells. Out of respect for the
silence in which his thoughts evolved, no bird had been allowed
within the enclosure, and even the bees had been driven away.
An enormous wall separated the garden from the rest of the

world, so that the wind that sweeps over dead dogs and corpses
on the battlefield would not dare brush the Emperor's sleeve.

The Celestial Master sat on a throne of jade, and his hands
were wrinkled like those of an old man, though he had scarcely
reached the age of twenty. His robe was blue to symbolize
winter, and green to remind one of spring. His face was
beautiful but blank, like a looking glass placed too high,
reflecting nothing except the stars and the immutable heavens.
To his right stood his Minister of Perfect Pleasures, and to his
left his Counselor of Just Torments. Because his courtiers, lined
along the base of the columns, always lent a keen ear to the
slightest sound from his lips, he had adopted the habit of
speaking in a low voice.

"Celestial Dragon," said Wang-Fo, bowing low, "I am old, I
am poor, I am weak. You are like summer; I am like winter. You
have Ten Thousand Lives; I have but one, and it is near its
close. What have I done to you? My hands have been tied, these
hands that never harmed you."

"You ask what you have done to me, old Wang-Fo?" said the
Emperor.

His voice was so melodious that it made one want to cry. He
raised his right hand, to which the reflections from the jade
pavement gave a pale sea-green hue like that of an underwater
plant, and Wang-Fo marveled at the length of those thin fingers,
and hunted among his memories to discover whether he had not
at some time painted a mediocre portrait of either the Emperor
or one of his ancestors that would not merit a sentence of death.
But it seemed unlikely because Wang-Fo had not been an
assiduous visitor at the Imperial Court. He preferred the farmers'
huts or, in the cities, the courtesans' quarters and the taverns
along the harbor where the dockers liked to quarrel.

"You ask me what it is you have done, old Wang-Fo?"
repeated the Emperor, inclining his slender neck toward the old
man waiting attentively. "I will tell you. But, as another man's
poison cannot enter our veins except through our nine openings,
in order to show you your offenses I must take you with me
down the corridors of my memory and tell you the story of my
life. My father had assembled a collection of your work and
hidden it in the most secret chamber in the palace, because he
judged that the people in your paintings should be concealed
from the world since they cannot lower their eyes in the
presence of profane viewers. It was in those same rooms that I
was brought up, old Wang-Fo, surrounded by solitude. To

prevent my innocence from being sullied by other human souls, the restless crowd of my future subjects had been driven away from me, and no one was allowed to pass my threshold, for fear that his or her shadow would stretch out and touch me. The few aged servants that were placed in my service showed themselves as little as possible; the hours turned in circles; the colors of your paintings bloomed in the first hours of the morning and grew pale at dusk. At night, when I was unable to sleep, I gazed at them, and for nearly ten years I gazed at them every night. During the day, sitting on a carpet whose design I knew by heart, I dreamed of the joys the future had in store for me. I imagined the world, with the Kingdom of Han at the center, to be like the flat palm of my hand crossed by the fatal lines of the Five Rivers. Around it lay the sea in which monsters are born, and farther away the mountains that hold up the heavens. And to help me visualize these things I used your paintings. You made me believe that the sea looked like the vast sheet of water spread across your scrolls, so blue that if a stone were to fall into it, it would become a sapphire; that women opened and closed like flowers, like the creatures that come forward, pushed by the wind, along the paths of your painted gardens; and that young, slim-waisted warriors who mount guard in the fortresses along the frontier were themselves like arrows that could pierce my heart. At sixteen I saw the doors that separated me from the world open once again; I climbed onto the balcony of my palace to look at the clouds, but they were far less beautiful than those in your sunsets. I ordered my litter; bounced along roads on which I had not foreseen either mud or stones, I traveled across the provinces of the Empire without ever finding your gardens full of women like fireflies, or a woman whose body was in itself a garden. The pebbles on the beach spoiled my taste for oceans; the blood of the tortured is less red than the pomegranates in your paintings; the village vermin prevented me from seeing the beauty of the rice fields; the flesh of mortal women disgusted me like the dead meat hanging from the butcher's hook, and the coarse laughter of my soldiers made me sick. You lied, Wang-Fo, you old impostor. The world is nothing but a mass of muddled colors thrown into the void by an insane painter, and smudged by our tears. The Kingdom of Han is not the most beautiful of kingdoms, and I am not the Emperor. The only empire which is worth reigning over is that which you alone can enter, old Wang, by the road of One Thousand Curves and Ten Thousand Colors. You alone reign peacefully over mountains covered in snow that cannot melt, and over fields of daffodils that cannot die. And that is why, Wang-Fo, I have conceived a punishment for you, for you whose enchantment has filled me with disgust at everything I own, and with desire for everything I shall never possess. And in order to lock you up in the only cell from which there is no escape, I have decided to have your eyes burned out, because your eyes, Wang-Fo, are the two magic gates that open onto your kingdom. And as your hands are the two roads of ten forking paths that lead to the heart of your kingdom, I have decided to have your hands cut off. Have you understood, old Wang-Fo?''

Hearing the sentence, Ling, the disciple, tore from his belt an old knife and leaped toward the Emperor. Two guards immediately seized him. The Son of Heaven smiled and added, with a sigh: "And I also hate you, old Wang-Fo, because you have known how to make yourself beloved. Kill that dog.''

Ling jumped to one side so that his blood would not stain his master's robe. One of the soldiers lifted his sword and Ling's head fell from his neck like a cut flower. The servants carried away the remains, and Wang-Fo, in despair, admired the beautiful scarlet stain that his disciple's blood made on the green stone floor.

The Emperor made a sign and two eunuchs wiped Wang's eyes.

"Listen, old Wang-Fo,'' said the Emperor, "and dry your tears, because this is not the time to weep. Your eyes must be clear so that the little light that is left to them is not clouded by your weeping. Because it is not only the grudge I bear you that makes me desire your death; it is not only the cruelty in my heart that makes me want to see you suffer. I have other plans, old Wang-Fo. I possess among your works a remarkable painting in which the mountains, the river estuary, and the sea reflect each other, on a very small scale certainly, but with a clarity that surpasses the real landscapes themselves, like objects reflected on the walls of a metal sphere. But that painting is unfinished, Wang-Fo; your masterpiece is but a sketch. No doubt, when you began your work, sitting in a solitary valley, you noticed a passing bird, or a child running after the bird. And the bird's beak or the child's cheeks made you forget the blue eyelids of the sea. You never finished the frills of the water's cloak, or the seaweed hair of the rocks. Wang-Fo, I want you to use the few hours of light that are left to you to finish this painting, which will thus contain the final secrets amassed during your long life.

I know that your hands, about to fall, will not tremble on the silken cloth, and infinity will enter your work through those unhappy cuts. I know that your eyes, about to be put out, will discover bearings far beyond all human senses. This is my plan, old Wang-Fo, and I can force you to fulfill it. If you refuse, before blinding you, I will have all your paintings burned, and you will be like a father whose children are slaughtered and all hopes of posterity extinguished. However, believe, if you wish, that this last order stems from nothing but my kindness, because I know that the silken scroll is the only mistress you ever deigned to touch. And to offer you brushes, paints, and inks to occupy your last hours is like offering the favors of a harlot to a man condemned to death.''

Upon a sign from the Emperor's little finger, two eunuchs respectfully brought forward the unfinished scroll on which Wang-Fo had outlined the image of the sea and the sky. Wang-Fo dried his tears and smiled, because that small sketch reminded him of his youth. Everything in it spoke of a fresh new spirit which Wang-Fo could no longer claim as his, and yet something was missing from it, because when Wang had painted it he had not yet looked long enough at the mountains or at the rocks bathing their naked flanks in the sea, and he had not yet penetrated deep enough into the sadness of the evening twilight. Wang-Fo selected one of the brushes which a slave held ready for him and began spreading wide strokes of blue onto the unfinished sea. A eunuch crouched by his feet, mixing the colors; he carried out his task with little skill, and more than ever Wang-Fo lamented the loss of his disciple Ling.

Wang began by adding a touch of pink to the tip of the wing of a cloud perched on a mountain. Then he painted onto the surface of the sea a few small lines that deepened the perfect feeling of calm. The jade floor became increasingly damp, but Wang-Fo, absorbed as he was in his painting, did not seem to notice that he was working with his feet in water.

The fragile rowboat grew under the strokes of the painter's brush and now occupied the entire foreground of the silken scroll. The rhythmic sound of the oars rose suddenly in the distance, quick and eager like the beating of wings. The sound came nearer, gently filling the whole room, then ceased, and a few trembling drops appeared on the boatman's oars. The red iron intended for Wang's eyes lay extinguished on the executioner's coals. The courtiers, motionless as etiquette required, stood in water up to their shoulders, trying to lift themselves onto the tips of their toes. The water finally reached the level of the imperial heart. The silence was so deep one could have heard a tear drop.

It was Ling. He wore his everyday robe, and his right sleeve still had a hole that he had not had time to mend that morning before the soldiers' arrival. But around his neck was tied a strange red scarf.

Wang-Fo said to him softly, while he continued painting, "I thought you were dead."

"You being alive," said Ling respectfully, "how could I have died?"

And he helped his master into the boat. The jade ceiling reflected itself in the water, so that Ling seemed to be inside a cave. The pigtails of submerged courtiers rippled up toward the surface like snakes, and the pale head of the Emperor floated like a lotus.

"Look at them," said Wang-Fo sadly. "These wretches will die, if they are not dead already. I never thought there was enough water in the sea to drown an Emperor. What are we to do?"

"Master, have no fear," murmured the disciple. "They will soon be dry again and will not even remember that their sleeves were ever wet. Only the Emperor will keep in his heart a little of the bitterness of the sea. These people are not the kind to lose themselves inside a painting."

And he added: "The sea is calm, the wind high, the seabirds fly to their nests. Let us leave, Master, and sail to the land beyond the waves."

"Let us leave," said the old painter.

Wang-Fo took hold of the helm, and Ling bent over the oars. The sound of rowing filled the room again, strong and steady like the beating of a heart. The level of the water dropped unnoticed around the large vertical rocks that became columns once more. Soon only a few puddles glistened in the hollows of the jade floor. The courtiers' robes were dry, but a few wisps of foam still clung to the hem of the Emperor's cloak.

The painting finished by Wang-Fo was leaning against a tapestry. A rowboat occupied the entire foreground. It drifted away little by little, leaving behind it a thin wake that smoothed out into the quiet sea. One could no longer make out the faces of the two men sitting in the boat, but one could still see Ling's red scarf and Wang-Fo's beard waving in the breeze.

The beating of the oars grew fainter, then ceased, blotted out by the distance. The Emperor, leaning forward, a hand above his eyes, watched Wang's boat sail away till it was nothing but an imperceptible dot in the paleness of the twilight. A golden mist rose and spread over the water. Finally the boat veered around a rock that stood at the gateway to the ocean; the shadow of a cliff fell across it; its wake disappeared from the deserted surface, and the painter Wang-Fo and his disciple Ling vanished forever on the jade-blue sea that Wang-Fo had just created.

Translated from the French
by Alberto Manguel

The Tree
by *Andreas Schroeder*

He was an old man, though just how old was quite impossible to tell; he belonged to one of those aboriginal tribes whose members grow old at an early age and then seem to stop having anything to do with time at all. He was introduced to me simply as a "displacer of stones", a man who spent most of his time down at the beach lifting and replacing the jagged chunks of coral in search of whatever he could find. It was mentioned that his father had lowered the first fishing nets into the Macumba River.

He was an unperturbed old man, almost always smiling and nodding his head, trying to interest me in this or that triviality, often raising his calloused, almost black finger and delivering himself of little wisdoms which were translated to me as "People have more fun than anybody" and "In the days after the Great Heat, the heron sticks his legs into his pockets and flies elsewhere" or even the more unfathomable "In a land of little water, men weep less but take more women". Day after day I saw him wading along the beach at low tide, patiently turning over rocks, his fingers making quick darts into the water as whatever lurked beneath the stones blinked in the unaccustomed light and was caught. He dropped everything he apprehended into a smelly brown flour sack which he dragged into his hut at the end of the day, then lowered the curtain. I was never able to discover what he did with all he caught.

It was several weeks after I had met him that I was informed: "the old man has been told". At first I couldn't understand the information and no one seemed to understand my incomprehension, but eventually I discovered that the old man's death had been "officially forecast" by the tribal fortune-teller that day. After that there were no more smiles. When I saw the old man later that afternoon, his eyes gloomed and his face hung dully from his skull like his empty sack. He announced to me sadly that he would soon be turning into a tree; that the fortune-teller had divined his fate by looking at the season to come through the eyes of a dying rooster.

I asked if he knew exactly when this would occur, but he merely shook his head and muttered that "one would have to be careful where one stood from now on; one would have to be careful where one stood".

From that time on the old man became increasingly clumsy at displacing his stones; his attention was constantly divided between the water and the land and he appeared always on the verge of making a dash for the line of trees just above the beach. Whenever he stopped to talk on the trail, villagers admonished him that "that is not a good place for a tree to stand", and he would hurriedly step aside among the bushes, continuing the conversation through the branches. His main concern was that when death became imminent, he would be able to reach an advantageous place where he could continue his life in tree form with relative comfort. For this reason he rarely dared to stray farther than a quick sprint away from such a spot.

Then the days began to grow longer and the tides receded farther from the land each day. Food grew more plentiful in the village and the fishermen risked deeper and deeper forays into the ocean's belly for sponge. Now, in the afternoons, the reef lay exposed for miles in every direction, baring an ever-increasing expanse of formerly concealed and mysterious sea-life. Every day saw the capture of new, colourful and obscure monstrosities which the villagers dried and added to their constantly growing string of temple gods. Only Katunga, the old displacer of stones, crouched near his tree-line and refused to hunt. The villagers made sympathetic, sorrowful clucking noises and brought the new spirits for him to see. Each time Katunga fingered the grotesque eyes and ornate scales of each new god, his eyes glowed darkly with the longing to join the search, as a displacer of stones should do. But he held grimly on beneath the trees, turning away.

It was one or two days after the kaantung, the Hottest Day, that I woke from my afternoon sleep to a frenzied shouting and clanging of pots through the village; children screamed, footfalls thudded rapidly past my curtain toward the beach, and everywhere I heard the name "Katunga". I pushed my curtain aside, the villagers pointed excitedly toward the reef and motioned me to hurry. Far across the treacherous maze of coral I saw a scattering of people straggling toward what appeared to be an unusually tall gaunt man flailing wildly about himself with his arms and legs.

"Katunga, Katunga" the villagers shouted, and as the tall gaunt man erupted into strange, jerking convulsions on the distant reef, I began to run.

As I jumped and stumbled across coral-encrusted boulders I remember thinking angrily, why couldn't he have resisted that temptation; should've stayed near the other trees where he was safe, the damn fool, to go that far out has to be madness, and I almost rammed my foot down on a cluster of poison-filled spine coral and realized I was running much too fast for my own safety; when I looked up again he was already twice his original size.

I stopped. Katunga staggered as if jolted by enormous bursts of electricity, like a giant epileptic; what I had at first assumed to be reflections of his arms in the trembling heat were in fact many arms, some longer than others, some already very thick; his torso grew wider, heavier, rippling with straining, rebelling muscles; he was trying to run, to return, but his legs had already become too stiff to give him leverage and he tottered about until his feet entwined in the coral and anchored him fast. Above, his head disappeared in a burst of leafy green.

Now the transformation slowed, the struggle appeared resolved, the tree had asserted itself and the only movement I could still discern was the steady rising and unfolding of its crown, like the opening of a huge flower in the first rays of morning sun. A tentative breeze from the ocean riffled through the branches, swaying it slightly, and I thought for a moment I could still see Katunga trying to find more solid footing on the slippery reef, but that might have been only my imagination. By the time the first villagers arrived, they found nothing more than an implacable tree.

A dark tribesman standing next to me shook his head with a mixture of impatience and sadness. "This is not a

good thing" he muttered, looking with some anxiety at
the sky. "He has chosen a foolish place. Tonight the winds
will be angry from the west, and the tides will leap high.
He will drown."

I hooded my eyes and looked back at the strange tree of
Katunga, standing improbably where in a few hours the
ocean would return and find him there, a giant plant in a
sea-meadow, clutching grimly to the rainbow molluscs
and rubbery brain-coral underneath.

"He will be swept away" the tribesman muttered again.
"It was a foolish place, he does not know the sea; he will
be swept away."

Women Born from Trees

by Lars Gyllensten

Women were born from trees—the old people have said this—the first women grew on trees like giant white marrows. They swelled forth naked in the foliage like soft pale fungi. They were there for all who visited them: stags, stallions, dogs, and small cat-monkeys clamped themselves over their hips, male swans enfolded them with their wings as they penetrated close, snakes twined up their thighs to seek pleasure in them and fructify them with their cold seed, all manner of birds and beasts had intercourse with them, excepting man, and they bore their young in a variegated flood that poured from their wombs, but human children they never bore. They had their pleasure and pain of this as long as they were young, but they aged rapidly from all this birth, were torn up by it, and worn out by the lust of all who came to them at will, since they could not defend themselves; and their pleasure was destroyed and only the pain remained, and their life was shortened so that they died of a surfeit of womanhood before they were eight years old. And when they died, they were dried up like old women, shrivelled and empty like orange peels in the sun.

Translated from the Swedish
by Keith Bradfield

Baraka

by Mohammed Mrabet

Since Baraka's father had two houses, he let Baraka live by himself in the empty one. It consisted of two ground-floor rooms and a kitchen and bathroom. The large room was fully furnished. Baraka preferred the small room, which had a mat, a taifor, a mattress and a wardrobe. On the taifor he kept a large bowl filled with a mixture of almonds, walnuts, honey and black jduq jmel seeds.

Afternoons Barka would sit and brew a pot of tea. He would eat two spoonfuls of the mixture and drink two glasses of very hot tea. A little later he would smoke a kif cigarette.

This story is not one that can be proven, but it is certain that he would shut his eyes and lie back on the cushions with his head against the wall, and begin to dream. He always dreamed that he was wandering in an orchard. It was a strange place, like nowhere he had ever been before. Wherever he walked there were roses under the trees. Roses in all directions; he could walk a kilometer and never cease to see them.

Sometimes he would reach a place from where he could see, far ahead, faint glimpses of another orchard where the trees were taller, and it seemed to him that he could hear a great crying of birds in the distance. The day he managed to get to the second orchard, the sight of it made him stand motionless. He watched the birds as they circled above the trees. Finally he sat down, leaning against a tree trunk, and listened for a long time to the sound of the birds.

There were two of them in the tree above his head. Soon they began to fly down and hover in front of his face without touching him. They would be there for an instant, and then they would dart up into the tree. For a long time they played this game with him. What do they

want? he wondered. He got up, and the birds disappeared
quickly into a hole in the tree-trunk.

That's strange, he said.

He stood for a while looking at the hole, and soon they
came out and flew away. This was the moment to look
into the hole. Inside was a nest with two featherless
fledgelings in it.

Allah! he cried. I was going to kill those birds if they
didn't stop their game, but they only wanted to get some
food for their family.

At that moment his eyes opened. He stood up and went
to the taifor, where he sat writing the entire story in a
notebook. Then he went back and sat where he had been
sitting before. He shut his eyes, took himself back to the
orchard, and began to walk again.

After a while he came to a hillside covered with trees.
There was a long path leading upward. He climbed slowly.
When he got to the top he saw a field where many mongooses were running among the bushes. When they caught
sight of him they all disappeared into their holes. He stood
and watched, and saw their pointed muzzles appear in the
openings, one by one. He sat down. Strange animals, each
one in his hole. When I first saw them they were all out
there playing together.

After a time he got up and walked toward the holes. The
mongooses did not not pull their heads in, but stayed
where they were, watching him. When he stopped over
they all ran inside.

These animals understand, he said to himself. I'm going
to keep looking. He sat down under a tree nearby and
waited. Soon their heads appeared in the holes again, and
they began to watch him.

Suddenly one of the mongooses came all the way out of
its hole. I wonder why he came out?

As he said this the mongoose darted forward and seized
a large snake that was crawling not far from where Baraka
sat. Baraka jumped up, crying: *Ay yimma!* and ran to find
a stick. By the time he got back the mongoose had bitten
the snake's head off and was running away with it. Then the
others came out of their holes and set to work eating the
snake. When they had finished it, they went back to their
holes.

Baraka opened his eyes. He got up, rolled himself a kif

cigarette, and wrote down what he had just seen. After a while he returned to the mattress and relaxed, in order to get back quickly to the orchard and see what would happen next.

He found the place where the mongooses had eaten the snake. I must go further, he thought, and see what's ahead. It can always be even better.

He cut across the hill, always walking among trees, and went downward to a river, whose course he followed until he came to a series of pools. The air was fresh and he could hear the river running nearby. He chose a pool and sat down beside it. As he looked into the water he saw two fish with brightly shining scales. He reached behind him, pulled up some plants, and tossed them into the water. The fish came up to the surface and nibbled at them.

Strange, he thought. Even fish eat weeds. Allah, what a garden! It's what all gardens should be. I can walk here, and yet no one has been here before me. What patterns the fish have on their scales! It would be a sin to eat such fish. They should be kept where people can see them.

It was a warm day. He reached out to feel the water with his finger. There was a sudden sharp pain, and he pulled back his hand. When he looked at the finger, he saw that half of it had been bitten away. With the blood running from his finger, he went in search of a plant with a yellow blossom. When he found one, he broke its stem. A milky liquid ran out, and he let it run onto his finger. It burned. He wound his handkerchief around the finger and went back to the pool. There were clots of blood in one part of the water. As he watched, another kind of fish appeared, silvery and flat, and sucked in the blood.

Strange, said Baraka. I never thought such a thing could happen.

It frightened him, and he decided these were not fish, after all. But what else could they be?

At that moment he opened his eyes. He was clutching his wounded finger, and the sweat ran down his cheeks. When he looked closely at his finger, he saw with relief that the flesh was all there. It was a dark purple color. He stood up and went over to the taifor. He found it painful to write, but he managed to put down everything that had happened. Then he went back to his seat and shut his eyes.

This time he passed the pools by the river and continued further. Soon he came to a forest of such huge trees that there was only darkness beneath them. He was convinced that there was something even more important in here. He began to walk between the trees in the gloom, feeling his way among their trunks, and going very slowly. He continued ahead in this way for a while. Finally he saw a pale sliver of light beyond. When he got to the clearing, he realized that it would be impossible for him to go further, because the roots of the trees formed a high wall. They rose up sheer and wet, high above his head. He tried again and again to get a foothold, but he always slipped back. He walked first one way and then the other, and found only the wall of roots.

Then in the air above his head he heard a sound. A great bird was flying down upon him. As it came nearer, one of its wings hit him, and he fell headfirst to the ground, striking his forehead. He sat up, put his hand to his face, and felt the blood. Then he leaned back against a tree-trunk, feeling faint.

The bird had its nest nearby. It stayed a while there, and then it flew away. Baraka opened his eyes a little, and from where he lay, he looked around. He saw the nest and got up. There were three large eggs in it. Then he noticed that the eggs were moving. This frightened him, and he returned to the tree.

Soon he saw one of the small birds break through its shell. As he looked, the other two also hatched. Two of them were healthy, and the other was feeble.

The parents arrived. Baraka watched them feed the young birds. The two healthy ones ate hungrily, but the weak one would not touch the food. When the father saw this, he seized the weak one in his beak, and the pieces of broken shell in his claws, and flew away with them. Soon he returned, carrying nothing.

Baraka opened his eyes. He was sitting forward on his mattress, holding his forehead and sweating. He got up and went into the bathroom. There he stood in front of the mirror, looking to see if there was blood on his forehead. The pain where he had fallen was so strong that he expected to see a great amount of blood. However, there was only a drop.

He went back to his mattress saying: Strange. Such things don't happen. Wait while I fill a cigarette with kif.

He made the cigarette. While I smoke it I'll drink a glass of tea. And then back to my place to see what happens next.

He put the teapot onto the mijmah to heat. When it was ready he poured himself a glass of tea and lighted his cigarette. Afterward he shut his eyes. Quickly he was back in the darkness of the forest, near the wall of tree-roots. He found the nest, and looked at it as he passed. There was nothing in it.

And now he discovered a way of getting past the wall of roots, into the other part of the forest. It was a narrow winding passage. As he pushed ahead, he became aware of a red light flickering in the distance. He watched it moving, and knew it was fire. After a while he came to where he could see the flames. There was a cave ahead, and in its floor was a huge hole, full of fire. As he stood looking, there was an explosion, and the fire belched up like red water out of the hole, higher and higher, until the roof of the cave was a glowing crescent.

This sight delighted Baraka, for he felt that he had come upon something marvellous. He walked on through the maze of roots. The passage led him out onto open ground at the top of a steep cliff. Far below there was another forest, but he would have needed a two-hundred-yard rope to reach the bottom. He saw that if he went for miles along the edge of the cliff he might find a way down.

Baraka stood for a while, letting his eye run over the landscape. Then he turned and looked down at the earth near his feet. Not far away squatted a large spider, covered with black hairs. Its eyes were bright blue. As he watched, it began to move toward him. Fear seized him, and the skin tightened all over his body.

Baraka began to run, back into the maze of roots. Several times he looked over his shoulder and saw the spider coming along behind him. When he got to the darkest part of the forest he stopped looking back, and merely ran. It took him hours to get to the orchard where the roses grew. Then he turned again to see, but as he was looking back he ran full tilt into a tree. There was a terrible crash, and he opened his eyes.

He was sitting upright on his mattress, staring ahead of him. His breath came in gasps and his clothes were drenched with sweat. He looked at the table. The spider was there, on the edge of the bowl of jduq jmel paste. Now that he had made it real, he was no longer afraid of it. He thought: Other men dream and return with nothing. But I've learned how to bring things back. *Hamdoul'lah!*

Translated from the Moghrebi
by Paul Bowles

74

I Sang in a Forest One Day

by Bob Dylan

i sang in a forest one day & someone said it was three o'clock—that nite when i read the newspaper, i saw that a tenement had been set aflame & that three firemen & nineteen people had lost their lives—the fire was at three o'clock too . . . that nite in a dream i was singing again— i was singing the same song in the same forest & at the same time—in the dream there was also a tenement blazing . . . there was no fog & the dream was clear—it was not worth analyzing as nothing is worth analyzing—you learn from a conglomeration of the incredible past—whatever experience gotten in any way whatsoever—controlling at once the present tense of the problem—more or less like a roy rogers & trigger relationship of which under present western standards is an impossibility—me singing —i moved from the forest—frozen in a moment & picked up & moved above land—the tenement blazing too at the same moment being picked up — moved towards me—i, still singing & this building still burning . . . needless to say—i & the building met & as instantly as it stopped, the motion started again—me, singing & the building burning —there i was—in all truth—singing in front of a raging fire—i was unable to do anything about this fire—you see— not because i was lazy or loved to watch good fires —but rather because both myself & the fire were in the same Time all right but we were not in the same Space— the only thing we had in common was that we existed in the same moment . . . i could not feel any guilt about just standing there singing for as i said i was picked up & moved there not by my own free will but rather by some unbelievable force—i told Justine about this dream & she said 'that's right—lot of people would feel guilty & close their eyes to such a happening—these are people that in-

terrupt & interfere in other people's lives—only God can
be everywhere at the same Time & Space—you are human—sad & silly as it might seem' . . . i got very drunk
that afternoon & a mysterious confusion entered into my
body—'when i hear of the bombings, i see red & mad
hatred' said Zonk—'when i hear of the bombings, i see
the head of a dead nun' said i—Zonk said 'what?' . . . i
have never taken my singing—let alone my other habits—
very seriously—ever since then—i have just accepted it—
exactly as i would any other crime.

The Polish Tree
by *Gunter Kunert*

There was a tree that stood outside the little town of Kielce but still in sight of it, not a famous tree at all, far from the world, always on the fringe of history.

Out of the foliage which clasps it, the deep green pinnacles, it is said, you can hear on some days a sound of weeping, like children's voices, when the wind blows through the tree, cries and whimpering, sighs which end in rattling sounds, in breathless silence. Not everyone, they say in Kielce, has the right ears to hear what sounds are being made in the trembling branches.

A German scientist, armed with a tape-recorder, lurked for a long time under the huge crown of leaves, without being able to record anything acoustically peculiar; and he assigns to the realm of fable what is said about the tree and the children. He says: apart from the oak-tree and two jays, everything else is scientifically baseless.

Translated from the German
by Christopher Middleton

The Sheep of the Hidden Valley
by R. Yehoshua Lovaine

There was once a tailor in a valley so small, and so far away, that you have probably never heard of it. The tailor was a man of great skill. His excellent material, perfect stitching and precision in fitting assured that his customers were always satisfied. When the clothes became torn, the tailor could mend them so that they were almost like new. Despite his great skill, the tailor was a troubled man. Even when he used the best of materials his clothes did not last fovever. They sometimes lasted out the life of a customer, but rarely was a suit passed down from father to son.

One night the tailor dreamt that he was wandering about the surrounding towns. Suddenly he found a valley hidden away from the eyes of the world. In this valley were sheep with thick coats of beautiful wool. In his dream, he spoke for hours with the shepherd who guarded the sheep. The man confided to him the many intricate details of raising sheep whose wool was fine as golden thread, soft as baby's skin, as shining as a star, and as firm when woven as the resolve of a wise man. The tailor awoke from his dream determined to seek out the valley and its sheep. For many years he travelled the countryside without success.

At last behind a waterfall at which he had stopped to refresh himself, the tailor found a hidden valley in which grazed sheep with marvelous wool. In the real valley, unlike the one of his dream, there was no shepherd to guide him in raising the sheep. In moments of deep concentration, the tailor was able to remember the special rules communicated to him in his dream. He dedicated himself to raising these sheep, and followed the rules for their care scrupulously.

Wishing to share his discovery with the villagers, his beloved friends, the tailor announced that he would sew new clothes for all adults in the village. He sheared his sheep, wove their wool into cloth, and began to sew the new garments. The tailor found to his surprise that he had just enough cloth to make clothes for every man and woman in his village. Although the tailor guarded them well, the sheep somehow disappeared within a week of their shearing, and no more clothing could be sewn from their splendid wool.

The new garments were a delight to the village. The people discovered that this clothing, so warm and snug in winter, was never uncomfortable even in the hottest heat of summer. The rain did not ruin these fine clothes nor did the years wear them thin. When they were torn through carelessness, it needed but a stitch to restore them. These were charmed garments, and the villagers of that generation counted themselves blessed.

A boy reaching the age of manhood approached his father in secret. He asked his father to acquire for him a fine suit of clothes like the ones owned by the adults in the village. He too would soon be a full member of his village, and, he argued, he should have as splendid a garment as any one else. When the father explained that there were no more miraculous garments, the boy cried bitterly. Finally the father, out of his great love for the boy, took off his own coat and gave it to his son. A great miracle followed. Having put on his father's coat over his own garments, the boy found that his clothing was transformed into the material of his father's garments. Soon it was discovered that whenever a child near the age of adulthood put on his parent's cloak, the child's own clothing turned to the cloth woven from the marvellous wool of the sheep of the hidden valley.

As the young people grew, they found the clothes changing to fit them. Arms lengthened, chests filled out, and at the same time the garments had longer sleeves and fuller breadth. However a person changed, if he became fatter or thinner, wider or narrower, straighter or more bent with age, the miraculous clothing fit exactly.

The village became famous throughout the area and many envied the fine garments. People in the surrounding towns began to gossip, and they whispered that wearing the same clothes continually showed the backwardness of the villagers. They said that it made the villagers boring.

Believing the garments worn by the young to be those of their parents, they bitingly asked: who wears the clothes of dead people? They did not know the secret of the garments or their source, so they did not understand.

After many years, some say generations, the trust of the village itself was undermined and many came to doubt what their own eyes had seen. The village became divided. Some sold or gave away their old garments, preferring to wear the stylish new clothing they found in the surrounding towns. These who bought new clothes found that they soon wore out. When they tore they could not be restored and had to be discarded. Their ancestral garments, when worn by others, lost their special properties. The garments, once the pride of the town, became rags for the poor in the neighboring towns.

Others in the village tried refashioning the old garments. They dyed the new colors, lengthened and shortened hems, and restitched the seams to fit the newer fashions. Their newly restyled clothes did not wear well and, as with the others, were discarded. Still others in the village desperately tried to prevent the slightest change in the clothing. They refused to allow the alteration of the garments even a stitch. But their clothes grew stiff about them, losing their ability to fit throughout the whole of a person's life. Finally, these garments too were discarded.

Fewer and fewer of the original coats were to be found. As the years passed many in the village began to doubt that there ever were such marvellous clothes. They could not believe in the funny story about the tailor, his dream and his hidden valley. Where was this valley? What proof was there that such a tailor had ever existed? Who trusts dreams? And most of all, where were these so-called magic garments?

The few who claimed to own original coats were regarded as half-crazy or deluded, or at the least as very poorly dressed. Among those who still wore the old coats there was a desire, born from the love of their neighbors, to restore the miracle of their special clothing. They alone knew the value of the clothing. They alone knew how much superior were the original garments to the new ones. There arose among them a question: will we, they asked, need once again a tailor who dreams of wondrous sheep, and can then find them? Or, they wondered, do we simply need to collect the worn rags and reweave them into the fine garments? They have not yet answered this question.

Translated from the Yiddish and Hebrew
by Tsvi Blanchard

77

A Myth of Asherah
by Howard Schwartz

Myth demands ritual.
—Rudolf Otto

This is a tale about a mystery that slowly revealed itself. Even now I do not understand it. What is certain is that I am drawn to it and filled with fear at the same time, for what I do know has blurred the boundary between myth and the world as I know it. I can no longer consign myth to the realm of the imagination.

I met Anath Bethel on bus 24 from Hebrew University. We were the only riders that day. I sat a few seats behind her and we did not speak. But she seemed to wait for me when we got off at the same stop, and we walked back together. It turned out that our houses were in the same direction. In a short time we discovered a great deal we held in common, especially a love of literature. In two or three days we became lovers, although I was far from certain that I was in love.

Anath had beautiful, sad eyes, a fact I came to attribute to her mother's experiences in a German concentration camp. Her father was a Sabra, a doctor. She admired him greatly. They lived in Haifa, and Anath felt torn between that city and Jerusalem. But she loved Jerusalem best of all. She was delighted to learn that I wrote poems. She also did, although she never showed them to me.

Anath took it on herself to show me Jerusalem, a city of worlds within worlds, many of them ancient. Most of all we talked. She was the eldest of six children, very close to her brothers and sisters, especially to the youngest one. She had had many lovers. At that time she had never traveled out of Israel. I asked her about her name, and she told me it appeared in the Bible once or twice, but nothing was known about that Anath. Her parents had selected the name at random from the Bible. Once, after we had made love, I took her hand and pretended to

265

read her lifeline, which was short. She said, "I'm not going to
live very long, am I?" I laughed and said, "No, your lifeline
isn't very long."

I was in Israel that summer to exorcize the ghost of an old
love. I had decided to attend her wedding, to know for certain
that she had married someone else. On the first of August I left
Jerusalem for the wedding in the North. Anath wanted to
accompany me, but I wanted to be alone. She was hurt but said
nothing. When I returned there were only three days remaining
before I was to leave Israel, and in many ways they were the
best.

On my last full day in Jerusalem Anath took me to one of the
underground tunnels that had been dug in the time of King
David to carry water to the city. The tunnel was too narrow for
more than one person to pass through at a time. The ceiling was
low, while the water rose to our knees. It was pitch black except
for the light cast by the candle that Anath carried. As we stepped
inside she hiked up her skirt to her waist, to keep it from
becoming wet. She never seemed more sensual to me than at
that time. At one point I blew out the candle and we kissed in
the dark. Then we had to find our way by feeling along the walls
and ceiling until we reached the place where the light of the
other entrance could be seen in the distance.

Our last night together was the most tender. We clung to each
other like authentic lovers, and just before waking I had a
mysterious and beautiful dream. In the dream Anath and I lay on
a round bed in a magnificent bedroom chamber, also circular.
We read together from a holy book we held in our hands, and
while we read a sacred presence rose up from the page. As is
possible in dreams, I was able to glimpse what was going on
outside the chamber without getting up from the bed. A great
celebration was in progress: hundreds of people in ancient dress
circled our chamber, chanting in unison and swaying from left to
right. Over and over they chanted the same word, "Asherah,
Asherah." The accent was strongly on the last syllable. At one
point in the dream I turned to Anath and touched her with my
hand, but she whispered that embracing was unnecessary, for we
had already passed beyond that realm. And there was no
denying the truth of what she said.

When I awoke it was dawn. Anath's eyes were open and I
told her the dream. Then I asked her what the word "Asherah"
meant, but she said she didn't know, although it did have a

distinctly Hebrew character. She guessed that I might not have remembered it correctly, but I was certain I had pronounced it right. Somehow the dream made a deep impression on us both. It sustained us all that morning on the journey to the airport and even after we had said goodbye.

By the next night, however, in New York, I already felt a great distance from Anath and Jerusalem. We wrote to each other only occasionally. Once a year passed without the exchange of a letter. Then I sent her my first book. She replied with a warm letter in which she told me that she was very close to an American she had met in the Hebrew class she taught in the Ulpan. She said that after a year of unsatisfying affairs this new love was a great consolation.

During that time I came across a book which claimed that prior to the codification of the Bible, a cult of Jews had worshipped, in addition to Yahweh, the God of the Jews, a goddess of Canaanite origin. This cult had set aside sacred groves for the goddess and set up wooden posts for her worship. For a long time—several hundred years—her statue had been present in the Temple in Jerusalem. The author proposed that this was not a form of pagan worship, but that the people regarded this goddess as the feminine aspect of God. But the rabbis feared that later generations would misunderstand this distinction and proclaim the goddess independent of Yahweh. So with stunning success the rabbis excised every reference to this goddess in the Bible but three. The name of this goddess was Asherah of the Seas. She was said to have had a daughter, whose name was Anath.

I lived with this coincidence, if that is what is was, for a few weeks, often thinking that I must write to Anath about it. But I didn't. Then, on the thirteenth of August, I had a dream that made me think of her again. In the dream it was the eve of an important but unspecified Jewish holiday. I was alone in my apartment, but I wanted to take part in the ritual. So I turned on the television set and saw the start of the ceremony. A large crowd had gathered at the shore of the sea and watched in solemn fascination as the body of a beautiful woman was dragged out of the water. Despite the apparent tragedy, grief did not seem evident in the faces of the people. Rather it was a sense of ceremony that dominated, as if the event were something that had happened before and would happen again. After the body of the woman had been carried out, the limp body of a

Siamese cat was pulled from the water. That was all I could
recall when I woke up. It was the first dream I had remembered
in several months.

Later that day I sat down at the typewriter. Since nothing
came to mind at first, I typed out the dream. Before long it
occurred to me that this dream might be linked in some way
with the dream of the last night in Jerusalem, three years before.
It was only a few weeks since I had read the book about the
goddess, and that dream came readily to mind. I recalled that no
complete myths of Asherah had survived. I decided to try to link
the two dreams to create such a myth. I worked on the myth for
more than three weeks, first expanding it and then condensing it
to half the original length. The final text appears as follows:

Every year, in the early autumn, a flashing meteor would
fall like a star on a certain day from the top of Mount
Lebanon into the river Adonis. Soon after, the body of a
beautiful woman would appear floating on the surface of
the river towards the shore. It had happened this way for so
long that her arrival had come to be awaited, and in time an
ample mythology emerged about her existence prior to the
day she returned. Each family had its own treasured myth:
some spoke of a journey through the stars; others told of an
exile that finally came to an end. During the seasons of her
absence these myths were repeated and enhanced, but in the
autumn the myths of her absence gave way to the longing
for her presence, and as far back as anyone could remember
they had never been disappointed in their hopes.

On that day a ram's horn would be heard in the city and
in no time a large crowd would assemble at the shore. At
first they could see nothing but her white gown and black
hair. Then, as she came closer, a powerful undercurrent
would cause her to submerge one last time before she rose
within reach of the maidens who had been waiting, their
arms open. All would crowd together to catch a glimpse of
her face. From the shore she was borne on a litter led by a
young priest to her place inside the House of Prayer, a
golden bed set down before the Ark. There she lay lifeless
while the priest prayed beside her and all the others circled
outside the chamber, swaying from left to right.

As the shadows started to lift, the color would return to
her face, and at last her eyes would open. At that moment
the priest would reach for the holy book that lay closed on

the altar beside him, and when the book was open it was as if they had embraced in the shelter of a House of Song. This change was somehow apparent to those who circled outside, and then they would start to chant her name, *Asherah*, louder and louder, as if in a single voice. And inside the room this chanting was like a flame fed by the silence that surrounded them, a holy presence emanating from the letters on the page that came to pervade the Ark and chamber, the House of Prayer, and all those chanting in celebration inside it.

When the myth was complete I was pleased with it, although I regretted not having found a place for the Siamese cat, obviously a symbol of the divinity, as in Egyptian lore. By this time I was very anxious to write Anath, to tell her the whole story, and vowed to write a long letter the next day. That night there was a folkdance troop from Haifa performing in the city. I went to see them and thought often of Anath, since Haifa was her home town. The next morning I received a handwritten letter from a Seth Suriel, whom I did not know. The letter read as follows:

I write to you with tragic news. Three weeks ago, yesterday, Anath Bethel, while vacationing in Norway, was killed in a bizarre and impossible accident. She had just turned twenty-five.

Anath spoke of you often, and I assumed that you should know about this.

I was deeply in love with Anath and planned on marrying her. She told me—over a period of many months—many facets of her relationship with you in Israel.

Anath's parents are broken over her death. As you may have known, she was the favorite of her parents, as well as being adored by her five younger brothers and sisters.

For myself (and, I suppose, Anath's closest friends as well) this is a time of tremendous pain and emptiness. Anath was the center of my life.

I am very sorry to have had to relay this sad news to you.

Sincerely,
Seth Suriel

In that moment, as so often happens, I saw Anath's face in my memory, more clearly than ever before. Soon, however, it started to fade and I developed a migraine headache. For a week

I found it almost impossible to function. Finally I found the strength to reply to Seth Suriel, and to tell him the things I would have written to Anath. For, in addition to my grief, I felt strangely cheated of the right to surprise her with all that I had discovered.

A few days after mailing the letter I was woken by a phone call early in the morning. It was Seth Suriel, who said he had tried to reach me until three in the morning the night before. He told me that my letter had disturbed him very much—not only because of what I had told him, but because of what he had not yet told me: how and when Anath had died. Now he told me the story.

Anath had traveled to Norway for a vacation. She had been living with a farmer's family in the North, earning her room and board by picking berries. On the fateful day she had taken a hike with the farmer and his son, with whom she had become friends. Normally hikers in Norway are careful to take along a rope and pick, but for some reason they did not bring them that day.

At one point it became necessary to cross a glacier. They crossed in single file, the farmer first, then his son, who was twelve, then Anath. Apparently the farmer stepped over an invisible fault, covered with a foot of snow, his son stepped on it but did not break it, and Anath fell through it, into a glacial pool about twenty feet below. She was not hurt from the fall, nor did she drown. Although the farmer and his son could no longer see her, they were still able to talk to her. But they had no rope to pull her out. Finally they took off their clothes and tore them and knotted a rope. They lowered this make-shift rope to her and she started to climb up it, but when she was halfway up the rope broke, and she fell back into the pool. Then they had nothing else with which to pull her out, so the son ran off to find help while the father tried to comfort Anath. But they had hiked into such a remote area that it was three hours before the farmer's son returned with others, and after the first hour she had fainted from the incredible cold of the glacial pool, slipped into the icy waters, and drowned. Her last words had been spoken in Hebrew, which the farmer, of course, did not understand. He thought, perhaps, that they were a prayer.

Now there was only one last detail to convey: the date of Anath's death. She had lost her life in Norway on August fourteenth; my dream, as I had noted in my letter to Seth, had taken place on August thirteenth. Calculating the difference in time meant that my dream had taken place on the same day that

Anath had drowned. I was terrified by this revelation. At first I was afraid that in some way I was responsible for Anath's death. But then I recalled the television set in my dream, and remembered that a television receives but does not transmit. I had been like a radar screen, picking up this information from Anath, or from whoever had transmitted it. I had been the witness.

As I thought over this sequence, one thing stood out above all others: the imprint of Asherah clung to these events. Had the goddess somehow planned all that had taken place, manipulating us like figures on a chessboard? And if so, why? All I could speculate was that the myth I had pieced together from my dreams was far closer to the truth than I had imagined, and that Asherah had sacrificed Anath in order to reenact her myth.

Others might deny the logic of the pattern I saw, but I myself could not refute it. With trepidation I reread the book about Asherah, and discovered in the notes that the mythic Anath had a consort—Seth. So too did I learn that there were priests, known as *Kedeshim*, who had lodged within the walls of the Temple in Jerusalem and sometimes acted out the myth of Asherah. At this point the presence of the goddess became all too real to me. Was it possible that Asherah had secretly found a way to reenact her myth every year since her exile? That she, so long forgotten, no longer worshipped, had found a way to see that the ancient sacrifices still took place? That at the end of every summer some girl, singled out from birth, drowned, so that the myth of the goddess might live on in secret? Now the act of naming Anath no longer seemed mere chance. The Hasidim say that a man's destiny is determined by his name. Somehow Anath's name had demarked her destiny.

But I became most frightened, even terrified, when I wondered what else this goddess might want of me. Surely I could no longer deny her existence; I would be a fool to do so. Somewhere, somehow, in some dimension, Asherah exists. But I refuse to pursue the mystery any further. I'm afraid of what I might find.

78

The Book of Vessels
by Howard Schwartz

> There shall not be found among
> you any one that maketh his son
> or his daughter to pass through
> the fire, or that useth divination,
> a soothsayer, enchanter, or a witch.
> (Deut. 18:10)

Before Noah Talvi became a Sinologist, he had attended a Yeshivah in Jerusalem. For a while he had believed his destiny to be purely in the study of the Torah and the Talmud and the other sacred Jewish texts. But he had changed his path. He had left the Yeshivah for graduate school. He had studied under Richard Wilhelm in Berlin in the last years of his life and had let him become his master, as the head of the Yeshivah had once been. And like Wilhelm he had devoted himself to the mysteries of the *I Ching*, the 4000 year old Chinese oracle.

Often Talvi would think to himself that the *I Ching* was in many ways like the Talmud. Both were commentaries on an earlier text. The *I Ching* was said to have evolved from an oracle read from the cracks of a tortoise shell burned in fire. Now it consisted of sixty-four oracles symbolic of all of the possibilities of being. There were many layers of commentary. The earliest attached meanings to the six broken and unbroken lines, known as hexagrams, of which each of the oracles consisted. These early commentaries were amplified in the Confucian period, much as the Talmud, itself a commentary of sorts on the Torah, combined two texts, the Mishnah and the Gemara. In both cases there were strata of commentaries, like an archeological dig.

Without a doubt, Talvi's Yeshivah training had prepared him to be a fine scholar. Even the kinds of commentaries found in

the Talmud were not dissimilar to those of *I Ching*. Both sought
to define and interpret life in this world; each drew upon the
wisdom of the greatest sages; and each approached the subject in
a methodical manner. And this was true despite the fact that the
Talmud is, on the surface, the most disorganized of books, the
compilation of the minutes of the debates of the rabbis, often
shifting from one subject to another. In the *I Ching*, on the other
hand, each oracle was highly focused on a specific phase in the
cycle of creation. This cycle ended in the 63rd oracle, Completion, and began again in the 64th, Before Completion. And the
commentaries were appended not only to the oracle as a whole,
but to each of the individual lines that made it up.

More than once, as he meditated upon the rich commentaries
of the *I Ching*, Talvi thought that Judaism lacked such a finely
crafted system of divination. Impossible as it might seem, Talvi
knew with certainty that the *I Ching* did indeed function as a
true oracle. And he did not question this, but gratefully accepted
it. Yet Judaism had explicitly rejected such an invaluable tool.
For it was clearly written in the Bible about diviners that
"because of these abominations the Lord thy God doth drive
them out from before thee." Diviners were in the same category
as witches, and the punishment for witches was clearly stated:
"Thou shalt not suffer a witch to live." And this even though
the high priests once read the future in the precious gems of their
breast-plates known as Urim and Thummin.

In time this thought became something of an obsession. The
truth was that Talvi was being called back to his Jewish roots,
although he had not yet recognized this. He continued to
imagine the effect of young Jews meditating on the lines of the
Torah or Talmud the way those who contemplate the Chinese
oracle do, knowing that their fate is written there, and trying to
decipher the full implications of its meaning. Perhaps it was
destined that he should decide to invent such a Jewish oracle, a
Jewish *I Ching*.

When the notion of creating such a book of divination out of
Jewish sources first occurred to him, Talvi quickly dismissed it.
The reason was obvious: it wouldn't work. The mystery of why
the *I Ching* served as a viable oracle had been obscured in the
4000 years since its creation. How it had been formed into such
a perfect vessel could not really be understood at all. And no
amount of scholarship could pierce the veil of this truth. How
could one man form another such perfect vessel?

But one day the thought came to him that it is not the *I Ching* itself that serves as the oracle, but a benevolent spirit that animates it, which always makes its replies inevitable, and never arbitrary. This spirit used the oracle as a vessel through which to speak. All that this spirit required was a vessel. The more perfect the vessel, the more accurate the reply. That is why the *I Ching* worked: it was a perfect vessel.

At this point Talvi thought of the wonderful myth of the Ari, as Rabbi Isaac Luria was known, about the Shattering of the Vessels. According to this myth, at the time the world came into being, vessels filled with light emanated from the essence of the Holy One. For some reason—not even the Ari seemed to know why—the vessels shattered and scattered sparks of that primordial light all over the world. According to the Ari, this was the reason the Jewish people had been brought into being—to gather those scattered sparks wherever they had fallen. Finding one of these sparks was, for the Ari, the same as performing a good deed, or *mitzvah*. He called this part of his cosmology Gathering the Sparks. Each spark raised up from where it was hidden was a step towards restoring the shattered vessels. This notion of scattered sparks had caught the fancy of Jews everywhere, who finally saw a purpose in their wide dispersal around the world, as well as a goal towards which to strive, the restoration of the primordial world.

Now Talvi wondered if he might somehow create a vessel through which the spirit might speak to his fellow Jews, alerting them to every kind of danger, as the Chinese oracle was able to do. The notion drew him on, even though he always recognized that it was a mad project, or at least that it would be regarded as such in the eyes of the world. What did the Jews want with a book of divination? They had their books, and they had decided long ago what to do with diviners.

At first Talvi did his best to put these thoughts out of his mind. But having thought of the notion, Talvi's imagination proceeded without his permission to conceive ways the oracle might be brought into being. For example, the *I Ching* consists of sixty-four oracles, known as hexagrams. And in the Kabbalah, the texts of Jewish mysticism, there is frequent reference to the Thirty-two Paths. At first Talvi considered creating an oracle of thirty-two vessels, but then he considered the fact that the process of the Ari's cosmology consists of two stages, the Shattering of the Vessels and the Gathering of the Sparks. If he retained the sixty-four oracles, he could divide half of them into oracles of the broken vessels, while the other half would constitute those in the process of being restored. This followed as well the basic assumption of the *I Ching*, that change is the primary law of the universe, and that there is a predictable pattern to this change. The meaning was obvious: if the oracle received was one of those of the broken vessels, the overall fate revealed a condition of unravelling, a world under the sway of the Fall; but if it fell into the second half, it revealed that the process of repair had begun, and the oracle would delineate how far it had progressed towards the restoration. This decision greatly pleased Talvi, because it enabled him both to remain true to the myth of the Ari and to the structure of the *I Ching*.

With this structure in mind, so similar to that he knew so well, Talvi began to create his oracle in earnest. One of his first major decisions was what to call it. It would not do to call it a Jewish *I Ching*. No, he would give a title that echoed the Kabbalistic treatises that so abounded in the Middle Ages, all of which were called the Book of Something or Other. Talvi considered several titles: *The Book of Paths*, after the Thirty-two Paths; *The Book of Facing*, because whoever used it would be facing his innermost self; and *The Book of Vessels*, since the oracles would serve as a vessel through which the spirit might communicate, and because of the teachings of the Ari. It was this last title that he chose, in its Hebrew version, *Sefer ha-Kelim*.

Now that he had a book with a title and a structure, Talvi began to collect material that he might insert into the various oracles. He intended to model the book fully on the *I Ching*. He chose passages from the Bible as the primary judgments. These were modified and explained by passages from later texts, such as the other books of the Bible, the Talmud, the Midrash and the texts of Jewish mysticism. Soon Talvi found himself deeply involved in reading Jewish texts, selecting passages that might serve as the kind of commentaries required for an oracle.

As his work progressed, very slowly, Talvi began to consider the futility of creating a sacred book in a secular age. It might well be regarded as nothing more than one man's invention. A mere pastime. Who would have faith in it as an oracle? And Talvi was certain that without this faith, the oracle would not function. For the divine spirit only responds if its existence is recognized. It was at this time that the thought first occurred to him of presenting the book as if it had been a recently discovered ancient text.

Over the ages many others had come to this difficult pass. In the first few centuries after the books of the Bible were codified, many books were written in the biblical mold in the hope that they would be added to the sacred texts. But they were not. These books were classified as Pseudeipigrapha, and included The Book of Enoch, among others. Perhaps the most famous case of such a literary fraud was that of Moshe de Leon, who claimed in the 13th Century to have discovered a text written by the 3rd Century sage Simeon bar Yohai. It was known that Simeon had spent thirteen years in a cave, hiding from the Romans, who had condemned him to death. What had he done all that time? Moshe de Leon supplied the answer: he was writing *The Zohar*. Remarkably, the hoax was accepted as authentic, even though there were a great many suspicions at the time that Moshe de Leon was the true author of the text. Even his wife had confirmed these doubts, asserting that he had composed the manuscript himself. Nevertheless, in a few centuries *The Zohar* had become recognized as the central text of Jewish mysticism.

Talvi began to explore the history of divination within Judaism prior to its being forbidden and afterward. He found, to his surprise, that not only had the High Priests of the Temple used the stones of their breast-plates to divine, but divination was widely practiced by the people in many ways. Not only by the flight of birds and by singing, but also by fire, water, earth and air, by dreams, by lots, by the staff or wand, by oil and by cups. Yet no well-structured book of divination had been created, since the practice was forbidden by the rabbis, obeying the biblical injunction. It was carried on by the people, though, much as were many other superstitious practices.

The more Talvi thought over the matter, the more it became apparent to him that the only hope of the book's being accepted as a sacred text was to attribute it to another, of an earlier age. Since the book drew on texts through the 16th Century, Talvi decided to attribute it to the Ari, Rabbi Isaac Luria, himself. Talvi studied the teachings of the Ari and those of his disciples, and in time it became apparent that rather than attribute the book to the Ari, who left no writings of his own, it would be better to attribute it to the Ari's primary disciple, Hayim Vital. It was while studying the career of Hayim Vital that Talvi discovered the title of a lost book of his, and he could barely believe his eyes: it was called *Sefer ha-Kelim*.

In this discovery Talvi read the hand of fate. He did not

imagine, of course, that his book was similar to that of Hayim Vital, but the fact that a book had existed with that title, by that author, and had been lost was perhaps too much of a coincidence. Talvi began to believe that in preparing his oracle for the world he was serving the intentions of the Divinity. It was at this point that he cast the *I Ching* and asked if his oracle was destined to be. The reply astounded him: "Ten pairs of tortoises cannot oppose it. All oracles—including those read from the shells of tortoises—are bound to concur in giving him favorable signs."

With this reply Talvi's resolve was confirmed. He would continue both in the creation of such a text, and in the effort to offer it to the world as the work of Hayim Vital. Thus, while he worked at a snail's pace in seeking out the sacred texts that would serve his oracle, at the same time he became a scholar of the school of the Ari and of his disciple, Hayim Vital, in particular. He held with his own hands the existing manuscripts written by Hayim Vital, and in the course of his readings he came across something that truly amazed him. For in one obscure kabbalistic text of the 17th Century it was noted that some claimed that the lost book, *Sefer ha-Kelim*, had been used as a book of divination. When Talvi first read this, a chill ran up and down him. And that was the first time he began to think that perhaps he was not inventing a book, as it had appeared, but rather restoring one that had disappeared, without any guidelines but his own intuition.

This discovery and its implications greatly affected Talvi. For one thing, it changed the emphasis of his wide research. From that time on he limited the texts from which he drew his sources to those mentioned in the writings of Hayim Vital or one of the other disciples of the Ari. Of course this in itself was a vast library, but it was also a highly focused one. And from the time this change in sources took place, a change also occurred in the manner of his locating the proper passages for his oracle. Now they seemed to leap out at him from the page. Soon he was able to dispense with reading the whole text from beginning to end. Instead he merely opened pages at random, selected in the same way a line to read, and inevitably it was one that he required for his work. So it was that Talvi came to think of himself as collaborating with a spirit, and in time this spirit became a very specific one, none other than Hayim Vital himself.

At first it had appeared that Talvi's project was to take him many years. He had estimated twenty. But all at once the pace of his creation quickened far more than he had ever expected. The lines that leapt forth each fell into the proper place. And Talvi found that he was working with an assurance far greater than he had ever known.

In the third year since he had conceived his strange project, Noah Talvi completed it. With trembling hands he cast the oracle for the first time, and received for the reply one of the very first lines of Genesis: "And he looked upon His creation, and He saw that it was good." And then Talvi knew that he had indeed served as a vessel, as he had hoped.

Now the remaining task that confronted Talvi was to present the text as a long-lost manuscript. This was the most difficult part of all, because it went against all of Talvi's well-developed scholarly instincts. He argued with himself over this, and even raged. And in the end he concluded, as he had at the first, that this was the only way the book would be acceptable to the world at large. For Talvi believed that he had truly created, or recreated, an oracle that could serve as well as the *I Ching* itself.

In his studies of the Ari and his circle, Talvi had learned that the center for kabbalistic studies had moved in the next century from Safed to Padua in Italy. Talvi had decided not to attempt to write a manuscript in the handwriting of Hayim Vital, for that could too easily be shown to be a forgery. Instead he planned to present a manuscript which would claim to be a copy of Hayim Vital's, deriving from the 17th Century.

Once he had made his decision, Talvi worked with the same single-minded determination that he had to create the oracle in the first place. He was able to locate paper and inks dating from the 17th Century, and he studied the handwriting of some of the minor kabbalists in the circle of Luzzato. When he actually wrote the text, Talvi felt inspired as he had never felt before, and his hand moved as if the spirit of that obscure scribe had taken possession of him. In less than a month the copy had been made. Talvi even included several easily detectable errors, since even the best copyists inevitably let a few errors slip through. Then he traveled to Italy, taking the manuscript with him, and on his return he announced that he had purchased it there.

In the world of scholarship news does not travel very fast, except in rare instances. But the discovery of a text attributed to Hayim Vital that was intended as a book of divination was quite remarkable, and the discovery was announced and discussed not only in obscure scholarly journals, but even in the newspapers of the world that found room for such strange tales. After all, the practice of divination had clearly been forbidden to the Jews, and yet here was a manuscript that seemed to demonstrate that divination had indeed taken root among the People of the Book.

As might be expected, the scholarly debate over the validity of the book was heated. Those scholars who were certain that the injunction against divination had been obeyed by the rabbis wrote seething attacks on its validity, while those scholars who had long suspected the kabbalists of having moved beyond the usual borders of mainstream Judaism claimed that they were not surprised, and tended to accept the authenticity of the book.

But it was not in the scholarly world, surprisingly, that the book had its greatest impact. In a short time it had been published by a small press in Jerusalem, and to the amazement of everyone, it went through half a dozen printings within weeks of publication. A brief article to this effect in *The Jerusalem Post* caught the eye of a visiting editor in Israel, and he quickly purchased the translation rights. Within a year the book had been published in English, French, and Spanish editions, and it soon became apparent that it was not being read as a scholarly discovery, but being used as an active oracle.

Noah Talvi, who viewed all this activity with considerable amazement, began to feel that he had restored to the world something that it had badly needed. But now that his work was complete he felt strangely empty, uninspired, and unwilling to undertake anything else. Although he received many invitations to speak on the manuscript he had discovered, and many requests for interviews, he rejected all of these, and added nothing to the ongoing debate.

The discussions among scholars are often intense, but they are rarely violent. Yet the debates about the authenticity of *The Book of Vessels*, as it was known in English, became most heated among the most religious Jews. By and large, these Jews angrily denounced the book as a forgery, since the penalty for diviners was clearly demarked in the Bible. Yet there was a small group of modern kabbalists among them who were able to recognize the logic of such a book among the disciples of the Ari. After all, the Ari had been able to divine mysteries from a flock of sparrows or in the trembling of the leaves of a tree. Nothing escaped him—he understood every sign.

These kabbalists began to use *The Book of Vessels* as it was intended—as an oracle—much to the chagrin of the others. Attempts were made at excommunication of those using the book in this fashion, and several bookstores were broken into, and all copies of the book taken away.

The opponents of the book would have preferred, of course, to burn it. But that option was not available to them, as one of their most honored rabbis was quick to rule. After all, the book consisted entirely of texts taken from sacred books, and sacred books could never be burned. Instead, all the copies of the book that were collected were treated like worn out holy books and hidden away in a secret *Geniza*. This action, however, outraged those who had come to strongly believe in the power of the book, and led to the first raid by Jews on a *Geniza* in Jewish history, in which all of the stolen copies of the book were stolen back. In this fashion the battle raged on.

During this time Noah Talvi was very restless, for he had not expected the book to create such a divisive controversy. To see for himself that the antagonism against the book was as great as claimed in the newspapers, he attended a rally against the book in Mea Shaarim in Jerusalem. Standing at the back of the crowd along with several other curious onlookers, Talvi was suddenly recognized by one of the religious opponents of the book, who had seen his picture in a newspaper. He screamed his discovery to the others, and all at once, as hysteria descended on the crowd, Talvi suddenly realized that his life was in danger.

Only a few seconds later the first stone struck him sharply in the head, and he lost consciousness. It was followed by a myriad of others, for all of those present wanted to share the guilt for that murder, since they regarded it as simply obeying the Law of God. Talvi's murder was reported around the world, and for a short time was much discussed, but before long it was dismissed as a strange convulsion such as sometimes occurs among the most fervid believers and was soon forgotten. No one was ever brought to trial.

Seven years later, in Safed, a *Geniza* dating from the 16th Century was discovered beneath the foundation of one of the synagogues of the Ari that was being restored. A handful of new manuscripts were discovered, including two written by disciples of the Ari. Among them was the lost book *Sefer ha-Kelim* of Hayim Vital. To the amazement of the scholars who found and confirmed this, the manuscript, written in the hand of Hayim Vital himself, was identical, word for word, with that published by the late Noah Talvi, except for a very few errors that had crept into Talvi's copy.

Isis

by Rachel Kubie

Here's your desperate madness, moving without hope through Egypt, frantic for loose fingers, a dusty tuft of hair, a shattered foot, a torn palm. Consumed by desire, in one bright mirage you find both eyes, clean and whole, their sight restored. Next day, good luck: you toe the busted heart out from a pile of stones. So little by little, piece by piece, he comes along. Sweet Isis, lucky you are beautiful. Lucky you are frantic in this endless search. We are plain and lazy, we women in our short skirts. We no longer care to make our lovers whole.

The Death of Rabbi Yoseph

by David Slabotsky

Rabbi Yoseph was astounded to discover that he was dead. Far below him, the crumbling ghetto of Zlochtov slumbered under a blanket of thick, wet snow, and a chorus of pious snores floated dreamily past him, wending their sleepy way to the Kingdom of Heaven. The snores were collected in a basket by a bird he had never seen before but had dreamed of once on the night of a Holy Day he no longer recalled. As in the dream, the bird wore curly sidelocks like an orthodox Jew and a skullcap embroidered with beads and small, round mirrors. Because of this odd familiarity, Rabbi Yoseph imposed upon the bird and begged permission to look through the basket for one particular snore, hinting that it was utterly important for reasons which he was obliged to keep secret for the moment but, at length, would reveal. The bird toyed with his sidelocks as he pondered the request and consulted a manual written in Yiddish and Hebrew and a language Rabbi Yoseph had never seen before. He furrowed his brow as birds will do when pouring over questions of a legal nature, moved the skullcap back and forth on his head, and grudgingly consented. At that, a nest fluttered down beneath him and, tucking his bill into his wings, he was instantly asleep.

Rabbi Yoseph searched through the snores with particular care. Some felt warm to the touch like tiny kittens, others tickled him so that he nearly cried out, others were so drenched with tears that they nearly slipped through his fingers like water and escaped completely, and then at last he came to the snore he was looking for, that of his wife, his Merriam, who lay sleeping beside his mortal remains in the nest of rags and shredded linen which had been their wedding bed for so many years. In the morning she would discover him there and at night her snores would be dripping, heartbroken snores like so many the bird had collected before.

He held the snore cupped tightly in his hands for a very long time, afraid that it might float away the moment he opened them again, but at last contrived a way of opening just one finger enough so that he could see it clearly but not enough so that it could slip out. The snore was warm, and grey, and wrinkled, with a mole on its chin. As it lay in his hands like a tiny bird snuggled safely in a shell, its gentle buzzing was sometimes interrupted by snatches from the tune of a Sabbath prayer, once by incoherent words concerning a poppyseed cookie so wondrous that it could only be baked in the kitchen of dreams, and once it spoke Rabbi Yoseph's name with such a rich and boundless love that the snore nearly consumed itself in a sigh.

Rabbi Yoseph addressed the snore tenderly, tearfully, recalling vows of love and years of devotion, finishing first with a kiss and lastly with a blessing. He was intending to send the snore back to the sleeping ghetto of Zlochtov, along the tumbling streets and laneways, up the creaking stairs, and down the dark, damp corridor to the room where Merriam lay with the dust of her husband. How she would rejoice to know that he held in his hands at that moment her gentle snore! Tears clouded his eyes and a terrible sorrow tugged at his heart. Overcome by grief, he squeezed the snore so tightly that it suddenly popped right out of his hands and before he could catch it again it was floating over the head of the sleeping bird who, awakening suddenly, gathered it into his basket like a hen with a wayward chick, took the handle of the basket in his bill, and flew off into eternity. Rabbi Yoseph watched him disappear and then looked down at his hands which only a moment ago had held his Merriam's warm and beloved snore. He pressed his palms to his cheeks and wept without shame.

In the moments which followed, Rabbi Yoseph struggled with a curious event: The entire ghetto of Zlochtov was tangled in his beard like a fly on a hot summer day. He looked down his nose which was hooked and twisted at the end as if the tip had rebelled against the rest and

taken a random course of its own, and screwing his eyes
up and straining until he was faint, he was obliged to accept
this strange occurence as fact, though with misgivings on
certain points. For instance, the ghetto of Zlochtov
which lay before him at the foot of the wayward hill of
his nose had not been diminished in size, and yet his
beard, which admittedly was long, was no longer than
usual, and he was certain, to the best of his knowledge,
that not even once in his lifetime had the ghetto of
Zlochtov even once grown tangled in his beard. The only
time it might have happened was on a certain Day of
Atonement when it had been an especially difficult fast and
many strange things had happened-or had seemed to have
happened; but since everything under Heaven was the
working of the Holy Name there had seemed little point
in trying to distinguish between the real and imagined
events of the day. Furthermore, it had always been he,
Rabbi Yoseph, who had been entangled in the ghetto
of Zlochtov, and much like a fly at that, a humble almost
unnoticed buzz in the life of that small community of
Jews who made a home for their God in the vast Dia-
spora. And finally, since he had enemies (What man
hasn't?) if this strange event had happened in the course
of his lifetime, surely his enemies would have reproached
him. Would Mendel the baker have spent one minute in
his beard, one second in his beard, without giving him a
slap? Or Hayim the tailor? And so it had never happened before and was happening now for the very first
time. How this had all transpired was beyond the range
of his intellect but within the bounds of belief, and utter-
ing special prayers for the occasion he gazed at the
ghetto of Zlochtov with new curiosity.

How very wonderful it seemed. How much like a
miracle. Merriam was still the most beautiful woman
and now he could see little prints of her feet showing
every step she had taken in the ghetto throughout her life,
the faintest being the smallest steps she had taken in
childhood, the brightest being the ones she had taken that
day to the market and back to their room. All her steps,
even the first, smelled vaguely of onions and fish and this
brought a deep, warm smile to his face as he closed his
eyes and remembered her.

Rabbi Yoseph was distracted by the sound of a wagon

rumbling towards him with a loadful of snores on their way to the Kingdom of Heaven. The wagonmaster was a pious frog with dark green sidelocks, a skullcap and the four-fringed vest of an orthodox Jew. Enquiring after the bird, Rabbi Yoseph learned that it had finally passed away and, since it had not appointed a successor, after much debate the task was given to the frog who rode on the wagon which stood before him. Rabbi Yoseph realized at once that a great deal of time had passed and instinctively put a hand to his beard and fumbled through it frantically for the ghetto of Zlochtov. To his dismay it had vanished without a trace. And where had it gone? And how had it gone? Loneliness came down upon him like a mountain collapsing on a fly and a giant, deadening ache overwhelmed him entirely. He looked around and saw as if for the very first time the vast expanse of the heavens. He gazed at the planets, and stars and constellations, and wondered whether in all that endless night there were Jews, or if there was a Sabbath.

In the years that followed, Rabbi Yoseph wandered from star to star and from world to world and returned to earth as a minor figure in a parable uttered by the Miracle Rabbi of Lublin. From tiny cracks in the story, Rabbi Yoseph looked out briefly into a world which reminded him of Zlochtov and fell in love with the rabbi's daughter whose name was not Merriam but might easily have been. Unfortunately, the Lublin Rabbi only recounted the parable twice in his life, once as a very young man and once on his deathbed, and since the Lubliner lived to a very ripe age, Rabbi Yoseph only managed to see his daughter twice, once as a girl and once as a very old woman. However, since his role in the parable was of a man who extolled the virtue of constancy, Rabbi Yoseph loved her faithfully all the time they were separated and praised her beauty the moment the parable rose to the lips of the dying Lublin sage.

Because of this, Rabbi Yoseph was given lives in other parables uttered by such great men as Lev of Grenoble and Raphael of Bershad and others greater still, and since the Jews were being driven from place to place, from cracks in their stories he managed to see a good deal of the world and in this way acquired a measure of wisdom of his own.

It was Rabbi Yoseph's honour to live in a parable

uttered daily by Rabbi Judah, the Lion of Minsk, who was told of Rabbi Yoseph's presence in a dream. For his special benefit, Rabbi Judah created such wide cracks in his story (often to the point where his own disciples considered him a fool) that Rabbi Yoseph was able to leave the parable completely at times and sit in the study hall disguised as a shadow or a draft of air.

Late one night, Rabbi Judah was astounded to discover that he was dead. Overcome with grief, he recited the parable in which Rabbi Yoseph had lived for so many years and found him suddenly there at his side. Rabbi Yoseph explained to him the pious task of the hare who collected snores in a barrow and how he had replaced the frog who had once collected snores in a wagon and how he had replaced the bird who had once collected snores in a basket. He showed Rabbi Judah the proper manner of searching through the barrow of snores to find the snore of his wife whose name, oddly enough, was Merriam, and how to cup it gently in his hands and peer at it by opening just one finger so that it would not float away. He showed him how to screw up his eyes to behold the ghetto of Minsk entangled in his beard and, when it vanished, clasped him to his bosom with heartfelt compassion.

Thus they became fast friends and wandered together from star to star and from world to world. Whenever they came to a difficulty, Rabbi Yoseph recited a parable which he had lived in and Rabbi Judah commented on it, whereupon Rabbi Yoseph related another parable, and so on, often for years at a time, until at last they reached the Kingdom of Heaven. The details of their journey are much like a dream and have no place in this story recounting the actual events of Rabbi Yoseeph's adventures following his death. It can be told, however, that as they approached the Kingdom of Heaven they were greeted by a smell which reminded them greatly of onions and fish. And this can be told because it was no dream at all.

The Glass Blower

by *Duane Ackerson*

Sometimes, despite himself, he practices on his wife. As they kiss, his breath, that animal that assumes so many shapes, leaves him without his seeming to even will it. His wife gasps; suddenly, she is filling with him as no wife, no matter how loved and loving, is filled with her husband. She begins to lift away from him, her skirt billowing, breasts swelling, each foot shedding its shoe like a small black tear as they rise to kiss the ceiling. What am I; what am I now? she cries out, carried away in spite of herself.

In casual conversation, an inspiration will sometimes come to him, and the most trivial remarks will appear encased in balloons like cartoon talk, detach themselves neatly at the end of a speech, and float to the ceiling and shelter. The balloons assume whatever form they want: a remark about the weather dressed in a coffin, politics masquerading in bombs and storm-clouds, or, as the sentences follow one another wearily, like German middleclass afternoons, we may see a series of link sausages. Sometimes the silences in which the mouth merely suckles the air will themselves take shape as giant breasts or brooding hens.

As he sleeps, each breath leaves his lips in a different shape: balloons, glass goblets, poodles, the most delicate of glass deer, mice, and horses. Each shatters after it has travelled a short distance from his lips. His wife has seen the shapes that shimmer out of him but is careful not to disturb his inspirations. She knows these bubbles must burst of their own accord, or some nearly perfect creations will not come to be.

The Chameleon
by Milos Macourek

At school children learn to draw cats and caterpillars and dead leaves, cabbage whites, pears and snails, but somehow no one ever seems to think of teaching them to draw chameleons. The reason lies in the supposition that it's too difficult to draw a chameleon. Nothing could be further from the truth. The chameleon is the easiest animal of all to draw, you needn't worry about what crayon to use for it, whichever crayon you choose, it's bound to be right.

And even if the chameleon comes and complains: What's the idea, drawing me in blue when I am yellow, you need only say: But, my dear fellow, this is your portrait of yesterday. You can say this with impunity, you risk nothing, the chameleon can't very well remember what he looked like yesterday, and he will therefore try to change the subject.

With a little diligence we can draw chameleon portraits in advance. Let's think ahead: supposing the chameleon chooses to sit on a checked tablecloth? Let's therefore draw checked chameleons as well, we can't possibly lose on it.

We can't profit by it, either, though. Chameleons aren't in the habit of buying their own portraits. This isn't really surprising, you see: they can't recognize themselves. And there's yet another unpleasant thing. If two chameleons meet, they hardly ever acknowledge each other. They don't see one another. And even if there is a whole group of chameleons together somewhere, it seems as if they weren't there at all. That's why the chameleon is considered a rare animal. Yet it's an animal just like any other and it belongs in the curriculum along with the snail, the cat, and the caterpillar. It's interesting to see that when dead, all those

beautiful orange, green and pink chameleons look exactly
the same. Pickled in spirits, they're all a uniform incon-
spicuous grey.

*Translated from the Czech
by George Theiner*

Mr. K's Favorite Animal

by Bertolt Brecht

When Mr K was asked which animal he prized above all others, he named the elephant and justified it thus: The elephant combines cunning with strength. Not the miserable cunning which manages to avoid a trap or sneak a meal by not being noticed, but the cunning attendant upon the strength needed for important tasks. This animal leaves a broad trail. For all that, he is good-natured and has a sense of humor. He is a good friend, just as he is a good enemy. Though very large and heavy, he is also very swift. His trunk conveys even the smallest morsels to his enormous body, even nuts. His ears are adjustable: he hears only what suits him. Besides he lives to be very old. He is sociable, too, and not only with other elephants. Everywhere he is both beloved and feared. A certain drollness enables him to be positively venerated. Knives buckle in his thick skin, but his heart is tender. He can grow sad. He can grow angry. He enjoys dancing. He dies in the heart of the jungle. He is fond of children and other small animals. He is grey and conspicuous only of his bulk. He is not edible. He works well. He enjoys drinking and grows merry. He makes a contribution to art: he provides ivory.

*Translated from the German
by Yvonne Kapp*

The Elephant

by Slawomir Mrozek

The director of the Zoological Gardens has shown himself to be an upstart. He regarded his animals simply as stepping stones on the road of his own career. He was indifferent to the educational importance of his establishment. In his Zoo the giraffe had a short neck, the badger had no burrow and the whistlers, having lost all interest, whistled rarely and with some reluctance. These shortcomings should not have been allowed, especially as the Zoo was often visited by parties of schoolchildren.

The Zoo was in a provincial town, and it was short of some of the most important animals, among them the elephant. Three thousand rabbits were a poor substitute for the noble giant. However, as our country developed, the gaps were being filled in a well-planned manner. On the occasion of the anniversary of the liberation, on 22nd July, the Zoo was notified that it had at long last been allocated an elephant. All the staff, who were devoted to their work, rejoiced at this news. All the greater was their surprise when they learnt that the director had sent a letter to Warsaw, renouncing the allocation and putting forward a plan for obtaining an elephant by more economic means.

"I, and all the staff," he had written, "are fully aware how heavy a burden falls upon the shoulders of Polish miners and foundry men because of the elephant. Desirous of reducing our costs, I suggest that the elephant mentioned in your communication should be replaced by one of our own procurement. We can make an elephant out of rubber, of the correct size, fill it with air and place it behind railings. It will be carefully painted the correct colour and even on close inspection will be indistinguishable from the real animal. It is well known that the elephant is a sluggish animal and it does not run and

jump about. In the notice on the railings we can state that
this particular elephant is exceptionally sluggish. The
money saved in this way can be turnèd to the purchase of
a jet plane or the conservation of some church monument.

"Kindly note that both the idea and its execution are
my modest contribution to the common task and struggle.

"I am, etc."

This communication must have reached a soulless official, who regarded his duties in a purely bureaucratic
manner and did not examine the heart of the matter but,
following only the director about reduction of expenditure,
accepted the director's plan. On hearing the Ministry's
approval, the director issued instructions for the making
of the rubber elephant.

The carcass was to have been filled with air by two
keepers blowing into it from opposite ends. To keep the
operation secret the work was to be completed during the
night because the people of the town, having heard that
an elephant was joining the Zoo, were anxious to see it.
The director insisted on haste also because he expected a
bonus, should his idea turn out to be a success.

The two keepers locked themselves in a shed normally
housing a workshop, and began to blow. After two hours of
hard blowing they discovered that the rubber skin had
risen only a few inches above the floor and its bulge in no
way resembled an elephant. The night progressed. Outside,
human voices were stilled and only the cry of the jackass
interrupted the silence. Exhausted, the keepers stopped
blowing and made sure that the air already inside the elephant should not escape. They were not young and were
unaccustomed to this kind of work.

"If we go on at this rate," said one of them, "we shan't
finish before the morning. And what am I to tell my
Missus? She'll never believe me if I say that I spent the
night blowing up an elephant."

"Quite right," agreed the second keeper. "Blowing up
an elephant is not an everyday job. And it's all because
our director is a leftist."

They resumed their blowing, but after another half-an-
hour they felt too tired to continue. The bulge on the floor
was larger but still nothing like the shape of an elephant.

"It's getting harder all the time," said the first keeper.

"It's an uphill job, all right," agreed the second. "Let's have a little rest."

While they were resting, one of them noticed a gas pipe ending in a valve. Could they not fill the elephant with gas? He suggested it to his mate.

They decided to try. They connected the elephant to the gas pipe, turned the valve, and to their joy in a few minutes there was a full-sized beast standing in the shed. It looked real: the enormous body, legs like columns, huge ears and the inevitable trunk. Driven by ambition the director had made sure of having in his Zoo a very large elephant indeed.

"First class," declared the keeper who had the idea of using gas. "Now we can go home."

In the morning the elephant was moved to a special run in a central position, next to the monkey cage. Placed in front of a large real rock it looked fierce and magnificient. A big notice proclaimed: "Particularly sluggish. Hardly moves."

Among the first visitors that morning was a party of children from the local school. The teacher in charge of them was planning to give them an object-lesson about the elephant. He halted the group in front of the animal and began:

"The elephant is a herbivorous mammal. By means of its trunk it pulls out young trees and eats their leaves."

The children were looking at the elephant with enraptured admiration. They were waiting for it to pull out a young tree, but the beast stood still behind its railings.

". . . The elephant is a direct descendant of the now extinct mammoth. It's not surprising, therefore, that it's the largest living land animal."

The more conscientious pupils were making notes.

". . . Only the whale is heavier than the elephant, but then the whale lives in the sea. We can safely say that on land the elephant reigns supreme."

A slight breeze moved the branches of the trees in the Zoo.

". . . The weight of a fully grown elephant is between nine and thirteen thousand pounds."

At that moment the elephant shuddered and rose in the air. For a few seconds it swayed just above the ground but a gust of wind blew it upwards until its mighty silhouette

was against the sky. For a short while people on the
ground could still see the four circles of its feet, its bulging
belly and the trunk, but soon, propelled by the wind, the
elephant sailed above the fence and disappeared above the
tree-tops. Astonished monkeys in the cage continued staring into the sky.

They found the elephant in the neighboring botanical
gardens. It had landed on a cactus and punctured its rubber hide.

The schoolchildren who had witnessed the scene in the
Zoo soon started neglecting their studies and turned into
hooligans. It is reported that they drink liquor and break
windows. And they no longer believe in elephants.

Translated from the Polish
by Konrad Syrop

85

A Capsulization (of the Odd-Numbered Chapters of the Novel *In Lieu Of* by Leroy Ortega Holcomb, from Chapter One to Chapter Twenty-Three)

by Robert Thompson

No Bow Lew was born in a hospital on the other side of town, a location which was a major inconvenience for his parents. His mother, Louella Lew, telephoned the hospital repeatedly to say she couldn't come due to the high transit fares, the growing crowds, the air, and various personal depressions. Though the doctors countered each of her excuses with offers of assistance, when the time came the operation had to be performed without her. It was successful, and though a brief flurry of national attention followed, as always, time passed, interest shifted, and what had been heralded as a modern miracle passed from the newspapers to obscure medical journals and then disappeared, leaving the business of getting No Bow from the hospital to his home uncompleted.

The hospital's first plan for the baby's homecoming was drawn up by Ms. Olmstead, a nurse who was authorized to deal with the parents, and her plan required the hiring of a taxicab. This taxi would drive Mr. and Ms. Lew to the hospital to fill out a few brief forms and then drive back to their residence with the baby, all cab fare at the hospital's expense. But when Ms. Olmstead made this suggestion to Ms. Lew over the telephone, invariably one or other complained of a poor connection and their conversation degenerated into half-sentences concerning who heard what. Ms. Olmstead was unable to get Mr. Lew on the telephone at all. This continued for a week and then Ms. Olmstead admitted at the staff meeting that she was blanked.

Therefore a second plan was formulated. So the new plan could be explained without any worries of interference, a separate telephone cable between the hospital and Ms. Lew's house was ordered. Also provisions were made for new telephones for Ms. Olmstead and Ms. Lew so that any guilt association that might have attached to the old telephones due to previous miscommunication was circumvented. The plan itself called for the collecting of several thousand chameleon skins, pressing them together and rubberizing the seams and filling the container with helium. This chameleon blimp would then be used firstly to float over to the Lew's home, secondly to take them to the hospital where the necessary forms could be initialed and the baby released, and thirdly to return them to their home, almost invisibly, and all at the hospital's expense.

86

The Garden
by Paul Bowles

A man who lived in a distant town of the southern country was working in his garden. Because he was poor his land was at the edge of the oasis. All the afternoon he dug channels, and when the day was finished he went to the upper end of the garden and opened the gate that held back the water. And now the water ran in the channels to the beds of barley and the young pomegranate trees. The sky was red, and when the man saw the floor of his garden shining like jewels, he sat down on a stone to look at it. As he watched, it grew brighter, and he thought: "There is no finer garden in the oasis."

A great happiness filled him, and he sat there a long time, and did not get home until very late. When he went into the house, his wife looked at him and saw the joy still in his eyes.

"He has found a treasure," she thought; but she said nothing.

When they sat face to face at the evening meal, the man was still remembering his garden, and it seemed to him that now that he had known this happiness, never again would he be without it. He was silent as he ate.

His wife too was silent. "He is thinking of the treasure," she said to herself. And she was angry, believing that he did not want to share his secret with her. The next morning she went to the house of an old woman and bought many herbs and powders from her. She took them home and passed several days mixing and cooking them, until she had made the medicine she wanted. Then at each meal she began to put a little of the *tseubeur* into her husband's food.

It was not long before the man fell ill. For a time he went each day to his garden to work, but often when he got there he was so weak that he could merely sit leaning against a palm tree. He had a sharp sound in his ears, and he could not follow his thoughts as they came to him. In spite of this, each day when the sun went down and he saw his garden shining red in its light, he was happy. And when he got home at night his wife could see that there was joy in his eyes.

"He has been counting the treasure," she thought, and she began to go secretly to the garden to watch him from behind the trees. When she saw that he merely sat looking at the ground, she went back to the old woman and told her about it.

"You must hurry and make him talk, before he forgets where he has hidden the treasure," said the old woman.

That night the wife put a great amount of *tseubeur* into his food, and when they were drinking tea afterward she began to say many sweet words to him. The man only smiled. She tried for a long time to make him speak, but he merely shrugged his shoulders and made motions with his hands.

The next morning while he was still asleep, she went back to the old woman and told her that the man could no longer speak.

"You have given him too much," the old woman said. "He will never tell you his secret now. The only thing for you to do is go away quickly, before he dies."

The woman ran home. Her husband lay on the mat with his mouth open. She packed her clothing and left the town that morning.

For three days the man lay in a deep sleep. The fourth day when he awoke, it was as if he had made a voyage to the other side of the world. He was very hungry, but all he could find in the house was a piece of dry bread. When he had eaten that, he walked to his garden at the edge of the oasis and picked many figs. Then he sat down and ate them. In his mind there was no thought of his wife, because he had forgotten her. When a neighbor came by and called to him, he answered politely, as if speaking to a stranger, and the neighbor went away perplexed.

Little by little the man grew healthy once more. He worked each day in the garden. When dusk came, after watching the sunset and the red water, he would go home and cook his dinner and sleep. He had no friends, because although men spoke to him, he did not know who they were, and he only smiled and nodded to them. Then the people in the town began to notice that he no longer went to the mosque to pray. They spoke about this among themselves, and one evening the imam went to the man's house to talk with him.

As they sat there, the imam listened for sounds of the man's wife in the house. Out of courtesy he could not mention her, but he was thinking about her and asking himself where she might be. He went away from the house full of doubts.

The man went on living his life. But the people of the town now talked of little else. They whispered that he had killed his wife, and many of them wanted to go together and search the house for her remains. The imam spoke against this idea, saying that he would go and talk again with the man. And this time he went all the way to the garden at the edge of the oasis, and found him there working happily with the plants and the trees. He watched him for a while, and then he walked closer and spoke a few words with him.

It was late in the afternoon. The sun was sinking in the west, and the water on the ground began to be red. Presently the man said to the imam, "The garden is beautiful."

"Beautiful or not beautiful," said the imam, "you should be giving thanks to Allah for allowing you to have it."

"Allah?" said the man. "Who is that? I never heard of him. I made this garden myself. I dug every channel and planted every tree, and no one helped me. I have no debts to anyone."

The imam had turned pale. He flung out his arm and struck the man very hard in the face. Then he went quickly out of the garden.

The man stood with his hand to his cheek. "He has gone mad," he thought, as the imam walked away.

That night the people spoke together in the mosque. They decided that the man could no longer live in their town. Early the next morning a great crowd of men, with the imam going at the head of it, went out into the oasis, on its way to the man's garden.

The small boys ran ahead of the men, and got there long before them. They hid in the bushes, and as the man worked they began to throw stones and shout insults at him. He paid no attention to them. Then a stone hit the back of his head. He jumped up quickly. As they ran away, one of them fell, and the man caught him. He tried to hold him still so he could ask him: "Why are you throwing stones at me?" But the boy only screamed and struggled.

And the townspeople, who were on their way, heard the screaming, and they came running to the garden. They pulled the boy away from him and began to strike at the man with hoes and sickles. When they had destroyed him, they left him there with his head lying in one of the channels, and went back to the town, giving thanks to Allah that the boy was safe.

Little by little the trees died, and very soon the garden was gone. Only the desert was there.

Asilah
1963

from *Green-sealed Messages:* 1
by H. C. Artmann

In the midst of a whim to stroke a cello is a repeating dream, and it lets loose a hope to gain money, then evolves until the whim is consumed by a quail, then the quail is consumed by a lamb, the lamb is consumed by a wolf, and this beast is finally consumed by a starving admiral, who has been set down near the coastal plain of Oregon by his mutinous navy. Then, as the cello sounds in the bowels of Admiral Boyd, you wake, and you write, with your own strange music still in your ear, the number one.

Translated from the German
by J. Rutherford Willems

from *Green-sealed Messages:* 88

by H. C. Artmann

That travelling on a whale's back is particularly conducive to dreaming has already been reported in the *Naturalis Historia* of Pliny the Elder. So if you've found refuge on top of such a fountain-carrier after a shipwreck, then send out the birds of the Ocean who trust you, that they may bring you soil, beakful by beakful, thus the ground brought you in this manner will in time suffice for a little garden. Thereupon send the good birds out for rose shoots. Plant these in the gathered soil, so they might grow into beautiful large bushes. Now if the whale sniffs the enchanting fragrance of the full blossoms, he will be overcome by a great yearning for the long-missed mermaids; and he will alter his course, will betake himself to the region between Rosalind Bank and Pedro Bank. But there you will cast your net, readied long since, for the whale's yearning is now in you as well . . . But instead of three, *eighty-eight* mermaids will become entangled in your meshes, the Caribbean sea will rage awfully, the whale will overturn like a dinghy, the garden with its rose bushes will sink into the furious night of the waves. You, however, will save yourself from this maritime harem in dream number 89.

Translated from the German
by Derk Wynand

89

A Considerable Purchase
by Wolfgang Hildesheimer

One evening I sat in the village tavern before (or more precisely, behind) a glass of beer, when an ordinary looking fellow sat down next to me and asked in a subdued and confidential tone, whether I'd like to buy a locomotive. Now it is rather easy to sell me something, I'll admit, because I simply can't say no, but for a considerable purchase of this type, caution seemed to be called for. Although I know very little about locomotives, I inquired about the model, the year of construction, and the bore of the pistons, to give the man the impression that he was dealing here with an expert, who wasn't about to buy a "pig in a poke." I don't know if I succeeded in giving this impression or not, but he quite willingly gave me the information I wanted and then showed me some snapshots of the locomotive from the front, rear, and the sides. It looked nice, so I ordered it, after we had agreed on the price. It was a second-hand article and, although locomotives depreciate very slowly, I wasn't willing to pay the "blue-book" price for it.

Already that same night it was delivered. Perhaps I should have been able to gather from this quick delivery alone that something fishy was going on, but it just did not occur to me. I'm so naive! I couldn't take my locomotive into the house; the doors wouldn't open wide enough for that, and the house would probably have collapsed because of the weight. So it had to be taken to the garage, which is just the right place for such a vehicle. Naturally it only went in half-way. However, my garage was high enough for it, because I had formerly kept my blimp there, but it had burst.

Soon after that my cousin visited me. He is a person who is disinclined to any speculation or expression of feeling, and will only admit naked facts. Nothing astonishes him, he knows everything; before you tell him something, he knows all about it and can explain it to you. In short, he's an insufferable person. To bridge the painful pause after shaking hands, I began, "These splendid autumn fragrances . . .," to which he replied, "Withering potato vines. . . ." So I gave up conversing with him and poured us some cognac, which he had brought along. It tasted like soap and I told him so. He replied that this particular cognac had won great prizes at the world fairs of Düttich, and Barcelona, and even the gold medal at St. Louis, which I could see on the label, if I'd only look. After we had silently drunk several cognacs, he decided to stay overnight with me, and he went out to put his car away. Several minutes later he came back and said with a quiet, and slightly trembling voice, that there was a large express locomotive in my garage. "I know," I said calmly and sipped my cognac, "I bought it recently." In response to his timorous question, whether I often drive it, I said no, not often, but one night recently I drove a neighbor lady, the wife of a farmer, who was expecting a blessed event, to town, to the hospital. She had given birth to twins that same night, although I doubted that that unusual birth had anything to do with the locomotive trip. All that was a lie, but I often cannot resist the temptation to adorn reality a little bit when the opportunity arises. I don't know if he believed me or not. He accepted my story in silence, and it was obvious that he felt uncomfortable near me. He became monosyllabic, drank one more cognac, and took leave. I never saw him again.

When shortly afterwards there was an announcement in the daily newspapers that the French National Railways had lost a locomotive (it had disappeared one night from the face of the earth, or more precisely, from the roundhouse), it became clear to me that I had been the victim of a disreputable transaction. For that reason I was reservedly cool towards the seller when I saw him in the village tavern a short time later. This time he wanted to sell me a crane, but I wanted to have no more dealings with him, and besides, what would I do with a crane?

Translated from the German
by Norman Kennel

90

The Tramp's Sin and Charlie Chaplin
by *Eugene Jolas*

In that gentle spot my friends and I lived with the sense of being in paradise before the fall. There was always a blue sky above the mountains, the wild brook burst cool-singing through the gorge, eagles flew around the crags. Nature was harmony, and beasts lived side by side, without warfare.

One day there arrived a party of tourists from America. Among them was the Tramp. They wanted to find a blessed land without machines, without materialism, without the feeling of money. The Tramp was in high spirits, let his little stick fly into the air, danced around the meadows near the ravine. He asked me to be his secretary. I accepted.

All the inhabitants walked through the summer landscape. On the terrace of a charming white house, reminiscent of the Colonial houses of the American South, we watched a young woman perform a solo dance in the sun.

We stopped in the hall of a palace-like building. The girl we had just seen dancing was lying on a couch arranging her hair. I turned to light a cigarette. Suddenly I heard a scream. I turned around and saw a little man, obviously the girl's lover, arguing violently with the Tramp whom he accused of trying to seduce the girl. I defended the Tramp.

We were seated at dinner, the Tramp and the other American guests. Charlie Chaplin appeared and I introduced him to the Tramp. He was evidently much pleased to meet him.

Now a man appeared in front of our table. He was the district attorney, he said, and was clad in black. He asked me to come along for an examination in the judge's chambers. The examination was brief and I was immediately released. I went to a table just outside and began to write down my impressions of the scene. As I returned to the table, there was much merry-making. Nobody thought to ask me what had happened.

The scene changed. I found myself standing in a dark night in the Roman Campagna. A pyramid loomed in front of me, but otherwise there was only darkness. Shadows now began to move in the half-gloom. Among them I recognized the woman who claimed that the Tramp had tried to seduce her. She tried to hide by running into a tunnel below a pyramid. Several other shadows followed her.

Once more the scene changed. I was in a small British town. It was night, impenetrable night. The whole town was surrounded by a cordon of police and secret service agents. I was at once taken into custody.

—Do you´ know where they have gone? I was asked.

—Who?

—The spectres, said an agent, and began to search me for poison I was supposed to be carrying. Then he gave me a few lashes with a whip.

—That's St. Fouettard all right, I thought.

I was desolate and cried for my mountain refuge.

91

Pyramid Criticism
by Isaac Rosenfeld

No one knows what heretic it was, what poet or philosopher, who first discovered and dared to reveal the true meaning of the pyramid, or how it was that the knowledge spread throughout the world. Moreover, his name cannot be known, for it was in the nature of things, first noted among the intellectual classes, that men lose their identity when they live forever. One is therefore obliged to speak broadly of the spirit of the age, and to declare that it was inevitable that the new condition of consciousness should turn upon itself—that the condition of life become the examination of life.

Soon it was recognized among the more advanced circles, among the radicals so to speak, that the pyramid was a figure of death, which conveyed death-feeling. Some actual scraps of evidence of the historical Egypt were unearthed by scholars; they stated their conclusions: Pyramids were known to mortal men. An effort was made to suppress their publications, but before it could succeed, the poets and intellectuals, the better minds of the time, were convinced that mankind, in reaching its ultimate goal, had returned to its original premise and that in the end lay the beginning—the preoccupation with death. Booklets, pamphlets, and brochures, the work of an underground press, were circulated among the population of the cities. In these forbidden publications, all that was known of the true Egypt was set forth plainly, to enable the people to grasp the real character of the age in which they were living. The unknown writers described the dynasties of the unknown Pharaohs, the death rituals, mummification, the arts of healing, and the cults of burial, making it clear that the pyramids were no more than great tombstones under which the Egyptians, fearful and obsessed, sought to defend themselves against death by preserving, against time, the corruptible objects of the known life. Certainly, there was nothing seditious in these writings, nothing that threatened the form of society that had been evolved through the ages, or the ultimate goal of life that this society had attained. But the implication was obvious: as pyramids signified the preoccupation with death at the dawn of man's history, so they cast the shadow of the same anxiety at the full blazing noon.

Mummification and Space Travel
by Britton Wilkie

Gazing on the unmoving calm of an ancient Egyptian face—the face of a body arrested in the process of death —fixed—secured from decay—I have been able to accept the idea that some form of life may yet dwell in those pitch-covered, linen-wrapped husks . . .

The idea of travel through space at the speed of light illuminates the image of the mummified pharoah—in order to allow for the constant speed of light in all frames of motion, the Theory of Relatively states that objects approaching that absolute velocity will contract in the direction of motion, gaining in mass as they contract and that, within these contracting. ever-more-massive frames of motion, time will gradually slow down—with respect to the time of a relatively stationary observer—and on reaching the absolute velocity will stop altogether. A brilliant flash through the void—as one voyager watched the other blink his eye, two thousand years passed on their home planet . . .

Now, in our state of motion, the mummy appears static —lifeless—but, if we consider him as a traveler at the speed of light—a passenger on the boat of the sun—he then assumes an entirely different aspect.

My colleague Martin Wolf believes that masters of yoga like disciplines in earliest dynastic times could induce in themselves a state of suspended animation, that the funeral practices of the later dynastics (disembowelment and preservation of the body attended by elaborate ritual) represent a degeneration of more effective earlier methods . . .

The Hot Cosmonaut
by *Gust Gils*

He was going to make a trip to the sun. They were getting him used to high temperatures. First (with increasingly hotter baths) to that of boiling water. As soon as he felt comfortable in it the heat was increased. He got used to boiling lead. Than there followed the more hot tempered metals. He finally could take a shower of liquid metal. He got a nice tan.

He adapted so well to it that great heat became a necessity. He became fantastically chilly: he already felt shivery when it was beneath 6000°. This confronted science with the difficult task of creating an environment for him wherein he wouldn't freeze to death. How would one maintain those temperatures aboard the sunship? How to build instruments which would function under such circumstances; and how would he take down his observations, on what kind of indestructible material? But, of course, the clever brains found a solution for everything, including a custom made diet for the eccentric testperson: liquid steel porridge (iron for the red blood corpuscles) with refreshing drinks of metal that had a lower smelting point. And while the hot cosmonaut sat on hot coals in his blast furnace the sunship (called Icarus I, what else) was finally completed. It was a day of triumph when the whitehot contraption rose straight up from the fiery orgasm of its exhaust and tore full blast away from the atmosphere of the earth.

The trip went perfectly. The cosmonaut transmitted his observations regularly. For a while he complained about the cold but that quickly got better when he saw his objective. Blazing enthusiasm! never had he been more in the heat of it and he thought it was wonderful! The landing on the sun went perfectly and he became almost crazy with rapture. 'It's great here, let my family come over,' he radioed to earth. And was shocked by the negative answer. An endless discussion ensued. 'Try it,' he argued, 'follow the same conditioning I did and come up here, you don't know what you're missing!' Like all other fanatics he became unreasonable. Even when they didn't agree with him he still wouldn't stop talking about it. When he was ordered to go back to busying himself with his observations (that's what he had come for after all) he simply refused! The heat had gotten to his head, reasoned the organisors. A pity of all that money and trouble but the experiment had failed and he better return, without any data. What, come back? The swearing which then flashed through the interplanetary vacuum from sun to earth did not have its equal in the history of space travel! You want to freeze me to death you bastards. Tyrants. Murderers! But it's not going to be that easy for you! I won't move an inch! I'm staying! I never had it so good in my entire life and you creeps begrudge me that, you deepfreeze pests! You'll never see me back again!

He meant it. He never went back. And though no one has ever received another signal from him, it is assumed that he is doing well. (He is sometimes visible when it is foggy weather or through a sooted piece of glass as the man in the sun.)

Translated from the Dutch
by E. M. Beekman

Left Out
by *Charles Schwartz*

Now that it is dark outside, now that you are sleeping, I can come out. Yes, this is me. I am the one you have locked up and hidden away for so long. I am the one who looks on helplessly when you enter the room; as you reach out to touch something with your favorite hand. I am the one who looks longingly as you feel the softness of a breast. I am the one left out.

For as long as I can remember my life has been lonely. I am separated from my brother by geography, but somehow, we are still connected. He is the chosen one: He provides for you; he lifts the fork to your mouth; he must also hold the hammer and the knife. What do you ask of me? It is I that must hold the rabbit, feeling its timid life quiver, while my brother cuts the throat. You make me hold the cucumber while my brother flits his blade faster and faster, slicing ever closer to my fingers. You don't care if I am afraid. You just dangle me from the end of your arm as if I were a second thought.

Other times, like now, when you are asleep, I can delight in my independence. Neither of you knows what I do. In sleep, I guide your dreams: I caress and convince you that a succulent beauty is taking you into her mouth. You fall for my tricks every time!

I know what you are thinking: You think I'm weak, and jealous; that I possess a filthy mind. You think that most of the time I just hang around while my brother does most of the work. But what else can I do? I depend upon you. I don't know how to live on my own.

Don't think that I don't know about my brother's scheming. He's as sly as a fox, always there first to open your doors, to brush your teeth, to comb your hair. I am even more cunning: I look on in satisfied silence as he burns his fingers. But then you place him lovingly between your lips and comfort him. Why couldn't it be me that you kiss?

The Master
by *Lawrence Fixel*

Of course the birth took place. For those whose interest centers on this, there are documents, witnesses and so forth. I have held in my own hands volumes in which the circumstances are described—in such fashion as to convince all but the most biased and self-seeking. One such volume I recall with a thick blue binding, on good paper, and with a number of clear, detailed photographs. Others I have looked at appear well-researched, comprehensive in their presentation of the facts.

But I learned long ago that the real interest of all these scholars, critics, commentators was in something beside the facts. This happened when I first came across the phrase: *born of the cruellest of fathers*. The writer's name, understandably, has been forgotten; but the sentimental and misguided intention—which put me on guard for what followed—has remained. For it was the starting point for a whole school of would be "analysts," making careers out of what their probing fingers pulled apart.

I will not put either that life or those words under that harsh, searing light. But repeat, what is beyond dispute, that the birth took place. And add a few words, not to explain anything, but to express my feeling about a presence that changed the course of my existence.

I am sometimes asked to comment on how it is that this terrible gift and burden appears so incredibly close to our own time. And yet as one considers it, could not have happened any sooner. One realizes that somehow it had to be in just that country, and after those particular wars. One can not help thinking of those tidal waves which, in their own time, reach the intended shore. Or to change the figure, of molecules already in the air, seeking the body which they have to enter.

Whether others would go quite that far, I can not tell. But at least there should be little disagreement on the force and significance of his presence. I have to call it a great *dividing line*—one of the greatest. Let those who would dispute this only look at their morning paper; let them take the shortest walk on our endangered streets. That is where they may test the clear-sightedness of his prophecy —on those destroyed faces, in the closed eyes of wandering, mindless children.

I am tempted to say the obvious: *his children*. For who else understood so well the role of corridors, of endless desks placed side by side? But it would not be accurate to present the prophecy that flowed through him as if it were, literally, the work of his hands. It was rather what he saw and felt and lived with—if we understand this in the proper way and in the proper dimensions—as far as our own limited minds can reach.

I claim for myself no more than this. With these few glimpses of what lies beyond, I am content now to return to my place among his readers. His words are preserved by now in countless editions. Let those who read make of them what they can. They have the printed pages; they can use his name wherever and however they choose.

What is missing of course is his voice. That was available only for a short time, and for those few to whom he gave so generously of his unique spirit. *His voice.* Those seated beside him at the same table . . .

The words go on; they flow through his silence. That silence which was his last considered choice. For wasn't it enough for them to know that he had been there; could they not have pooled their memories of his presence? But this was not to be. The hand of one of those closet to him sifted among his belongings, fingers tightened on sheets covered with black ink.

We have read those words—read and recited over and over again—and understood nothing. The experts still express astonishment that he could speak of the Garden as if he had been there in person. Some of them even revel in the opaque, counting the tiny prisms made with the points of their pens.

They can not grasp what goes deeper than their lives. Not a choice for darkness, but for the earliest light: before the forest awakens, before the intruder arrives.

The True Waiting
by *Elie Wiesel*

Having concluded that human suffering was beyond endurance, a certain Rebbe went up to heaven and knocked at the Messiah's gate.

"Why are you taking so long?" he asked him. "Don't you know mankind is expecting you?"

"It's not me they are expecting," answered the Messiah. "Some are waiting for good health and riches. Others for serenity and knowledge. Or peace in the home and happiness. No, it's not me they are awaiting."

At this point, they say, the Rebbe lost patience and cried: "So be it! If you have but one face, may it remain in shadow! If you cannot help men, all men, resolve their problems, all their problems, even the most insignificant, then stay where you are, as you are. If you still have not guessed that you are bread for the hungry, a voice for the old man without heirs, sleep for those who dread night, if you have not understood all this and more: that every wait is a wait for you, then you are telling the truth: indeed, it is not you that mankind is waiting for."

The Rebbe came back to earth, gathered his disciples and forbade them to dispair:

"And now the true waiting begins."

Soap

by Jerome Rothenberg

When two men had a disputation one man argued for the use of soap.

The other, who was a stranger in that town, countered question with question.

"Will the man who gets clean love his neighbor?" he demanded, & again, "When Moses was forty years in the desert, did he not bathe with hot sand; & were not the odors from his loins wafted to Jehovah as a living sacrifice?"

The first man grew silent though his finger still pointed to Leviticus.

The Angel of the Garden was crying in his throat.

The Unmasking of the Apocalypse
by Cecil Helman

On the day before the Apocalypse, the streets are strewn with discarded masks.

We step among the piles of torn paper masks, their cheeks gaily painted, scattering in the winds. With them lie the plastic and professional masks of judges, officials and others; some stern, some with frozen frowns, others still plumply benevolent. In the dusk running feet crunch the porcelain masks of fashionable women, and trip on the hessian faces of the poor. One by one we peel the masks off our faces; tear off the smiles and sneers, moulded in rubber or wood, and throw them out of the windows. In the streets they are collected and carried to bonfires, where soon the flames flicker up through their mouths and empty eyeholes. Everywhere in the smoke there are the clicks of locks unlocking, as people unhinge their black iron masks and throw them heavily to the ground. Silence deadens the thud of their falling. . . .

As the twilight of the last day reddens, we see—and recognize—one another for the first time, for the last time. Now only one mask—different from all the others—remains glued to our faces. It is that strong transparent mask which we can see only on others, not on ourselves; which we can only pull from the faces of our friends, but not from our own. Within this final mask the air thickens slowly in our lungs. Our eyes meet in the dusk; we reach out across the voids between us. But our fingers are clumsy in the dark, and the mask is tightly glued. As we struggle and fumble we know that if only we can remove it now, the Apocalypse may never—need never—arrive.

Threatening Letter
by *Maria Luise Kaschnitz*

Each day he hurries through his mail to see if the threatening letter he's been expecting a long time has arrived. He does not know on what kind of paper the letter is written and what format it has, maybe on the long side, maybe red. Possibly it is an ordinary business envelope, green, with a window, which is hardly to be assumed since it is, after all, a matter of a quite personal letter. What is written on it he does not know either, of course. There is much for which he could be called to account, his lethargy, his cowardice, these above all. Maybe on an otherwise blank page there is only a question mark (he, called into question), or an exclamation mark (Careful, careful) or quite simply: a period.

Translated from the German
by Derk Wynand

Period

by Zbigniew Herbert

In appearance a drop of rain on a beloved face, a beetle immobilized on a leaf when a storm approaches. Something which can be enlivened, erased, reversed. Rather a stop with a green shadow than the terminus.

In fact the period which we attempt to tame at any price is a bone protruding from the sand, a snapping shut, a sign of a catastrophe. It is a punctuation of the elements. People should employ it modestly and with a proper consideration as is customary when one replaces fate.

Translated from the Polish
by Czeslaw Milosz

About the Authors

Kobo Abé was born in Tokyo in 1924. He received a medical degree in 1948, but he has never practiced medicine. In that same year he published his first book, *The Road Sign at the End of the Road*. In 1951 he was awarded the most important Japanese literary prize, the Akutagawa, for his novel *The Crime of Mr. S. Karuma*. In 1960 his novel *The Woman in the Dunes* won the Yomiuri Prize for literature. His novels also include *The Face of Another, The Ruined Map, Inter Ice Age 4*, and *The Box Man*.

Duane Ackerson was born in New York City in 1942. He presently lives in Pocatello, Idaho, where he teaches at Idaho State University and independently edits *The Dragonfly*. He has published three chapbooks of poetry, including *UA Flight to Chicago* and *Works*, a volume which also includes the fables of Russell Edson.

S. Y. Agnon was born in 1888 in Galicia, the southernmost district of Poland. He received a traditional religious

319

education, and at the age of twenty left home for Palestine. Agnon's novels and stories became classics of Hebrew literature in his lifetime. Six of his books have been translated into English: *The Bridal Canopy*, *A Guest for the Night*, *Two Tales*, *In the Heart of the Seas*, *Twenty-One Stories*, and *Days of Awe*. The last is a collection of oral and written legends pertaining to the High Holy Days. Agnon shared the Nobel Prize in 1966 with Nelly Sachs. He died in Jerusalem in 1970.

Hans Christian Andersen was born in 1805 in Odense, Denmark. His father was a poor cobbler; his mother took in laundry to help support the family. In 1819 he went to Copenhagen, where he tried ballet, singing, and acting and all but starved. In 1829 his first play, *Love on St. Nicholas Tower*, was performed in the Royal Theatre. He then published *The Improvisatore*, a veiled autobiography and a psychological novel, *O.T.* It is his fairy tales, of course, that have made him immortal. The first he wrote were based on Danish folk tales he had heard as a child, but the vast majority are original. Among his most famous fairy tales are "The Snow Queen," "The Ugly Duckling," "The Emperor's New Clothes," and "The Princess and the Pea." He died in 1875.

Juan José Arreola was born in Ciudad Guzmán in the state of Jalisco, Mexico, in 1918. His stories first appeared in little magazines in Guadalajara in the early 1940's, and his first book came out in 1949. Two volumes, including his bestiary, appeared in the 1950's, and all three volumes were brought out under the title *Confabulario Total, 1941-1961* in 1962. A translation of this book, under the title of *Confabulario*, which means a collection of fables, has appeared in the United States.

Antonin Artaud was born in Marseilles in 1896. In 1920 he came to Paris and took part in the Surrealist movement and was also active as a stage and film actor. In 1927 he broke with Surrealism and developed his idea of the Theatre of Cruelty. In 1936 his experiments with peyote left him in a shaken condition, and for the next ten years he had many stays in mental hospitals. His most notable play is *The Cenci*, and he is the author of several works relating to the theatre. An edition of his *Collected Writings* has been published in London, and his primary nontheatrical writings were collected in America in the *Artaud Anthology*. Artaud died in 1948.

H. C. Artmann was born in Vienna in 1921. His first writings were detective stories he passed out at school under the pseudonym of John Hamilton. In 1940 he was drafted into the German army, and the next year he was wounded. He wrote poems and prose in a military hospital and returned to the war in 1943. In 1945 he was taken prisoner in Regensburg and had access to a library which contained works of the pre-Expressionists, Expressionists, and Dadaists. He returned to Vienna in October, 1945, and in the next few years gave successful readings on Radio Vienna. In 1962 he returned to Berlin, where the play *Dracula, Dracula* was performed. He is the author of five collections of poetry and short prose, none of which has yet appeared in English.

Pierre Bettencourt was born in 1917. He is a poet, painter, illustrator, essayist, publisher, and printer. Nearly all of his published work consists of short texts printed in limited editions by himself, sometimes illustrated by himself, many written under various imaginary designations. None of these collections has been translated into English.

Jorge Luis Borges was born in Buenos Aires in 1899. His family moved to Europe in 1914, and to Spain in 1918, where Borges was in close touch with the young vanguard-ist poets, especially those of the so-called *ultraista* group. In 1921 Borges returned to Buenos Aires, where he was quickly recognized as one of the principal poets of the Argentine vanguard. In the early thirties, after a long illness, his literary activity tended more and more away from poetry and toward the essay and short story. It was the publication of two volumes of his stories, *Ficciones* and *El Aleph*, to which Borges owes his international fame. In 1961 he shared the Prix International des Editeurs with Samuel Beckett. Borges is widely regarded as Latin America's most influential prose writer, and all of the major South American writers of the current generation, such as Gabriel García Marquez and Julio Cortazar, have acknowledged their debt to him. His first collection of stories in English was *Labyrinths*, and since then a number of volumes have appeared, including *Ficciones*, *The Aleph and Other Stories*, *A Personal Anthology*, *Dreamtigers*, *Dr. Brodie's Report*, and *In Praise of Darkness*. An edition of his *Selected Poems* has also been published. Borges died in 1986.

Paul Bowles was born in New York City in 1910. He first had a career as a composer, writing opera, orchestral pieces, and film scores. In 1952, Bowles moved to Tangier, Morocco, and began to write novels and short stories that explore the harsh cultural incongruities between primitive and modern modes of life. These works include the novels *The Sheltering Sky* and *The Spider's House*, and the collections of stories *The Delicate Prey* and *A Hundred Camels in the Courtyard*. Bowles has also translated the writings of important figures such as Mohammed Mrabet and Rodrigo Rey Rosa. Bowles' *Collected Stories: 1939-1976* was published in 1979.

Bertolt Brecht was born in 1898 in Augsburg, Germany. When the Nazis came into power in 1933, he became an exile from Germany and sought asylum in a series of countries—Russia, France, Norway, and finally the United States, to which he came in 1941. During this period many of his plays, radio plays, and poetry were on anti-Nazi themes. His collaboration with the composer Kurt Weill on *The Threepenny Opera* produced the work that made him most famous. He is now recognized as the major German playwright of his generation. His major dramas are *Galileo, Mother Courage,* and *The Caucasian Chalk Circle*. Brecht was also well known as a poet, and he published one collection of short stories, *Tales from the Calendar*. He died in East Berlin in 1956.

Martin Buber was born in Vienna in 1898 and raised in

Galicia in the home of his grandfather, Solomon Buber, a noted Hebrew scholar. It was here that he was exposed for the first time to Hasidism. He studied philosophy and the history of art at the Universities of Vienna, Berlin, and Zurich. In 1900 he joined the Zionist movement and made the decision to dedicate his life to the cause of Judaism. Buber's first book, *I & Thou,* is a major philosophical-theological statement about the relationships between man and man as well as between man and God. His later books are primarily concerned with various facets of Hasidism and Jewish thought. He edited the classic collection of Hasidic stories and tales, entitled *Tales of the Hasidim* (Early Masters and Late Masters), and his other books include *The Prophetic Faith, Two Types of Faith, Eclipse of God*, and *The Origin and Meaning of Hasidism.* Buber was also the author of one novel, *For the Sake of Heaven*, and of a book of short stories, *Tales of Angels, Spirits, and Demons.* Buber died in 1965.

Italo Calvino was born in San Remo in 1923. When the Germans occupied northern Italy during World War II, he joined the partisans, and the stories which resulted from these experiences won wide acclaim. An essayist and journalist, and the author of many stories, he has had seven books published in English: *The Path to the Nest of Spiders, Adam One Afternoon and Other Stories, The Baron in the Trees, The Nonexistent Knight & The Cloven Viscount, Cosmicomics, T Zero,* and *Invisible Cities.* This latest book is, in the editor's opinion, the best single collection of parables to be published since Kafka's *Parables and Paradoxes.* Calvino died in 1985.

Elias Canetti was born in 1905 in Russe, Bulgaria. He moved from Bulgaria to Vienna at the age of six, and was educated in Vienna, Zurich, and Frankfurt. Since 1939 he has lived in England. He is the author of one novel, *Auto-da-Fe,* which may be described as a cross between Kafka and Cervantes. It is certainly one of the major novels of the century. He is also the author of one sociological study, *Crowds and Power,* and two plays, which he sometimes gives readings of, playing all the parts. Canetti's method in *Crowds and Power* has been described as "eclectic, poetical, sociological, anthropological and philosophical." As such, the book has not endeared itself to traditional sociologists, but has attracted a wide and diverse audience.

Marvin Cohen was born in 1931 in Brooklyn. He is the author of six books. Two are novels: *The Self-Devoted Friend and Others,* and *Including Morstive Sternbump;* three are books of parables: *The Monday Rhetoric of the Love Club, Fables at Life's Expense,* and *The Hard Life of a Stone;* and one is a book on the metaphysics of baseball, entitled *Baseball the Beautiful.*

Kirby Congdon has worked as a literary agent's assistant, editorial assistant at Collier's Encyclopedia, and, far more times than he wishes to recall, he says, as a secretarial-typist for a temporary personnel agency. Currently, he works on the staff for an encyclopedia of the history of art. He is the author of three books of poems, *Iron Ark, Juggernaut, A Key West,* and of *Dream-work,* a collection of parables.

Julio Cortazár is an Argentine who was born in Brussels in 1914 and has lived and worked in Paris since 1952. His first novel, *The Winners,* was published in the U.S. in 1965, and his second, *Hopscotch,* in 1966. A third novel, *62: A Model Kit,* is based on the sixty-second chapter of *Hopscotch.* He has also published three books of short stories and parables: *The End of the Road, Cronopios and Famas,* and *All Fires the Fire.* Cortazár died in 1984.

Marco Denevi was born in Sáenz Pena, Argentina, in 1922. He is best known for his novel *Rosa at Ten O'Clock,* which was made into a motion picture. In 1960 his novella *Secret Ceremony* won the major "Life en Espanol" literary contest, a contest that considered work from writers from all of Latin America. These are the only of his many works that have been translated into English.

Isak Dinesen is the pseudonym of Karen Blixen of Rungstedlund. Born of an old Danish famliy, she has made contributions both in Danish and in English. Her style is elegant and precise, yet intense. In 1914 she was married to a cousin, Baron Blixen, and she accompanied him to British East Africa, where they established and operated a coffee plantation. Her book, *Out of Africa*, records many of her experiences during this period, and is one of the most widely read of memoirs. Prior to *Out of Africa* she had published one collection of stories, *Seven Gothic Tales*, and several collections, all first rate, followed, including *Winter's Tales*, *Last Tales*, *Anecdotes of Destiny*, and *Ehrengard*, this last her only novel under her primary nom de plume. She was also the author of the novel *The Angelic Avengers*, written under the pseudonym of Pierre Andrezel. Baroness Blixen died in 1962.

Fyodor Dostoevsky was born in Moscow in 1821. His mother died in 1837, and his father was murdered a year later. In 1849 he was arrested and sentenced to death for participating in the "Petrashevsky circle"; he was reprieved at the last moment but sentenced to penal servitude, and lived until 1854 as a convict in Siberia. Out of this experience he wrote *Memoirs from the House of the Dead*. Most of his important works were written after 1864: *Notes from the Underground, Crime and Punishment, The Gambler, The Possessed* (also translated as *The Devils*) and *The Brothers Karamazov*. Dostoevsky died in 1881.

Bob Dylan is the name taken by Robert Zimmerman, who was born in Hibbing, Minnesota, in 1942. Dylan is the author of one book of fiction, *Tarantula*, from which "I Sang in a Forest One Day" has been excerpted.

Russell Edson lives in Stamford, Connecticut. He handset his first books himself, and eventually New Directions published a collection that gathered the best stories from them, *The Very Thing That Happens*. Since then Edson has published three major collections, *What a Man Can See, The Childhood of an Equestrian,* and *The Clam Theatre*. He recently published his first book of plays, *The Falling Sickness*.

Lawrence Fixel was born in 1917 in New York City and was a member of the Federal Writing Project. He is the author of three books of prose, *The Scales of Silence, Through Deserts of Snow,* and *The Edge of Something,* and of one book of poems, *Time to Destroy/To Discover.*

Gabriel García Márquez was born in Aracataca, Colombia, in 1928. He attended the University of Bogotá and later worked as staff reporter and film critic for the Colombian newspaper *El Espectador.* He currently lives in Barcelona. García Márquez is the author of *One Hundred Years of Solitude,* the most famous of the many fine novels to come out of Latin America in the last ten years. The book has had an international success, and the Chilean poet Pablo Neruda called it the finest book in Spanish since *Don Quixote.* Two collections of stories by García Márquez have also appeared in English: *No One Writes to the Colonel* and *Leaf Storm and Other Stories.* His new novel, *The Autumn of the Patriarch,* was recently published in Barcelona.

Gust Gils was born in Antwerp in 1924. He has published poetry and three collections of parables, which he calls "paraprose." He now writes songs in English and performs them himself in cafés in Antwerp, accompanying himself on guitar. None of his books has been translated into English.

Nicolai V. Gogol was born in 1809 at Sorochintzy, in the Ukraine. He turned to writing at an early age. In 1829 he published, under the pseudonym of V. Alov, an idyllic poem, *Hans Kuchelgarten,* but this work was so ridiculed by the critics that Gogol destroyed as many copies as he could. Only after the appearance of his play, *The Inspector General,* however, did he think seriously of literature as a life work. In 1840 the first part of *Dead Souls* was finished, and Gogol took it to Moscow for publication. At the same time it appeared, in 1842, he published the first collected edition of his earlier works, which included the famous tale "The Overcoat." This period marks the apex of Gogol's career. Later he came to think of *Dead Souls* as an epic of which the second part would show the regeneration of rogues, but after a great deal of work he burned the manuscript. After this both his mental and physical condition became worse, and he died in Moscow in 1852. *Dead Souls* and collections of his short stories are readily available in English. Gogol's work was a great influence on subsequent writers, including Dostoevsky, and is especially the inspiration for much of the literature of the Absurd that has appeared during this century.

Lars Gyllensten is the Swedish author of the novel *The Testament of Cain,* which consists of a series of linked parables.

Cecil Helman was born in 1944 in Cape Town, South Africa, the grandson of rabbis. He graduated as a medical doctor at the University of Cape Town in 1967. Since then he has been self-exiled from South Africa and has lived in London. He has studied anthropology at the University of London, and at various times he has been a ship's doctor, illustrator of children's books, picture salesman, astronomer, and museum guide, and is currently working as a doctor. His collection of parables, as yet unpublished, is titled *The Revolution of the Pin-ball Machines.*

Zbigniew Herbert was born in Lwów, Poland, in 1924. In his late teens he fought in the underground resistance against the Nazis. He later studied law, economics, and philosophy at the universities of Cracow, Torun, and Warsaw. He has published three volumes of poetry in Polish, and his *Selected Poems,* including a number of parables, was published in the Penguin Modern European Poets series. Among those in the West who are familiar with his work, an unusually large number of poets and critics are of the opinion that he is the greatest living poet. His awards include that of the Polish Institute of Arts and Sciences in America and the Austrian Government Prize for European Literature.

Wolfgang Hildesheimer was born in 1916. A German expatriate, he now lives in southern Switzerland. He is prolific writer of poems, plays, and short prose, but very little of his work has been translated into English. He is best known here for the story "A World Ends," which can be found in many anthologies.

Enrique Anderson Imbert was born in Argentina in 1910. He has taught at many universities in Latin America and the United States, and is now the Victor S. Thomas Professor of Hispanic-American Literature at Harvard University. Anderson Imbert is one of the foremost contemporary critics of Latin American literature, and is credited with writing short parables long before Jorge Luis Borges approached the form. He has had more than a score of books published, including novels, short stories, essays, literary criticism, and a book-length collection of parables. A translation of many of his stories and parables has been published under the title *The Other Side of the Mirror*.

Edmond Jabès was born in Cairo in 1912. Being Jewish, he had to leave Egypt at the time of the Suez crisis. He now lives in Paris, where he received the Prix des Critiques in 1970. One of his books, *Elya*, has already appeared in English, and another, *The Book of Questions*, is being prepared for publication.

Eugene Jolas was born in New Jersey in 1894 and grew up in Lorraine, France. He wrote mostly in English, but also wrote trilingual poetry. He edited the magazine *Transition* during the 1920's and the 1930's, where he advocated surrealist-related programs like Verticalism. He died in 1952. His books include *I Have Seen Monsters and Angels*.

Franz Kafka was born in Prague in 1883. Kafka took his law degree in 1906 at the German University of Prague and later secured a minor position with the Austrian government. During his lifetime only a small portion of Kafka's writings were published. Before his death, of tuberculosis, in 1924, Kafka requested of his friend Max Brod that he burn his remaining manuscripts. However,

Brod published all of them, and later edited Kafka's diaries. Many of his letters and notebooks have also been published. There are several editions of his stories available, including an edition of his *Complete Stories*. His three novels, all unfinished, are *Amerika, The Trial,* and *The Castle*. His *Parables and Paradoxes* is certainly the classic volume of parables to be published so far in this century.

Marie Luise Kaschnitz was born in 1901 in Karlsruhe, Germany. In 1955 she received the Georg Büchner Prize, and in 1964 the Georg Mackensen Literature Prize. Since 1960 she has had a professorship in poetry at the Johann Wolfang Goethe University, Frankfurt. She has published six books of poems and eight collections of fiction, none of which has been translated into English.

Daniil Kharms was born in St. Petersburg in 1905. His real name was Yuvachev, but he liked to use various pseudonyms; Kharms was the one under which he wrote most often. Kharms was the leading member of the avant-garde literary group called Oberiu, and he wrote in Leningrad during the late 1920's and 1930's with no hope of publication. He was arrested just before World War II and died in prison in 1941 or 1942. His manuscripts continue to be privately circulated in Eastern Europe, where George Gibian discovered them and translated a number of Kharms' stories and a play, *Elizabeth Bam*, along with works of Alexander Vvedensky in the book *Russia's Lost Literature of the Absurd*.

Heinrich von Kleist was born in Frankfurt in 1777. He was a dramatist and short story writer. Several translations of his story "Michael Kohlhaas" are available in English, and one collection of his other stories has appeared, entitled *The Marquise of O*. Kleist killed himself as part of a suicide pact in 1811. He has had great influence on later generations of writers, including Kafka. Kafka acknowledged this debt by visiting Kleist's grave.

Jerzy Kosinski was born in Lodz, Poland, in 1933. He arrived in the United States in 1957, where he completed his graduate and postgraduate education. Despite his late emigration, Kosinski writes only in English. His first novel, *The Painted Bird,* won the French Prix du Meilleur Livre Etranger for the best foreign work of fiction. His second novel, *Steps,* won the 1969 National Book Award. His other novels are *Being There, The Devil Tree,* and the recent *Cockpit.* Kosinski's non-fiction works include literary criticism and two volumes on collective behavior, *The Future is Ours, Comrade* and *No Third Path,* which were written under the pen name of Joseph Novak. His books have been translated into every major language.

Rachel Kubie was born in St. Louis in 1968. She has edited small literary magazines and published in small journals.

Günter Kunert was born in 1929 and now lives in East Berlin. His work includes poetry, short stories, parables, and TV scripts. Selections of his work have appeared in the magazine *Dimension,* but none of his books has been translated into English.

Pär Lagerkvist was born in Vaxjo, Sweden, in 1891. His early works included the parables in this anthology and longer stories utilizing folk elements, such as *The Eternal Smile.* His early work also included poetry and drama, and his accomplishments in these genres were also considerable. Lagerkvist's reputation began to spread beyond Sweden with publication of the novel *The Dwarf,* which appeared in English in 1945. His novel *Barabbas* brought him the Nobel Prize in 1951. His other books include *The Marriage Feast, The Sibyl* and a book of his poems, *Evening Land.* He died in 1974.

Tommaso Landolfi was born in 1908 in the province of Frosinone, which lies between Rome and Naples. He attended the University of Florence and took a degree in Russian literature. Landolfi published his first book of stories, *Dialogue on the Greater Harmonies,* in 1937. Nearly a dozen other books have since appeared, including *Rein Va,* an imaginary diary. Landolfi will release no information about his personal life. Two collections of his stories have appeared in English, *Gogol's Wife* and *Cancerqueen.*

Reinhard Lettau was born in 1929 in Erfurt, Germany. He studied at Heidelberg, and, later, at Harvard, where he received his Ph.D. He now teaches at the University of California at San Diego. One collection of his stories has appeared in English, entitled *Obstacles*.

Jakov Lind was born in 1927 in Vienna. He was evacuated to Holland for safety in 1938. At the time of the German invasion he obtained false papers under the name of Jan Overbeek, returning to Germany as a deckhand on a Rhine barge. At the end of World War II he emigrated to Palestine, but returned to Europe a few years later. His first book, *Soul of Wood*, was an international literary sensation and was translated into fourteen languages. His subsequent books include two novels, *Landscape in Concrete* and *Ergo,* and three volumes of autobiography, *Counting My Steps, Numbers,* and *The Trip to Jerusalem.* "The Story of Lilith and Eve," which reveals an entirely new direction the author has taken, is from an as yet unpublished collection of parables and one long story entitled *The Stove*.

R. Yehoshua Lovaine's identity is something of a mystery. The translator, Tsvi Blanchard, received the original parables without any specific information about the history of the author. Mr. Blanchard hazards the guess that R. Yehoshua Lovaine is either a nineteenth century Kabbalist who wrote in Yiddish or else a living Jewish writer who wishes to keep his identity hidden.

George MacDonald was born in Aberdeenshire, Scotland, in 1824. He obtained degrees in natural philosophy and chemistry, then became a minister in the Congregational church. When he was twenty-six, despite the success of his preaching, he resigned from the ministry and devoted the rest of his life to literature. His first and last novels, *Phantastes* and *Lilith,* are adult fantasies that make explorations into the unconscious mind far in advance of their time. MacDonald is also one of the greatest authors of children's fantasies and fairy tales. His children's books include *At the Back of the North Wind, The Princess and the Goblin, The Princess and Curdie, The Light Princess,*

The Lost Princess and *The Golden Key*. MacDonald virtually originated the fantasy genre, and was a great influence on writers such as C. S. Lewis, David Lindsay, and J. R. R. Tolkien. He died in 1905.

Miloš Macourek was born in 1926 at Kromeriz, Czechoslovakia. After studying at a school of music and drama, he held various jobs as a factory worker, scene shifter, warehouseman, publisher's editor, university lecturer on literature and art, story editor for Czechoslovak Films, and lately also as a screenwriter. He writes poetry and prose, as well as plays, Apart from his children's books, his only book of prose is *Zoology*, from which "The Chameleon" is taken.

Christoph Meckel was born in 1935 in Germany. He writes poems and stories, and is also known for his graphic work. To date none of his many collections has appeared in English.

W. S. Merwin was born in New York City in 1927. From 1949 to 1951 he worked as a tutor in France, Portugal, and Majorca. Since then he has made the greater part of his living by translating from French, Spanish, Latin, and Portuguese. He is the author of one book of parables, *The Miner's Pale Children*, and of eight books of poetry, including *The Moving Target, The Lice, the Carrier of Ladders,* and *Writings to an Unfinished Accompaniment*.

Henri Michaux was born in Namur, Belgium, in 1899. He is equally famous as an artist and as a writer of short prose. Michaux was first published in 1920, but was ignored until after the war when André Gide recommended that he be "discovered." His first exhibition of paintings took place in 1937, and from 1946 onwards each year he had one or more shows of his paintings, drawings, and book illustrations. In 1955 Michaux began experimenting systematically with hallucinogenic drugs, especially mescalin, and these experiments resulted in the book *Miserable Miracle*. A selection of Michaux's writings from 1927 to 1959 has been published in one volume, *The Space Within*. This book was translated into English as the *Selected Writings of Henri Michaux*. He has also written a travel memoir entitled *A Barbarian in Asia*. Michaux died in 1984.

Barton Midwood was born in Brooklyn in 1938. He has been employed as a jazz musician and as a counselor in a treatment center for disturbed boys. He has published one novel, *Bodkin,* and one book of stories, *Phantoms,* from which "One's Ship" was taken.

Mohammed Mrabet was born in Tangier of Riffian parentage about 1940. Like many Moroccan boys he preferred the freedom of living in the streets to the discipline involved in remaining at home. In 1965 he met Paul Bowles, who began to tape the legends and invented tales he constantly recounted. His first novel, *Love with a Few Hairs,* was published in 1967. Two years later a second novel, *The Lemon,* appeared. He has also published two volumes of stories, *M'Hashish* and *The Boy Who Set the Fire.*

Slawomir Mrozek was born in Bozerin, near Cracow, in 1930. He studied architecture, painting, and Orientalism for a few terms. His first job was on a Cracow newspaper as a writer and cartoonist. While still a journalist, he began to write satirical short stories and it was with a first collection of these, *The Elephant,* that he achieved an early success. These stories were followed by others, and by a book of cartoons, *Poland in Pictures.* He abandoned journalism in the late fifties and his first play, *The Police,* was first performed in 1958. Eight more short plays followed before he wrote *Tango,* his first full-length play, first performed in 1964. A selection of his stories has appeared in English under the title *The Elephant.*

Multatuli is the pseudonym of Eduard Douwes Dekker, Holland's greatest nineteenth-century writer. Dekker was born in Amsterdam in 1820 and spent a considerable number of years in the Dutch East Indies. In 1852 he returned to Holland and made his first attempts to become a professional writer. These efforts failed, and after a return to the East Indies Dekker travelled around Europe for several years. In 1860 he published *Max Havelaar*, his first novel, which has since become a Dutch classic. At this time Dekker took up permanently his pseudonym, which is Latin for "I have suffered a lot." His works are generally unavailable in English, although a selection of his aphorisms and parables has been published under the title of *The Oyster and the Eagle*, and *Max Havelaar* has appeared in an English edition. Multatuli died in 1887.

Rabbi Nachman of Bratslav was born in Medzibuz, Poland, in 1772, the great-grandson of the Baal Shem Tov, founder of Hasidism. He became a prominent Hasidic rabbi, who, on Friday nights would tell his disciples stories he had invented during the week. The disciples would retell the stories to each other all during the Sabbath, when they were not permitted to write, and Nachman's disciple Nathan, who served as his scribe, would write them down when the Sabbath was over. The entire body of major tales that has come down is only thirteen, but the stories are in every sense exceptional and in advance of their time. Two translations of Nachman's tales have appeared, one by Martin Buber entitled *The Tales of Rabbi Nachman*, and one by Meyer Levin entitled *Classic Chassidic Tales*. Rabbi Nachman died in Uman in 1810.

Paul van Ostaijen was born in 1896 in Belgium. As a young man he fled Belgium because of political entanglements. In Berlin he met a number of Dadaists, and it was Dadaistic iconoclasm that first inspired his satires, which he called "grotesques." He wrote in Dutch. His writing did not bring him financial success and he began experiments with cocaine. In 1921 he returned to Antwerp only to be immediately drafted and sent back to Germany as a soldier in the Belgian occupation forces. After his discharge he started an art gallery, which failed, and then tried supporting himself as a journalist while continuing his writing. In 1928, at the age of thirty-two, he died of tuberculosis. One collection of his stories has appeared in English, entitled *Patriotism, Inc. and Other Tales*.

I. L. Peretz was born in 1852 in Zamosc, Poland. Though raised in the orthodox tradition, he also absorbed worldly knowledge. He was a prodigy, being advanced enough at the age of six to begin the study of the Talmud. He passed the bar in 1877, and, for a decade, had a thriving practice in his home town. In 1890 he secured a position as a secretary to the Jewish community of Warsaw, a position he was to retain for the rest of his life. Though he experimented with Polish, Hebrew, and Yiddish, it was the last that was to become his chief literary medium. His poem "Monish," published in 1877, first demonstrated that Peretz was a literary craftsman. Before long stories by Peretz began to appear regularly in the Yiddish dailies, and his popularity became immense. At his funeral in 1915 more than a hundred thousand mourners followed his coffin. Several collections of his stories, which were often based on folktales, have appeared in English, including *In This World and the Next, The Book of Fire,* and the recent *Selected Stories of I. L. Peretz.*

Edgar Allan Poe was born in Boston in 1809. Poe is the father of the detective story ("The Murder in the Rue Morgue") and the horror story ("The Fall of the House of Usher," etc.) and he also did pioneering work in the genre of fantasy, of which "The Oval Portrait" is one example. He wrote one novel, *The Narrative of Arthur Gordon Pym,* and collections of his stories are available everywhere. Poe died in 1849.

Isaac Rosenfeld was born in Chicago in 1918. He took a degree at the University of Chicago and then moved to New York, where he briefly studied philosophy at New York University and began to publish short stories. His novel, *Passage from Home,* appeared in 1946. After a period of teaching at the University of Minnesota he returned to Chicago, and soon thereafter, in 1956, he died of a heart attack. A posthumous collection of his stories, *Alpha and Omega,* appeared in 1966.

Jerome Rothenberg was born in New York City in 1929. He is the author of more than a dozen books of poetry, several books of translations, and four major anthologies. His books of poetry include *Poems for the Game of Silence* and *Poland / 1931.* His anthologies include *Technicians of the Sacred, Shaking the Pumpkin,* and *America, A Prophecy.* His is currently editing a "big Jewish book."

Andreas Schroeder was born in Hoheneggelsen, Germany, in 1946. He emigrated to Canada in 1951, and set up home base in British Columbia several years later. He is the editor of the journal *Contemporary Literature in Translation*, which was the source for many of the parables in this collection. He also works in the capacities of poet, fictionwriter, columnist, critic, filmmaker, and translator. His books include *The Ozone Minotaur, File of Uncertanties, uniVerse, The Late Man,* and *Shaking It Rough.* He is also co-editor of the anthology *Stories from Pacific and Arctic Canada.* He has been the recipient of numerous prizes, grants, and awards.

Charles Schwartz lives in Eugene, Oregon, where he attends the University of Oregon. He writes short stories and screenplays. Several of his stories have appeared in *Avenue*.

Howard Schwartz was born in St. Louis in 1945. He is the author of three books of poetry, *Vessels, Gathering the Sparks,* and *Sleepwalking Beneath the Stars,* and of several books of fiction, including *The Captive Soul of the Messiah* and *Rooms of the Soul.* In addition to *Imperial Messages: One Hundred Modern Parables* he has edited the anthologies *Gates to the New City: A Treasury of Modern Jewish Tales* and *Voices Within the Ark: The Modern Jewish Poets.* He has also edited three volumes of Jewish folklore, *Elijah's Violin, Miriam's Tambourine,* and *Lilith's Cave,* as well as *The Dream Assembly: Tales of Rabbi Zalman Schacter-Shalomi.*

Miguel Serrano was born in Chile in 1937, into a family of diplomats and writers. For nine years he served as Chilean ambassador to India. Since leaving India he has served as ambassador to Yugoslavia, Bulgaria, Rumania, and Austria. He now lives in Switzerland. He is the author of *The Serpent of Paradise, The Ultimate Flower, The Visits of the Queen of Sheba,* and *C. G. Jung and Hermann Hesse: A Record of Two Friendships.*

Isaac Bashevis Singer was born in Radzymin, Poland, in 1904. Singer is widely recognized as the last great Yiddish writer. In Poland he worked for the Yiddish press, and since 1935 he has been a regular contributor to the *Jewish Daily Forward,* the principal Yiddish newspaper in the

United States. His novels include *Satan in Goray, The Family Moskat, The Magician of Lublin, The Slave, The Manor, The Estate,* and *Enemies: A Love Story.* His collections of stories include *Gimpel the Fool, The Spinoza of Market Street, Short Friday, The Seance,* and *A Crown of Feathers.* He has also written many children's books and one memoir, *In My Father's Court.* Singer is the brother of the late I. J. Singer, also a great Yiddish writer, whose most famous works are *The Brothers Ashkenazi, Yoshe Kalb,* and the memoir *Of a World That Is No More.*

David Slabotsky was born in 1943 in Montreal, Canada. He is the author of four books of parables: *Parables, The Girl Without a Name, The Wandering Jew,* and *The Mind of Genesis,* this last his collected parables. His work has been published in periodicals in Canada and the United States, and has been produced by the C.B.C. television and radio networks.

Robert Thompson was born in St. Louis in 1944, and died in Columbia, Missouri in 1988. His stories, which are still uncollected, were published in *The New Yorker, Harper's,* and *Kenyon Review.*

Roland Topor is a French artist and author. He is best known as the co-author and artist responsible for the surrealist animated film, *Fantastic Planet.* A collection of his short prose, *Stories and Drawings,* has been published in translation in London, while in the United States only a short collection of his drawings, entitled *Panic,* has appeared.

Krishna Baldev Vaid was born in India in 1927. He was educated in India and at Harvard, where he obtained a Ph.D. in 1961. He is currently a professor of English at the State University of New York at Potsdam. He has published several novels and collections in Hindi, and has served as his own translator into English. His publications include *Steps in Darkness, Bimal in Bog,* and *Silence and Other Stories.* He is regarded as one the most important and controversial Hindi writers.

Marguerite Yourcenar (pseudonym of Marguerite de Crayencour), was born in Brussels in 1903. She was the first woman member of the Academie Francaise, inducted in 1981. Best known among her novels, critical essays, plays, and poetry was the novel *The Memoirs of Hadrian*, an erudite reconstruction of the personality of the Roman emperor. Other works in translation include *The Abyss*, *Fires*, *The Dark Brain of Piranesi and Other Essays*, *Oriental Tales*, and *Two Lives and a Dream*. She died in 1987.

Elie Wiesel was born in 1928 in the town of Sighet in Transylvania. He was still a child when he was taken from his home and sent to Auschwitz and Buchenwald. After the liberation he made his way to Paris, where he studied at the Sorbonne. His work as a journalist took him to Israel and finally to the United States; he now makes his home in New York City. His books include *Night, Dawn, The Jews of Silence, The Accident, The Town Beyond the Wall, One Generation After, The Gates of the Forest, A Beggar in Jerusalem, The Oath,* and *Zalman: Or the Madness of God. A Beggar in Jerusalem* won the French Prix Medici in 1969.

Britton Wilkie was born in Texas, and has traveled and lived for long periods in Mexico. His books include *Mirrors of Time* and *Limits of Space and Time*. His illuminated manuscripts have been published in *The World* and *Fits*. He presently resides in Canada.